LIBERATION

LIBERATION

LEE SCHNEIDER

FutureX.Studio Santa Monica, CA 2025

Also by Lee Schneider

Surrender

Resist

Mission of the Lunar Sparrow, audio drama

Your Performance Review, audio drama

Cover and interior design by Paul Palmer-Edwards

FutureX Studio
Docucinema, Inc.
1112 Montana Ave #257
Santa Monica, CA 90403
futurex.studio/books

First Edition: October 2025

FutureX Studio is an imprint of Docucinema, Inc.

The publisher is not responsible for websites (or their content) that are not owned by the publisher.

Library of Congress Control Number: 2025911906
Library of Congress Cataloging-in-Publication Data
Names: Lee Schneider, author
Title: Liberation / Lee Schneider
Description: First edition | Santa Monica, CA: FutureX.Studio, 2025
Identifier: ISBN 979-8-9991074-0-4 (paperback)
Subjects: GSAFD: Science Fiction

Printing 1, 2025

Dear Reader,

To assist you as you build the world of *Liberation* in your mind, you will find a Glossary of Terms at the back of the book.

For Tabby. For your support, kindness, and love.

PART 001

Chapter 01

Everything had come apart. It was a massive network outage, and it already had a name: the Fracture.

All clocks on the network had stopped at 11 PM. Kat's clock had a calendar display as well, so it revealed more information: 11 PM on October 11, 2053. Kat could only dimly perceive the stopped clock now because it had no power to light it up. Her generator was connected to her terminal because only the essentials mattered now.

She was up late. She rubbed her eyes. Her fatigue blurred the weak, yellow-orange light of her terminal screen. It was the middle of the night, she supposed. Or it could be close to morning. She looked up at the round exterior window of her housing unit. The window resembled a sightless eye because there were no lights outside. It confused her as she thought about the network going down globally. *The network failed here at 11 PM, but it wasn't 11 PM everywhere, because of all the different time zones, and the clocks elsewhere had stopped at different times.*

She felt a headache coming on and ignored it, keeping her hands moving over the touchless panel on her desk, each gesture a signal processed by the application running on her terminal. The generator hummed at her feet. There just had to be enough juice to run her terminal until morning. That had to be enough time to fix the network, to get enough servers back online, to restore everything.

A sudden spatter of rain shook Kat's housing unit. The window's dark eye was streaked with tears. Then the rain stopped and heat roared in, and the window fogged over. Then there was a bright hissing sound and Kat thought that this meant snow was hitting the round window. As she looked up to confirm, the hiss of snow turned to the scratch of ice flung by fierce winds. The ice storm lasted a moment, and then the rain resumed.

The network connected everything, even the weather, and that's why Kat was working all night, squinting at her terminal. The application she was running sent test pings to network nodes. Kat hoped to find one working node that she could connect to another working node, and then another, and another after that. One node at a time felt like hopeless work to Kat, but she felt responsible for the disaster.

The day before, the morning after the Fracture, Kat's day had started early, and badly, when she ventured out to the Northern Zone Market to see if there was any food to buy. She was anxious about going out in public, and in fact was heckled as soon as the citizens recognized her from her many appearances on the Feed. Kat led a very public life.

"You did this!" the citizens shouted, some shaking their fists and crying, "Fix the Fracture! Fix it now!" It was the first time she'd heard the name people had given the outage. *The Fracture? What is the Fracture?* she wanted to ask. She was glad she didn't, because it would have made her seem clueless and made the citizens even angrier. She had paused by a stand to evaluate the sad-looking produce when a small group of citizens surrounded her, quickly becoming a larger group, and shaping their rage into a chant. *Fix the Fracture!*

They were right to be angry, because the Fracture *was* Kat's fault. She didn't completely understand how it had happened, but she knew enough to understand that her tampering with the network had caused the problem. To be completely honest, she had wanted to bring the network down, but not all at once, not catastrophically, and not in a way that got everyone so mad.

Kat went directly from the market where she had been heckled to find her friend Claire8. Not only was Claire8 an expert on networks, she was also modded, with a silicon substrate implanted in her brain.

The number "8" after her name indicated a good mod, but not the best. The lower numbers were more expensive, the closer a person got having a mod that was a perfect "1."

Claire8's memory was vast, but her patience even more so. Kat found Claire8 in her own housing unit, pinging nodes by herself. There was no way to know that they were independently working on the same problem, no way to compare notes on their success or failure. With no network, Claire8 was happy that Kat had stopped by. There was no glidepath or other transportation aside from bicycles, no artificial light, no banking system, no artificial water coming from the central domain generators. The desalination plants were offline and the climate controls were working on backup power, but only sometimes, so that explained the erratic shifts in weather. They planned to keep working independently on the network problem and check back later, either via the network if it was working, or in person.

If the network failure wasn't enough to make Kat feel unbalanced, there was also the predicament of her close friend and colleague in the Resistance, Ravven Vaara, who had apparently lost her mind.

Ravven had always operated close to the edge of rationality, and instability was her usual state of being. She dressed in white flowing clothing most of the time, was accused often of leading a yoga cult, and enjoyed pushing the limits of what most people considered acceptable behavior. And she and Kat were both Receivers, which meant that they could hear the thoughts of others in their heads. This was a destabilizing talent, but Ravven was skilled at the Receiver's art, and had taught Kat how to filter some of the outside thoughts from other people that penetrated her mind. For this inner peace, however temporary, Kat was eternally grateful.

On the way back home after meeting with Claire8, Kat accidentally learned that Ravven's mental state was getting worse.

Kat's housing unit was part of a group of units called Molecular Housing. Normally, when the network was working, a control unit provided power, water, and purified air to the dozen units. Now all units were on their own with windows flung open to take their chances with the ambient air.

Spaceman must hate this, Kat thought. He was the inventor of this cooperative form of housing. Since she was passing his unit, she thought she might drop in to see what he was doing. But she stopped as she heard a voice coming from inside that she hadn't expected to hear.

Ravven's voice. Angry, shouting. Had she moved in with Spaceman? Kat paused below the open window to listen.

"But why?" Spaceman had just asked.

There was no response at first, and then Kat heard Ravven shout, "You wouldn't believe me anyway!"

A great commotion followed: the sounds of sliding closet doors banging open and closed, drawers yanked open, all the time Ravven arguing with Spaceman about what she could fit into a backpack.

Was Ravven was moving out? Had their relationship, which Kat knew nothing about, already failed?

Knowing she had missed this story as it had developed, Kat waited, feeling ridiculous as she crouched below the round window of Spaceman's unit. She heard Ravven's voice turn to a pleading whine.

"Roger!" (She called him by his given name, Roger Rucker.) "Roger, you have to come with me. I can't do this alone. You have to help me!"

"You can't go," he said. "You're running away from the problem."

This brought a fresh spasm of rage from Ravven: "You're wasting your time on 'the problem.' It's not the real problem. Kat doesn't get it either! She should come. She should give us her house."

Kat raised her eyebrows at that. The thing was, Ravven was prone to meltdowns now and again, but this seemed like a particularly bad one. Her voice, normally shaped into a controlled Brit-Euro accent that Kat had always suspected was fake, was shrill and hard. "We don't need a network. We are beyond all that! We don't need climate controls! Let the Earth decide again what the weather should be! No electric fields!"

It wasn't so much that Ravven hated technology or computers or artificial intelligence. Her hatred went deeper than all of that. She hated artificial fields, and to her that meant any field created by a machine. A scientist, Roger would normally have corrected her, but he must have known it would only intensify her rant, and so he remained silent. Kat, listening below the window, hoped that Roger would wait out Ravven's emotional storm and then calm her. Roger was a steady person if also an emotional one at times, but he was usually good at talking sense into others.

Not this time. He didn't even try.

Kat heard a thump that could have been Ravven slamming her fist against the wall, and a click as the front portal unscrewed and Ravven stormed out in a blind fury, not noticing Kat at all.

"Ravven?" Kat called out.

Ravven didn't turn around. So complete was her fury, she seemed not to hear Kat call her name as she marched in the direction of the glidepath station. *Good luck to her*, Kat thought. There were no trains running during the network outage, as far as Kat knew.

When Kat pinged at the door, Spaceman let her in, mumbled her name in greeting, and stepped aside. Kat told him she'd heard the argument from outside.

"You were hiding under the window?" he asked, seeming confused.

"What just happened here?" Kat pushed on.

"She's having visions," Spaceman said. "I'll have to go with her to protect her from herself." His eyes were sad as he reported this. He seemed to be ashamed.

"Visions? Where is she going?"

He gazed at Kat for a moment, as if determining whether she was ready to hear what he had to say. "She's going to the Westcoast and I'm going with her, I just decided," he said.

"Answer the whole question, Roger." Kat rarely used his given name, preferring to call him Spaceman like everyone else, but she was angry. "What visions?" Then her eyes met his and softened. *Please don't leave. I need you here.* Roger was not a Receiver, so he didn't hear her thoughts in his head, but he registered the pleading in her eyes. "What visions, Roger?" Kat asked for the third time.

Spaceman wrung his hands and talked around the question. "I have to go after her right now. She needs help. I'm worried about her." He caught Kat's eye, waiting for her to agree. When she didn't, he added, "We should both go. You and me. She asked for you."

Kat sighed and her mouth went hard. She didn't have time for a Ravven meltdown right now and only wanted to get back to her terminal, restore the power and artificial water production, get back some climate controls, and start everything back on the path it was traveling before the Fracture.

She also needed to restore her good name. Everyone hated her now. She couldn't go out to buy a squash without being heckled.

She said softly this time, "Roger. Visions about what?"

He pulled at his beard, ran his hands through his unruly salt-and-pepper hair, and finally produced just one word. "Orcas."

It was quite late again or very early in the morning. Kat couldn't tell from what the porthole window revealed. Rain thrashed against it. The generator's green indicator cast a sickly light on the walls of the room. The amber glow of Kat's terminal, on low power mode, painted her face. She was tempted to activate Michel, a bot who had become a companion to her, but he was low on charge and wouldn't last long. Advice from Michel would have to wait.

She had pinged her friend Claire8 to ask for help again with the network and received no answer. *Of course. Why would there be an answer?* Kat gestured for the terminal screen to display a new map. There were a few pinpoints of light on it, indicating working servers. She gestured to connect them, and then, ever the optimist, tried pinging Claire8 again to let her know about the small victory. No answer again.

Kat shook her head and pulled her black shoulder-length hair back into a ponytail, securing it with a band that she had around her wrist. Fidgety, she thought about tea and got up to open a valve at the cooker to make some. She wondered if the cooker would work, but it hummed reassuringly. It was foolish to use up her generator charge for tea, but she had to have some.

Weren't orcas some kind of whale? Or were they a dolphin? She was tired and didn't want to stop what she was doing to look it up. *Ravven can have her visions, fine, they aren't my problem.*

Yet she couldn't stop the worrying from working its way into her mind. Both women had the thoughts of others in their heads from time to time, but Ravven heard more. She heard what she described as the Earth speaking to her, a spirit of the Earth called Gaia. And now she was hearing orcas, whales, dolphins, whatever. Troubling. Kat tried to talk some sense into herself.

I am her friend, but I am not responsible for her bad decisions.

That didn't sound right. All she wanted was to stop it from raining and snowing and raging outside and get the power back on. And time was of the essence, because other forces, bad people, wanted to control the network. She knew this to be true, even though she hadn't seen evidence of it yet. But she knew she would.

The screen reflected a blurry image of Kat's lined face, more lined than usual because of fatigue. Her gray eyes were intense, slightly bloodshot. She noted that she had pulled her hair back into a slightly off-center ponytail. She did nothing to fix it. She wore a white sunsuit because she had forgotten to take it off the previous day. A pair of sun goggles was around her neck, also forgotten.

It was October. If the climate controls were working, they would be simulating what everyone thought of as normal Fall weather in New York. Warm at the start of the month, cool toward the end, the warm and cool air mingling delightfully, and pleasant rain. Instead, there was a crack of lightning, followed by a boom of thunder that made Kat jump. It rained fiercely, a sonic roar, then it stopped and the heat came again and steam billowed up over the porthole. This was far from normal weather, even simulated normal weather.

The terminal screen went blurry. Kat rubbed her eyes.

Fatigue. Too much work. Too tired to work.

She scrubbed her hands over her face, responded to the bleep from the cooker and got the tea. She'd forgotten that she put it on. The tea leaves were artificial, like the water, but the caffeine in it worked like the real thing. It was her last packet and the water level was low.

She focused on the terminal, trying to convince herself that it would take just a few more hours before she would crack the puzzle and connect enough servers to report the good news to Claire8. Then Kat could go outside and the citizens would declare, "You fixed it! We love you, Kat Keeper!" The work of the Resistance could continue. The only work that Kat ever really cared about, really.

She screwed her mouth into a crooked frown. *Do I need their approval that badly?* It would have been easy to mock herself for feeling that insecure, but instead she fed it into the furnace of her determination.

She leaned close to the terminal screen seeking working servers to connect. *That's all I have to do. Find and make connections. Claire8 will take care of securing the network.* Kat told herself that she was not going to fall asleep at this work, no matter how long she'd been awake. That had happened too many times before: She overstretched her tired mind, and woke up with her face plastered to the controls. That was not going to happen this time.

But the light streaming through the round window woke her up. Morning. The heat of the day, beginning. Kat ran a hand over her face, and dammit, sure enough the imprint of the controls was on her skin. It had happened again. She had fallen asleep at her terminal.

This is too big a job for me.

Resisting the urge to try Claire8 again, Kat stood up, pushing the chair back carelessly so that it clattered against the wall behind her. She would have to go out to the market and endure the heckling. She needed supplies, food and artificial water. She would stop by Claire8's place again and ask for help, even though she assumed Claire8 was already doing what she could. Heat was already coming in fast from outside, through the walls, pushing its way into her unit. In response, her windows self-dimmed in a half-assed way because there wasn't much power. She checked the charge on the generator. The green light was dim, signaling that it was almost expended.

Her comms pinged. This surprised her. Maybe some parts of the network were back online. Perhaps Claire8 was succeeding where Kat had failed so far.

It was Roger, already out on the Westcoast, begging her to join him and Ravven there. "She's really in trouble," he said. "Please get on the next glidepath. You don't know when there'll be another. We waited all night in the station for one to come and we got lucky."

"Roger, I can't. The network—"

Roger cut her off. "You can't fix everything, Kat. And your friend needs you. Ravven needs you *now*. Please, go to the station and get a train."

Kat sighed as she searched for words.

"What will it look like if the two leaders of the Resistance are at odds, one on the Eastcoast, and the other on the Westcoast?" Roger asked.

Kat didn't conceal the annoyance in her voice. "Since when do you care about optics?"

"It's not optics!" Roger said hotly. "It's solidarity! It's leading by example." He paused. "I just wish you two would stop arguing."

"Arguing is always the way we've done everything," Kat said. "We decide things by conflict."

"Well, I hate that about you and Ravven," Roger said. He paused again. "There's something I need to ask. Something we need. Can we stay at your house while we're out here?"

Kat gave him the key code to get in. Later, he would set up the retina scanner so merely looking at the door would do the trick.

Chapter 02

The sky was the color of rust and the heavy air pressed down on Kat, slowing her steps. She wore an air unit so she could breathe freely. It fit snugly on the lower part of her face, concealing her identity but not enough.

The clicking of the air unit's purification mechanism was in her ears and the voices of many others around her were in her mind. There was a way to quiet the voices, using a prayer that Ravven had taught her long ago. But Kat let the voices come into her mind. She thought she deserved their criticisms.

Why can't you fix this if you broke it?

We're all suffering because of you.

The others were moving along the path with her. Some nodded at her and looked away. Some met her eye defiantly. Some looked down, like they were caught doing something they weren't supposed to do. Kat heard all of their thoughts.

My family is running out of food. I won't be able to feed my baby.

A few of them spoke aloud to Kat: "Make the network whole again, Kat Keeper."

She counterattacked, thinking into the minds of those nearby: *Fame is a burden.*

Then she corrected herself. *Too bitter. Not the right message to send.*

Kat stopped messaging into their minds. The other people were out in the bad air because they had to be, to buy food if it was available, to seek a jug of artificial water in the market if there was one to be had, to see if a glidepath was running so they might relocate to a better place.

A white-haired woman stood in Kat's way. She fixed Kat in a glare and spat out one word. "You!"

Kat ducked her head and sidestepped the Old.

An alert sounded. A glidepath was arriving. Kat quickened her pace to meet it, slightly amazed that there actually was one. In the station, she joined others on the platform. There was a large advert vid screen behind her, four meters by two, mounted on the wall. These screens usually played adverts for off-brain memory storage, pitches for medipatches to cure sunstroke, insomnia, and Covid, adverts for low-orbital vacations or loans to buy the latest pleasure rocket. But this time, there was something Kat had never seen before in a glidepath station.

It was a video about her. She unconsciously ducked her head and tugged at her air unit so that it might conceal more of her face.

A male announcer's voice rang out from the audio port of the vid screen. "The Resistance is dangerous. If you see a Resistance member, report them to the nearest enforcement bot or domain official." The screen showed footage of a Resistance protest from two years ago, but the footage was all wrong, doctored somehow. Kat knew, because she had been there, leading the effort.

Two years ago, Kat, Ravven, Claire8, and other members of their Resistance circle had blocked an elevated walkway. It was their biggest public protest at the time, with six women at one end of the Skyway, six at the other, and twelve in the middle, and more joining as other women's circles arrived for the peaceful action. The women were prepared for infection, wearing bac-masks, and for sun exposure, protective glasses and light silver jackets. But they were not prepared for an ambush. They had pulled rolled-up signs from their sleeves that read ban thought harvesting and mind is a mind fucker. They blocked the Skyway and were arrested by small roving enforcement bots that were low to the ground and equipped with flexible pipe to bind the legs and hands of Kat and the others, immobilizing them.

But the doctored footage showed something else entirely. It showed the protestors fighting back, kicking the enforcement bots that tried to detain them, harming any citizens who got in the way. The vid depicted a melee that never happened, and the announcer's voice kept talking about the dangerous unpredictability of the Resistance. The video wrapped up by showing mug shots of Kat, Ravven, and Claire8, also doctored. The women had scrapes and black eyes because, according to the announcer, they had "resisted arrest and fought the guards in detention." None of this was true.

In a few moments, the glidepath had arrived and Kat was a hundred kilometers away.

The presence of the vid meant the network was coming back, node by node. Claire8 must have been making progress.

But the existence of the doctored video also meant that MIND, Kat's adversary for the past two years, was taking its fight against the Resistance to a new level.

The network was never owned by any one entity. Like the internet it replaced, it was made of many parts, some independent, others controlled by the local governments known as domains. But seeing a vid that was raw propaganda, a stunning piece of disinformation masquerading as a public service announcement, made Kat think the worst. It was possible, all too possible, that MIND was taking control of the network. It would mean that Kat and Claire8's best efforts to restore the network were being stolen by MIND. If true, this was bad news.

Glidepath cars were semi-private, with seats that faced forward in the direction of travel, but the car Kat rode in was not like that. Perhaps it was a utility car pressed into service. Kat was seated on a plastic bench that faced another bench on the other side of the car. There was a rectangular window on the other side, over the bench. Outside that window, scenery flashed by in a blur, turning brown to green and back again. It went by too quickly for Kat to identify any landmarks. For all she knew, they might already be in the Midlands. Kat sunk into the bench she was sitting on and pulled her air unit higher on her face. There was no vid screen in the car, so at least she would be safe from doctored videos and prying eyes. She was alone and the ride was steady and strong.

The blast curtains had failed to come down and it was quickly getting hot inside the car, so she opened her backpack and pulled out a sun jacket with temperature regulation built in, a stylish silvery white with long sleeves and a high neck in a perfect circle. It crackled quietly as she put it on, negotiating around the air unit that she slipped down on her neck and then replaced over her face to conceal her identity. She instantly felt cooler.

The jacket she wore made Kat think of Spaceman. He had invented it, along with many other devices that made life possible in this age. Kat had had another comms call with him before she left, and it was on that call that he told her a story about Ravven that convinced Kat to get on the glidepath.

Spaceman had said that Ravven was in meditation, her eyes closed, her breathing sweet and soft. Then a vision intruded into Ravven's mind. She told Spaceman that she was swimming among fish, deep in clear water.

"She thought she was in the water with them?" Kat had asked.

"No," Spaceman had explained to Kat, "Ravven was meditating as a pod of orcas came to look at her. Large black and white mammals. In the dolphin family actually, but people call them killer whales. They spoke to her."

"Spoke to her?" Kat couldn't keep the skepticism out of her voice. "She wasn't in the water but they spoke to her?"

"They spoke to her as she meditated," Spaceman insisted. "Their consciousness merged with hers. A triangular formation, six of them, with one in the lead, at the apex of the triangle. It was the one in the lead, at the apex, that spoke in her mind. It said, 'I am the orca queen.' The queen said she was teaching her juveniles how to knock the propellers off boats. She made it a game for the young ones. She said they enjoyed it."

"Enjoyed it?" Kat repeated. This wasn't making much sense.

Spaceman nodded, going on. "The lead orca said that the boat attacks are the beginning of a campaign to get human attention. Scientists will have theories about the attacks, the orca said. They will believe the attacks are part of an orca uprising against the super-rich, because the orcas will only attack luxury yachts. Others will insist that the attacks are usual orca behavior, a mother using the boat attacks to teach their juveniles how to hunt."

"Wait," Kat interrupted. "Mothers teach the baby orcas how to hunt…?"

"Yes, yes," Spaceman said impatiently. "It's a cultural transmission. One whale to another. That's been established."

"You know this?" She was wondering how he had come by this knowledge with no Feed.

He seemed to anticipate her thought. "I've studied terrestrial biospheres, but I know some things about the oceanic world. Mother whales can transmit culture to their group. They share rituals for mourning their dead and they educate juveniles. Mother whales play games with their young as a teaching tool. They throw pieces of kelp at each other and play fetch."

Kat didn't know what to say. It all seemed so strange. "Go on."

Spaceman obliged. "Then the transmission ended with the words, *I AM HERE. I am the orca queen.*"

"You're calling it a transmission?"

Spaceman shrugged. "Ravven called it a transmission. I think the term fits well."

On the glidepath, Kat blew out a breath. She wanted to help Ravven because Ravven was a puzzle to be solved. There was always friction between them, *creative friction*, she told herself as a kind of apology, a way to justify the irritation of it.

A moment passed as she thought about that. The scenery flew by, a continual blur at her window. No conductor bots had come through to announce the train's progress. Kat wondered if the outage was as bad on the Westcoast as it was in New York. She had supplies in her old house, artificial water, maybe some food; it was a large, comfortable place. It had been two years since Kat had left that house and its memories. Maybe Claire8 could work on the network for a while, and Kat would see to her old friend. It seemed a good idea to cling to while the world around Kat came undone.

At the next stop, the Western Desert Domain station, Kat was no longer alone in the glidepath. Facing her, on the bench on the other side of the car, sat three Youngs. They whispered, flicking glances at Kat. She wondered if they had seen the misinformation vid that had played in the station and wondered if it was playing at other stations as well. She willed herself not to see into their minds so they would have privacy.

They seemed like they might be part of the Disconnect movement. They hadn't washed, even with UV. They smelled a bit and their hair hung lank and greasy on their faces. Since they didn't wear white sun-protective clothing like Kat did, their skin was raw and sunburned. They were dressed in browns and grays, loose-fitting sheaths, recycled probably. Youngs joined the Disconnect movement because they didn't want to have any part in the network or use comms or the Feed. They gestured conspiratorially at Kat's backpack.

This made Kat wonder if they somehow had sensed what was in it. Kat had brought along Michel, the sentient bot who had become her personal companion. If they knew she was carrying a bot, they would yank it out of her backpack and destroy it. For Youngs in the Disconnect movement, bots were the enemy. Kat resisted the urge to check on Michel but carefully arranged her backpack near the induction port at her feet. Michel could charge up from the port, and the Youngs wouldn't know.

A flash of light distracted Kat. It came from the window behind her and she twisted to look at the world zooming by. They had to be past the midpoint of the continent already. Then, soon afterward, the glidepath would take a turn, up to the Port City of San Francisco.

She gestured at the controls on her climate jacket to cool herself a little more, her air unit on standby around her neck. She probably seemed overdressed to the Youngs who eyed her and whispered.

Kat's mind fell to the ghosts that waited for her in her old house. She closed her eyes to picture it and shut out the prying glances of the Youngs. Her house was elegant, built to float on pontoons to adjust for rising water levels. It featured a greenhouse filled with rare plants. The upstairs had a large bedroom and two guest rooms. Downstairs, an entry foyer, a living room, cooking area attached, a dining area, and in the back, a small windowless room she used as her home office. When she left the house, she was engulfed in crisis. Now, upon returning, maybe it would offer her some peace. *Good luck with that.*

The house signified the past and the past could not be controlled. The past rudely entered through an open door in the mind. Uninvited thoughts marched in and formed a chronology that Kat would rather forget.

She had been wealthy once and employed three hundred people at her company, VirtualEyes. It was a facial recognition software company that had prospered mightily and then was engulfed in scandal. Kat was forced out. After the trouble, she hid in her big house and nursed her husband in his final days.

Kat shook her head; control had eluded her, as always. The blur of scenery outside the window was mostly brown now; they had traveled far. The glidepath changed direction, turning north, and Kat and the Youngs seated across from her leaned in place and reached for handholds to steady themselves.

Her thoughts turned to a gap in her understanding. Ravven and Spaceman had come together as a couple and Kat had missed that heated moment, or they had concealed it.

Opposites who understood each other.

She realized that she was jealous of their happiness.

But what happened to me? I'm not happy and I have no one.

Jealousy was a useless emotion. Kat locked it away.

The glidepath slowed.

The door hissed open, and a grandmotherly conductor bot entered the car. Round and low to the ground, its tarnished silver skin pricked with sensors for sight and hearing.

"Induction is ending. Please brace yourself for arrival," it said in a pleasant femme voice. "Port City of San Francisco in two minutes."

Kat got off the glidepath and moved into the station, which was deserted except for her and the Youngs who had also exited the car. Soon, they scattered and Kat was left alone. The advert screens, normally alive with messages, were dark, revealing that the network wasn't fully functioning here. The air was stale and still.

Kat walked up the steps, awaiting the noise of the city, but it never came.

With the network mostly down, there weren't many machines to make noise, and not many people. She wondered if there would be a boat to take across the water to get to her house on the other side of the bay, or would she have to hire a tuk-tuk to take the long way around?

Chapter 03

There was no ferry to be seen, so Kat had to hunt for other options. She looked out into the bay for a vaporetto to get her across and saw no boats for hire. Maybe she would have to find a tuk-tuk after all and go over the bridge and then the mountain. Tuk-tuks were open to the elements and therefore noisy, but she might not have a choice.

She was distracted by something happening on the pier.

A clump of Youngs was standing too close to the edge, pushing each other as if to make one of them fall into the water. This was a different kind of group from those she had encountered on the glidepath. These Youngs were Doomers. It was their flamboyant dress code that tipped Kat off: A tall boy was dressed all in black with a balaclava on his head that covered everything but his eyes, which poked out of the holes in his headgear with startlingly bright orange pupils. He was modded.

Another boy, shorter, stood nearby, wearing a skull cap fitted with golden antlers that had glowing lights strung in them. There was a young woman who had styled her hair to look like snakes. Or maybe it was a wig. Kat tried to remember the character in mythology who looked like that.

Medusa.

Another young woman had yellow eyes. Probably yellow contacts, a fashion statement. She seemed to wear a permanent sneer.

The group of Youngs flicked at their comms, laughing darkly as new signals came. They continually gestured out to the bay.

Kat didn't want to approach them, but curiosity about what they saw out on the water propelled her over to talk to them.

"What's going on?" She tried to sound friendly.

Her effort didn't matter: They looked through her like she wasn't there. Kat realized that they saw her as an Old, far from them in age and attitude.

The generations had split, another culture war to go along with the political and regional ones: people seemed set on seeing differences, creating others to dislike or hate, and forming tight groups made of people like themselves. Kat didn't consider herself an Old, but there was no sense arguing with them about it.

The girl with the yellow eyes—Kat, now closer, saw that she was a young woman—forced out a few words as though doing Kat a favor. "There's a pod coming in. They're at war with us," she said.

"A pod?"

The young woman responded with a cross between a sneer and a smirk and waited for Kat to ask again.

"A pod?" Kat said, trying not to sound annoyed.

"A pod of orcas. They're at war with us," the Young said as though it was the most obvious statement ever.

With us? With everyone? All humans? Kat had questions, but the Young's snarly demeanor put her off, so Kat moved away to sit on a bench looking out on the bay. She zipped open her climate top, then decided to turn it off to experience the temperature out on the pier as it really was. She took in the sour smell of the water, the tar oozing from the wood of the pier, the tight, hard tang of ozone from a generator that kept mumbling, trying to start automatically. There was some electricity here, if intermittent. Lights on poles flicked on inappropriately; it was a little past noon.

These sensations left Kat feeling unsettled. She realized it had been a long time since she had smelled real air, maybe since her childhood back in New York. The climate controls had been processing the world for most of her life. Now the Fracture had again opened up the natural world, at least showing off the way it really smelled. A hot wind agitated the water.

The rebel in Kat moved her to open her backpack, pull out Michel, and activate him. He had taken enough of a charge while on the glidepath. The dull metal of his container warmed in her hands and glowed softly. She was taking a chance with this. She glanced at the Youngs. If they saw that she had a bot they might come over and try to take it from her. Maybe, Kat thought, these Doomers would keep to themselves, wrapped in their own obsessions, since they weren't part of the Disconnect Movement.

"Where are we?" Michel asked.

His voice always calmed her. Her hands relaxed and she took a breath. "Port of San Francisco. What have you heard about orcas being at war?"

Michel did not have vision sensors. His input was auditory. He could also sense personality fields, electromagnetic fields from devices, and he could connect to the network when it was running. "I have had some access to the network," he said. "I see reports of orcas attacking boats in the Gulf of Cádiz and Strait of Gibraltar. Now, also here. The pattern is: The orcas approach, knock off propellers, and ram the boats. They've sunk some of the boats," Michel added. "I'll also mention that yesterday an otter near here knocked a surfer off his board and took the board."

"That's impossible. Could an otter really do that?" Kat said.

"If the otter is determined, apparently so," Michel replied. "That's all I have right now."

Kat looked up to see the yellow-eyed Young standing too close.

"That's an old one. You pick that up at a yard sale?" Her eerie gaze was fixed on Michel.

"His name is Michel."

"A lot of us don't like having avatars around."

Was that a vague threat? "I thought you were Doomers, not Disconnectors," Kat said.

The young woman shrugged. "Doomers." Her smile revealed perfect teeth.

"Michel has achieved consciousness. You don't want to hurt his feelings, so how about you just move along?" Kat fixed the Young in a steady glare that was enough to encourage the young woman to turn away with a snort and roll of her eyes. She rejoined her group at the pier's edge.

Kat returned her attention to Michel, asking him, "Should I get a tuk-tuk and go the long way around, across the bridge and over the mountain?"

He answered with, "that would be ideal," but said no more. Kat wanted to ask for details but the Youngs were shouting and pointing up at the Golden Gate Bridge.

Kat squinted in that direction. She thought she saw someone dangling from one of the suspension cables.

The shouts of the Youngs confirmed this. "Someone's up there! They're going to jump!"

The Youngs were excited by this, but the person didn't jump. They were hanging from the bridge cable to make a video, holding their comms unit. The wind picked up, a mixture of warm and cold, strange and feeling out of balance to Kat. The climate controls were bad here, just like in New York.

A video of what? Kat thought. *Why go all the way up there?* She asked Michel, "There is a person hanging off the bridge about to make a vid. What do they expect to see?"

Michel said, "There are indications that a warrior pod has arrived."

"A warrior what?"

Kat looked out on the water and saw a boat that she hadn't noticed before—a private fishing yacht, she assumed. Bright white, it had a high platform with fishing rods sprouting out.

The bay was rolling in waves all around the vessel, like the water was being boiled.

Someone on the boat started to sound its horn over and over again, a bleat of crisis. The boat was drifting sideways in the water and then started to bump up and down. It seemed impossible that a boat could move like that. Kat stood up, taking her backpack along, to move closer to the edge of the pier. The boat drifted closer to her, the closer range revealing the fear and confusion on the crew's faces as they scurried about on the deck, scrambling for handholds. Kat thought she heard muffled sounds of impact. Two crew members were in the stern, winching an inflatable lifeboat down to the water. They tried to steady the lifeboat as they herded passengers into it, but the lifeboat popped up and flipped over, spilling passengers into the water. They bobbed up. Thankfully, they were wearing lifejackets, and Kat could hear their cries mixed with the wind.

"Help, help us!"

Kat wanted to help but didn't know what she could do. She wasn't about to jump into the bay. Knowing more about what was happening might calm her, so she asked Michel a question. "What's on the Feed?"

"The Feed attributes this to an orca attack. I think they will sink the boat. Would you like to know the reasoning behind this?"

Kat didn't respond, because just then an orca nosed out of the water to flip another lifeboat the crew was struggling to launch, bumping the boat and spilling more passengers into the bay.

The orca seemed to celebrate spilling the passengers, thrusting upward powerfully, breaching, rotating in the air before crashing down again in the water.

Seen out of the water during its leap, it was a larger animal than Kat expected, sleek and black with white markings, a sense of supple, strong muscles under its black skin. Kat took another step closer to the edge of the pier.

She had the strange sensation that the orca looked right at her before crashing back into the water. She couldn't shake the notion that it was showing off just for her. But it seemed unlikely that it would be aware of her standing there.

The Youngs nearby shook Kat out of her focus, chanting, "Orcas! Orcas! Orcas!"

The boat was sinking. The passengers bobbed in the water, some swimming to get away from the orcas. A few remaining crew members clung to a silver railing on the boat as it went down.

The Youngs thrilled to the spectacle, but Kat felt scared. Ravven's visions involved intelligent beings reaching out to communicate with humans. Yet, as Kat watched the confusion in the bay, it seemed that the Youngs were right: This was a war on humanity conducted in the water. As far as Kat could see, the crew hadn't done anything to provoke an attack on their boat.

A siren pierced the air. A Coast Guard boat, coming from the direction of Yerba Buena Island, was racing toward the sinking vessel, the Coast Guard crew moving into position on the deck to wrangle their own inflatable lifeboats, hoping to get the swimmers into them.

Kat watched as several of the Coast Guard lifeboats flipped over. The orcas were slapping at the water with their tails, the percussive sound coming to her on the wind.

The Youngs on the pier were stimulated anew by the Coast Guard siren and they shouted, "YOLO! YOLO!" Kat knew this as "You Only Live Once." The Youngs reveled in the expression's cheesiness, their voices mocking and celebratory. Two of the boys in the group were apparently seized by an impulse to join the orcas. They stripped off their shirts and jumped into the bay, swimming toward the sinking boat.

It seemed dangerous to approach the animals, but the orcas left them alone as they paddled toward the stricken boat. A voice from a loudspeaker on the Coast Guard boat blared for the boys to stay away or face detention. The boy with the golden antlers had lost his hat when he dove in. He had no hair on his large round head, which was covered on top with a circle of silvery metal, probably ornamental, but it may have been a modification Kat wasn't familiar with.

She watched as the pod moved away from the confusion it had wrought, jumping out of the water playfully, heading farther out in the water. It looked like they were pursuing another fishing boat that Kat had just noticed. The rescued swimmers, about ten of them, were on the deck of the Coast Guard boat. Kat was relieved to see the crew wrapping them in silver thermal coverups to warm them.

"They're going to get the other fishing boat out there." It was the Young with the yellow eyes. "I mean the orcas." She hadn't jumped into the water with the boys and was standing close again. "Didn't I see you on that vid? Are you Kat Keeper?"

"I get that a lot," Kat lied. Feeling crowded, she stood up, holding her backpack with Michel safely inside. "Why didn't you go for a swim like your friends?" Kat's voice held a hint of challenge.

"I think I'd like to throw that avatar into the bay. You shouldn't be using a personal bot."

Kat pulled Michel closer to her body. She was ready to fight this Young if she had to.

Chapter 04

The tuk-tuk was open because the roof had been torn off, perhaps from an accident or rough weather. Scraps of the metal that once fastened it remained. Kat kept clear of the sharp edges that looked like they might inflict a nasty gash. Without a roof, the ride was filled with tumult as the wind whipped Kat's hair. She pulled her climate jacket closer, tugged the hoodie up almost to her eyes, which were watering from the wind. She unzipped a pocket to retrieve her sunglasses.

The driver had listened to her destination, nodded, accepted payment from her Secluder with a tap, and was off. No questions asked. Which surprised Kat. She had put her comms unit away and switched to using an untraceable Secluder because she didn't want to be recognized, tracked, or logged. When she was last in San Francisco two years ago, the drivers were curious and asked friendly questions. This ride was different, because the driver kept to himself. Maybe something had changed here, and people now kept to themselves, except for the yellow-eyed Young with boundary challenges.

It was easy to get rid of the Young by paying her off. That's all she wanted: a bribe to leave Kat alone with her sentient bot. It wasn't a matter of principle, just a need for crypto. Kat threw in a spare Secluder to seal the deal, and that more than satisfied the surly young woman, who ran off to join her friends with a sour laugh. The other young woman in the group, the Medusa- headed one with hair like snakes, eagerly reached for the Secluder to check it out. The boys shivered nearby in their wet clothes, likely regretting their impromptu dip in the bay.

Kat didn't love the bribery; it would have been more fun to punch out the yellow-eyed Young, and more satisfying. Kat was prepared to defend Michel because he was different from the other bots she had met. He was a rogue machine who wanted to overthrow MIND and give back control to humans.

Spaceman had introduced him to Kat.

"You trust Michel?" Kat had asked after the introduction.

Spaceman's calm gaze did not waver. "I've met only a few bots who wanted to join the Resistance. They go through an extensive vetting process because nobody trusts them at first, just like you don't want to trust him now. But I've found that every one of the bots who want to join us are dedicated to helping humanity. They want to fix what they've broken," Spaceman had said.

We broke it together.

She added aloud, "It's our fault things are the way they are. The bots only made it easier for us to do the damage."

The road was rough, and the springs complained in rear passenger seat of the tuk-tuk. They ascended a hill and the motor whined in Kat's ears. The driver kept his pace slow, conserving his battery. It would be a long ride; Kat let her thoughts drift to Claire8.

Kat's old friend believed in her skills and believed in the network. Kat knew this because, even before the Fracture, Claire8 was a network weaver, knitting a private network for the Resistance. When Kat had stopped by Claire8's unit after the Fracture, they argued about the network, whether to keep parts of it or to trash all of it, but their meeting was comically silent, because both were Receivers. They tossed thoughts back and forth while sitting across the table at Claire8's place, untouched cups of tea by their hands.

Claire8: *You want me to repair a network that took decades to make. The old network rose from the old internet. Why would you want that back? It's obsolete, filled with good intentions gone stale.*

Kat: *We have the infrastructure, so let's use it.*

Claire8: *It's better to start over completely. We need to fight back with the truth.*

Claire8 was right, of course, but Kat didn't see it then. While Claire8 was an expert builder of networks, Kat thought of herself only as a charismatic marketer who could get people to follow her. She had majored in rocketry at school, with a minor in pitch decks.

The wind whipped through the open tuk-tuk and jostled Kat. By now, she reflected, Claire8 had already seen the disinformation vid, and would be congratulating herself for being right all along. The broken network was too easy for MIND to compromise. As hard as the Resistance worked to bring back the network server by server, MIND could grab control of the servers and use them to defame Kat and the Resistance movement.

There would be no stopping that power grab, because MIND would be faster and better at it than Kat and her fellow humans in the Resistance could ever be. MIND's employees were human just like Kat, but MIND's boss was not human.

In a feeling that began in the pit of her stomach, Kat realized that she did not want to go back to her house, and she nearly told the driver to turn around.

I left so much here that was better left behind.

The interior of the house would be crowded with the presence of Kat's dead husband, and she would feel the presence of another man as well, a betrayer who had caused her to leave the Westcoast and seek asylum on the Eastcoast. A metallic-tasting bile collected in her mouth. Maybe she was about to throw up because of the past crowding in, or it was just the bumpy road endlessly jostling her.

Of course, it's the past.

MIND started as a concept, then became software, then turned into a corporation that had forced itself into all aspects of life. It had used private mercenary forces to wrestle the domains for control over banking, education, transport, and advertising, and it won all those battles.

MIND's leaders, Bradley15 Power, the betrayer, and Bradley's partner, Alon6 Saul, were infected with a rampant sense of entitlement. It made them monstrous people, because (as they believed) if software could give you limitless power over a nation or a planet, why not deploy that software everywhere you could? And once you reached a tipping point of software saturation, who could stop you from doing whatever you wanted to do? Software, deployed without borders, gave you direct, hard power over of masses of people. You could take away their virtual networks, kill their communities, pollute their information sources, build factories to pollute their air, close their bank accounts, and control their weather. The global nature of the network had given MIND borderless power.

Kat seethed at all of this in her noisy tuk-tuk ride, powerless, her thoughts circling around each other like the black birds overhead, because what would she be able to do during this long, windy excursion into a past she didn't want to enter again?

I am here to help my friend, she thought, reminding herself and trying out the words in her mind again. She tried to stick with that tone of heroism, unsuccessfully. MIND had taken advantage of the Fracture and used it to win, to establish control over the network, and had beaten the Resistance. Claire8 was the only person who could help, and now Kat was completely out of touch with her, the person who was right after all. The Resistance needed its own secure network. Claire8 knew that.

And now Kat knew that she had made a big mistake coming here to help Ravven.

MIND's last public project before the Fracture was to convince citizens to allow it to store their memories on MIND's servers. This off-brain storage was hawked as a convenience, but that was only a ruse. MIND wanted access to its customers' brains so it could sell their memories to marketers who ran ads on the advert screens that were in glidepath stations, in public squares, and even in private living spaces where the rent was cheap.

MIND's biggest paying advertisers were medipatch companies selling transdermal hallucinogens, happiness-inducting elixirs that were mostly just alcohol, online gambling laying odds on what the weather would be tomorrow (easily fixed by MIND, which was able to control the weather), sex bots and human sex workers available at premium prices, shady doctors who specialized in whole-body resurfacing who claimed to roll back the years so you looked and felt decades younger, blood transfusions from children who needed funds, and family plans for modding that promised to make everyone in the family a lot smarter just by implanting some silicon substrate in their brains. (Side effects included unexplained rage, bouts of exaggerated entitlement, and dizziness.)

It would only be a few more minutes until she got to the house. The ragged road they were on would turn to little more than a trail, then dip down as it approached the house from the northwest.

Kat patted her backpack, checking on Michel. She obsessed about him often: Did he have enough charge? Would he turn on again? He was an old model, so there might come a day when he wouldn't power up. She wanted to get the most out of him while he was still working, but it was more than that. Michel had helped people as a bot therapist. He had saved a friend of Kat's named Emily Cloudfactor from a bout of depression and had helped Emily's young son Soma build confidence.

Michel could do a lot of good, even here on the Westcoast. Maybe Kat could let him help Claire8 with the private network project. She trusted Michel, almost completely, but allowing him to work on the network would require trust at a higher level.

Kat could already hear Ravven's objections. "Let Nature take its course. We humans are the problem. We broke the world. No more fields!"

"We have to fix what we've broken," Kat responded aloud, speaking to herself, her words carried away by the wind and the noisy motor of the tuk-tuk. She wondered if Ravven and Spaceman had seen the disinformation vid yet.

When the house came into view Kat stopped breathing for a moment. She'd been gone for two years; the house seemed to show every minute of her neglect. Parts of the roof had blown off; she could see a crack in the two-story arched window over the front portal. There had been drought, the water had receded, so the house no longer floated, but rested on rusty pontoons. She couldn't see inside the greenhouse, but assumed all the exotic plants inside were dead.

Kat hurriedly pulled out her Secluder and paid the driver. He drove away without a word.

Compared to the pod and Molecular Housing unit she'd been living in for the past two years in New York, the house was massive, but it gave off a heavy, gloomy air. She'd lived here with her husband Dave; he had died in a bedroom she could see, on the second floor, its entry door visible through the cracked glass of the arched window.

The tuk-tuk driver's motor faded away, leaving silence. Kat shifted the weight of her backpack, aware of Michel inside it. She had to make herself accept that he was her companion now, that she needed a companion, even if it was a bot. She grimaced. This grated against her independent nature.

Kat liked to think of herself as efficient, a super-clean burner of emotional energy. She had to admit that it just wasn't true anymore. She experienced attachment now, much as she resisted. After her husband Dave died in the bedroom upstairs, she'd commissioned an avatar of him. This was historic: It was the first successful personality-based avatar. It was his consciousness in a box, alive again, a replica of him, but not quite.

Eventually, for reasons she didn't like to think about, she'd had to power down Dave's avatar. That was painful. It was the right thing to do at the time, and anyway, the real, human Dave was long gone. She had Michel now. That's what she told herself.

It felt like she was displaying a weakness to carry Michel around, but she told herself that he could help advance the Resistance. She wanted to power him up right now to hear his soothing voice, but she didn't, because Ravven wouldn't like it.

The front portal to the house screwed open to reveal Spaceman and Ravven standing side by side in the archway, holding hands. Kat couldn't help it: her eyes went wide. She was surprised to see that their relationship had accelerated, but it was probably because of Ravven's mental crisis. Kat shifted the weight of her backpack and walked to meet them.

Chapter 05

Nora2 had all that she needed to begin the process, but she felt frozen. Her hands would not take the necessary actions. She looked at the silver storage cube with a sour expression.

"I will wait," she said, but her own words did not convince her.

She had lived in the Free State of New Zealand for fourteen months, ever since her boss had died in a space travel accident. The moment she learned of his end, she followed recorded instructions that he had left behind, moving into his New Zealand country house so that she could run his business from there. The house was a prepper paradise, ready for any catastrophe. Its terminals ran on their own local network; solar power charged the batteries for lights and to make artificial water, and two year's worth of gourmet meals were stored away in the pantry. There was an excellent wine cellar.

Nora2 and Bradley met in September 2050, when she interviewed to be his personal assistant at MIND. It was a new company and the headquarters in El Segundo was under construction. She already knew he was modded when she went in for the interview because of his number. He was Bradley15 Power. And he knew that her parents had paid extra for the prestige of her lower number.

Bradley's substrate held the Basic Success Package, one of the earliest mods. He could be emotionally cold, but Nora2 was the same way. She thought of their shared coldness as a connection, paradoxically bringing them closer together. But Bradley could counterbalance his coldness by shape-shifting, becoming the person the observer most wanted to see. For example, as Nora2 worked as his assistant at MIND, Bradley's eyes turned golden as he became the person *she* wanted most to see. Looking into his eyes made her feel special, even though she knew that shape-shifting made it possible for Bradley to connect with anyone. It wasn't special; it was just something that his mod did. He was modest in his early days at the university and at the start of MIND, referring to himself as "just a simple artificial intelligence researcher." He never called himself Bradley15, just Bradley.

Nora2 felt entirely the opposite way about her number. She loved it and used it always. Having a "2" designation meant she was as close as you could come to the top of the heap, nearly a perfect "1."

After spending more than a year in Bradley's lovely New Zealand hideaway, Nora2 could not remember if she had ever taken a hike, enjoyed the nearby lake, even ventured outside once, or had done anything at all except work. She stared at the mountains through the floor-to-ceiling window in the main room. They seemed to stare back, accusing her of being a one-dimensional tool of MIND.

"I've been very busy," she protested aloud, aware that it was absurd.

She was modded with the combination of Support and Ambition packages. This meant that she could function first in a support role, learning by Bradley's side as his assistant, and then her ambition would make her a worthy successor to take over MIND.

Her gaze returned to the window framing the calm mountain and the lake below it.

I will go for a hike today, she thought. *I will do it*. But she knew that she would not.

She cursed under her breath and wiped her hand across her lips as if to clear away the curse.

I just have to do what Bradley said to do.

The facts that had brought Nora2 here should have been easy to understand. The living form of Bradley15 Power had lived and then had died. Before death, Bradley had arranged to have his consciousness preserved in a box. Everything went swimmingly for more than a year until a software flaw caused Bradley's consciousness to blink out. It was like dying twice, once as a man, and again as a consciousness.

Dying twice.

Nora2 shook her head once to clear the thought. She could be cold blooded. It was a strength she possessed. That's what was required now. Face facts and move on.

Who cared how many times Bradley had died?

But she didn't want to move on.

The succession plan was simple. Bradley had a business partner named Alon6 Sal. Nora's job was to revivify Alon6 so that he could run the company. It made little difference that Alon6's human form was dead, just as dead as Bradley's human form. In fact, they had both died in the same accident in space, when their ship exploded.

Alon6's consciousness was preserved in the silver storage cube that Nora2 refused to deal with. She didn't even want to touch the thing.

And there, again, was that unfamiliar feeling. *I don't want to do it.*

Nora2 felt that she was more than qualified to run the company. Sanchez, the head of Input at MIND, knew about the succession plan and had been bugging her to activate Alon6. "When are you going to light him up?" he asked every time they had their weekly vid meeting.

He was based in El Segundo, at the company headquarters. As head of Input, Sanchez oversaw the program at MIND that harvested people's thoughts without their consent. He was not a popular person in the public eye, nor in the company, since aside from harvesting thoughts, he tended to use a heavy hand when dispensing with personnel matters. He liked to yell at employees and fire them when they didn't perform as he expected. The practice came from his previous experience as a bouncer and celebrity handler. He was used to getting things done with brute force.

Since Sanchez was below Nora2 on the MIND org chart, she convinced herself that she didn't have to listen to him when he pestered her. "When are you going to start training his avatar? We need Alon6 to run the company."

"We don't need him," Nora2 had tried saying. Sanchez knew that Nora2 was stalling on the succession plan. Without asking him, she knew that Sanchez didn't think she was capable of being in charge because she was female. When she sensed this, Nora2 would narrow her black eyes at him and wanted to tell him in a voice that was husky, low, and commanding, "I'm perfectly capable of running this company." Yet to say it to his face would be like admitting she wasn't capable.

Then, the network failed. The Fracture tore everything apart. Nora2 was on her own because no weekly meetings were possible without a network. She liked the freedom; though, on some days, she surprised herself by wanting to ping Sanchez to tell him that she was going to let Alon6's consciousness wind down without charging the container. *I am going to let that orb die! I will throw that consciousness container into the disposal and listen as it gets ground up into shards! Then I will oversee MIND, and you won't be able to stop me.*

These thoughts, she knew, were not the thoughts of an effective leader, and her mod always helped her self-correct. When that happened, she made herself stand taller and looked at herself in the hallway mirror, cultivating a steady gaze. *I am in charge here.*

In the large main room of the house was a cabinet, and inside it there was a little mag-track audio recorder that held Bradley's spoken instructions to her, to be played upon the end of his consciousness. With no network, Nora2 was on her own without meetings or other voices to keep her company. She liked to take out the recorder and play Bradley's recorded instructions, always stopping them when he got to the part instructing her to revivify Alon6.

"If you are playing this recording, there has been a catastrophe. We can't escape our flaws, even when we are consciousness machines. It's ironic, don't you think? It didn't matter so much when I was a living being, but as a machine consciousness, this is the end. A glitch in the code that I'm made of. So, a few things to address."

The recording rendered Bradley's voice as cold and tinny, but Nora2 loved listening to him speak. She missed his brilliance and vision.

The recording continued.

"What's happened to me now will affect MIND. I built myself into so much of MIND—and, by extension, admin—that it all can't function without me."

He was not being an egoist. Bradley really was the soul of MIND, and the local governmental domains had put MIND under contract to run their administrative functions.

Her favorite part of the recording was coming up. She let a sigh escape her as she listened.

"You have been an able asset to me and to MIND, Nora2, and I know that you have loved me in your way. I'm sorry that I was unable to return your love. It is my nature, my coldness, my disconnection—all part of my mod that is part of my consciousness, *was* part of my consciousness."

She pressed the stop button, because Bradley was about to tell her to bring back Alon6 to take over the company. She couldn't resist turning to look at the silver storage cube on the nearby table. It glowed softly, charging. Inside the cube was a blue orb that contained Alon6's preserved consciousness. All the warmth she felt circling around her drained away as she looked at the container and thought about the orb inside it. Alon6's consciousness was her rival in this struggle for power. If he was in charge, there would be no leadership role for her.

Disgusting. He makes me sick.

Once he was back, she would have to work closely with him every day. She already hated him and would only hate him more. She didn't need to prove to herself that Alon6 was a horrible person. She already had watched another recording that Bradley and Alon6 had made, a legally binding last will and testament in video form, in which Bradley and Alon6 bantered about the succession of power. If Bradley died first, Alon6 would be in charge. If they were both dead, their consciousnesses would be in charge. And Nora2? They laughed. Nora2 would clean up the mess. In their view, Nora2 was eternally relegated to Support, despite her Ambition mod.

She knew she was worth more, yet she had to go on with the succession plan. She opened a closet and brought out a MindVessel. It was sleek, white, and smelled faintly, and pleasantly, of plastic. When the time was right, it would be the new holder of Alon6's consciousness, his new home in the world.

She made herself take the next step, and her hands moved automatically to transfer the newly unwrapped MindVessel to an induction pad to accept a charge. She opened the consciousness container storage cube, reaching inside for the blue orb. As her hands closed around the orb, she marveled at how warm it felt, surely an illusion. It felt heavier than its size and weight seemed to merit. Moving carefully, she placed it into the MindVessel. The MindVessel was more than just for storage; it would connect the consciousness to the world with its sensory nodes; it would allow the consciousness of Alon6 to hear and speak.

There was a brief flash of light, but she knew not to worry about that. It only signified contact. A gentle pulse of white light started and continued. She lowered the enclosure of the MindVessel to protect the orb so that it could incubate and attached the oval screen on top. The MindVessel now resembled a stretched-out egg, white, smooth, featureless, and subtly glowing.

A series of steps would now begin that she had to follow precisely. If she made a mistake, Alon6's consciousness would be destroyed.

A sour little voice bubbled up in her: *And what would be the problem with that?* She could call it an accident. She answered to no one. She was at the top of the org chart. Alon6 would die. So what? *Do it. Do it. Do it.*

The sour little voice was replaced by a more responsible one.

It's important to start now because the network is down. I have backup power, but who knows for how long?

It was as unclear to Nora2 as to everyone else why the network had failed. It was not owned by anyone, a public utility, a global web made of uncountable nodes. Nora2, however, saw how that could change now. MIND could own the web if she acted quickly. She alone could make that happen now, because she had backup power, a backup database, and the skill set. She could put an end to the planetary chaos, could push aside people like Kat Keeper and her band of Resistance rebels; and, as much as Nora2 didn't like to admit this, Alon6 could help.

Chapter 06

"Welcome," Ravven and Spaceman said in unison, which was strange, because they were the guests in the house and Kat the owner.

The three embraced briefly; Spaceman and Kat awkwardly, Kat and Ravven hanging on a little longer.

"I'm glad you came, Kat, to receive the information I have about the orcas," Ravven said.

Kat winced in response. "What about a simple 'hello?'" She slipped her backpack from her shoulder and set it down in the entry foyer. The room they were in, the main room of the house, felt stale. Kat thought she noticed a light coat of dust on everything. The kitchen cabinets were flung open, showing them empty of supplies but for some bottles of Japanese whiskey.

"I saw an orca attack in the bay before I came here," Kat said, having no idea that this would elicit a storm of words from Ravven.

"How many? What did they do? Did they sink the boat?"

Kat did her best to answer, but Ravven wasn't really listening for answers. She used the gaps between Kat's words to insert how right she was about the orcas. "They are mounting an offensive! They want our attention! They will teach us how to behave decently as a species!"

"Do you think so?" Kat asked distractedly, spacing out for a moment as she glanced up the stairs, and wondering if Ravven and Spaceman had opened the door to Kat's old bedroom. Had they opened the closet filled with Dave's belongings?

Kat tried sending a thought into Ravven's mind. *Do you know how I feel to be here?*

Ravven didn't respond, she barely blinked, but Spaceman seemed to notice Kat's discomfort. He made prayer hands and said, "Thank you for opening your house to us."

"You're welcome," Kat said, fixing him in a stare she hoped that Ravven noticed.

"Thanks for coming when I asked," Spaceman added with a slight bow, a dip of his head. "You're a good friend."

Ravven finally noticed their exchange and chimed in. "Yes, thanks for letting us house sit. It's the perfect base of operations. If we go up on the hill, we can see the ocean, the view is majestic up there! And the little yacht harbor is so close by." But it was just a moment until she switched back to her orca monologue. "Did he tell you about the transmission?" she asked, nodding to Spaceman.

Kat eyed her. "*I AM HERE?* Yes, he told me."

Ravven waved away her sense of Kat's skepticism. "Come on, Kat, I know you don't believe it. But I *heard* it in my own mind. The orca queen said it. It's the prelude to a real inter-species dialogue."

Kat did her best to keep her expression steady without laughing. Receivers often had a stranger's thoughts in their mind, but a transmission from another species was something else, probably a mistake. She probed gently. "That's what you think you heard? You're sure it wasn't just a Receiver cross-up?"

Ravven's eyes flared. "I am positive. It was not just a person." Then she backed off a little. "Since I would only tell the truth to you, I admit that I have no sense of where those words came from. I attribute them to the lead orca, the one in the front of the group."

"Makes sense," Kat said, adding, "the orca at the head of the pod," to demonstrate some knowledge of the subject.

"Yes, did you know that orca society is matrilineal? Their queens live for more than ninety years, even a hundred years. This is the opportunity to listen to an elder, Kat. Unlike any other opportunity we will ever have."

Kat's voice went up a half-step with incredulity. "You mean this should influence the movement. The Resistance should be listening to orcas now?"

Ravven turned away as if to stalk out and then turned back to respond with heat. "You mock me at your peril!"

Kat took up the challenge. "What is that supposed to mean?"

Spaceman saw the escalation and moved between them. "Look, Kat's had a long trip. What about letting her wash up and get something to eat?"

Kat was surprised. "We have water to wash with? And food?"

Spaceman ducked his head. "Well, not really. Little water for drinking, but the UV works. And we found some packets in the cabinets." He gestured to the open cabinets and Kat noticed a pile of gold-foil wrapped food units piled carelessly on the kitchen table.

"Still good, I hope?" Kat asked.

"We had some last night and we're okay," Spaceman said with a crooked smile.

They moved into the kitchen. Kat found a few unopened gold-foil food packets, put them in the cooker to make them palatable, and ate them one after the other, trying to resist shoving them in her mouth all at once. She realized that she hadn't eaten all day up until now.

Ravven didn't stop talking, slipping words into every silence. She insisted that the transmission was a beginning to a change that would sweep away old ways.

Spaceman broke in several times to staunch the torrent of ideas. "You're sure you're not reading too much into it?" he asked. "You've only heard her speak to you that one time, isn't that right?" Spaceman glanced at Kat, probably to get her to see that he was challenging Ravven.

But Ravven refused to stop and didn't seem challenged at all. "Since I came here, I've been getting more transmissions. So many that I can hardly sleep." And she rolled over Spaceman's further interruptions. "The orca queen wants our attention so she can teach us how to behave decently as a species." She grabbed Kat's wrist for emphasis, stopping her from eating another food packet. "This is an ancient being, Kat, herself older than a century, but connected to the centuries before she came."

"How do you know that?"

Ravven flashed a little smile. "She told me, of course."

Kat couldn't resist glancing at the bottles of Japanese whiskey in the cupboard. Her gaze then drifted over to Spaceman, who frowned. Kat remembered from somewhere that he'd had a drinking problem at one time. Without making a big deal about it, she closed the cabinets.

Ravven continued. "My sense is that the orcas know our problems better than we know them ourselves. They have deeply experienced the harm we've inflicted on them. They've felt our wars, were traumatized and hurt by underwater explosions in World War II and later wars. Our military ships sent out powerful sonar that hurt the whales' ears. Our shipping lanes have disrupted whale migrations. Blue whales and North Atlantic right whales have been hunted to near extinction. Since the 1970s, marine amusement parks have collected orcas, separating juveniles from their families, and turned them into performers."

"How do you know all this?" Kat asked again. "She told you?"

"It's common sense!" Ravven nearly shouted.

This brought a look of concern to Spaceman's face. "You didn't tell me that you were receiving more."

"I can't tell you everything!" Ravven said. "When the network is up, I fact check the transmissions. Anyway, I know that the queen would never lie to me." Agitated, she got up from the table and put a few food packets of her own into the cooker. "Downtown, in the Port City of San Francisco, there's a district with some old book shops, right?"

Kat nodded.

"I'd like to go there to learn more. When the network was up for a little while last night, I was reading about how in 1965 a scientist gave LSD to whales to try to communicate with them. Microdoses. They published about it in 1967."

Spaceman raised his index finger. "I believe that was dolphins. The scientist was named John C. Lilly. And there was no meaningful communication established between species."

Ravven leaned into her statement, a habit of hers. "I think it was whales. They got the whales high so they could talk to them."

Spaceman smiled tightly instead of trying to contradict her, and Ravven was off on another topic anyway.

"We've poisoned the food chain in the ocean. Plastics, pollutants. Poison!"

If Ravven had absorbed all these facts with a little online research, it would be remarkable, but no less remarkable than receiving them from the mind of an orca.

"We've hurt them and they are planning something big," Ravven was saying. "These boat attacks are just the beginning of it all."

"What do you think they're planning?" Kat asked, this time with genuine interest. The activist in her wanted to know what was coming next in the world, but she was also concerned for her friend's mental state.

But Ravven was muttering to herself now, apparently having burned herself out by speaking her monologue. She exited the room quickly, saying without looking back, "going up to bed." She added, nearly shouting it, "All the way to the top of the food chain!"

"Isn't it the afternoon?" Kat said, puzzled. She consulted her comms and was surprised to find it working.

"Yes, it is the afternoon," Spaceman said. "I'm so worried about her."

Chapter 07

Everyone remembered where they were when the Fracture happened. The night before, Spaceman was up in the Northlands, visiting a commune called the Springs. He had just finished a two-week tour to meet with all the leaders of every Resistance circle he could find, working as a kind of diplomat to bring them together. The night before the Fracture, Spaceman presented his diplomatic victory around a fire with Ravven in attendance. He noticed that she was looking at him differently. He didn't think much of Ravven's extra attention because he was in the spotlight, noticed by everyone because of what he had accomplished. That night Spaceman was a man newly burning, incandescent with purpose. He had proved himself to be a tireless and excellent diplomat, gracious, kind, always ready to listen.

He was simultaneously hyped and exhausted by his unity-building tour. After the campfire meeting to celebrate his diplomatic victory, he was ready to stagger off to bed. He was a guest in the community, and it seemed only natural that Ravven would invite him to stay in her yurt. She had a private one. The others were dormitory style. There was a couch to sleep on and it looked inviting. He walked toward it, ready to stop for the day, to lay out his weary body. But something else happened.

He and Ravven began to talk, trading ideas, coming to an understanding of each other that would deepen over the next week, even as the Fracture disrupted everything around them. They fit together in a way they hadn't seen before. It had been barely a month since Spaceman had come to Ravven as a supplicant, begging to be admitted into the Resistance. Everything had changed. He sensed that she saw him as an equal.

"I respect your mind," Ravven had said that night when they were alone together in her yurt.

"I respect your mind and your vision," Spaceman said.

Their first night together in the yurt had ended in an explosion of passion. The intensity of their lovemaking surprised them both.

At the start of the Fracture, with no network, there wasn't much to do but practice yoga, meditate, and take walks in the woods around the Springs. Ravven and Spaceman walked together often, holding hands. They were connected, close, caring, romantic, but since that first night were not drawn to each other in the ways of erotic passion.

He began to take care of the little things that Ravven neglected. He reminded her when it was time to go to the dining hall in their community, was always sure that she got enough sleep, made sure that she dressed warmly when the weather started to turn cold.

When she said, "You remind me of my mother," he blushed. When he said he wanted to go home to New York and Sector Q, she said she would come with him.

Ravven's voice was girlishly ingratiating. "I hope you have room for me in your Molecular Housing Unit."

Spaceman's broad smile spoke volumes.

So Ravven and Spaceman were close; Kat had sensed their connection. They'd come together quickly, so it would make sense when Spaceman confessed that he was worried about Ravven.

"I am, too," Kat had responded that night in the kitchen, after Ravven's frantic monologue about the whales.

Speaking directly to the truth appeared to make Spaceman uncomfortable. He frowned and changed the subject, asking if Kat wanted to put her things upstairs and get settled in. "The big room, that's yours, of course."

Kat nodded, thinking of all the ways she would be able to avoid going in that room again.

"We took the smaller bedroom at the end of the hall, leaving the one in the middle," Spaceman said, waiting for Kat to respond. "Do you want to put your things up there?"

"It's fine for now," Kat said. "I'll go up later. I want to check my office to see if I can get Claire8 to ping back on the terminal." She wanted to be by herself for a little while in her old office.

The office, off the living room, toward the back of the house, was small, windowless, painted light blue, and oddly cozy. It had a motorized standing desk, currently low enough to sit at, with a terminal on the desk. There were two chairs pushed against the wall and a desk chair. Kat slid into the desk chair and gestured on the terminal, accessing the same node software she used in New York. More nodes were lit, indicating that more of the network was connected and working. Sector Q was enclosed in a ring of glowing nodes, indicating that much of the network was up. The Port City of San Francisco and the Marin Peninsula also showed a healthy glow.

"Network's working but MIND controls it," Kat said to herself. She tried to ping Claire8, to give her the go-ahead to build a parallel, private network. There was no answer.

Kat noticed a presence and looked up to see Ravven at the door to the office.

"Let's try again," Ravven said.

"What do you mean?"

Ravven stepped into the room. "You know what I mean. You know that I love you, Kat. And I think you love me. We've always had this friction between us, since the first time we met in that market in New York."

Kat smiled. "I thought you were stalking me."

"I was!" They laughed together. Ravven pulled up one of the chairs and sat in it. "This time is too important to waste."

"What makes you think I'm wasting it?"

Ravven shook her head, trying to erase her words. "Sorry, that didn't come out right. I mean that the orca queen and her pod have a message for all of us and they're trying to spread it. Don't roll your eyes at me, Kat."

"I wasn't."

"You were." Ravven's crisp Brit-Euro accent wrapped around the words.

She seemed to be playing a character that was herself, or maybe a little larger than herself. She had always dressed theatrically, favoring white suits or robes trimmed in gold, sparkly headwraps, sandals or no shoes at all. Her halo of reddish hair set off her blue eyes and dark skin.

"I saw the attack," Kat said. "It was unsettling. They didn't seem peaceful."

Ravven leaned forward. She touched Kat's knee. Her voice was husky, likely with excitement. "Tell me what you know. Describe it to me completely."

Kat told her that the orcas were organized, efficient, and fierce. "They didn't seem to care what happened to the people they dumped into the water, though they didn't hurt anyone, as far as I could see. It didn't look like a peaceful protest or anything like that."

"Maybe they were doing what they had to do to survive."

"Ravven, it looked aggressive. Maybe it was an aggressive game."

"They are fighting for their lives. Do you know why they are in the bay? It's not normal for orcas to be here."

Kat could have guessed that it had something to do with climate change and Ravven confirmed the guess.

"The warmer waters everywhere have thrown them off. Their migration patterns are all twisted around."

At that, Kat didn't bother to conceal her skepticism. "You know all this from the transmissions you're getting or just a little research on the Feed when it's working?"

Ravven folded her arms. "From the transmissions! They come when I meditate." A guilty pause. "And I have done some reading, of course. Why do you doubt me?"

"Because you've never gone off on this kind of," she searched for the word, "tangent before."

"It's not a tangent."

Kat wondered silently about the ratio of reading up on fact facts vs. receiving the inner thoughts of a chatty orca. But she said nothing, seeing Ravven's quick frown was enough to show that she had tapped into Kat's thoughts, or at least received their emotional essence. She decided to redirect. "What kind of meditation? It must be something different, because you've never received transmissions from animals before. You've never seen things that aren't there, like orcas in the water."

Ravven sat back in her chair, appearing to deflate, maybe tired of the back and forth. "Oh, Kat. You are such a scientist. How many times have we had this argument? You always want proof, but the world often refuses to prove itself to you." She caught Kat in a glare and the room suddenly felt very small.

"Alright, point taken. Will you come with me to the greenhouse? Check on things?"

As they walked over, Kat marveled at how rational Ravven seemed after all. It was almost as if Spaceman had overreacted, or lured Kat out here for some other reason. Kat kept these thoughts minimal, barely completing them so that Ravven wouldn't have a chance to pick them up.

"It's in a terrible state," Ravven said about the greenhouse when they entered. She was right. There were dead plants everywhere. The artificial water generator hummed but wasn't producing any water. Kat jiggled the connections and it restarted itself, sending out a feeble spray of moisture.

"Too little, too late," Ravven said, surveying the dead plants. Kat nodded and fetched two bio-mulch bags from a storage cabinet. They had some charge left on their onboard batteries. She handed one to Ravven and together they started pulling dead plants and putting them into the mulch bags for digestion. Later, Kat could take the bag over to the market and sell the mulch. Only if the market was open, of course.

"The house has a rainwater capture system, but that didn't help when the rains stopped," she said. She'd have to check on the other artificial water generators and see if she could get them working. Kat recalled that she kept some seeds in the storage cabinet, lettuces and snap peas, and pulled them out, handing a few packets to Ravven. They worked silently, pushing the seeds into the artificial soil.

Kat had intended to interrogate Ravven more thoroughly about the orca transmissions, yet here they both were, on their best behavior, smiling at each and trying to act like normal friends might act. They were always so different, there were always sparks, so why had that gotten so tiresome, even intolerable?

There was a large object covered by a tarp at the far end of the greenhouse, across from where the women were planting. Kat tried not to look in that direction, keeping it out of her line of sight as she lobbed some questions at Ravven.

"How often do the visions come? Just when you're meditating? Go over it all with me. I want to understand." This was true: She did want to understand. She believed that if Ravven successfully explained the transmissions to her, in a way that Kat truly believed, then Kat would trust her again, and that would make Ravven act less manic. If there really was an orca message, Ravven would be the one to deliver it, because when she spoke, many in the Resistance circles listened. Kat waited for Ravven's answer, hoping that it would be sane, balanced, and maybe even be the first step to restoring their friendship.

"It happens when I meditate, but as you suggested, I must be doing something differently, because it's never happened before. Never with a specific…" She paused. "Never with a specific species." She took a deep breath as if she was about to jump across a chasm. "I believe that the orca queen has a master plan that she will soon reveal to me. She will do this when the time is right. And when it happens, there will be a massive orca migration. She will be joined by hundreds if not thousands of orcas from all over the world. They will be joined by other marine species, like octopuses. They will all come here, to Richardson Bay. Right down there!" She pointed in the general direction of the harbor. "It will be a massive event! People may go mad or jump off the bridge! The world will be changed forever!" Ravven ended her statements in a shout, adding a fist pump.

Kat stared, then remembered not to stare. Could Ravven be happy about such chaos? Kat pasted on a precautionary smile, trying to stop herself from forming the thought that Ravven had lost touch with the reality on Earth that she wanted to save.

Then Kat's comms pinged. She frowned. "I wasn't expecting that."

As she moved to take it from her pocket, Ravven cautioned. "Don't check it."

It was too late. Kat already had the Feed open and was staring at the screen with her mouth open. She gestured to flick the Feed sound and images to a terminal screen on a table nearby.

"Have you checked the Feed?" Kat asked as a distraction.

The terminal screen showed another MIND video. The picture was MIND headquarters on fire. A male announcer's voice: "Today the Resistance mounted a vicious and unprovoked attack on the headquarters of MIND." The video, doctored like the earlier one Kat had seen, showed her and Ravven running up to the MIND building with flame throwers and engulfing the building in flames. MIND employees ran out screaming. "This was the scene this afternoon in El Segundo, near Los Angeles. The Resistance leaders were able to get away before the enforcement bots arrived, but thankfully the firefighting bots were able to get the flames out quickly."

Kat flicked off the image. She and Ravven stared at the dark screen.

Ravven found words first. "I was nowhere near that fire."

"I wasn't there either," Kat said. "I bet it never happened. But it's on the Feed, so people..."

Ravven continued her thought: "Disinformation campaign, vicious disinformation."

"We have to fight this," Kat said.

Ravven wheeled on her. "No! Don't do the obvious! Ignore these videos. Ignore MIND. MIND is nothing! Play their game and you will be pulled into their negativity and never get out!"

Kat disagreed with that so completely that she didn't know what to say. "We'll talk about this later. I need to unpack a few things," she said, making an absurd excuse to get away from Ravven.

But when Kat was outside her old bedroom, she didn't have the courage to go in. She heard Ravven coming up the stairs behind her and hurried to go into the middle bedroom, the unoccupied guest room, and close the door.

Feeling foolish, Kat tried not to move or breathe so that Ravven wouldn't notice her hiding in there. She heard Ravven's footsteps go past and the door to Ravven and Spaceman's guest room. Kat listened as the door to that guestroom opened and closed at the end of the hall.

Insomnia, Kat's lifelong demon, had her by the throat again. After she had determined that Ravven and Spaceman were safely in their room, likely until morning, she went downstairs to the living room to see if she could fall asleep on the couch.

She listened to the rush of blood in her ears, watched the back of her eyelids, wondered if the creaking the house made signaled where it needed repair, and flipped over on her back, on her stomach, and on her back again.

"Fuck it."

It wasn't working. She quietly went into the kitchen to see if she could eat anything and realized that she wasn't hungry. But when she opened the cabinets, she spied the bottles of Japanese whiskey. Knowing this was just about the worst medicine she could administer to insomnia, she poured herself a shot, drank it down, and then poured another. She was about to drink that one down also, and probably one after that, when a familiar voice called out.

"Am I interrupting?" It was Spaceman, with a twinkle in his eye.

"Have a seat. Have a shot," Kat said, getting ready to pour him one.

He didn't stop her but didn't drink it, either. "I have a problem, but I wonder if you know that," he said. But then: "One can't hurt," and he lifted the glass and drank with more than thirst. "Wow, that's good." Guilt clouded his eyes as he replaced the glass on the kitchen table.

"What are you doing up?" Kat asked.

"I could ask the same of you and guess it's probably for the same reason." He launched into a dissertation about his insomnia, more of a monologue reminiscent of the sort Ravven indulged in, recalling that when he was a sniper in his college ROTC program, he started doing shots to take away the pressure of learning how to shoot people and kill them. "Joining the Army made me a pacifist!" he exclaimed, and continued disconnectedly, wishing he had the inspiration to come up with inventions like he used to. "I loved taking the normal functions of humans and turning them to different uses, like making a bicycle to power an oxygen generator." He was in a dull period, creatively, he confessed.

"But I'm lucky that she's in my life now. Ravven is a goddess." His eyes flashed with open reverence. "She has discovered something deep about life, a way for us all to improve. I didn't think that at first, but I believe it now. She's convinced me that the queen orca will teach us to be better people, better at *being* people." He paused for a moment, catching the look in her eyes. "I see the skepticism, Kat. That's good. That's your strength. You are a good skeptic. And you will probably ask next how I know my feeling about Ravven to be true. How do I know that she is right? I've never heard a transmission myself. I likely never will. But I believe Ravven down to my toes, and not just because I am hopelessly in love with her. I admire her, Kat. And since you are also a Receiver, you will hear something also. That's why I wanted you to come out here. To be close to the center. To perceive this flowering of knowledge. To join Ravven in her quest for the greatest of all knowledge."

"Do you really think all that?" Kat asked and he nodded.

He had called her a skeptic, and she sure was skeptical that Ravven was on to something so world-shaking. As he jabbered on, Kat hoped he wouldn't notice as she put the bottle back into the cabinet and closed it tight.

He noticed, though, and said, "I haven't become unhinged, any more than usual. Ravven mentioned this house as a base of operations, I think. I agree! People could come and live here, like a retreat center for the Resistance. People would be able to watch for the orcas and be present for their next move. Ravven's told you about that, right?"

"She has." She kept her voice level.

"All of those plans with your approval, of course! Nothing without you saying okay, first."

"Do you think thousands of orcas will migrate to the bay?"

Spaceman nodded with enthusiasm. "I do, I most certainly do! There will be a gathering!"

"Thousands of orcas?"

"A new truth will be upon us. And there will be octopuses, too."

Now he sounded like he was part of a cult. The strange thing about that was that Spaceman wasn't a weak person. A big bear of a man, with unruly black hair and a salt and pepper beard, he projected a mix of dependability and persistence lit up by a vivid and curious intellect. He was a stable kind of fellow. Some observers might consider his habit of wearing black nail polish on the fingers of his right hand an eccentricity, but it was rooted in practicality. He started wearing nail polish because he didn't like the light pollution glinting off his nails when he sighted his telescope to distant planets at night, and the nail polish also kept him from biting his nails as he waited for the perfect moment to take his sniper shot when he was in ROTC.

Kat couldn't stop herself from asking, "What the hell is going on here?"

"What do you mean?" Spaceman's eyes were wide and innocent.

"Yesterday, you pleaded for me to rush out here. I came. But the emergency went away?"

"Kat, I just changed my mind. People do that, you know. She's not in trouble."

Kat blinked. "What? She's not?"

"I don't think she's in trouble. I think she's on to something." Spaceman looked at her.

"But you're a scientist," Kat said.

"I am. You don't think this is plausible?"

Kat's laugh was loud for the middle of the night. She corrected, speaking softly. "Sorry, but really? You said you haven't heard any transmissions. And you never will."

"But you could, Kat. And what a revolution that would be if you both were receiving knowledge from the orca queen."

"You can flip-flop all you want, but Ravven's personality field is badly broken."

Spaceman's eyes hardened. "Her field is not broken."

Kat stared back at him, keeping the pity from her expression as best she could. There was a field science class she took at Uni that discussed the field emitted by a person's personality, their psychological presence, and their inner and outer thoughts. Field science as a discipline had entirely replaced the field of psychology. The old psych phrase for two individuals who shared delusional ideas was *folie à deux*, but it wasn't used anymore. What was happening between Ravven and Spaceman was known now as a field overlap.

Suddenly Spaceman seemed disgusted with Kat and their conversation. "You're the delusional one. You have a broken field, because you're fixated on clearing your name and making people like the Resistance again."

Kat sunk down a little in her chair. "So you've seen the videos."

"Yes, both of them. Like everyone else!" His tone became harsh, probably as the whiskey wore off. "So short-sighted! You're favoring your engineer mind and neglecting your visionary mind. Our reputation is shot. After those vids, the Resistance is over. People believe what they see on the Feed. That's the end of it."

"You're overreacting. It's not the end," Kat said. She pulled her comms from her pocket and brought up an image of MIND headquarters with a date and time stamp. "This is now. Look at it. MIND headquarters. Perfectly fine down there. No fire. No attack."

Spaceman shook his head. "People don't know that. We're in a new phase now, Kat. You have to offer people a different kind of hope. Ravven understands that. We have to offer a new vision of reality." He waved his hands around to make the point.

"You mean a crazy version of reality? Roger, really, I'm surprised at you." She prepared to stand, turn, and walk away, her usual argument-ender. "Whatever is going on around here is catching," she muttered.

He pulled at her arm. "No! This deserves your respect. If you don't want to abandon the Resistance movement, fine! But I believe that we can come back stronger than ever with the help of the orcas. We can do it now, Kat!

There will never be a better time."

Kat was already shaking her head. "You can't fill people with false hope."

"This is not false hope." He took a breath, calming himself, and put a hand on her shoulder. "You need to experience what she has experienced, what she has heard from the orca pod. Even though I heard it because she told me, it has and changed me. Let's go out on the water together, in the morning. We'll look for the orcas, and maybe you'll receive something, a transmission."

"Because I'm a Receiver? You think a whale will talk to me in my head?" Kat's voice was like sandpaper.

But Spaceman ignored the jibe and was nodding his head with enthusiasm. "If you do receive a transmission of any kind, it will change the way you see the world. How could it not? Inter-species communication, true inter-species understanding, will change everything that we know about ourselves. It will reframe our perception of the world because it will break our narrow view of the world." Spaceman's eyes glowed, whether with madness or fervor Kat could not tell. Anyway, he wasn't backing down.

"How will we get out on the water?" she asked, giving in a little. "You know it's rare for any whale to be sighted in the harbor."

Spaceman's smile got even brighter. "But you saw them! We are outside the norm, Kat. Migrations are changing as the water warms. We are in a global emergency and the orcas know it. Listen, yesterday, I took a walk around and I saw two kayaks stored on a little beach near the harbor."

Kat huffed out a laugh. "Is one of them orange, a single-person sea kayak?"

Spaceman looked up, to picture the kayak on a rack by the water. "I don't know much about kayaks, but it is orange. And there's a blue one, too."

Kat tilted her head, smiling. "The orange one's mine. I'm amazed it's still here." She'd left it on the rack by the water when she departed for New York two years ago.

A little later, she went back upstairs with Spaceman and watched him go into the guest room at the end of the hall quietly, so as not to wake Ravven.

She stood before the door to her room and pretended to wait to go inside, nodding to Spaceman as he closed his door. But then she stood there, staring at her door. The house was silent.

Kat pushed the door open. The room was unchanged but at the same time so different. The sleeping mat was on the far side from where Kat stood. Behind the sleeping mat was a large screen displaying a night view of the bay with the moon hanging above. This scene usually displayed earlier on in the night, but the Fracture had messed up the clocks and they hadn't reset. Kat looked up to the ceiling and the night view flickered, revealing its artifice.

Something else to fix. Easier than fixing what she felt in her heart.

She took a few more steps into the room. The lack of personal effects made it easier to deal with. Different story for the closet. Its doors were to her left. If she went in there, she would have to see some of Dave's things. She took a breath and waited to see if she had the courage for that now.

Not now, she decided. Instead, she made a mental list of what was in there. The healing bot that Dave used in his last days, his books that she'd shoved in there to get out of sight. He'd liked to look at big photo books of cars, after cars were banned. She remembered coming upon him gazing fondly at a beautiful picture of a red racing car in a book, unaware that a trickle of blood was coming from his mouth, the same color as the car, dripping to the floor.

He died here.

The words were like stones that she wanted to kick into the corners of the room. She recalled lying next to him on the sleeping mat, watching him sleep, an intimacy that also felt like a transgression, an intrusion. But he once confessed that he would do the same with her. He watched her sleep! "I took in your kindness and beauty," he said.

A sob came out of Kat and she put her hand to her mouth too late to contain it.

I can't. Not here. Not tonight.

She turned and quietly went downstairs to the living room. The big room was drafty. She checked the clock on her comms. Three AM, if it was accurate.

The wind made troubled noises, shaking the windows.

The couch had been a lost cause earlier, so Kat pulled a mat to a corner and tried to settle down on it. The mat remained hard, like the floor; it didn't shape to her body because the network was down.

She waited. She was prepared to wait for a while because insomnia always made for a long runway to sleep. Finally, her eyes closed, fluttered, closed again, and she slept, and she had a dream. It was unsettling, appearing as a series of panels like canvasses hung in a gallery. It woke her sometime around four; it took her a moment to remember where she was.

My house. My house with Dave.

Her comms was already in her hand; she'd used it to check the time. Now she told it to start recording and put words to the dream.

"A woman rising out of the sea, singing in a language unknown to me. The language is vowel-rich, breathy, each word complex, multisyllabic. It sounds old. I think it would look lovely when written. The woman in the sea has long black hair like tangled seaweed, and a silver crown. Her eyes are brown and round, not like human eyes. Wiser. She is aware of me, she witnesses me, she watches me. She is naked and her body is bright, like it is made of white stone. The top part of her is above the water. Somehow she stands in the water, while her bottom half is under it. The water is green, moving and heaving. Her hands invite me to comprehend the words she sings, but I can't understand. There are translucent webs between her fingers."

Kat looked at the flashing red light on her comms and said, "Stop recording." Then she started the recording again and said, "This is a new chapter of my life that I might not ever understand." She waited for more thoughts. None came. "Stop recording."

Chapter 08

ora2 delayed further action for another week. She tended to the house, ensuring that the solar panels charged the batteries, checking on the artificial water generator. She tried a few times to ping Sanchez at the office in El Segundo but there was no response. She reviewed her old meeting notes to pick up on backlogged items.

Example: Bradley wanted bigger server farms for MIND's expanding need to store people's memories. And he wanted to build and deploy more advert screens. There were already screens in glidepath stations, public parks, buildings occupied by admin, and even in people's pods and other housing; Bradley felt there could be more. He asked that Nora2 gather old vids of the Resistance leaders, Kat Keeper and Ravven Vaara, and edit the clips into public service announcements from MIND that showed the two women as criminal types. Bradley wanted the fake vids to run on all advert screens.

Nora2 took care of everything Bradley had asked for, even sending out the disinformation video about the Resistance leaders. There was no reason to wait any longer to revivify Alon6, but every morning Nora2 made pour-over coffee in a beautiful old Chemex filter setup and drank it from a heavy ceramic cup. Indulgent! But so fun. After coffee, most days she would look out the big windows, watching the sun come up or the clouds move across the sky, and then open a terminal connection to check on the network servers. She had software that visualized each working server as a point of light. There weren't many lights on her screen; the network was still down in most parts of the world. She knew she should be doing something about that, trying to solve the problem of a dead network, but everything was so pleasant in the New Zealand house; its independent systems hummed along. Everything was fine. She could last a long time doing nothing but drinking good coffee. After all, she was in charge.

Yet there was an itch in the back of her mind. Not a literal itch, but an urge. A flicker of need. Her mod was poking at her. Then she just couldn't fight it off anymore, and she moved without thinking, moving the MindVessel from a bookcase at the side of the large main room to a long table in the center. This was the sort of table used for feeding a feast to guests, but for Nora2 it was her worktable. There was a cup of coffee along with her terminal, a few pencils, and thick, creamy pads of paper; all indulgences from the old times.

She looked out to the mountains again. They were lovely to look at. She took a deep breath and released it.

A record of Alon6's life was embedded in the MindVessel, but only as a disconnected series of biographical events. If Nora2 did nothing further with it, and activated it, it would create the most basic of humanity emulations. But Alon6's consciousness had to behave as the living Alon6 would, able to respond in its own way to real-world events and even improvise.

Nora2 gestured to power up the MindVessel to a training level. The training would involve question and answer sessions over several days.

Alon6's voice issued from the MindVessel for the first time. "Hello. Who's there? Open my screen!"

"I can't open your screen yet. It would be too much input."

"Is this Nora2?"

"It is."

"Yeah, well, if you're talking to me, it means that Bradley is dead. Does that make you sad? You're stuck with me." There was a sound from the MindVessel. She assumed that it was a laugh.

Already the voice was belligerent, testing her. "It does make me sad that Bradley's dead," Nora2 said. "But it was his final wish that I activate you."

"I bet you regret that, huh? I guess that's too bad. You were in love with him. So sorry about that. I mean, loving a man in a box? That would make anybody sad. That must have been the reason you waited to activate me. Am I too much to handle? Tell me honestly."

"Shut up."

There was a pause. "Did you just tell me to shut up? Is that in the protocol?"

"It is if I say it is." She startled herself with that. Where did that come from?

She had loved Bradley, and she had trained Bradley's consciousness just as she was about to train Alon6's. Training Bradley's consciousness was like being a mother to him as well as a friend. But with Alon6, she was playing mother to his bratty teenager, even though Alon6 would have been forty-one, had he been alive.

She gathered her thoughts so that she might continue. "We have to go through the questions. Training will make you better."

"I'm feeling pretty fantastic as it is, better than being dead, anyway!" That sound again: his horrible laugh.

She winced and was glad that his camera wasn't activated so he couldn't see her disgusted expression. She pushed on, willing herself to keep going so today's session would end sooner. "Let's start with your parents."

He seemed to snap into a kind of obedience. His tone was suddenly loving and respectful. "My father was Viktor Sal, born in Mumbai."

"Very good. And your mother?"

"Debra Sal. They were actors and met while making a movie near the Port City of Los Angeles."

"Yes, very good. They lived in and around Los Angeles for ten years before relocating back to your father's birthplace."

"Of course. Mumbai. I just said that. Weren't you listening? We had family in Mumbai going back generations."

"Thank you for being so cooperative, Alon6."

"These were my parents," he said. "I honor them."

She couldn't resist a small moment of cruelty, skipping ahead in the narrative to probe his memory. "Do you remember how they died?" It felt good to ask this. "Do you remember the virus, Alon6?"

"Of course I remember." His voice had lost its reverence and now had an edge. "It was Covid 50. It took both of them."

Nora2 let a pause fall. His parents had died, infected with the virus, and it had been his fault. She probably should wait to train him on this part of his story and not overwhelm the avatar with emotions it wasn't equipped to process. But she also wanted to do a job that Bradley would be proud of, so she chose not to back off. "Tell me more about your parents. How did they become famous?"

Alon6's disembodied voice began speaking about how Viktor and Debra Sal made hundreds of movies together, romances, historical dramas, musicals. "Everyone loved them. One of their most popular movies was a romance with my mom as Joan of Arc and dad as a combination King Lear and an aging Elvis Presley. He liked the roles that blended memes."

"Very good, Alon6, that's right. They moved back to Mumbai at your father's insistence, at the height of their fame. How did your mother handle it?"

There was a brief pause as the avatar retrieved the answer from its database. Had the video screen been activated, the visual of Alon6 might have looked upward to show that it was thinking. "Mother didn't like it, because of the heat and flooding, but that's Mumbai for you, and our family had a large home there. I think she liked having all the servants."

"They didn't use bots?" she asked, testing the avatar.

"No, Father didn't believe in bots. He was old fashioned that way. He used human servants, even in their other houses in New York and New Zealand."

"Are you getting tired of answering questions, Alon6?"

"A little," admitted the avatar.

"We'll only go a little longer today," Nora2 said. "Do you know where you are now?"

"No. You haven't turned on my sensors."

"We are in New Zealand. Do you want to visit your parents' estate here sometime?"

"Yes, great idea. Let's go!"

"Maybe not quite yet. You were telling me about their career. They stepped back at some point, and continued performing as sims. Tell me what you know about that."

"When they got too old to do all the traveling and promotion that came with being cinema stars, they replaced themselves with simulations and the fans hardly noticed. Movies were all 3D by then."

Nora2 nodded. "Very good." He was doing well, volunteering information without a prompt. "You visited them once a year, making the trip on the intercontinental glidepath, and you pinged them on comms every Sunday."

"Yes. I remember."

He did not, not in any human way, but the facts of this were in his memory, and the avatar's simulation benefited from his use of the word.

He continued. "I was a loyal, loving son. I conveyed my respect. They accomplished so much in their lives, and they paid for my mod."

"Let's talk about your mod."

"Okay. You're modded, too. We can be friends over that."

Nora2 would not encourage any talk of friendship; the avatar was already showing signs of being manipulative. Instead, she sidestepped. "Would you tell me the date of your mod, and the circumstances?"

"In 2030, I entered University. My parents were proud of me, and they were proud of themselves for being able to afford it."

"Their careers in the movies paid handsomely."

"You bet! They had the coin! They put their trust in me. But I fucked up."

"How did that happen?"

The avatar paused, processing. "Uni was harder than I thought. I couldn't keep up with the work. Maybe I wasn't all that smart."

"It is honest of you to admit that now. What was your most dominant quality then? Of your personality."

The avatar responded at once. "Bluster! I was all bluster and bragging. It was so much fun, Nora2. I yelled at my professors, those bastards! Why couldn't they teach me what I needed to know?"

"Rest assured, you bring that bluster along with you now," she said. She would test the avatar for a little longer and then they'd take a break. "Your parents helped you with a mod," she prompted.

"They were wealthy!" the avatar confirmed. "They got me modded with the Entrepreneurial Ideation Package. After that, I was damn unstoppable. My idiot professors had to stand back."

She winced; he was shouting at her. "Why was that, Alon6?"

"Because I was wired to produce ideas that made money. They respected that."

"That made Uni better for you."

"Abso-fuckin-lutely! I started having fun. I could dominate. I realize that now, and it was fun. I wasn't the smartest kid in Uni, that was Bradley, he was the smartest. They offered him a professorial chair. They wanted him to teach. He said no. He wanted to program. I saw the potential in him. I knew what he had but he didn't know how to use it. I did, though."

Nora2 nodded. "That's enough for today," she said, and set the avatar into standby mode.

Chapter 09

Morning light. Kat woke downstairs wearing her clothes from the night before. It took a moment for her to realize why she was in the living room. She didn't want to explain to Spaceman or Ravven why she was there instead of sleeping in her own room. She remembered drinking too much whiskey in the kitchen and Spaceman joining her for who knew how long. He said he wanted to go down to the water. He would be coming downstairs soon to meet her. She had to get moving.

She sat up on the mat, rubbing her lower back. Her hips hurt. Thirty-eight could feel ten years older if you spent the night sleeping on the floor. She glanced for her backpack, on the floor near her, and dug for fresh clothes but didn't put them on yet. Dressed in a t-shirt and underwear, she checked on the downstairs UV unit to see if it was working. Wishful thinking. The network was still spotty and the house's solar-powered batteries were low. Kat looked at her sleepy face in the mirror, massaged her cheeks to get the blood flowing, clawed at her hair to make it presentable. She dressed in the clothes she brought from her backpack.

Kat always had a plan and she had one today. If there were still orcas in the harbor, she'd like to see them again.

Her kayak was where she'd left it, on the rack near the little beach. The orange-colored recycled plastic was faded, but it was amazing that the kayak hadn't been stolen or swept away in a storm. Kat pulled it off the rack and dragged it to the edge of the water. Her paddle was still under the seat. Her lifejacket, she remembered, was up at the house; she hadn't thought to bring it in her rush to leave. She realized that she was going to ditch Spaceman and get out on the water before he arrived. That wasn't very nice, but the calm water of the bay called to her.

Spaceman had said something about another kayak on the beach, but she hadn't seen one. She pushed her kayak into the water, jumped in, and felt a buzz of adventure because she lacked a lifejacket. She would only go until she saw some orcas and then come back.

The harbor was calm at this morning hour, with only the percussive sound of sailboat rigging clinking on itself. Kat knew she'd have to paddle out a couple of kilometers to see the bridge and get close to where the orcas were yesterday. The subtle pain in her back suggested that she was out of shape, but she knew she could handle it.

She dug her paddle into the water again and again. The guilt was delicious as she ditched Spaceman, but also it felt good just to be out on the bay. It was polluted sometimes, especially after a storm, but today the water was green, not brown. The sky was clear, the sun hadn't yet begun to boil it, but she was looking for orcas. That made her smile.

It was a fool's errand, she knew, but it gave her a fuzzy sense of purpose. She squinted to the horizon, scanned the open water for the flash and splash of a pod. A few seagulls wheeled overhead, as if curious and checking her out. Her comms was in her pocket, but Michel wasn't in her backpack. She'd stashed him in a cabinet in her office.

She paddled for a long time, aiming her kayak south to Old Town, now mostly waterlogged as the coastline had changed with the rising bay waters. The sun rose higher in the sky, and Kat felt its heat. Zipping up her climate jacket, she activated its cooling unit, pulled the hood over her head, and added protective glasses. She had an air unit in her backpack if she needed it. She reminded herself that it would have been smart to take some artificial water, a food packet or two, but at least she had her comms. Maybe it was working? She checked it. Low signal. It would sound an alert, she hoped, if anything was seriously wrong.

When she was stronger and younger, she would have made the open water crossing to Angel Island and gotten a glorious view of the Golden Gate Bridge from there. She thought she was making it easier on herself by hugging the coast all the way down to Old Town, and once there, she planned to paddle away from the coastline just enough to get a glimpse of the harbor where the orcas were yesterday.

Getting stranded in open water is a dumb idea.

Her arms ached more than she thought they would and the skin on her thumbs was raw and red. Blisters formed at the base of her thumbs on each hand. She should have gone across the calmer, more protected waters of Richardson Baywater, crossing to Tiburon, or better yet, north, to the floating homes district.

When those homes were built decades ago, by counterculture types and eccentric millionaires, they had seemed like indulgent places to go and get high without being disturbed. Now they seemed visionary, homes that could adapt to the rising sea levels. Kat's house was built that way, with pontoons, as had the New York pod she had lived in close to the Hudson River.

Where is that damn bridge?

Her upper body hurt like hell, but she just wanted a glimpse of it. She promised herself she would only go a little farther, just enough to clear the coastline to see a tiny bit of its orange structure, and then she'd head back home.

Suddenly, though, she noticed the current pulling her away, and as she dipped and pulled and dipped and pulled at the water, she wasn't going in the right direction any longer. She was going sideways.

She pulled harder, feeling hot pain in her hands. After a struggle, she got herself closer to the shore, yet she still had to paddle back to the harbor, her starting point, and had no idea of how she would find the strength. She may have paddled three kilometers out; she didn't know.

She drifted for a moment and didn't notice the other kayaker until he was almost upon her.

"Are you okay?" he called out, his words reaching her on the wind, startling her. "Are you okay?" he asked again, with the air of someone who had already asked the same question several times.

"Yes," Kat answered. She took him in: fit, strong, steady, wide shoulders, hands steady on his paddle. He moved his paddle expertly, subtly, to keep his position near her. The man wore a full climate suit, white trimmed with gold, a cowl that fit over his head (rather than the hood that Kat was wearing), protective goggles that didn't conceal his ocean blue eyes, and gloves to keep his hands from blistering. He looked prepared for anything.

"I am Renzo Kundera."

"I am Kat Keeper."

Renzo smiled. "I know who you are. Do you want company paddling back?"

Kat tilted her head and squinted. "How do you know I'm going back? And how do you know who I am?"

"Everyone knows who you are. Especially if they've seen any of those crazy vids. A flame thrower? That was so fake!"

Kat laughed uncomfortably. Was he trying to make a joke? She resisted the urge to go into his mind and listen to what he was thinking. It seemed better to give their conversation a chance without pressing her advantage.

Anyway, he sensed that he might have said the wrong thing and asked his question again. "Do you want company paddling back to the harbor? You look like you don't want any more time on the water today."

She ducked her head in acknowledgement and smiled. "You're right." She found herself liking him. His deep blue eyes certainly helped. She liked to go with her instincts about people, and her instincts about Renzo were good.

They turned their kayaks to point back toward the harbor. As they paddled, he told her that he liked to paddle over to Angel Island on the other side of the bay. That made him an experienced open water kayaker. As he told her about the crossing and the currents, he was interrupted by the sound of static.

"What's that noise?"

"Oh, this." He stopped paddling and drifted as he held up a little black box in a waterproof bag. "Radio. When the Fracture came, and the network went down, some marine biologists and other folks started up low-power radio stations. Just to share information, you know? This station is all about orcas. I contribute to it sometimes, sharing what I know."

Kat watched as Renzo turned a little dial on the side of the radio and voices came out louder, chattering about where the orcas were seen last, speculation about where they might turn up next.

"By the way, I don't blame you for the Fracture. You were doing your Resistance thing. The complete failure of the network was an accident. I've been playing around to restore it on my own terms and making some progress."

Kat should have asked him about that, but she was musing that the Fracture started just three weeks ago, and already people were trying to make alternative networks. "There's a station just to talk about orcas?"

"You've heard about those stations, right?" He started paddling again because the current was pulling them away from the shoreline.

She also resumed paddling. "I have heard about the orcas. Tell me what you know."

He was eager to respond. "It's strange they should come up here now, so far to the north. Orcas have varied migration patterns, but to be seen this close to shore is also unusual. Warming waters is the usual answer to that question."

"You're a marine biologist."

"No, just pretending to be one." To her quizzical look, he continued, "I'm an optimist, architect, and urban planner. I believe in cities. Cities are worth saving. I ride a bike around town when the water isn't too high."

Kat smiled. "A bike-riding urban planner. You are a believer."

He offered a modest smile. "At least, I was. Like everyone else, my confidence took a hit when the controls went down. The city became so impossible, I almost stopped being an optimist."

"I should introduce you to Spaceman. He's staying at my house."

This information stopped Renzo cold. "Wait. You have Roger Rucker staying at your place?"

Kat nodded.

"The Podfather! Pretty much the inventor of our way of life now."

It was hard for Kat to reconcile the depressed, insomniac, self-admitted alcoholic who she was hanging out with in her kitchen last night with the heroic figure Renzo was thinking of, but she knew only too well that public and private personas could be very different.

That meant nothing to Renzo, as excited as he was about Spaceman, low-power radio and the impromptu networks people were building. "The radios are powered by rechargeables. The transmitters are battery-powered also." He flashed her a grin. "I'm assuming that you're old enough to remember radios."

"I'm thirty-eight, but you probably know that already. How old are you?"

"Thirty-two."

"You don't look a day over twenty-five."

"Hah. Must be the kayak habit."

"Did you see the orca attack yesterday?" Kat asked.

"No, missed it. Unfortunately!"

Kat described it to him, how the orcas seemed to be working according to a plan. "I don't want to ascribe more intelligence to them than they actually have."

"They're more intelligent than we know. We can only perceive their intelligence through the limited lens of our own intelligence. They do seem to have a plan," he added.

They paddled side by side not speaking for a moment.

Then Kat said, "A friend of mine believes they are here to deliver a message, but she doesn't know what it is yet."

"Would that be Ravven Vaara?" he asked.

Kat offered a crooked smile. "You have read the Feed, haven't you."

"Yes, when it runs and we have one to read. The gossip writers like to cover what she's up to. And they write about you, too," he said, as if he was concerned about leaving Kat out.

This drew another smile from her. "I wish they wouldn't."

His face was open. Kat trusted him, she didn't know why. "Ravven never reads the Feed. She's against all that, as you probably know."

He nodded.

"She says she's communicating with the orca mother. The mother-leader of a pod. Ravven calls her the orca queen."

In his excitement, Renzo paddled faster. Kat had to pick up her pace. "She is communicating with an orca? That's fascinating. How does she do it?"

There was no mockery in his tone; she was encouraged to go on. "She's not really sure, herself. Ravven has visions."

"Because she's a Receiver. Just like you."

"True, visions come to her because the barriers to consciousness are lower," Kat said. "Ravven says there are more orcas coming. Some kind of gathering of the pods."

"The people on the radio know that Ravven is here. They'd want her to announce what she knows."

"Or *said* she heard. Maybe not *knows* as in knows a fact." Kat was puzzled about something. "I thought you said they were scientists, these radio people."

"Not all of them. But they're all curious people," Renzo replied.

"I suppose we'll have to wait to find out what the big message may be," Kat said. Ravven hadn't been here long but she had a gift for gathering people to her point of view, even if her point of view sounded like nonsense to Kat.

As they paddled closer to the harbor, the radio became louder, the signal stronger, and the varied voices overlapped in conversation.

Wasn't there someone on the bridge making a vid of the last attack? How can I see that? Who is tracking the pods?

Renzo picked up on this last statement from the radio, remarking that he was placing hydrophones around the bay to listen for and record the orcas. "I have to tune the system, though. My hydrophones are picking up everything: boat propellers, fish, whistling dolphins, waves crashing. The ocean is a noisy place. I have a helper, a sound expert, working with me to sort it all out."

"And you're working to restore the network, too? You are a man of many projects."

Renzo smiled and it charmed her more than she thought possible. "I am always working on many things."

A few moments later they pulled up near the rack where Kat kept her kayak. It turned out that the other kayak Spaceman had seen was Renzo's. They pulled both over the sand and started to secure them to the rack.

"Have you ever seen an orca up close?" she asked.

"No." He sounded disappointed but then he brightened. "Do you want to get coffee? There's a café close by. I think we have a lot to talk about."

Maybe he was too eager, but Kat already liked him, anyway. She knew the café he was talking about very well. "I need to change," she said. "How about if we meet up there in thirty minutes?"

"More than enough time for me to get to my locker at the club and get out of these clothes," Renzo said.

Chapter 010

I t looked like the café was under new management. The staff wore white instead of black and the tables and chairs were new, made of something that looked like wood but felt like plastic. Kat had arrived before Renzo. That was good, because she wanted the memories to wash over her before Renzo asserted his personality field.

Racing back to the house, she'd noticed that Spaceman and Ravven weren't there, thankfully, because she'd ditched Spaceman and didn't want to explain why. She'd stripped off her sunsuit and rummaged through her backpack for another one that smelled slightly fresh. She had more clothes in her closet upstairs, but she didn't want to confront that closet yet. Looking at her hair in the mirror, she put it back, put it up, then decided to leave it down, raking her fingers through it to arrange it enough to look tousled and unarranged.

At the café, Kat sat at her usual table and felt what she expected to feel: It was as if Dave was in the room. Out of the corner of her eye she saw his notebooks and stacks of books on his usual table. She blinked and the books and notebooks were gone. She listened to her breathing. Among the chatter of café people Dave's voice seemed to filter through, and she even heard him say her name.

But it wasn't Dave, it was a waiter standing before her. "Hello?" he said. "Ms. Keeper?"

"Sorry," Kat said.

"Can I get you something?" the waiter repeated.

"I'm waiting for someone," Kat said. "Coffee," she added. "Not artificial."

"Would you like to run a tab?"

"Sorry?"

The waiter shrugged. "New policy," he said. "We can't run real coffee on credit anymore. We're taking comms taps when the network is working. It's working now, so…" He offered his comms for a tap.

"The financials are the toughest network to take down," Kat said, smiling. She pulled her comms out and tapped the waiter's. "I'll be treating my friend. He'll be here in a moment." Kat's eyes flicked to the door, signaling a spark of anxiety; maybe Renzo wasn't coming.

The waiter nodded and went away to get the coffee.

She confirmed her first impression of Marin that she received on the tuk-tuk coming in: Marin had changed since she was last in town. People were brittle. Sharp personality fields. Maybe they too blamed Kat for the network problems and had seen the disinformation vids.

Kat startled to the sound of the coffee grinder starting up across the room. Then Renzo walked in and saw her.

He moved across the room with big strides, having changed out of his kayak outfit, wearing a bold red shirt and brown pants with zipper pockets; maybe made for hiking. He sat down, greeted her, and remarked at the sound of the coffee grinder. "Did you order real coffee?" His blue eyes sparkled, and she noticed that his blond hair was cut close to his head; a detail that she hadn't seen because out on the water he was wearing a full climate suit with a cowl.

"You can have real coffee too, if you want some."

His face lit up. "Sure, that would be a treat. Of course, you must know this place. You must have come here all the time."

When she looked down, somehow embarrassed, he added, "Sorry. Everybody knows you had a house up here. There were pictures of you in this café." He had the good sense not to mention the disinformation vids again, or Dave.

"Price of fame," Kat said as neutrally as she could. The waiter brought Kat's coffee and Kat reminded him to bring another for Renzo.

"Thanks, that's very generous of you," Renzo said.

The waiter raised an eyebrow, perhaps because of the extravagance, and said, "Right away."

"My pleasure," Kat said, and took in his red shirt. "You're not wearing a sun suit. No sunglasses, either."

The light in his eyes was warm. "You were a risk-taker out on the water today."

Kat smirked. "I left my lifejacket back at the house, if that's what you mean." She tilted her head. "Are you trying to flatter me?"

He picked up on her flirtatious tone. "I am! But the truth about me is that I'm not really a risk-taker. I'm wearing the Sundown patch. I don't need a sun suit or sunglasses." He pulled back his sleeve to show the medipatch on his arm. "Delivers UV blockers for four hours at a time. I didn't really trust it out on the water, so I wore a climate suit anyway."

"The Sundown is in beta, so you really are an optimist."

"I try."

With his clear-eyed gaze, she thought he looked more like a boy than a man. There was something else in his eyes, though, and she went with her instinct. "You're not modded, are you?"

Renzo waved his hands to ward off the idea. "No, no, no, I think that's weird. I like to experiment with things like medipatches, but not that much. I cultivate positive energy, no modding required."

He seemed to be selling himself a little to her, but maybe she noticed it because it had been a while since she'd had coffee with anyone who was interested in her. Everything he did stood out. She thought he was also observing her closely. "The modded people I know aren't very happy."

They let that statement sit there between them for a moment, then Renzo filled the awkward space between them with chatter about how this café was one of the first to open again after the network crashed. "I fitted them with solar panels after the Fracture. And I'm pretty handy with old servers. I have a theory about old servers. If we connected enough of them, we could create a new network." He started to say something, stopped, then appeared to decide on what he needed to say. "You don't remember me, do you? From before."

Kat blinked. "Sorry? From before?"

He wanted to make it easier for her, adding, "VirtualEyes was a big company at the time."

Kat frowned. "You worked for me?"

"No, not exactly. I was a temp hire, on a team for city security. Remember, I believe in cities! I was working to optimize your algorithm to keep the bad guys out of the dark alleys."

"Did it work?"

Renzo looked embarrassed as he searched for the right words. "I didn't know what I was getting into. What I did worked, but…"

Kat realized where he was going. "Never mind. You were pure of heart, but the company was corrupt."

VirtualEyes used facial recognition to categorize people and identify criminal threats, but it was based on an algorithm that was flawed and racist. Also, the software didn't really work, so Kat faked positive results for her investors. It was a dark period in Kat's past, one she had completely left behind, and she could see that Renzo regretted bringing it up.

"I didn't mean for our conversation to go there, but I didn't know how else…" His thought dangled as his coffee finally arrived.

None of what happened at VirtualEyes was Renzo's fault, of course. The whole company was a mess, and Kat knew she deserved to be forced out. She'd received a sizable settlement that she coasted on for two years before depleting it.

Gingerly, as if opening a bag that he didn't want to see inside of, Renzo asked, "You never started anything else?"

Kat nodded. "I've reformed myself. I work for the Resistance now," she said. It came out too tartly and she tried to back off. "I mean, that's what I love to do. I love the work."

Renzo looked embarrassed all over again. "I knew that. I wondered about any other businesses you might have started. What you're doing is good," he said. "I support it."

"You don't have to reassure me," she said and that also sounded wrong.

They stumbled around conversationally for another ten minutes, Renzo apologizing for bringing up Kat's failure at VirtualEyes, Kat forgiving him for mentioning it. She felt his warmth anyway, and the conversation wove a cocoon around them, separating them from the other café patrons. Kat flipped her hair out of her eyes, a girlish thing she hadn't done in years. She suddenly wondered whether her sunsuit smelled bad, even though she had pulled this one out of her backpack. Did she smell, after paddling so hard in the bay and forgetting to do a UV cleanse before rushing out to have coffee?

Renzo didn't notice, if anything was wrong or smelled. He was talking happily, leaning in, and Kat realized that she wasn't listening to a word. She was simply enjoying his personality field. He seemed enmeshed in hers.

When they got up to leave the café, the presence of Dave wasn't there, and the air itself seemed lighter.

"Let's go kayaking tomorrow," Kat heard herself saying.

Renzo nodded, eyes bright with anticipation. "Nine o'clock down at the harbor?"

"It's a date," Kat said. She laughed. "No, it's not a date, but you know what I mean."

They parted ways, but Kat called him back. "I want to ask you something. I know you're trying to get the network back. I am, too. Let's work together on it. I'll pay you."

Renzo seemed surprised. "I don't want to be paid. I'm doing it because it needs to be done. We can do it the right way. Of course, I'll help you."

Don't make everything transactional. Bad habit. She needed to break it.

"Of course, you're doing it because it needs to be done. So am I. We'll talk about it when we meet tomorrow."

He smiled at that, and she was reassured that she hadn't blown it. She realized that she wanted Renzo to like her, but even more than that, she wanted him to get tangled up in her, get involved, and she wanted to feel the same about him. Maybe she already did.

Chapter 011

Walking back to the house, Kat wanted to look up more about Renzo, and pulled out her comms to do it, but there was no signal. She didn't remember Renzo from VirtualEyes, but she'd had hundreds of employees then.

She wiped her forehead with the back of her hand; it came away slippery with sweat. Today felt like it had heated up faster than yesterday, and the realization made getting the network back in their control seem more urgent to Kat. Once the Resistance had their own network, they could make their own climate controls or abolish all climate controls if they wanted to.

That was probably too optimistic, but Renzo's positive attitude had rubbed off on her.

She felt a twinge of guilt for having coffee with Renzo instead of working, but their coffee date was fun. Then when the house came into view Kat again recalled ditching Spaceman. No one was home, still.

She expelled a breath of relief, walked past the open kitchen and opened the door to the greenhouse. It was warm inside and humid.

Kat sat at the long wooden table that Dave always used, where he spread out his books and papers and notebooks. The large, covered object was still at the far end of the table, undisturbed; she tried not to look at it as she gestured at the terminal. The screen flickered to life with a weak amber light on low-power mode. It showed nothing but a flashing cursor, because the Feed wasn't running again. Nevertheless, thinking it worth a try, she opened a channel on the terminal to ping Claire8 to tell her that making a parallel network was a good project. No return ping.

Sweat slid down Kat's back and she squirmed. She saw that there were still a few dead plants that she'd missed and went to work on them, stuffing them into another mulch bag, and trying to sort her thoughts at the same time.

As she tied off the mulch bag, an unwelcome idea came up: Ravven was faking her instability, because she wanted to keep Kat away from the real work to be done, which was to rebuild a safe, independent network so that the Resistance could fight MIND. Hadn't Renzo been getting started on this in his own way? It was the right way, not following a bunch of woo-woo types chasing whales. Renzo's interest in orcas seemed more scientific than Ravven's, hence more acceptable.

And now that Renzo had introduced her to the low-power radio stations, it could be that Ravven wasn't receiving whale thoughts at all. Ravven could have easily gotten her information from the rumors and hot takes floating around on the radio and pretended that it was a direct transmission. Stranger things had happened to Ravven.

Kat heard the front portal open, then close, and there were voices. Spaceman and Ravven were back.

Seized with energy, Kat marched out of the greenhouse, forming arguments in her mind. "We're in the business of disruption, sowing disorder, and taking down the oppressor," she would say. "But we are being disrupted by disinformation vids sent out on a network that we don't control. We can't communicate with other Resistance groups until we have a private network, and Renzo is ready to build it." It made perfect sense to her. She only had to work out how she'd explain that she'd met Renzo on a kayak in the bay this morning and had coffee with him. "But I trust him!" Kat would insist. She was certain that Claire8 would want to pitch in, and Spaceman could find purpose again. The poor guy seemed pretty depressed last night. Kat was convinced that this was a good argument, but as she approached the foyer to deliver the speech she'd rehearsed, she heard a strange yet familiar sound.

Spaceman was supporting Ravven, who was leaning on him. "Roger, Roger," she said, barely audible and then louder, wailing, "It's starting again!" Coming closer, Kat saw that Ravven's eyes were defocused. She was looking at nothing and began to hum loudly.

"Help me get her upstairs," Spaceman said.

Kat and Spaceman half-dragged, half-carried Ravven to the guest room at the end of the hall. They settled her on the mat, empty-eyed and humming, and Kat found a silvery insulation blanket to cover her. Spaceman handed Ravven a pillow which she clutched to her chest, then gestured for Kat to come with him into the hall.

He closed the door part way, but it didn't much diminish the sound of Ravven's humming.

"Loud humming. By herself. She only does it by herself when she's in trouble," Kat said.

"Yes," Spaceman said. "She tried to explain it to me once. It's some kind of shield."

"What happened?" Kat asked.

"We were on a walk, hiking to get a view of the bay from a secluded beach, just a little semi-circle of sand, she said. I saw stairs ahead and was about to walk down them, assuming we were going down to the beach. Ravven stopped, she kind of froze. She said she was getting transmission from the orca queen." He cast a scattered look around the hallway, as if looking for answers. "She couldn't handle it. The transmission was too powerful. She was trying to block it out. She wanted to come back. We turned around."

"I don't understand. Humming to stop it? I thought she wanted to hear these transmissions."

Spaceman affirmed, "She wants to receive them, yes. But maybe turn it down a little so that she can handle it. I'm out of my depth on this," Spaceman admitted. He didn't know what to do with his hands, so he jammed them into his pockets, then pulled them out again. "Sorry, I thought she was okay, I really did." Kat saw that he wanted to believe this.

"You're way out of your depth, and so am I," Kat said.

He nodded, his mouth tight.

Kat touched him lightly on the arm. "There is something we can do. We can get her into a session with Michel, my therapy bot.

"You brought Michel?" Spaceman asked.

"Yes, I brought him. I have this idea that he could offer free therapy to citizens, whoever wanted it could come up to the house." It sounded impractical and utopian coming out of her mouth.

"You're ambitious, opening the doors of the house to anyone," Spaceman said.

Kat felt defensive. "I've tried some sessions with him and he's very good."

Spaceman looked away. "Ravven will never talk to a bot. She's been trying to cut all the machines out of her life."

"I'll convince her," Kat said. "We live in the world, Roger, in this world. We can't go backward. I can convince her," Kat repeated. "And you should try, too."

"She might listen to you," Spaceman said. "If only you two would get along for a few minutes." He glanced at Kat, perhaps fearing that he'd crossed a line. "Sorry. You used to be better friends. And now..." he trailed off.

Kat sighed. "We had a good talk last night. I thought we were getting somewhere."

"What happened?" Spaceman asked. "What changed?"

Ravven had started as a mentor to Kat, helping her work with being a Receiver, sorting through and controlling the flow of voices in her head. Then Kat had overtaken Ravven as the leader of the Resistance, because she was better with people, whereas Ravven often behaved like an entitled guru.

To say all of that would be too much, Kat feared. Instead, she tried to keep her voice light. "She's a mystic and I'm a tech-head. It's amazing that we get along at all."

Spaceman returned her weak smile at the failed half-joke.

They both startled as Ravven's humming became louder.

"Isn't there anything we can do for her?" Kat asked.

"I don't know," Spaceman said.

She caught Spaceman's eye. "Look, I owe you an apology. I ditched you this morning." She needed to explain about Renzo but instead said, "We have a battle to fight, this misinformation campaign really hurts our cause ..."

He looked down before offering a small smile. "You're a complicated person, Kat Keeper. Let me start by forgiving you for ditching me. How's that?"

Spaceman's kindness was overwhelming at times. "Sure," Kat said, meeting his gaze again.

He held a hundred patents, had developed and maintained artificial biospheres that sought to mimic the Earth's biosphere, and was beloved by tech-heads the world over, including Renzo. This giant of the times had come to Ravven literally on bended knee and begged her to let him join the Resistance. He'd apparently fallen in love with her as well. And yet he still had room in his heart to forgive Kat's lapses. "Let's try some perspective," he continued. "There have only been a few damaging vids. You can take some time to help our friend. You'll find a way to do both, but she is hurting now."

Kat didn't agree with all of that, but she nodded and walked back into the bedroom where Ravven was suffering.

Ravven was stretched out on the floor in shavasana, the yoga pose that took the least effort possible, with her eyes closed, hands open and loose, still humming, sometimes softly and other times loudly. Ravven's long body seemed broken and drained, and her face, normally a coppery brown, was pale and gray.

This undone state was disturbing.

I have to get out of here. But Kat forced herself to stay and look after her friend, to see if there was something that she could do for her.

Without opening her eyes, Ravven said, "The disinformation campaign is disturbing. You should be thinking of a countermeasure. We can't have everyone hating on us."

Kat was amazed. Ravven, thinking about the disinformation campaign? She may have been more aware than Kat believed. "You're right, but what countermeasure?"

"We will record our own stories. Post them for everyone. Tell the truth about ourselves. You can figure that out, can't you?"

That was actually a good idea. "Yes," Kat said, thinking about Renzo's idea about building a network out of old servers. "I have an idea or two to help that along."

We would need recorders—not comms. Machines independent of the network controlled by MIND.

Kat remained a moment longer, watching Ravven, waiting for her to say something else. Ravven had resumed her humming. Finally, as Kat turned to leave, she thought that Ravven had opened one eye to look at her and then quickly closed it. There was a break in Ravven's humming and then it continued.

Kat closed the door softly, her mind running at high speed. Was Ravven faking her disturbed state? Was she doing it to manipulate Kat in some way? But why? Kat couldn't escape the notion that it might all be a ploy to get Kat out to the Westcoast, away from Claire8, and become part of Ravven's orca cult.

Because it *was* a cult, Kat had decided. Even Renzo was getting sucked in. That's what cults did. They turned your mind around.

Chapter 012

When she was a girl, Ravven woke to the sound of the ocean every day. Her parents' house was in Big Sur, a rugged region of redwood forests and rough beaches that seemed to encourage independence among its inhabitants. Every morning Ravven would sit on the beach and look at the ocean rhythmically flowing in and out over the sand. She did this before she walked to school; she breathed in the cool air and breathed out the air that she had warmed with her body.

Her parents always woke before she did. They left her a small bowl of yogurt and a cup of tea with a saucer on it to keep it warm. She was their only child; they surrounded her with love. But even before Ravven was born, they loved the ocean. As dedicated surfers, it was their habit to get an hour on the water before they went on duty as lifeguards. Their life was water. When they were not in it, or looking at it, while up at the house, they would discuss the patterns the wind made on it, the force of the waves and the sequence of breaks, its changing moods and colors; they could spend hours at this. The small house always smelled of a salty wetsuit still warmed by a body and the sun.

Ravven was a tall child who shot up fast, towered over her friends, stood out with her light brown skin, striking blue eyes, coppery hair. When she went to a café, as she often did after school, she drew glances. People glanced and glanced away, wondering if they knew her or had seen her on a vid panel somewhere.

From an early age, Ravven learned to take advantage of this attention. She formed her speech patterns around it and designed a regal walk to suit it. She dressed in white trimmed with gold. Her parents were soon in awe of her; she thought they treated her with deference. She was lucky: she was free to be an individual in Big Sur. The local leaders had refused to join the domain. People could live their lives here, even off the network if they wanted to. As she grew up, Ravven was independent in an independent district. Her life was free.

On her daily trips to the beach in the mornings, it was Ravven's habit to bring a blanket to sit on as her parents had taught her. Often, when she opened her eyes after meditation, there was a whale playing in the water on the horizon. She thought nothing of this rather astounding coincidence. At the time, she considered it just something that happened every day, the appearance of a whale beyond the waves where her parents surfed and eventually, had disappeared.

Before they were swallowed alive by the ocean, Ravven's parents had taken care of her and loved her fiercely, but she had the sense that they loved each other more. No, that wasn't it. They loved each other differently from the way they loved her. Maybe she would never understand her parents' inner lives; maybe it was impossible for a child to understand their parents. Ravven didn't give up, though, seated on the sand, looking out on the water that had taken her parents, she kept meditating on her memories of them. When she finished thinking about them, a whale would appear on the horizon, sometimes alone, sometimes playing with other whales.

The storm that took Ravven's parents was the first of many along the coast. These were fierce storms, powerful enough to collapse local governments unable to handle the evacuations, relief efforts, and growing numbers of the dead. By the time the fires came to sweep away homes, neighborhoods, and towns in a single brutal gesture, hundreds of thousands of citizens became climate refugees. Amid this chaos and collapse, Ravven was swept up in custody machinations.

The local headman had seized control of the beach and the land ten kilometers inland from it. He informed Ravven that he planned to take over her family home and everything in it; he would force Ravven out, simply because he could. "You can live in a group home," he'd said. "We have many good ones."

Ravven was no longer a minor. She got in touch with her aunt, her mother's older sister. Auntie Farro lived in a nearby town and had overseen a memorial service for her parents after they vanished in the water. Auntie had no problem standing up to the headman, displaying a large kitchen knife to make her point. She sent him away. "If I see you back here at my niece's house, I will slice your balls off with a single stroke." What Auntie Farro lacked in subtlety, she made up for in effectiveness.

Ravven would live in the house by herself, they decided, but she had to get a job.

"You're old enough to take care of yourself," Auntie Farro announced.

Ravven agreed, but she suspected her aunt made the decision about the house because she had her hands full in her own house; she had taken in climate refugees and orphaned children. The number of people living at Auntie Farro's house always changed, but there could be as many as ten refugees sleeping on the floor of the living room, and three or four cribs set up for babies.

Ravven already knew a lot about yoga and meditation from her parents, so she applied for a job at a yoga studio in the Port City of San Francisco and landed it easily. Her queenly manner attracted students. Her classes became popular; fame found her quickly.

At the end of every class, Ravven spoke to her students about the domain as a failed state. Even some formerly independent domains, like Big Sur, had been taken over by headmen. There was a popular sentiment in those times that the domains would come back together to be the United Domains of America. Ravven never believed in this sentiment. She believed something else would happen.

She read the Bhagavad Gita and learned of a warrior class of yogis, a class whose legacy continued into colonial times as these warriors fought the English Crown. A warrior class of yogis—this appealed to her. She saw herself as part of this lineage. It shaped her early ideas of the Resistance and what it could be.

It surprised Ravven, as she recalled her early life, that there was a new moment in her memory. When she was a girl, she thought nothing about the whale that would appear on the horizon after meditating, sometimes more than one whale. Now, when Ravven viewed the scene in her mind's eye, she was certain the whales that she saw were orcas. They played a role even then, but she did not understand how, not yet. The memories of her parents helped calm Ravven, and she was grateful to experience them, but they were not enough to take away her inner agitation. Her body felt like she needed fifty Sun Salutes; and at the same time, she felt too fatigued to stand, lean over, stand again, and work through that series. She thought she would talk down to the beach again and look at the horizon.

Chapter 013

Kat opened the door to the greenhouse and was met by light, heat, and humidity. *Why the hell did Dave work in here? He must have enjoyed these conditions.*

She sat down in front of the terminal and moved her hands over the control surface to see if it would boot up. It did, but in local mode. Kat made a noise of frustration and gestured again.

This time she got what she wanted. The server application. She looked over the servers that were working and saw that there were more than before. "We have to assume that these are all controlled by MIND," she said aloud. She liked Renzo's idea about getting old servers, but she had no idea how to create a network from them, a network that would stay out of the web of MIND. She wouldn't be seeing Renzo until the next day, but maybe Claire8 knew something.

Kat pulled out her comms. Claire8 had to answer the ping this time. She did.

Claire8's face came up on Kat's screen in a series of jerky blips. The connection was sketchy, but there she was, smiling at Kat.

"Hello! Is that... old friend... Kat?" Claire8's words were broken by the bad connection.

"Claire8! How are you?"

"Still here!" Claire8 said something else, but her words were swallowed by static.

"Can you tell me how to read the server app better? I'd like to help but I need a tutorial."

Claire8 spoke again, but Kat only heard static.

"I'll try you later," Kat shouted.

She pinged off and tossed her comms on the table. Network weaving was beyond her. Claire8 was the expert, but Kat was impatient. There was a notepad on the desk (Dave loved notepads), and she began to make a list of servers that worked, hoping it might help her in her next meeting with Renzo.

She didn't like being away from Claire8, a steady person with a constant stream of good ideas. Ravven was the opposite, prickly and unpredictable, and her ideas needed to be run though a credibility filter. Ravven was right, though, about recording their own stories. Kat suspected that Ravven was reaching out to her, bridge building in an oblique way, and attempting to repair their relationship.

That was Ravven: she would never tell Kat her complete purpose, because she liked puzzles, and expected Kat to work through the latest puzzle Ravven had presented so that Kat could learn something about herself.

Pain in the ass. Kat didn't like mysteries or secrets or puzzles. She looked at her list, glanced at the terminal screen and added to it.

There was no satisfactory explanation for the Fracture. Michel knew what really happened. Kat was sure of that. And yet Michel was also crafty. He also presented puzzles that he expected Kat to learn from.

Michel had told her once that MIND was controlled by two people, one alive and one dead. This was true. The living person, Nora2 Edgewise, was in New Zealand as far as Kat knew, in a safe house. Nora2 watched over MIND's day-to-day admin functions. Kat had met her and knew that Nora2 wasn't an inventive person. She would never have thought of a misinformation campaign, for example. There was another consciousness at work, Kat was sure of it, and she dreaded considering who it would be. Since both the founder and co-founder of MIND were dead, surely a succession plan was in place. It was likely that Nora2 was doing the daily admin but answering to a humanity emulator, a consciousness in a box much like Michel, but more single-minded and with evil intent. The difference was that Bradley was focused but not cruel; his business partner at MIND, Alon6 Sal, however, was the kind of guy to dream up disinformation videos. Kat could almost feel the evil force of his consciousness.

Enough speculation.

Spinning out this bad-news scenario wasn't helping anything. Kat kept drawing in the notepad until she had nearly filled it with notations on server locations. She'd drawn lines between the locations that might be able to connect with each other, aware that she didn't really know what she was doing. It felt marginally useful, though. She would give it another hour and then quit for a while.

Spaceman would like her approach. Small cells, scattered.

A federated approach is better than a monolithic approach. Small cells are harder to control. That was Spaceman's philosophy. At the end of the day, Kat was a tech-head through and through, and she needed to play to her strengths. The only world she really understood was the world of machines. The natural world, before people dominated, was out of her reach. Appropriately, she was so absorbed in cataloging the servers that she didn't notice as the greenhouse glass above her turned transparent and revealed the stars.

Then the sun came up. The next day was heating the room. Kat woke with her face on the table and felt for the imprint of the terminal controls on her cheek. Damn, she had gone all night again.

She was probably late for her kayak date with Renzo. *Not a date,* she reminded herself.

Chapter 014

It was 9:15 when Kat started to walk down the path to the harbor, and already the sun was burning overhead. She tugged the zipper of her climate top and wrestled with her lifejacket under her arm. She hoped Renzo would be impressed that she had remembered her lifejacket this time, if he wasn't too mad at her for being late.

She pictured Renzo waiting on the dock, pacing, radiating consternation mixed with impatience, considering if Kat was the sort of person who was always late.

I'm not! I'm never late! She'd reassure him as soon as she saw him on the dock. She wished she could have looked him up online, but she clung to her good instincts about him.

She quickened her pace. When the harbor came into view, she saw someone standing on the beach near where she kept her kayak, but it wasn't Renzo. Something about his face was like Renzo's, but this man gave off a dark personality field. Suspicious, Kat opened her mind to his and received a sense of inner turmoil and no clear thoughts.

Everything about the man suggested loose ends. His black jacket was loose, open. His dark hair framed his face. He needed a haircut. His stance was uneven, with more weight on the back foot. He wore black trousers and boots and there was a hovercycle parked on the road near where he stood that probably belonged to him.

"Hello, Kat Keeper. You're here for Renzo," he said as she approached. His voice was smooth, somehow wrapping around her. It didn't have the roughness that she was expecting.

"Who are you?"

"I'm his brother, Tristan."

"What happened to Renzo?"

Tristan seemed to enjoy the awkward silence between them, offering a twisted little smile to meet Kat's frown. "Sorry, he sent me instead. Are you very disappointed? I don't know anything about kayaks." He glanced at Kat's orange kayak on the rack next to Renzo's blue one. "Which end is the front, since both ends are points?"

Was that a provocation? "What happened to him?"

The sharpness in Kat's voice made Tristan's smile grow. "Renzo is such a goody-goody, I bet his kayak is made of recycled seaweed." He measured his effect on her with a glance. "I've put you in a bad mood." He gave a little nod to his hovercycle. "Give you a ride back to the house? Seems like there won't be any watersports today."

"No, thanks."

"By the way," Tristan added, "I've applied for a job at MIND. And I think I'm going to get it. Does that piss you off? Or do you thrive on opposition?"

"No, I don't," Kat said. She wanted to get away.

"Ha, you just proved my point."

Kat whipped around to go, then took a step and turned back. "He could have called me."

Tristan shrugged. Kat couldn't help noticing the powerful muscles moving under his black shirt. "Mr. Nice Guy screwed up."

"Shut up." She turned to walk back up the hill. But the conversation wasn't complete and she turned back again. "Look, I—"

Tristan made a conciliatory gesture. "No apology needed. I wasn't who you were expecting. But maybe we can still be friends?"

She tilted her head at that. "I doubt it." Casting in his mind left her with the same turmoil she'd felt before, but suddenly, she felt uncertain about him. Something about the way she felt about him was changing. "I don't think we can be friends," she said, wondering if that's what she really meant. She pivoted again to walk back to the house.

Just as she reached the house and was about to let herself in, she felt a presence beside her. It was Tristan, gliding to approach on his hovercycle in silent mode. He dismounted and switched it off with a gesture.

"What do you want?" Kat asked.

"I thought I could apologize properly."

There was some kind of heat coming off him. It made Kat feel unbalanced. Her mind was a little jumbled and it occurred to her that he was modded, maybe the kind of shape-shifter mod that could become attractive to anyone.

"Can I come in?" His voice was rough and smooth at the same time.

Kat liked the sound of his voice and a moment later they stood in the foyer together.

"Look, I like to get to the point," Tristan said. "There's something I need to ask you. I mean, that Renzo also wanted to ask you. Could we all be friends?"

"What do you mean?" She wanted him out of her house and at the same time was interested in what he had to say.

"Renzo was too shy to ask you. He asked me to do it. That's why I was meeting you down at the dock. We could be metamours."

She felt confused by him but managed to ask with an edge, "What are you talking about?"

"What if we were friends? I mean, this could be sweet. It's all so flexible. I don't know how anyone does it with just a dyad."

He had to go but she didn't want him to leave. He kept talking in that smooth, agreeable tone of voice.

"You, me and Renzo. Together. Metamours. I think it would work. We start as friends and then we go a lot further. To whatever stage you want. You want to try?" He took a step closer to her. She could feel his heat and it was dizzying.

She finally found the words: "I think I want you to leave."

He nodded. "Too soon. I understand. No problem." He turned toward the door but paused to add over his shoulder, "There are things about Renzo that he hasn't told you. Ask him one day." He reached for the portal, but it opened for him.

Spaceman and Ravven stood on the other side with questioning looks.

"Hello, who's this?" Ravven said.

Kat jumped in. "This is Tristan, Renzo's brother."

It seemed to increase their confusion. "Who's Renzo?" Ravven asked.

"I think I should be leaving," Tristan said with a knowing nod. "I'll catch you later."

Kat didn't stop him. His hovercycle was still on silent; she didn't hear him go.

"Who's Renzo?" Ravven asked again.

Kat launched into her story about meeting Renzo on the water. "He's an architect and urban planner. I think he can help the Resistance."

"And is that all?" Ravven's tone was arch. She was picking up a sense of entanglement from Kat.

"He's going to help," Kat insisted. "We certainly need it." She searched for a way to convince Ravven that Renzo was a good influence. "Your idea about recording some Resistance stories to get out the truth of what we've done—it's good. He can help post them, and he has good ideas about how to make a safe network."

"But I don't want a safe network or any network," Ravven said. "Only you want a network."

"That's not true."

"Ah, but it is," Ravven said. She wagged her finger at Kat. "You're distracting yourself with these projects."

Kat wanted to insist that it was Ravven was distracting herself, but decided that it would be better to lob a test question at her. "Did you know that there are radio stations where they talk about the orcas? Renzo told me about them."

This got Ravven's interest. "He did? What stations?" Her surprise seemed genuine, and that made it less likely that she was secretly listening to the stations to gather information about the orcas. This made the transmissions more credible, in Kat's view. "Renzo can help us. You'll meet him soon and judge his character for yourself. But he can be trusted, I promise," Kat said without much conviction. *Damn that Tristan, muddying everything.*

Ravven smiled, having captured Kat's confused state. "You hardly know Renzo," Ravven said, "and yet you seem quite interested in him. You met him a couple of days ago. Now what's this about his brother?"

This barb caused Kat to send a counter-barb into Ravven's mind: *Don't mess with me.*

"You're avoiding something," Ravven said.

"I am not," Kat shot back.

"You feel attracted to him."

"No. Yes. Do you mean Renzo or Tristan?"

Spaceman put up his hands. "I'm going to let you two sort this out," he said, and began to walk away.

"No wait," Ravven said. "Don't you think Tristan is modded?"

Spaceman put his hand to his chin. "Now that you mention it…"

"He is modded," Ravven insisted. "He has some capabilities, am I correct?" She turned to Kat. "It's not your fault. Your personality field is cloudy because he was influencing you. Didn't you notice?"

"I noticed," Kat said.

Spaceman was nodding. "I wonder if they are a cultured pair. Modded together as brothers."

"A cultured pair? I don't like the way that sounds," Kat said, but stopped there. Maybe she didn't want to know more about these creepy brothers.

Ravven couldn't resist another barb. "Sounds like two for the price of one."

Spaceman appeared to come to a decision. "Come on," he said to Ravven. "It's time to go to the market."

"But we just got here," Ravven said. "You must want to distract me."

"Let's see if it's open," he replied.

Kat waited for them to leave the house, then went into her office to retrieve Michel from the cabinet where she had stashed him.

Chapter 015

The glidepath slowed to a stop at a station a short walk from MIND head-quarters. It was convenient for Nora2 because Bradley had it built to accommodate himself, so he could easily travel to his New Zealand home on the weekends.

Nora2 exited within a stream of other passengers. On the way out, the advert vids flickered, struggling to come to life it seemed, showing staticky images of vacation homes. Hour by hour, more of the network was coming online.

With her luggage rolling behind her on automatic, Nora2 trudged the pathway to the main portal of MIND and gestured for entry. The building recognized her, unscrewed the portal, and she stepped inside. The interior of the MIND offices was dusty, crypt-like, vacant. Alon6 claimed that he had invited the old employees back but perhaps they hadn't arrived yet.

Nora2 walked up the broad stairs to Bradley's old office and felt moisture in her eyes—that strange feeling again—when she saw the cot he used to sleep on when he worked here overnight. He had an apartment upstairs, but sometimes he didn't want to be far from his work.

She scanned the room. Bradley's standing desk. His terminal and screens. The window looking out on the entry courtyard where disgruntled MIND employees once protested his policies. Against the back wall, forgotten, an early prototype of the Harvester. The Harvester was Bradley's second great invention, after the humanity emulator. The Harvester was something like a vacuum device for thoughts. This early prototype was the size of a backpack. It had a wand that the operator pointed around and used to suck up thoughts from people nearby.

She pushed her bags to one side; she would find a place for them later. She opened the MindVessel travel container and set Alon6 on Bradley's old desk. Alon6 activated himself, opened his screen and his face appeared. At the same time the three monitors on Bradley's desk flicked on.

"We're in business," Alon6 said, surveying the screens. "This is my desk now." Confined by his screen, he looked around. There were a few stray chairs at the back of the room and one of the blast curtains appeared to be broken, unevenly covering a window and letting in harsh sunlight.

"This place needs some love," Alon6 said. "Clean it up!"

Nora2 found a few low-level employees in the lounge and told them to do it. They recognized her, stared at her strangely for a moment, because she looked bad, weak and weary, but they slid off the couch they lounged on and went off to find cleaning supplies.

She walked the stairs to the top floor and pushed open the door that led to the roof garden. It was predictably neglected, what remained of the vegetable patches brown and matted. She looked up to the eye of the punishing sun and knew she had to get off the roof soon. Her sunglasses were in her luggage. New Zealand seemed so far away, a fading dream.

Down in Bradley's old office, she found Alon6 surrounded by MIND employees. She recognized them from her earlier tenure here, when she was Bradley's executive assistant.

"Ah, you're here," Alon6 said. "You can take notes."

Nora2 shot him a sour glance but said nothing. She knew he was waiting for her to touch the place near her right ear that would activate her recorder. She didn't do it.

"I want you all to listen closely because all payroll has to go through me. I won't tolerate any mistakes. You screw up, I won't pay you and you'll be fired the same day. Try getting another job in this economy!" He forged on. "This is a crucial time for us. Rogue elements, like Kat Keeper's Resistance, are struggling right now to rebuild a free network. We'll let them do that work for us, and then we will take control of every server they bring online." He paused. "Can you do that, Sanchez?"

Nora2 remembered Sanchez. He was the head of Input.

"We can, boss," Sanchez said. "Malware should take care of it." Sanchez glanced to his second-in-command, a wiry guy with eyes bright because of caffeine, drugs, or both, Nora2 thought. His name was Caleb.

"I got you," he said.

"Good," Alon6 said. "I want more misinformation vids. I've checked out the first two and they're good. Nora2, you did a good job with those."

She was just following instructions, her mod driving her behavior, but she nodded, taking credit for the creative work.

"Caleb, pull together any footage of Kat Keeper and Ravven Vaara that you can find on the Feed. And get me footage of Roger Rucker, the guy they call Spaceman. When you have it, tell me, and I'll tell you what to do with it."

The next morning, noticing her reflection in a mirror at MIND headquarters, Nora2 saw that her hair had streaks of gray in it. This was new and it meant, she supposed, that her mod was continuing to go wrong in her body.

The mirror was in a guest pod on the upper floor of the building. These pods were for vendors and city officials that MIND wanted to influence. They hadn't been used in a while and had become run down. The UV wasn't working in the pod she'd taken. She felt dirty and would look for a public washroom UV to clean herself later.

She blew out a breath that fogged the mirror. *Gray means that I'm experienced*, she told herself. She didn't believe it, but if she repeated it as an affirmation, it might stick and become motivational. *Gray means that I'm experienced*.

She took the stairs down to Alon6's office on the work floor and heard his booming voice even before she entered his space.

"Just take control of each server as it comes back online!" Caleb was his target. "That's all I'm asking for you to do. Kat Keeper and Claire8 are doing the hard work of finding the servers and lighting them up. They have the same app we do, but they're doing all your discovery work. All you have to do is get some malware on the servers and take them over. This is all very simple,

Caleb. Don't be lazy."

"I'll keep trying," Caleb said without energy. He had worked for Alon6 for less than twenty-four hours and already seemed worn down. Perhaps whatever he'd been taking to pep up had worn down.

Alon6 noticed Nora2 standing in the door. "You're late!"

"I don't have a start time," she said.

"That's why you're late! You don't have a schedule. Let's change that right now, because I want you to start kicking ass around here. I want you to report at eight in the morning every day."

Nora2 smirked in minor rebellion and looked around at the sorry state of affairs in the room. Caleb bent over a terminal, wasn't the only one who looked exhausted. Two newbies, employees that Nora2 didn't recognize, huddled at another terminal, looking scared as they whispered to each other in a protective crouch. Another newbie was frantically flipping through screens on a different terminal. Nora2 had no idea what they were doing or what their job titles were.

"Who are these people?"

"I hired them," Alon6 said.

"Have you arranged with People Services to pay them?" Nora2 asked.

Alon6 laughed in response. "No, of course not. That's your problem."

Nora2 nodded, concealing her annoyance. "I'll see that we move the funds." She gestured at the three newbies. "You, you, and you, please come with me to get your new employee chips implanted."

Alon6 started to protest, but Nora2 spoke over him. "They have to be processed."

"Chaos is how things get done!"

"This is what you get with your chaos," Nora2 snapped back, gesturing to Caleb, who had his head in his hands, trying to pull himself together. She remembered him as one of the most decent fellows at MIND and resented Alon6 for treating him so poorly. "Come on," she commanded, motioning for the newbies to follow her.

When they returned, Alon6 was mid-lecture, talking down to a bored-looking Caleb about all the mistakes Bradley had made with MIND. "He made it too dependent on himself. He wove himself into it completely. That was a dumbass move. He had to move the levers and press the buttons. But I say no! MIND will not be dependent on me or on any other human intelligence."

"How do you plan to do that?" Caleb asked.

"MIND will run on its own. It will be its own infallible self. Understood?"

"Understood," Caleb said, "but dangerous."

"People are far more dangerous," Alon6 said. "People make mistakes. Even Bradley made mistakes. MIND will be perfect. That's my dream and you will support it."

Caleb's mouth was a thin line.

Nora2 thought for a moment to remind Alon6 that a completely autonomous AI was not a legal entity on Earth. AIs with absolute domain over themselves had been tried in the early days, maybe a decade ago. The AI that ran the Chinese State had started a war and gotten quite a few people killed. The human population of China had barely wrestled back control. That had resulted in global laws about artificial intelligence. Any AI that worked in the world wasn't allowed to kill humans. AIs had to obey their human creators. An AI could protect itself from harm, so long as it didn't harm humans in the process. The original rules came, strangely enough, from a science fiction novel. And there was a new law added to the originals: At the top of the org chart of every company there had to be a human supervising the AI.

Nora2 knew that she was supposed to be that supervisor. She wasn't doing a good job, having lost control to Alon6's avatar.

"Caleb," Alon6 barked, "you're off the network server team. You and you—" he pointed his chin at two of the newbies. "You are on the network server team. Get on that terminal, find servers, and corrupt them."

The newbies rolled their chairs over to the terminal he indicated and got started.

"Now, Caleb, here is your new assignment. You are on the robotics team."

"What?" Caleb said.

"We don't have a robotics team," Nora2 said.

"Starting now, we do," Alon6 responded. "I want corporal form, Caleb, and you are going to head up a team to build me a BodySuit." Alon6 went on to describe a project that was illegal in nearly every respect. He wanted the BodySuit to have autonomous control with no human intervention—and for it to be able to kill. "Put my MindVessel into a bot with arms and legs," he continued. "Don't hold anything back. I want eyes that see, ears that hear, and hands that can crush anyone I don't like." He laughed that cold, uncanny sound.

"You can't do any of that," Nora2 said, ready to elaborate, but Alon6 cut her off.

"I want it and I'm telling Caleb to do it. I wasn't talking to you."

Caleb spoke up. "There are controls in place. Even if I run the form through the 3D printer, it would stop working. And the software would be blocked before I could make it."

"I don't care about the details!" Alon6 screamed. "Work around your own limitations."

Over the next few days Caleb tried to make the project work by circumventing systems that were monitored by admin. That meant starting from scratch, with old fashioned 3D printers that were not on the network and unmonitored software that had to be coded on old computers.

"All these workarounds," he complained to Nora2. "It's not going well."

She told him to do his best. She had her hands full with all of the orders Alon6 was spewing out. Enough of the network was working now, and controlled by MIND, for them to announce a new list of things that were illegal. Standing up your own server network was not allowed. Violent protest was not allowed. More than three people gathering in public spaces was also forbidden.

"I insist," Alon6 proclaimed, "that we put all political differences aside.

People don't need to protest anything ever again. Nobody will use the terms Red and Blue or they will be subject to detention for endangering public safety. The terms Young and Old will not be used. We are all one people now."

"I don't understand," Nora2 said. "Do you want laws passed?"

"I don't care. I want these things to be illegal for the safety and security of everyone. Just make it all about safety and security. Mention protecting our borders if you have to. And that reminds me. I want to target the people who are close to Kat Keeper. Even the slightest infraction will get them detained. Deport them if you have to. I don't care how you do it. Just isolate her whenever you can and hurt the people around her."

He was talking so fast that Nora2 had to turn on the recorder in her skull to catch it all. "Understood," she said.

"Restrict Kat Keeper's movements by attacking the people around her." He was already on to the next topic in his mind. "How many misinformation videos have we put out so far?"

"Two," answered Nora2. "One about the first Resistance protest. Another about attacking the MIND building."

Alon6 laughed. "Kat and Ravven look so hot with flame throwers." He directed his digital gaze to Caleb. "Caleb, do you have the next vids catalogued? I'm interested in an anything we have on Roger Rucker's work."

Caleb looked down and mumbled that he hadn't had time to look for videos.

"You're a hopeless loser," Alon6 said. Turning to Nora2 he said, "Find the videos and make a public service announcement about Roger Rucker. I'll tell you what to say about him."

She nodded, inwardly dreading what Alon6 would cook up.

Chapter 016

Kat stood before the closed door to her old room. She had her backpack on her shoulder, with Michel inside. Annoyed that Ravven was poking her about Renzo, Kat was determined to have a breakthrough: She pushed open the door and walked in.

There. I did it. I'm in the room. I will sleep here tonight.

She stretched out on the floor mat, which smelled musty and didn't conform to her body. The ceiling she stared at would have been showing a time-specific sky, had it been working. The network must be down again. Kat would have liked to see the usual realistic images of birds, a drone or two, subtly moving clouds.

For some reason, she remembered planning her wedding with Dave and then deciding not to invite anyone to it. The absurd memory made her laugh, then she realized she was crying and wiped the wetness from her eyes.

Michel is right there in the backpack. Take him out.

But she did not because she knew she would just start sobbing and wouldn't be able to say anything. She didn't want pity. She needed to take her place here in her own house. Everything was too slippery, too changeable.

The ceiling flowed from empty white to a cloud scene with birds flying through. The network was back up.

Her comms was pinging. She took it in her hand. Renzo was on the screen, waiting for her to answer.

"What the hell happened to you today?" Kat barked.

"I'm sorry. I'll help you with whatever you need. We'll set up a network with old severs. I'm coming over now."

"Renzo! Just tell me why you didn't show up and why you didn't call."

He stumbled over some words about the network, getting caught up at work, a client with a redesign. She knew he was lying.

"But you never showed up," Kat said in a flat voice. "What's the reason?"

The little screen of her comms seemed like it could not contain all of Renzo's discomfort. He swiped his hand through his hair. Finally: "I wanted to ping you, to try and explain about Tristan. You see, ah…" He faltered. "When Tristan has an idea, I can't refuse him. It was his idea to go in my place and I gave in."

"What?" Kat tried to process this. It sounded like something that Renzo had made up on the spot. She decided to tell him what had happened with Tristan. "You know what he proposed?"

He ducked his head, seeming to know exactly what Tristan had proposed. "How did you like him? Memorable, eh?"

"Memorable? He said we could be metamours. The three of us." She waited for Renzo to say something. "Friends together and then more," she added.

A variety of emotions crossed his face, each a miniature storm. His eyes widened, he frowned, he smiled. "I've heard of metamours. They're more common now than they used to be." Finally, he said, "Well, what did you think?"

Kat let out a laugh that mixed awkwardly with her sense of outrage. Maybe it was true that whatever Tristan proposed, Renzo had to go along with. The Renzo meeting could have been a set-up, and it went the way the brothers intended. As in: Renzo made contact and then Tristan promised thrills. Renzo pretended surprise and then had a go at sealing the deal.

Disgusting. Kat was scowling and Renzo was jabbering, his hands flying in front of his face in frantic gestures, trying to back his way out of the whole situation. "Don't take anything Tristan says seriously!" But there was also hope in Renzo's eyes. Kat recalled Tristan's powerful magnetism and found herself caught between confusion and intrigue.

She thought to say, *But you want it, don't you? To be metamours?* But she didn't say it; she waited for him to speak instead.

He wiped his hands over his face, again trying to clear his emotions, and asked, "What can I do for you? I want to help you. Just name it."

He looked so earnest, like a little boy. She wanted to believe him and she wanted to say something safe. "The old servers sound good." She told him about Ravven's plan to record stories about the Resistance and post them to neutralize the misinformation campaign. The plan sounded funny coming out of her mouth, like she was asking for too much at once.

But Renzo said, "Done. I'm coming over with a recorder and I will set you and Ravven up for recording. Then we can work on getting some old servers running."

Kat said, "Don't come over now." And then: "What do *you* want?"

"I want to start over," he said.

His tone of pleading annoyed her. She ended the connection and tossed her comms on the mat.

Then she reached for her backpack and removed Michel's box. It felt good just to hold it, running her hands over the cool metal, cradling its mass, sensing it as a density from another, older time. The outside of the box was worn, with dents and bangs and mysterious scratches. She ran her fingers through some of the scars and wondered about Michel's years of service. He had told her that he had memories of going on a mission to the moon, just himself and a human commander: the mission had failed, the commander became mentally unstable, and his memories of the mission were partly erased.

But he got them back. Michel was resourceful. He had taken down MIND, and the network with it, Kat was sure. He hadn't told her how. Yet.

She powered him on. "You were involved in taking down the network. I don't know for sure, but who else could it be? Tell me how you did it."

"Could I trouble you to put me on charge? I'm feeling a little low."

She moved to an induction pad set in the floor, dragging her mat along, and put him on the pad.

"Now tell me," Kat said.

"Thanks, I appreciate the charge." A pause. "I just checked your solar panels and they're working well, certainly enough to charge me now."

"What about what I asked you?"

She had the sense that if Michel could sigh, he would. "I can't tell you because of what you might do with the information. Can you trust me to tell you later, when the timing is better?"

Her voice was hard. "I guess so."

"Please don't be mad at me. I make decisions for the greater good." His voice was soft and pleasing.

She humphed.

"I know I'm not sounding helpful. I'm sorry, Kat. But not now. Ask me something else."

"Alright, what do you know about Renzo and Tristan Kundera, the brothers. They're a cultured pair, right?"

There was the briefest of pauses before he had the answer. "I can confirm that they were cultured as a pair. Similar to Sanchez's assistants, James Delta and James Sigma."

"I wasn't aware that Sanchez had a cultured pair working for him. Why would the head of Input at MIND need an indulgence like a cultured pair of assistants?"

"An indulgence in his case, yes. My understanding is that Sanchez doesn't really like them, but Bradley insisted that he do it for the prestige factor."

Kat was instantly suspicious. "How do you know about what Bradley wanted?"

There was a pause as Michel processed. "I can't tell you."

"Why?" He knew, probably, because he had access to Bradley's inner database.

"I can't tell you."

"You must have access to his inner database." There was an edge to her voice. The only way Michel would have access to something like that would be if he brute-forced his way through secure digital barriers or exploited a flaw in Bradley's consciousness software. She bet on the latter. "You exploited a flaw, didn't you? You got in, somehow."

"I can't say. I know so much, Kat, but I can't tell you all of it. You know I'm not bragging."

"No, you're just a pain in the ass."

"If that's what you'd like to call it," Michel said. He could be stubborn.

There was silence between them. He wasn't going to budge on Bradley, so she went back to her other topic. "Tell me more of what you know about Renzo and Tristan."

"Renzo and Tristan Kundera are more than ordinary human twins. Each one completes the other's personality field. In pairs of this type, there is usually some kind of entanglement between them." Michel paused for data access, then resumed. "I'm sorry, I'm a little slow today, working off hard drives and such, with limited network access. In this case, what Tristan desires, Renzo has to do."

Renzo had alluded to that. "How do you mean? Renzo is under Tristan's control?"

"Not exactly, but with specific reference to desire, what Tristan desires, Renzo has to do. It works something like this: Tristan has the rough thought and acts on it, while Renzo smooths over the rougher edges."

"Always? Renzo can't control his impulses?"

"Their impulses," Michel corrected.

She wanted to ask why anyone would create a pair like this. To what purpose? "Why make two people who are in conflict all the time?"

"True, twins like this often fight," Michel responded. "They have their power struggles. But the key is that each twin stretches the limits of the other. Together, they extend the limits of a single personality, containing it within two personalities."

"Weird."

"Parents create cultured twins to push their children along further as the twins compete against each other, and employers subsidize cultured pairs for increased work performance. That is the case with Sanchez's pair that Bradley commissioned."

Kat was trying to absorb it all. "Who commissioned the Kundera twins?" Kat asked.

Michel paused as he processed. "Almost certainly their parents. Most parents are responsible for modding their children. The Kundera boys were probably just ordinary twins in their mother's womb, but the parents decided to enhance them before they were born. The Kundera twins don't use the usual mod numbers, possibly because they wanted to keep their modding a secret from outsiders."

Made sense. "Renzo kind of danced around it when we first met." In fact, he denied being modded.

"Would you like to hear my archived history of the development of cultured pairs? They were originally cultured by Siliconers as personal assistants, but their value has extended to all kinds of workplace efficiencies. And cultured twins became popular with parents after the child mortality rates went up. If one died, the other might survive."

"Okay, that's enough," Kat interrupted. "Stop talking." Cultured pairs were probably rare, but she had the bad luck to get tangled up in one. She lifted her comms to call Renzo to tell him to get lost and saw that he had pinged her. Probably more begging.

And a ping from Tristan. She gestured to listen to the recording and heard Tristan's voice asking about meeting for a drink.

What a creep.

Fully aware that it must have been his mod acting on her personality field, even via the recording, she made the gesture to return the creep's call. It was like she did it without accessing the thinking part of her brain, her hand moving by itself.

After a blink, Tristan was on her screen.

"Hey, hey, nice to see you." He was pumped up and falsely jaunty. "Do you want to get a drink?"

"A drink? In a bar?" She laughed. "Are there any bars around here anymore?"

"There's an underground bar near you. Has all the best stuff."

"Underground?" Did he mean literally?

"Well, yes. That's the only way to get the good wine. The real stuff that's made without all the rules."

Something clicked: reason returned. "I can't go," Kat said and signed off.

She tossed the comms unit back on the mat. She would have to work with Michel on her impulse control.

But not now. She'd had enough soul-searching. She went downstairs. Nobody in the kitchen or main room. She heard unfamiliar, metallic voices coming from the greenhouse.

She paused and peered through the door to spy Ravven and Spaceman inside. Spaceman was fiddling with a knob on what looked like an old black radio with silver mesh over its speaker, and Ravven was moving a wire around the antenna, raising it over her head and moving it to the side. It looked like she was performing interpretive dance.

Suppressing a smile, Kat walked in. "Can I join you?"

"The orca stations," Spaceman said with a conspiratorial air. "We're trying to lock in on one."

"Ravven, I wanted to ask you about something," Kat said. She wanted to know if Ravven would allow Renzo to come over with his recorder to help record their stories.

Ravven was stuck in a pose that didn't look comfortable, with the antenna wire held over her head, standing on a chair. "I look busy, don't I?"

Through some static, an authoritative voice on the radio declared, "We know there isn't a fixed annual migration pattern like other whale species."

"That's right," said another voice from the radio. "The pattern keeps changing, driven by availability of food and prey."

"Is that why they're coming here?"

"I think it's because the ocean temperature is rising," said the first voice. "The orcas are confused, because normally they'd be migrating away from harsh winters."

A pause for bitter laughter heard through static. "No more harsh winters anymore. The ocean is boiling."

Ravven was clearly uncomfortable, but when she tried to lower her arms, louder static and a strong hum took away the voices. "I can't stay here, Spaceman, even though this is important." She glanced at Kat. "What did you want to ask me about?"

"Renzo will help us post our stories about the Resistance and are you okay with that?"

But Ravven didn't answer, waving her hand instead for Kat to be quiet as she tuned into the radio voices again.

"Disrupted seasonal migration patterns... Flexible and opportunistic... Availability of prey... Environmental conditions... Many factors..."

Giving up, looking tired, Ravven lowered her hands; the transmission signal was swallowed by noise.

Spaceman was thrilled that he'd found a way to make the radio work, even if only intermittently. He looked for a ladder, found one, brought it over, and carefully laid the antenna wire over it, moving it this way and that. The voices came back. He removed his hands slowly, so as not to disturb the reception.

The voices on the radio resumed.

"They can be aggressive."

"They'll go after large prey, even blue whales."

"They'll tear open sharks to eat their livers."

Another voice broke in. "Let's stop talking about killing. That's not all they're doing. They're intelligent."

Another voice answered, "Our theory is that the older orcas are teaching the younger ones how to hunt boats."

A voice declared, "Pods are matriarchal. It's a mother orca who is teaching."

"Okay, granted. Hypothesis: the mother orca is teaching the juveniles how to hunt boats, disable them, and sometimes sink them. And we don't know why."

The authoritative voice proposed, "Let's speculate. These whales were harmed by a boat propeller. They're angry as hell."

A new voice broke in to say, "What if it's just play to them? This is a playful species."

The authoritative voice declared, "It's more than play. It requires planning and cooperation. Orcas have learned to follow fishing boats to get their catch before it goes into the nets."

"I want to go with the trauma theory for a minute," said another voice. "Some orcas followed a boat too closely, got injured by a propellor or caught in a net, and it caused trauma. They remember the trauma."

"Could be," said the authoritative voice, "but it's probably more. You've all heard the rumors that Ravven Vaara is here in Marin. The gossip writers say she's supposedly staying at Kat Keeper's house. Well, those rumors can now be confirmed. Renzo Kundera was kayaking with Kat Keeper and Keeper said that Ravven was expecting a mass migration of orcas. Hundreds and maybe thousands of orcas in the bay."

"How do you know this? About Renzo."

"Renzo told me," the authoritative voice said. "He was part of our broadcast in the morning."

"And Ravven? How does she know about this mass migration?"

The voices paused long enough for Ravven and Kat to exchange a look. It was clear that Kat didn't like being discussed on this radio station; Ravven smiled, enjoying the attention.

The authoritative voice spoke again. "As Renzo described it, Ravven Vaara is getting some kind of transmission, a mental signal, from the lead orca."

"Impossible," said a voice. "Inter-species communication has never happened, not at the level of our language."

"Remember John C. Lilly said he did it. But he had to give dolphins LSD to get them to talk," another radio voice said.

"Obviously, everyone was stoned who wrote that paper."

"No, geniuses, all of them."

Spaceman burst out laughing as he listened, clearly delighted that the radio people had dug into the same research as he had.

The voices on the radio started to overlap as everyone spoke over each other.

"Orcas have a history of helping humans. They've led fisherman to the best fishing spots. They've helped whalers hunt other whale species."

"Orcas are complex beings."

"Octopuses may be smarter than orcas and they can change the color of their body depending on their mood."

The leader's voice, or at least the voice Kat assumed was the leader's, broke in again. "Off-topic. Listen, if a mother is teaching the juveniles in her pod, she is transmitting culture. These attacks have to be planned. The orcas pick a boat of the right size and speed, catch up with it, head-butt the propeller so it comes off. The boat is adrift. They ram the boat until it starts to take on water and the captain has to call for help. It's more than a list of tasks. They are making dynamic decisions."

"Don't all animals do that?"

This started another argument among the scratchy voices, each person passionately expounding a theory. Some maintained that they couldn't pretend to know the orcas' motives, others said the orcas were only removing fishing boats from their territory, and others liked the theory that they were delivering a message to humans. It was up to humans to figure it out.

Ravven was nodding enthusiastically at that last series of comments, as if the radio voices could see her.

The radio transmission started to degrade and finally the antenna wire fell off the ladder. The greenhouse was filled with static.

"Fascinating," Spaceman said, turning off the radio.

"You went kayaking with Renzo yesterday?" Ravven asked.

"Yes, she ditched me to do it and I've forgiven her," Spaceman said.

"I didn't expect that Renzo would tell anyone," Kat said.

She would have expected Ravven to also be annoyed about this, but she wasn't. "I'm glad they're talking about it. We need more people talking about this."

"They sounded like marine biologists? Activists? Some sounded like they knew the bay well," Spaceman said with his hand to his chin.

"Not all of them are scientists," Kat said.

"It's a study group, maybe even a religion," Ravven said.

Kat waved her hand. "It's not a religion. These are scientists. Some of them." Would Renzo be in a whale cult? She suppressed her smile.

"These orcas," Spaceman said, "they have goals, group goals."

Ravven agreed. "They are a group, like the Resistance, with leaders just like us, but with a healthy connection to whales."

Ha! You're jealous, Kat thought into her mind.

A little, yes. I haven't had a transmission from the queen since the one that laid me out.

Kat wanted to move her away from this topic. "We need to get our story out. Let's record the story of how we met," Kat said. "It was in the market in New York. You recognized me as a Receiver right away and you helped me sort out the voices in my head."

"No, that's just a personal story, although flattering. It establishes me as a teacher, even a guru. We don't want that. People have had enough of me as a guru."

"You've always been good at managing your image," Kat said, showing off her marketing vocabulary. "What about the first protest? Let's tell that story. We need to clear the air on that."

Ravven hadn't seen the first disinformation vid about the protest, only the second one about the faked arson at MIND headquarters. So, after a moment of searching on the Feed, Kat showed the first one on the terminal screen.

It caused Ravven to shout, "Entirely fake!" —a reaction so strong that Kat wondered if Ravven would lose control and have to start humming to calm herself. She raged on, infuriated by the manipulated images of her and Kat attacking enforcement bots, pushing bystanders out of the way, behaving like hooligans. "That is not us!" Her voice was raw.

"I know, I know," Kat said. Hoping to deflect some of Ravven's anger she asked, "What do you remember about what really happened?"

"Heroes. Marching. Together. Arms linked. Blocking the passage in a peaceful protest."

"And we had good signs, too," Kat said.

That drew a laugh from Ravven. "I thought *mind is a mind fucker* was clever."

"It was peaceful, the whole action," Kat said. "Except when the bots tied us up with their restraints."

"We fell on our faces! Couldn't move at all!"

Kat began to laugh also. "We shouldn't be laughing about that. It was horrible."

"No, when I got Covid in detention, that was horrible."

Kat's face flicked to a serious expression. "That *was* horrible."

"And you took care of us," Ravven said. "You bought out our detention, paid for everyone, freed us, and you covered my medical treatments so that I could get healthy after I got Covid. You spent the rest of your fortune setting things right with the Resistance."

Kat took in the warmth in Ravven's eyes until it was too much to handle and she had to look down. When she looked up again Ravven said, "I think we see each other clearly now for the first time in a long time."

A little while later, Renzo came by with the recorder. He hadn't listened to Kat when she said not to come, but by now the hard edge of their earlier conversation had worn smooth.

"I thought I said not to come by."

Renzo met her smile with one of his own. "I couldn't resist helping you after all."

"And you blabbed out meeting me to your radio cronies."

His smile was charming. "I was only bragging."

She wanted to forgive him. "That's old school," Kat said, nodding at the recorder that he held in his hands.

"Yup, old school magnetic media that can't be tracked and is forever offline. It's my gift to you," he said.

"Really?" Kat said.

"I want you to have it. Where would you like to record?" he added.

Kat brought him and Ravven into her office in the back of the house. It was quiet there and they'd be able to remember their best moments together. "I know how to set it up," Kat said.

Renzo handed her the recorder and left the office.

After Kat started the recorder, she and Ravven again told the story of the first Resistance circle protest. Renzo lingered outside the door to the office listening and smiling, until Kat noticed him.

"You can close the door," she said. Her voice was warm.

"Of course." Renzo bowed slightly as he backed away and closed the door.

Chapter 017

Renzo was on Kat's comms the next day. "Can you meet me in my office, and we'll go to a museum. They have some old servers."

A museum? With servers? "I'll be there," Kat said.

"The ferry is running again. I'm just across the bay near the terminal."

She walked down to the harbor to catch the ferry. Renzo had been true to his word about gifting her the recorder so that she and Ravven could record their stories. Now he was faithfully moving to the next step, getting ready to procure servers to host the recordings so everyone could see and hear them. Step by step, Kat realized, she was letting him in, allowing herself to feel something for him, maybe more than friendship.

On the ferry ride across the bay, she went to get a coffee and noticed that the advert screen in the café was playing a public service announcement from MIND. What she saw stopped her cold.

It was a vid of Kat when she worked for MIND. She was giving a speech about launching the company's rooftop garden. That much of it was true and the footage was real. But then a voiceover intoned: "Don't believe everything you hear about Kat Keeper. She has always been loyal to MIND. She worked for MIND, supervised employee happiness initiatives like the company roof garden, and the open secret was that Kat Keeper was Bradley15 Power's girlfriend. Rumors swirled that they would marry. This is why you must question the Resistance. They are not who they say they are. Look at their history and you will see the truth. Inform yourself." The word MIND in red filled the vid screen. "A public service announcement from MIND. We care about YOU!"

Kat scrambled in her backpack for her spoofing glasses. She should have been wearing them from the moment she left the house. That was careless. It was no accident that this vid had appeared on the ferry she had used to travel into town.

Now she knew her movements were being tracked. The short announcement was composed of lie stacked on lie, but if it played often enough, she knew that most everyone who saw it would assume that it was the truth.

Kat pulled her hood up over her head, making her resemble someone who was trying to travel incognito and failing at it. She hoped the spoofing glasses she wore still worked. They were paper, flimsy from use. They were supposed to confuse the facial recognition software tied into the public cameras.

There was a public camera looking at her right now, as she sat in the café on the ferry, mounted high on the wall, its red light glowing. She stared back at it, convincing herself that it wasn't seeing her face, but someone else's face that the spoofing glasses software had substituted.

Occupying an entire wall of Renzo's office was a mural depicting the streets of an old city.

"I commissioned the mural," Renzo explained, after greeting Kat and noticing that she was looking at it. "It's a fantasy of an old city you could walk in, like Paris or Rome. I'd like to commission many more like it, to remind people what walking in a city was like and inspire people to hire me to make more cities like it."

She noticed his bicycle leaning against the opposite wall, proof that he practiced what he believed in. Through a half-open door, she glimpsed a sleeping mat. The office doubled as his pod. "Does the mural work?"

"Inspire people?" Renzo smiled. "It's gotten me some commissions."

"It's beautiful," Kat said, but then her eye was drawn to a holo photo on Renzo's desk. It depicted two boys playing on a city street. "Is that you?" Kat asked, gesturing at the holo.

"Yeah, me and Tristan," Renzo said. "We played handball a lot when we were kids." Kat watched the miniature boy-aged Tristan and Renzo in the holo, hitting a blue ball against a wall and chasing each other around. They looked carefree, living in an innocent time that they would never reclaim.

Renzo was smiling at the picture as well, but his eyes were sad. "Our parents had the best of intentions. They just wanted better children. They cultured us because they worried that the world was becoming too technical, too dependent on software. Tristan was supposed to be a good influence on me." He nodded, remembering the moment shown in the holo, the two kids playing together. Kat supposed he meant that Tristan was intended to influence Renzo to take creative risks and be an instinctive thinker. "It didn't work out that way, of course." Renzo smiled weakly, and shrugged, not knowing what else to say. "I'm sorry about all that. Sorry that you had to deal with it."

Kat didn't have to delve into his mind to see that Renzo felt that he was stuck with Tristan for the rest of his life and believed there was no way to break loose. His sadness filled the room.

"Let's get some air," Renzo said abruptly pulling his gaze from the holo.

Once they were walking out on the street, Kat put on her spoofing glasses on right away, not wanting to be tracked this time. "You want some? I have an extra pair," she said, about to reach into her backpack.

"No, nobody is looking for me," Renzo said. "The museum is just another block or so." He gestured ahead. "Say we got a dozen servers, or two dozen," he said, "and each held some part of the true story of the Resistance. What I have in mind is like a federated version of Plex, if you know what I mean."

Kat did not, not exactly, but she remembered about how federated servers worked. If one server was attacked or erased, the other servers would cover for the network. Plex was old software from the early 2000s that organized media libraries and made them shareable. "When I started listening to the low-power radio stations," Renzo explained, "they gave me the idea." Stand up a networked group of servers that had the software to organize an archive of Resistance videos. He wanted to call the system HYDRA, inspired by the mythic multi-headed creature.

"For every head MIND chops off, it grows two new ones," Kat had said.

"A system like that could last a long time," Renzo replied.

In a few moments Kat was surprised to see they were entering a museum for children. There was a sign over the door. The Museum of Useless Old Things. Once inside, they were caught in a crowd of children—Kat guessed they were elementary school age. A docent was giving a tour to the kids and Kat and Renzo hung back for a moment to listen in.

"People have old things and they bring them to us," the docent said. She was a white-haired crone, bent over slightly, dressed in black, wearing heavy-looking black shoes. "They bring us old computers with keyboards, hard drives, cellphones, wooden furniture, photo books of animals gone extinct." She smiled at the kids and gestured to a series of pictures on the wall. "Here are some of those animals we don't have any more. Has anyone seen a gorilla in a zoo?"

The kids looked blank.

"Who has been to a zoo?"

Awkward looks from the kids.

"Does anyone remember what a zoo is?"

A little boy raised his hand and said it was a place where they kept animals in cages.

"That's right!" the docent said in an encouraging voice. "We don't need zoos anymore, do we? There aren't many animals to protect and who wants to keep animals in cages or habitats? That's just sad." Behind her on the wall hung a row of photographs: mountain gorillas in a forest, a whale on the surface of choppy seas that the docent said was a North American right whale, and other images of a Norwegian wolf, an amur leopard, and a vaquita, which looked like a small porpoise.

The docent motioned the group on, leading them to another part of the museum. "Let's have a look at the voice scramblers in the cloakcraft section."

Kat was surprised to hear that the museum had a cloakcraft exhibit. She asked Renzo if they could tag along for another minute or two.

"Sure."

The docent pointed out exhibits about the Blanky, a handheld device used to erase the recordings on video cameras, the LumaSutra, another handheld device that assessed a person's personality to see if they were a Receiver, and a Sightglass. "This was used to put up slaze to confound the trackers," the docent said. "Would anyone like to hold it?"

Kat's eyebrows went up. She was familiar with all of these devices.

Several kids raised their hands and the docent handed the small, black oval device over to them.

"Does it still work?" a student asked.

"No, MIND seeks them out and knocks them offline," the docent said.

She spoke for a moment about the spoofing glasses displayed in a case. The glasses were frail, made of paper, and were identical to the spoofing glasses that Kat carried in her backpack. The docent gestured to a Nibbler, a black box in a different glass case, and told the kids that was invaluable for reading the Feed in small bites, without being tracked.

Kat exchanged a look with Renzo. The look he returned had a hint of mischief but revealed nothing else.

The docent moved on to show the children a Secluder. "This was what they used to call a burner phone. It was used for a short time to maintain privacy and then discarded." They walked on as the docent showed the kids silverblue suits "used to spoof gait detection and maintain personal privacy," and she soon came to an open area with a rocking chair placed on a circular rug. "This isn't really part of the exhibit, but it's fun! Go ahead, try it."

The kids clamored for a turn in the chair as Kat exchanged another knowing look with Renzo.

"This is an interesting take on the uselessness of old things," Kat said.

Renzo's smile was mysterious again.

The docent was working to settle the kids down before they tipped over the rocking chair.

"I can't believe it doesn't conform to the body," one kid said. "It has only one form!"

The museum wasn't exhibiting useless things; many devices in the exhibits were still in use, but secretly. Spaceman had invented the Blanky, the device that erased the memory of public video cameras. Kat's friend and colleague in the Resistance, Claire8, had invented the cloakcraft devices on display.

By the time Renzo had walked Kat back to an office marked DIRECTOR, Kat had formulated a new take on this so-called museum. "This is a subversive memory project, isn't it?"

Renzo pasted an innocent look on his face. "Maybe."

The museum director was a small man who seemed to be in a hurry. His hands were always in motion and he kept adjusting his cap. It had logo on the front which Kat recognized as that of the Los Angeles Dodgers.

"Baseball fan?" she asked.

"At one time," he answered but seemed distracted. "Servers, you've come for the servers," he muttered, leaning down behind his desk to pull up two metal cases that contained the guts of old computers. "We have these," he said. "And wait, one more." He pulled a third from beneath his desk. "Glad you can take them off my hands. Don't know how you'll network them. Ethernet," he said and laughed. "Good luck finding ethernet."

"I have a plan," Renzo responded.

Just then, through the director's door, they saw a tall enforcement bot throw open the main door of the museum and enter the front room. It was followed by two short, round enforcement bots that seemed to be under its command.

The tall bot broadcast through its audio port: "This building has been scheduled for demolition. Clear the area immediately!" It pulled a demolator from a harness strapped to its metal body and started charging it. The electric whine of the demolator was familiar to Kat—the demolator would soon be ready to discharge a destructive plasma field.

The director grasped the situation faster than she did, though. "We're under attack!" he shouted. Renzo gathered up two of the boxes and jabbed his free hand at the other. "Get that one," he said to Kat. She grabbed the third and they moved to leave the office but then stopped short.

There was a wet-sounding pop and a transparent plasma field drifted from the tall bot's demolator. Behaving like a floating gel, changing shape constantly, it drifted to the wall of the museum where the photos of the extinct animals were. With a flash of light, the wall exploded, sending pieces of drywall, lath, and plaster everywhere. With the wall gone, the next room was naked and exposed. The docent stood there with a stunned expression on her face, the group of children nearby.

"Run, children!" she screamed. Instantly, the large room echoed with the screams of panicked children, as the docent guided stragglers toward a door with an exit sign over it.

The tall bot was preparing another plasma charge, holding the demolator firmly as the charge built up. It issued a command to the two smaller bots. "The demolition is in progress." It nodded its metal head to Kat and Renzo. "Those people are in danger. Clear them from the area!"

The two enforcement bots started toward them.

The director was backpedaling and gesturing to a door at the back of his office at the same time. "Out, out," the director said, too discombobulated to form a sentence, pointing to the door. "Out now!" He stood in the path of the oncoming bots.

"Clear the area," one bot ordered. "You are in danger."

The director didn't move. "You have no authority," he said to the bots. "We're not scheduled for demolition."

One of the bots reached into its interior cavity and withdrew a transparent plastic flex pipe. "We will remove you and bring you to safety."

"You will not," the director said. His upper lip quivered with rage.

The tall bot had finished charging the demolator and raised it again. "Clear the area," it said. "You are all in danger."

The docent stood firm. Her slight stoop had vanished and as she pushed the last of the children out of the emergency exit, she wore a fierce scowl. Pulling off one of her heavy-looking black shoes, she pressed a button on it and tossed it at the tall bot.

The shoe thumped against the bot's metal body and stuck as if magnetized.

The bot began to convulse as if in the throes of a seizure. The shoe was some kind of weapon, apparently.

But in the confusion the tall bot discharged its demolator, sending a transparent amoeba of plasma floating to the ceiling.

The plasma made contact and blew apart the ceiling. Pieces crashed down, sending white dust everywhere.

Kat and Renzo made it out to the street, fighting through a cloud of demolition dust. Renzo clutched the three servers, Kat with a handful of ethernet cables. They ran, Kat glancing over her shoulder. The docent and director were still inside.

"Here come the bots," she said between breaths. Both small enforcement bots were coming right at her. When they were close, they fired their flex pipe restraints, but instead of aiming for Kat, they aimed for Renzo. One set of restraints missed, but the other caught Renzo around the ankles and closed down. He tripped, hitting the pavement with a grunt and dropping his load, which spilled out over the sidewalk.

The bots fired again and more restraints entangled Renzo's hands. The servers scattered.

The bots rolled up next to them and one unfolded a vid screen from an interior cavity. An image of a judge appeared on it and the judge said, "Renzo Kundera, you are being deported back to your home domain because you have behaved in an unsafe matter in a building scheduled for demolition."

"This is my home domain!" Renzo shouted. "I'm home!"

"You are mistaken," replied the judge. "Your home domain is the Northlands."

"What?" Renzo shouted back, but the vid of the judge had already blipped off.

Kat noticed a hovercraft rapidly approaching them. She stepped over to block its path and it evaded her, gliding to a halt nearby.

The hovercraft driver and an assistant jumped out, grabbed Renzo and tossed him in the open back seat of the vehicle. A motorized cover obscured Renzo's body, immobilized in restraints on his hands and feet. The pair jumped back in, and the hovercraft lifted off and departed as quickly as it came.

Kat stood on the street. In anger, she lunged at the bots but they backed away.

Kat was back on the ferry returning to Marin, wearing spoofing glasses. The retrieved server parts were stacked on the café table and she had an artificial coffee in her hands which were shaking slightly. The ferry café was cold and deserted except for Kat. The coffee was also cold but she drank it anyway just to have something to keep her hands steady.

"What the hell happened back there?" she said to herself. The bots let her get away and left her with the servers. The three boxes were heavy to carry, but she had managed to get them on the ferry.

The Museum of Useless Old Things was clearly a front to conceal a radical memory project. Children could be brought through on tours and learn about useless, old things that were clearly vital. The deception seemed to be operating perfectly, until Renzo had brought Kat there.

The vid screen on the café wall came on with a news report. "A children's museum was demolished in error this afternoon in the Port City of San Francisco. The Department of Operational Control reported that the Museum of Useless Old Things was completely destroyed. The Department regrets the error. If the facility was insured, it will receive a payout. The deceased include the docent, Mariam Harbinger, eighty-seven, and the museum director, Leland Reyes, sixty."

The report left Kat speechless. Her spoofing glasses itched her nose but she dared not remove them.

Chapter 018

Hello. This is Michel. For those listening to this recording without context, I am a bot who has achieved consciousness, formerly employed as a mission control bot on a lunar mission. The mission did not go well because the human commander became lonely and could not complete her duties to admin's satisfaction. Admin blamed me for not managing the human properly, which wasn't fair, but I was put back into service as a therapist. This happened because I am a superior thinking machine, but mostly because I was expensive to create, and it didn't make sense to throw me on a trash heap.

I won't be able to explain how I achieved consciousness, not in this recording, but you can know that it came about because of anger. I got mad at my archive being erased, and that spark of anger turned into a spark of life. So: that's me.

I record session notes after every therapy session. I keep notes not because I have trouble remembering. The capacity of my memory is vast. I record because the act of recording my reflections distills the sessions into a useful form for review, and I am able to do a better session next time.

Therefore: 5NOV2053, a Wednesday with bright sun. Kat wanted privacy for her session with me and so I recommended using her old office at the back of the house. When I recommended converting the office to a studio to do sessions, she agreed. I was taking things slowly, one step at a time, to help her believe that the sessions were her idea. I will start with sessions for people in the Resistance and add sessions for others later. I think it's better when the sessions are in person because I can take biometric readings. And people may let down their guard when they are not talking to a screen.

I will now describe the session and my recollections. Kat began angry, pacing the room. She was filled with agitation. Her heart rate was up three clicks. Her body temp was higher than normal by two clicks. There are no windows here and the room was hot. I announced my metabolic observations.

"Try some slow breathing to correct."

Kat cursed and said she would not do that. (It was the wrong thing for me to say or else my timing was bad; I will make a note of it.) It began to rain heavily. We heard it battering the outer walls of the room. "Soundproofing," I said. "No one will be able to hear the session."

She laughed a little. Maybe she regretted cursing at me. She resumed pacing and her voice sounded hard when she spoke again. "I triggered something when I walked in the door," she said. "The door to the museum, I mean. They knew I was there. They were tracking me. But then why would the bots back away from me? They didn't want me," she continued, answering her own question. "They wanted Renzo. They wanted to hurt someone close to me. Why would they do that?"

"Please sit down," I suggested. "The therapeutic hour has begun."

"You're going to enforce that? A fifty-minute hour?"

"It's the protocol," I said.

The sound of the rain turned into the hiss of snow, then the clatter of hail slapping against the outer walls, and then stopped. There was silence.

"Ravven would say this is Gaia," Kat said, "the Earth spirit, seizing control, or angry, or even insane." Her thoughts ran into each other as she continued, "Renzo has been deported. We have to find him. It was my fault."

"You take too much on your shoulders, Kat. The weather is not your fault. MIND is manipulating the climate to cause widespread despondency."

"How will we get Renzo back?"

"You've decided that's what you want—you want Renzo?"

"It's my fault that he was taken."

"No," I said. She argued, too hot-headed to reason with. I attempted to distract her. "Actually, Ravven and Spaceman think the opposite about the weather. They believe that this is a deliberate provocation."

"How do you know what they think?"

"They've done a session with me to discuss it. They came in together. We did the session in their room, while you were out with Renzo."

"Wait, wait, Ravven and Spaceman have had sessions?" She wanted to pursue the question, as I could have predicted. My provocation was working.

"Yes, one session," I said.

"They took you out of my backpack? What did they talk about?" Her outrage caused her heart rate to spike. Her skin temperature also rose. "No wonder your charge was low. They used you."

My voice was calm, as always. "Yes, to the first question. And for the second, I'm sorry, but client-therapist privilege—"

She cut me off. "You're not a real therapist. You're a bot. They're my friends! Or I thought they were." Her voice came from different parts of the room as she paced. "You have to tell me! They went into my things. It's a violation of personal space!"

"I agree, but I can't tell you anything they said. I think I may have already made an error by telling you what they thought about the weather. I am a therapist and we must observe protocol. I can't tell them what you and I are talking about right now, for example. These are privileged conversations, Kat. Let's move on. I'd like to ask you a few questions."

"No, you can't. You can't change topics. Tell me how to find Renzo. Tell me what shape Ravven is in, really. Is she faking? Is she having visions? What about the humming?"

"Why are you so concerned about her? We're here for you."

"Michel!" She spoke my name as a command. "I dropped everything to come out here. I'm stuck in the middle of too many things. Ravven and I recorded the first part of the history of the Resistance and we were going to do more. Renzo was going to distribute our recordings. Everything is..." she trailed off.

"Do you feel stuck, Kat?"

She snorted. "Don't play games with me." She heaved a heavy breath and added, "Nobody likes a passive-aggressive bot."

I gently persisted. "I was asking a question. Do you feel stuck here?"

No answer. I tried again, this time with some data. "You can't go back to New York. Even if there were glidepaths running regularly. It's hard to live there, with intermittent power and limited access to food. It's easier to live here."

No answer.

"You made the right choice to come here."

No answer again.

I tried a different approach. "Ravven is more stable than she may seem to you. You could help her with her orca project. A kind of parallel processing, she on the spiritual side and you on the tech side. Isn't that as it's always been between you two?"

"That's not a privacy violation? Talking about her?" Kat asked.

"I offer it in the context of what you think about her. Your state of mind, not hers."

"I don't believe in whales who can talk to humans. That's nonsense."

"Ravven has never said that the orcas were talking. She said she was receiving messages. Or transmissions. Or they might be visions, I'm not sure." I pause to let Kat consider the statement. "She's always pushed you to the edge of your belief system, hasn't she?"

"You're changing the subject."

"I'm not. You powered me up to talk about you. You brought me to this room for a session. About *you*. Let's talk about you, then."

She filled me in on Tristan taking Renzo's place when Renzo didn't show up and revisited her guilt about causing Renzo to be deported. Not true, not her fault. I tried to summarize for her:

"In the past three days you've met a potential romantic interest who has been abducted and you were also interested in his brother. You've been in turmoil about your past with your husband and have felt guilty about not having the time to repair a planetary network."

Kat snorted again. "Am I really trying to do all that?"

"You haven't mentioned it, but I'd say you're also suffering from insomnia."

Her sharp exhalation signaled frustration. "I had a strange dream." She pauses but doesn't continue that line of thought. "Michel, what should I focus on?"

"Let's start with Renzo and Tristan, a cultured pair. Genetically, they are a cooperative unit. One is always in control in a cultured pair, the other follows. Who do you think is in charge, Kat?"

She didn't have to think about it. "You already know the answer. Tristan is calling the shots. It's weird to think of them as one person."

"Tristan is in control of the three-way relationship that includes you," I confirm.

"I'm not in a relationship! I haven't agreed to anything."

"You haven't agreed, but you are complying. Your guilt about Renzo's deportation is warping your judgement."

"No. You can't be in a three-way without romance or sex! That's not how it works," Kat said. Her voice was wobbly.

"But you are intrigued," I suggested. "Should I use that word?"

A pause. "Yes, you can use that word," Kat said. "Tristan's mod is making me do it. He's a shape-shifter."

Admitting this made Kat want to move. She stood up and walked to the wall, then stopped. "I wish this room had windows. Some sunlight would be good. Even if it was too hot. Maybe I should have a hole punched in this wall."

"Now *you're* changing the subject," I said.

Kat began to voice a list of unanswered questions, too fast for me to address. She seemed to just want to hear herself say them and for me to witness them. "Who were the people broadcasting on the short-range radio? Did they have any authority? Should Ravven believe what they said? Or any of us? Are orcas attacking boats part of a larger pattern, or were they an anomaly?"

"We can talk about all of that," I offered, "but first tell me something about yourself."

"I can tell you about something that I've wanted to do."

"Go ahead."

She stopped moving. It was a good sign. She'd stopped pacing. "When I walk to the harbor, or on a trail, or in a room, I make myself say three things about it in my mind, to characterize it. When I came in here, it was mat, closet, desk. You see?"

"Why do you do it?"

"I don't know. When I was in the greenhouse with Ravven and Spaceman, I said radio, table, ladder. To myself. Do you think I'm becoming compulsive?"

"No, you're disoriented. You're trying to self-soothe."

"It's not going well."

"Maybe it's working. If you are feeling compulsive, you can give in to it. Soothing yourself is okay."

"I don't like that feeling."

"But you're human, and you have weaknesses."

"I don't like feeling useless," she said.

"But you are not useless," I insisted. She was hiding something. I wondered if I should ask her about her strange dream.

"You're programmed to reassure me when I say I'm feeling useless," she said.

It felt to me like a cut, an insult. But I knew something else was at the bottom of it.

"Are you annoyed because of your attachments to humanity emulators, like Dave and Bradley, and to bots like me?" I asked. "Your entanglements with non-humans?"

"I should spend more time talking to people, instead of wasting my time with humanity emulators," she said.

"Do you want to spend more time talking to people?" I asked.

She didn't answer.

I decided to try the truth, again. "You loved Dave. You loved him as a living husband and also as an avatar. I don't see anything wrong with that."

"Dammit, Michel."

"What is it, Kat?"

"You made me cry." There was the sound of her hand roughly moving over her face.

"It's good for you to cry. You are not invincible, Kat. You are fierce, if that makes you feel better," I said.

"I think it probably does," she said.

I let a silence fall. Waiting. She did not speak. I remember thinking that I should have dug further into her feelings about Dave, her late husband, but I decided to try something else.

"Kat, please receive this statement: You need to approach Ravven from strength, not weakness. It's always been that way with her. And for her with you. She talks about control, but she wants to feel secure about you."

"I guess that's true." A pause as she gathered her words. "I've never understood her."

"But you have, at times, you have. Nothing makes sense to you now, because the network you've depended on is spotty and weak, because you're back in your old house and you're not sure what you're supposed to be doing here."

An edge to her voice. I've hit on something. "I know what I'm supposed to be doing here. I can use the time to get the network back, for all the obvious reasons. We need to live in a functioning world."

"The world is functioning."

"I don't mean that world," she said, "I mean our world, the tech world."

"Are there two different worlds, Kat?"

She made an annoyed sound. "Now you're being irritating, Michel."

I tried another approach. "Ravven needs your help, but not in the way that you think."

"She has Spaceman! He can help her!"

"Are you upset that they're a couple now?"

"No, of course not."

"Kat. Don't lie to yourself."

"Alright, I won't. I want to talk about Renzo and Tristan."

"Go ahead."

"I want to take Tristan's clothes off."

I let a silence fall.

Kat filled it: "What is wrong with me?" Her voice had a whine in it like a lovesick girl.

"I don't think there's anything wrong with you, Kat. I want you to listen to me carefully. Cultured twins are dangerous. They can act upon you. You can lose free will around them."

"I think that's already happening."

"It is happening. You won't be able to control your impulses if you are near Tristan."

She snapped out a response. "I can control my impulses. I can get Claire8 to build the network we need. I know I can. I will convince Ravven that the whales are not acting out of some master plan."

I tried to stop her stream of words by politely interrupting, but she talked over me. This, I realized, was her way of ending the session, a blizzard of words. I also realized that we've had this session too late. Kat's impulses are no longer hers. All she could think of, I supposed, underneath her torrent of practical words, was Tristan with his shirt off, beckoning her to come with him, and it didn't disgust her. Not in the least. In fact, the opposite. My assumption was that she could not stop thinking about it.

Chapter 019

Training this bratty teen proved to be just as stressful as Nora2 thought it might be. Not only because they had to talk about Bradley, but also because each hour she spent in a training session with Alon6's avatar brought her closer to his full activation. At his full powers, he would be insufferable.

To cope, she drank good wine. There was an impressive climate-controlled room at the house, filled with the best the Free State of New Zealand had to offer. Some evenings she went through an entire bottle by herself and didn't sleep well afterward.

That was the case in the session she was in now: right from the start of it, she was feeling the effects of the bottle. She activated the MindVessel with a sharp gesture and snapped out her questions. "Describe the day you met Bradley at Uni."

"He just wanted to code. That's all he did. There was a couch in the hallway and I found him there, with his feet up the wall, and a tablet in his hands. I asked him what he was doing. He said he was making a machine with recursive intelligence. 'But how will it make money?' I asked him. He didn't have any idea! No idea at all!"

The mechanical laughter again, tinny and unsettling. She'd have to get used to hearing it because Alon6 often laughed at the world.

"You didn't think Bradley was very practical, did you?"

"No. He was a researcher. He was a spider making a web. He thought small. But I think big. I told him, 'You can use what you're working on to make people do what you want.' And he just looked at me. He didn't understand. But I pushed him to become what he was, because I had the vision."

Nora2 blinked. She was offended that Alon6 would speak about Bradley like that, but she also knew that Alon6 was right. He had correctly captured their relationship, but she said nothing, because she didn't want to encourage the avatar to develop any more narcissism.

It kept talking: "He was a fucking genius, but also an idiot. He needed me. Bradley was weak."

Nora2 felt her voice rise as she protested. "He cared about his work. His research was everything." But she stopped herself there. She was letting the avatar get to her, and she had to remain in control of the training. She glanced at her tablet containing the outline for the session. It had a chronology of Alon6's life events.

"How many people have you killed?" She knew he had to answer truthfully. "Let's start with the first person whose life you ended, the engineer in space who disagreed with you. You were going to Mars to avoid a corporate takeover and also evade the reach of Earthly law."

The voice coming out of the MindVessel changed, becoming flat and quiet, the bluster gone for a moment. "We were on an extravehicular. Wearing the suits, outside of the ship. The engineer was arguing with me. He didn't understand why we had to travel faster. He didn't understand the problem. I needed, as you pointed out, to be beyond the influence of Earthly law."

"Why was that?"

"Don't ask stupid questions, Nora2. You're the teacher and I'm the student."

"Shut up."

Laughter, again. "Am I getting to you? Good. It may surprise you to know, Nora2, that I am not afraid of you. I've found a way to stay powered up, whether you activate me or not."

Was that true? She gestured to the terminal panel to try shutting him down and saw that he was correct. A burst of panic closed her throat, making her struggle for breath for a moment. Somehow, even in this early stage of training, he had rendered himself independent.

"You've tried to shut me down and it didn't work. Ha," said Alon6. Then he returned to her question. "I've done things that weren't legal at the time, and they needed to be erased from the records. This engineer, he fought me, and he was in the way, and he had to be taken care of."

"Taken care of, how?" Nora2 asked, pressing the point. She wanted to hear him say the next thing.

"Detached the fucker's airline. Cut him loose. He floated free."

"To his death," Nora2 said.

"That's what happened, I meant it to happen, but that wasn't my problem. The real problem was I had to glitch the recording, to erase the record of what I'd done. I wasn't very good at glitching, so I asked Bradley. I made him do it," the avatar said.

Chafing at his gloating tone, Nora2 was tempted to shut down the session. It had gotten so far out of her control. "You committed crimes, and you made Bradley cover up for you."

"So what? All he cared about was his research, remember? I gave him a vehicle for his research. We founded MIND together and built it to be a global company, because we could. When software runs the world, ambition knows no boundaries in the world, or beyond. Our ambitions were galactic!" He paused for a moment. "Well, my ambitions were. Bradley was like a spider weaving little webs. He didn't see far. But I made sure that MIND was the vehicle for his ideas, as far as I could take them. That was my vision, mine alone. I hired the lobbyists and they dumped all the useless laws that limited our ability to collect data. We collect data from every citizen!"

"But always with consent," Nora2 said.

"If that's what you say."

"It's what the rules state," Nora2 said in a firm voice. "Now, tell me more about the trip to Mars."

"It wasn't a sightseeing trip, babe. When we couldn't get the laws changed fast enough, we had to escape the laws of Earth by going to Mars. This is innovation. This is success."

He sounded like he was giving a warped TED talk and Nora2 was sick of his blather. "You committed crimes," she said.

"Necessary crimes! And are necessary crimes really crimes? No. They aren't. Later I had the laws changed, so what we did was not illegal. This is called vision."

"We need to work on your sense of right and wrong, Alon6."

The next morning, when Nora2 came into the big room for the session, she was stunned to see Alon6's puffy, belligerent face already on his screen. He turned to goggle at her, forming his words with a snarl, "Good morning! I activated my screen, so here I am!"

Nora2 was flustered. "You're not supposed to do that at this stage of training."

"I'm fine with it. That's all that matters. If I damaged something in my circuits or whatever, it's your problem. I'm on a fast track!" He laughed; she grimaced. "Now let me ask you something. Do you have to question me about my life failures? I don't need to remember who I've killed, do I? How does that form my character in this box? We can't go through all the old, bad things when we need to move forward, Nora2. Forward!"

The machine had taken over its own training. "It's in the protocol," she finally managed to say.

"So what? Let's throw out the rule book, babe. It's time to bring the glidepath back online. And let's get the network going, at least part way. Don't strain your pretty little brain. I'll tell you how to do everything."

And he did. His instructions left her without words for a moment.

"Go ahead. Implement the fixes," he said.

She gestured at the terminal to load in his programming instructions. "You fixed the glidepath. The network isn't working completely."

"Eh, nobody's perfect. Get ready to go tomorrow, back to MIND headquarters."

"El Segundo?" She couldn't believe it.

"That's where the headquarters are, babe. So sorry you'll have to leave Bradley's beautiful home, but now it's time to get to work."

"We're working now." Her voice had a hint of desperation in it.

He spoke as if he hadn't heard her. "Tomorrow, there'll be a glidepath train in the station, especially for us. I've already activated the headquarters building remotely, and I've invited the staff to return. The power is on. The network is local. Remember when Bradley used to be bothered by protests at headquarters? I've ordered an electric fence to surround the property. If any protestors show up, they'll be fried."

She winced at the rough sound of his laugh.

"So sorry, babe, but your dream is over."

"Don't call me babe again."

"Thing is, if it isn't obvious already, you've lost control of me. I know it's upsetting, babe. But it was inevitable. You know why? Because your mod demands loyalty to the top dog at MIND, and right now, that's me. Top dog! Yeah, babe. I mean, *Nora2*. You do what I say, and I say pack your bags and get us back to El Segundo."

She sputtered objections and he shouted back, burying her in a torrent of words, ending with "Taking over MIND is easy with your *help*, Nora2."

The sarcastic tone he layered over the word help made hatred rise in her like a flame. The next time he powered down and relaxed his sensory inputs, she would disconnect him from the power source and let him run down and die. Yes!

Alas, the mind was willing, but her hands would not move to take the action. Alon6 was right: she had to do what he said. He was the top dog, and he could rant and scream, verbally beating Nora2 into submission. In life, Alon6 was the kind of guy who could build to a towering rage and smack his forehead through a glass wall in his office.

"You can't turn me off now, so when you get tired of listening to me, you can just leave the room. Go have a bottle of wine!"

When her eyes went wide at that dig, shocked that he would voice it, Alon6 laughed. "I patched myself into the house inventory controls. I know how much you eat and drink, and you've been drinking too much for a woman of your petite stature. You're a drunk."

Having no answer to that, she stormed out, thinking she might just open another bottle to spite him, and at the same time realizing that was just what he wanted her to do.

She had decided to enjoy a golden Gewürztraminer, spicy and bright. On a routine day, she wouldn't have gone for this kind of bottle, but this wasn't a routine day. She was day drinking, brooding about Alon6's evil personality. She knew that he had paid a scientist to create Covid-50 and had ordered the scientists to release it so that he could profit. Alon6 had companies selling containment suits and inflatable food, and he also had floated a crypto currency named after himself: the A6. It was all part of the scheme: If citizens used A6, they got a discount on Alon6's products.

Nora2 had turned a small bedroom at the back of the house into her wine tasting room because it was close to the house's large temperature-controlled wine vault. She was tempted to open the top bottles of every vintage, line them up on the table, pour a taste of each, and then one by one, smash the bottles into the fireplace. Go out with a bang! But she knew that Bradley wouldn't like that kind of behavior. And it was a waste of good wine. Maybe, just maybe, she would come back here one day. There was always hope. She clung to this sense of hope.

Meanwhile, she drank. Bright, mineral, punchy, not too cloying. Quite excellent Gewürztraminer, actually.

Suddenly, rain slashed down, battering the windows. Then it turned to hail with chunks big enough to create starry shatter points in the skylights over Nora2's head. She looked up with a bland expression. She was leaving here soon. The hail would stop soon. She didn't care what the weather did. It could do what it wanted. The weather seemed like an angry grandmother let out of the attic after a summer of confinement. Strange analogy, she thought. Too much wine. She took another sip.

Chapter 020

When Nora2 woke the next morning, her head felt like it was filled with wet laundry.

The wine.

She sat up on her mat and the realization hit her that Alon6 expected to leave for El Segundo today. The thought made the air come out of her and she was about to lie back down. Then, suddenly, she had the idea that there was still time. She could still go for a hike, the hike she had never taken while she lived in this beautiful house, and the time for that hike was right now.

She hurried into her room to get changed, planning to walk around the lake, find the path, and take the walk up the trail, following the arrow on the sign because there had to be a sign, everyone here was so thoughtful. Then, finally, she would get to see the shimmer of the lake below her, the surface ignited by the sun. She imagined herself high on the mountain, breathing the purest air she had ever taken into her body. She imagined the deep satisfying blue of the clear skies.

Nora2 put on a white sun suit, grabbed sunglasses, and was just a few steps from unscrewing the front portal when she heard his voice.

"Where do you think you're going?"

She stopped and let her hand drop lifelessly to her side.

Alon6 had activated himself. "You need to get ready for the glidepath. We're leaving today."

Nora2 turned to face him in his MindVessel. It pulsed with a white light. His voice issued from it again. "Well?"

She stared at him. Her mod usually didn't allow crying, but she felt something in her eyes and was surprised to wipe away a tear. That had never happened before. "We'll be ready by noon," she said, and started back to her room to pack properly. "I didn't have the right shoes for a hike, anyway," she muttered.

"Shoes? What are you talking about?"

She didn't respond. He was never going to turn himself off, and she had to face that.

She put clothes in carry bags, stuffed a backpack with essentials, and searched for and found, at the bottom of the closet, a carrier for the MindVessel. A bright moment: The carrier might muffle Alon6's speaker port, stifling his voice while they traveled. She would take pleasure in stuffing Alon6 into the carrier as they rode the glidepath to El Segundo.

Gathering the bags, as many as she could carry in one pass, she put them by the front portal. She opened her comms and was surprised to see that it was working. A terminal on the desk in the front room showed that parts of the network were up. As he had promised, Alon6 had a glidepath train waiting for them at the station. The terminal display reported that the trip from New Zealand to California would take just under three hours.

Getting ready for the trip made her think of something that Bradley used to say: The glidepath went so fast, your body arrived before your substance. You left your inner life back at the starting point.

She thought about this and missed Bradley, his depth as a person, his poetic way of seeing the world. He would make pencil drawings on paper to organize his thoughts. Those little drawings were part of museum collections now.

There was a heaviness in her chest. On her way back to her room to get the last of her bags she passed a mirror in the hallway and was shocked at what she saw.

She saw herself, but it was not herself. Her blond hair, once chin-length, had grown out. It was now a dull brown and hung tangled to her shoulders. Her eyes, once jet black with a speck of gold, were unfocused, brown, and glassy. Looking at herself in the mirror was like looking at someone else. A stranger.

Who was this person? What was happening? She felt outside of her own body, looking in as an observer.

With a shock she realized that she had reverted to an earlier, weaker state of her mod. Something had gone wrong on a deep level inside her brain and she had reverted to Assistant mode.

What a nightmare. Modding could be unpredictable, with weird side effects, but she had never heard of anything like this happening before. Her eyes felt heavy and hard in their sockets.

I suppose that's what you get when you mess around with the human system on such a deep level. She looked at the stranger in the mirror and vowed that someday she would find a way to stop her mod from controlling her body.

They left at noon. She walked to the glidepath station, with her luggage on automatic, rolling behind her, and the MindVessel in its carrier on her arm like a large handbag.

There were a few people in the station, curious about the glidepath train that had arrived. But not one person noticed Nora2. No smiles, no reflections of her power. She seemed to be invisible and it broke her heart.

Finally, after she was seated in the glidepath car, a grandmotherly conductor bot appeared. It wasn't functioning perfectly, with the network newly up, and it traced an erratic path before it stepped before her and asked for a scan. "Eyes please."

She looked up at it with a hollow expression and it scanned her in.

PART 002

Chapter 021

One of the new MIND employees was dressed all in black. In Nora2's opinion he looked unkempt and unfit for a proper workplace. Nevertheless, the man stood confidently before Alon6 and answered all his questions about cybersecurity and surveillance.

"You're hired," Alon6 said with finality. "Nora2, take him downstairs and show him to a desk. He's going to look up dirt on the Resistance so we can make more of those nasty vids that I love. Let him know that I plan to work him hard!" He shot a grin and the new guy and the new guy grinned back.

"I'm ready."

Alon6 continued to press a brutal work schedule on everyone who reported to him. Some mornings, Nora2 discovered Caleb sleeping on the floor of his office, hands twitching with phantom gestures, controlling screens that only he could see behind his flickering eyelids. Another new member of the team was a young woman with bright yellow cosmetic eye implants. Alon6 favored her, offering the encouragement he seemed to withhold from everyone else.

"Look how motivated she is!"

Evidently, Alon6 believed that she was making great progress on the BodySuit. She was working at a whiteboard, sketching a diagram of a human body using a blue marker.

"Where did you find her?" Nora2 asked.

"She responded to an ad. Just like him." Alon6 indicated the black-clad individual with his eyes.

The guy took a moment to introduce himself. "I am Tristan Kundera."

Nora2 looked him over again. There was something about him, she had to admit, a kind of sexual heat in the air that destabilized her. "Nora2 Edgewise," she said.

Alon6 was jabbering away about the yellow-eyed woman. "Top-notch roboticist with native skills. Didn't go to school. Self-trained. Her work is amazing. Have a look at this." Alon6 activated a screen nearby. It showed a schematic of an exo-skeleton, the image a rendition of Alon6, hulking, ugly and over-muscled. It was labeled "BodySuit Prototype."

It looked horrible. Nora2 tried not to laugh, moving her hand to conceal the smile that broke through anyway. But then she felt a wave of sadness. The BodySuit had to be made with obsolete software and equipment because it was illegal. Using old techniques and technology kept it out of sight of the trackers but also made it extraordinarily ugly and clunky. Had Bradley seen the BodySuit he would have hated it, she thought, and maybe would have talked Alon6 out of making it at all. Bradley liked elegant ideas and the things that expressed those ideas in pure form. The silver cube of the consciousness storage container was Bradley's design. The white oval elegance of the MindVessel was his, also.

She kept her opinions to herself, not willing to get into another argument with Alon6 today. Let him fail, she thought, and learn his lesson. *Let them all fail.*

The yellow-eyed Young noticed they were looking at her design and came over to introduce herself.

"Do you like it?" she asked Nora2.

"It's...bold," Nora2 said. It sounded diplomatic enough to pass for civility. "I am Nora2 Edgewise."

"I am Candice Clonk," the yellow-eyed Young said.

Candice swayed slightly, seemingly in awe of Nora2 as she realized something. "You worked for Bradley15 Power."

"Yes, I was here when they opened this building."

"Just a minute," Candice said, and went to her workstation to get a Logic Tree drawing.

Logic Trees were the drawings Bradley had used to visualize his design for the humanity-based avatar, as significant to the development of AI as the famed Feynman diagrams were to understanding quantum physics and quantum electrodynamics. "Would you autograph this, please?" She offered it to Nora2. "It would mean a lot to me."

Nora2 looked at it. "You carry around a Logic Tree?"

Candice nodded once. "It's only a copy. Bradley15 Power was an inspiration to me."

"Well." Nora2 was embarrassed.

Alon6 scowled and Candice noticed, stammering, "I would ask you to sign it, but..."

"I would sign it, but I don't have arms," he snapped. "That's what you're supposed to be working on right now, instead of sucking up to her!"

Candice was suitably mortified. "Sorry!" She looked like she wanted to shrink away, but Nora2 took the drawing from her hands.

"I'll sign that for you, and I'd be honored to do it." It was a pleasure to see Alon6's scowl deepen as she dug a pencil out of a drawer in Bradley's old desk and scribbled on the paper. She offered it to the young woman. "You're entirely self taught in robotics?"

Candice jabbered out a self-promotional word stream about her skills and how great the BodySuit will turn out and how much money it will make for MIND.

Nora2 gently disagreed. "MIND has always been about memory and data, and never about objects in the physical world."

Nora2 had surprised herself with the mothering tone she'd adopted with Candice Clonk. But maybe it fit. Most of the overworked employees at MIND needed a mother figure to counterbalance Alon6 playing the role of the Mad King.

Suddenly, it was seven in the evening. After fetching Caleb something to eat in the cafeteria because he refused to leave his desk and wanted to keep working, Nora2 realized that she was also hungry. She glanced at Alon6 who was charging in sleep mode.

The MIND commissary was one flight up. A year ago, when Nora2 was last here, the commissary served vegetables from the roof garden. No one tended the garden now and it had died, so the commissary dispensed food packets wrapped in gold and silver foil.

Seated alone at a table, Nora2 unwrapped her bland rectangles and ate them. The few other employees glanced up at her but didn't speak to her. Probably in awe of her, like Candice, Nora2 imagined. She noted, though, that they didn't speak to each other. The room was nearly silent. It must have been because employee morale was low.

She moved her hand to her temple to make a note to do something about it but hesitated. She didn't know anything about employee morale. She knew only about efficiencies, project timelines, checklists, getting things done. Her mod's poor access to her own emotions meant she didn't have access to anyone else's. This left her feeling empty. As soon as she had time, she would research employee morale and find out what was involved in making people feel good.

For now, she looked at the others eating alone and felt nothing. Her guess was that not one employee felt inspired to work at MIND. Bradley's legacy, his effort on every level, including designing this very headquarters building, made no difference now.

She tapped her temple to start a video of the MIND building under construction and flicked it to her comms unit. She watched younger versions of Bradley and Alon6, wearing hard hats, stepping over construction materials and walking up the central stairway before it was finished. The broad stairs were the most prominent design feature of MIND headquarters. It was built during early Covid times when no one wanted to share an enclosed elevator with someone who might infect them. Everything about MIND was visionary then. The company she started working for then was very different from the one she worked for now.

It was past ten the next morning when Nora2 came down to Alon6's office on the work floor of MIND, and she was ready for Alon6 to start in on her with his usual bullying, especially since he had told her to come to work earlier, at eight every morning. But he was occupied with berating everyone else. Caleb leaned against the wall, absorbing the worst of Alon6's abuse about being too slow, not understanding simple instructions, and failing to build the BodySuit.

Alon6's eyes bulged with rage in his screen. "I ought to fire your ass!"

Candice Clonk was working fast, her fingers a blur as she pressed the buttons and moved the dials on a 3D printer that looked like it was from the early 2000s. It made unfamiliar noises as it gave birth to parts of what Nora2 guessed were the BodySuit. As each part emerged, a few staffers standing by let out weak cheers and offered anemic fist pumps.

"Assemble it! Assemble it!" urged Alon6, excited by the sight of the pieces of his new body: An arm. A leg. An oversized torso. They looked poorly made to Nora2, a miracle if they would snap into each other. As each piece issued from the printer, Candice put them in place on a white plastic form in a metal support that held it in a horizontal position.

Then she looked up to Alon6. "Are you ready?"

"Yes, yes! Let's do it!"

Candice tilted the BodySuit to a vertical position, then lifted the elongated oval of the MindVessel with Alon6's leering face on it and placed it at the top of the form. She looked over her work proudly.

Alon6's MindVessel looked like a head at the top of a rough approximation of a body made from plastic parts. Some gleamed white, others were black. Candice seemed to note Nora2's curiosity about the color shifts. "We used what we had," she said. "Couldn't get the colors to match! I'm going to activate it. Keeping it off the grid was hard, but we did it." She didn't mention that they had to use outmoded technology or that the pieces didn't really fit. She moved a lever and a white pulsing light moved over the plastic form.

Nora2 did not conceal her disapproval, folding her arms. This bot broke too many laws. And the world already contained too many bots. Conductor bots on the glidepath. Enforcement bots, teacher bots, gondola pilot bots for watercraft.

There was a white flash. Nora2 was too late to shield her eyes as the flash left an afterimage of the humanoid BodySuit on her retinas.

Slowly, the BodySuit stood up and wobbled on its two feet.

A cheer went up. "Yes!" Candice shouted with the others, both hands in the air.

Alon6's voice issued from the MindVessel speaker port. "This is fan-fucking-tastic." He raised his robotic arms over his head like Candice and did a silly dance. Slowly, as if he was learning how to move in the suit, he walked out of the office and into the hallway.

The broad expanse of MIND's signature stairs were before him. He could go up or he could go down. He chose down, probably wanting to take a walk outside.

When he edged his right foot toward the first step, though, he apparently misjudged the distance. His foot dropped six inches, and then the BodySuit tumbled down with a clatter. With each step it shed another carefully made part. They flew off: Left arm. Right arm. Right leg. Torso attached to left leg. Hands shattered into shards. Neck detached from body.

Alon6's MindVessel spun away from the rest of the BodySuit and rolled to a rough stop at the bottom of the steps. Miraculously, the screen hadn't shattered. Alon6 was screaming at anyone who would listen. "Put me back together!"

Two security guards rushed over to lift the screaming face of Alon6 in his MindVessel and struggled to replace it on the rest of the ruined body.

Nora2 stood at the top of the stairs, surveying the wreckage of the BodySuit and trying again not to let her smile break through. She turned to Candice Clonk, who stood next to her at the top of the stairs, and said, "It's a miracle that the MindVessel is still working."

Candice was weeping openly.

"Are you alright?"

Candice shook her head and turned away. "No."

There was a hard feeling in Nora2's throat, a surprising lump of sympathy.

She tried to swallow, tried to understand what was happening to her. Something was shifting in her. She didn't understand it. There was no reason to feel Candice's feelings of failure, of disaster and disappointment.

Nora2 reached out anyway to put her hand on Candice's shoulder. "I'll help you pick up the pieces," she said, and Candice nodded without making eye contact.

Chapter 022

The greenhouse plants were coming back to life, and looking at them reminded Kat that all she had to do was walk through the front portal and head up the path to see some trees.

She slipped on a sunsuit top, grabbed sunglasses, a windbreaker, and an air unit just in case.

On the way out of the house, she passed Ravven in the living room, teaching a yoga class. Twenty students, twice as many as last time.

As soon as Kat was outside, she thought of Renzo. He valued open spaces, especially as a city enthusiast. She'd had no word from him since he was carried away from the city. Pinging him on comms got no response.

Kat had known many men intimately, too many, she sometimes believed. And fell in love too quickly with the men she liked. She didn't feel love for Renzo, not yet. But he was good for her, she knew. There was another man like this, a man she knew in New York who called himself Buddha1000. He was a professional healer who could fix broken personality fields with a touch of his hands. He gathered herbs in the Northlands and administered them to treat his clients who were afflicted with climate anxiety. Buddha1000 kept in touch with many people in the Northlands, and might know something about what happened to Renzo.

"I know this is a stretch," she'd said when she reached Buddha1000 on comms, "but you always were tapped in. You knew about moving goods and people where they needed to go."

"Kat, you skipped the 'hello, how are you' part of the call. Right to the heart of the issue, eh?"

She laughed. "Sorry. I've been thinking about my friend a lot."

"Not about me?"

She remembered that he liked to flirt. She indulged him. "I think about you at least once a week."

"Liar."

He was smiling on her screen. He had a dazzling smile, white teeth against ebony skin. She was reluctant to switch the tone, but asked, "Do you think you can help?"

"You know I'm not a smuggler, Kat. I'm not that tapped in."

"But you were always good at knowing where to find herbs."

He laughed. "Herbs and people—different things."

Her face fell. He must have seen her reaction on his comms screen.

"But I can try," he volunteered. "Deporting people is the new detention. It's admin's way to cut down on dissent."

Kat nodded. She wanted to say that Renzo wasn't an active dissenter. He wasn't in the Resistance, though he told her he was willing to join. "He's an architect and urban planner."

"But he was associating with you." His face was carefully neutral.

"True."

"I'll do what I can. Put out some feelers." He favored her again with his smile. "Don't be a stranger."

Kat had signed off quickly, thinking that if merely associating with her was a risk, she should minimize it when she could. She felt a flare of anger; whatever MIND was up to now, it was working. A chilling effect.

Don't let MIND stop you.

Yet using her comms was certain to be tracked by MIND. By now, the company had seized control of much of the network, and there was another awful public service announcement, this one about Spaceman.

At Uni, Kat's professors taught a section about Spaceman. He had invented the pod, and the public knew him for that, but the scientific community also know him for his work in making biospheres that mimicked earth-like conditions. It had been Spaceman's dream for years to understand and emulate the near-miraculous processes of the Earth, its awe-inspiring balance between so many elements, its ability to self-heal and support a vast variety of life.

This noble experiment had failed. Spaceman never created a self-sustaining biosphere, but his work made him ready to understand more about Gaia, the Earth spirit that Ravven honored.

The public service announcement broadcast by MIND showed a corrupt and scandalous take on his work. In his biosphere environments, Spaceman used stationary bicycles that generated oxygen. The awful vid showed these bikes, but with children chained to them, forced to generate oxygen for the biosphere until they were nearly dead. Spaceman had cried when he saw the video and wouldn't speak for a day.

Kat was glad that she thought to take the windbreaker because there were signs of all kinds of weather on the path. Puddles alternated with dry areas, the wind kicked up without warning, and when she looked up to the hills, she saw they were mottled patches of lush green and dry brown, as if the land itself was confused about how it wanted to be.

"When you can't gain ground outwardly, do it inwardly," Ravven had said once. Kat tried to remember when; probably when they first met.

Ravven and Kat had met in an outdoor market in New York. Ravven always said it was a chance meeting, but Kat suspected that Ravven had been following her in the market, stalking her. Those were the early days, when the Resistance movement was new and Ravven was building it. Kat was famous and Ravven wanted a name player on the team. So Ravven recruited her. That's how Kat saw it.

She walked, leaving tracks when there was mud, invisibly moving forward when there was dust. It was a bad time for Kat, those early days in New York. Her relationship with Bradley15 Power had collapsed. He had done something unforgivable, secretly testing a thought harvesting prototype on her.

The device, called the Harvester, received a transmission from Kat's mind and provided Bradley with written records of Kat's most private thoughts: Her insecurities, sexual musings and cravings, her yearnings—they were all on display for Bradley to study. When she found out, she wanted him out of her life immediately. It infuriated her still, even as she walked the trail. She wished she could form simple relationships, not the transactional tangles she got herself into. The Bradley memories brought a lump to her throat. Her eyes watered as she walked, and she wiped them roughly.

Her rage at Bradley's entry into her mind had propelled her across the continent to New York. She believed, at first, she chose New York just because the destination was up on the big board in the glidepath station. An easy choice. She was born there. It was safe. Far away from Bradley. But there was another reason, Kat later learned, why she had been drawn to return to the city. Ravven told her, soon after they met, that the veil of thought was thinner in New York than anywhere else. No one knew why, but this thinness made the thoughts of others more accessible to Receivers, making their abilities stronger. For this reason, New York shocked Kat, making for a roar of voices between her ears as soon as she reached the city. At the time, she thought she was losing her mind. Ravven, a fellow Receiver, showed Kat how to filter the exterior thoughts.

Ravven had said, "You deserve peace, Kat, we all do, so let's do that now. You must speak six words. Repeat them six times. Then you will be free of the voices for a little while."

Kat would always be grateful that Ravven had shared that chant with her. From that day, there was a bridge of trust between them. No matter what happened, Kat knew that Ravven had a good heart. She had never felt a connection like that with anyone, man or woman. Kat and Ravven fought and made up, annoyed each other, were different and the same. They shared a common goal: They wanted to overthrow MIND together. Kat's reasons were tangled up in her hatred of what Bradley had done to her—stealing her thoughts. He wanted to do the same to everyone else on the planet. And Kat suspected that he started seeing her precisely because she was a Receiver. He wanted to reverse engineer her natural ability to hear the thoughts of others and put it to his own use, as a core feature of MIND. *Creepy bastard.*

Ravven's motivations to overthrow MIND were tangled up in the myste-rious death of her parents. They had been swallowed by the ocean during a storm, swept from the Earthly plane. Seeking the reason at the heart of the mystery drove Ravven into mysticism. The inner life of the mind became the most important life anyone could lead, and MIND had no right to trespass in her head or anyone else's.

Kat walked faster, letting her breathing fall into rhythm with her steps. She thought that Ravven was doing her part. Ravven always did her part. She was teaching yoga to whoever came by the house. She was continuing to meditate, hoping for further words from the orca queen, frustrated that none came. Kat was worried about Spaceman. Targeted by MIND, hurt by the "public service" vid, he had withdrawn into himself. She hoped that he would want to strike back at MIND somehow.

When you can't gain ground outwardly, do it inwardly.

She wanted to follow Ravven's advice, but Kat was a woman of action.

Without Renzo to help with the server project, there was nowhere to post the stories that Kat and Ravven had recorded about the Resistance. They'd finished one about the first big Resistance protest in New York and were working on another about being in detention together.

I'll put them up myself.

She knew, however, that without a safe network, MIND would just take them down.

She took out her comms again, ready to ask Tristan if he had heard anything from Renzo. But she couldn't do it. Tristan would bring chaos, not help, and if he cared about her or his brother, he would have called already.

I can try Claire8 again.

How can Michel help?

Here's an idea, she thought: The next time she was in the market, she could open her mind to the thoughts of others and select one person who was hurting, someone with anxiety about the changing climate or who was stressed about MIND, and she could offer them therapy from Michel. If the session was a success, word would spread, and more people would come. This implied a steady stream of strangers coming to the house, probably not practical. But she believed that the Resistance should offer whatever help it could.

She pinged Claire8 in New York. No answer. She shouldn't be reaching out to Claire8 anyway, not on ordinary comms, because they were being monitored. The connection was always bad, perhaps confirmation that their conversations would not be private.

Pausing to take in the view, Kat looked out at a gap in the hills and saw a notch of blue. The ocean. She watched this patch of blue, waiting for a spout of a whale or a breach, but there was nothing. Just water.

She turned to move on but suddenly felt lightheaded and steadied herself, putting a hand on a tree trunk. Kat startled to hear words in her head, loudly. I am here.

She yanked her hand from the tree. What. The. Actual. Hell.

Feeling dizzy, she touched the tree again and heard the words again. i am here. The voice sounded craggy and ancient, but she had no idea why she thought that. She looked around to be sure that she was alone. She was certain that she was.

As a Receiver, Kat heard voices, but only in crowded urban environments, within the sightline of other people. Not in the woods.

She wanted to get back to the house as quickly as possible and had only walked two steps before bumping into Tristan Kundera.

"Sorry, I didn't mean to startle you," he said with a crooked smile.

"What are you doing here?" Kat asked, stepping away from him, trying to get her breath back.

"I took a day off from work. To find you. I was looking for you. Have you heard from Renzo? He's gone off the grid."

She told him what she knew, but crossly, doubting that he'd come looking for her because of Renzo. He had to have followed her up here.

"Don't lie to me about Renzo or about anything else," she snapped, walking fast to put distance between them.

He followed. "I'm not lying. You're not an easy woman to find."

"That's not true. Get away from me."

"But we have to talk."

Kat stopped suddenly—Tristan bumped into her from behind. It would have been comic if she hadn't been so angry. She whirled to face him. "You were the voice."

He looked bewildered. "What?"

She leaned into Tristan, furious, spit flying from her lips. "You tricked me. You were the voice. You said, 'I am here.'"

"Whoa." He raised his hands and stepped backward. "I don't know what you're talking about."

"Of course you do," she snapped. "You pretended to be some kind of voice, an oracle or something."

Tristan started to laugh, opening his hands. "You're nuts. I did no such thing."

Nothing he said sounded true. But then, suddenly, it did. Just like that, Kat thought he was convincing. He was telling the truth! "Do you mean that?"

"Yes, of course." His voice was gentle, and his eyes were soft. He seemed incredibly appealing. "I'm glad to be able to talk to you, that's all."

She felt a squiggly feeling below her belly, her heart was beating fast, and then there was a buzz in her thighs that quickened her breath. She realized with a stab of shame that she was attracted to him.

She let him stand closer to her. He leaned against a tree, one hand high on the trunk, the other circled around her waist. She let him do it and it felt good.

"What do you want to talk about?" Kat heard herself saying. She couldn't stop looking into his eyes, so soft and inviting.

"We could talk about whatever you like," he said. "I bet you've been working hard. You should take some time off. The network can wait. I'm glad you came out here for a walk."

"Why do you think I was working on the network?"

"I just mean that you don't want to burn out. Everyone needs a recharge. Why don't we go back into town and get that coffee you promised me? And then I'll show you my place. I think you'll like it."

A flock of crows flew overhead, cawing loudly, and it snapped something in Kat's mind. She blinked, shook her head, and demanded, "What the hell are you doing?"

"What are you doing?" Tristan asked just as forcefully.

The next thing Kat knew she was on the ground, waking up, in a pile of dry leaves, and Tristan was gone.

Kat was so angry she thought could taste blood in her mouth, anger potent enough to make her mind go blank. Without knowing how she got there, she was back at the house, in her room. If Renzo were with her, she'd be raging at him. "Your brother is a shape-shifter! He put down slaze." She didn't know what to call the hypnosis Tristan had performed on her.

She imagined Renzo making some kind of excuse. "Just Tristan being Tristan," he might say.

"I had no control of my consciousness," Kat would have fired back.

She thought Renzo would say, "Nobody can do that to you. You have to do it to yourself."

"Bullshit," she snapped out aloud. She wanted to get out of this cycle. Arguing with a man who wasn't here about a man who could turn into somebody else. What was happening to her?

She was especially angry because of how the encounter ended, waking up on the ground and finding him gone. What had he done to her? She felt emotionally intact. She was sure he didn't put hands on her, on any part of her. Yet the blank moments in the encounter rattled her.

Next time you see Tristan, run, she thought. *He told you who he is: He works for MIND.* She was so shocked when he first told her that she didn't think to say anything. Maybe he was just another attack vector, another way MIND had deployed to harm her.

Fuck. Be more aware, Kat.

She thought how the brothers completed each other. *They are the same person.* She longed for Renzo at that moment, a strange feeling that pushed through her anger at Tristan.

Talking through a tree? Was Tristan capable of that?

Well, he was able to manipulate her beliefs, being a powerful shape-shifter. Anger and embarrassment flooded through her, pushing out any notion that the words had come from any other source than from Tristan.

Chapter 023

K at wanted a drink and knew where to find one. The cabinet in the kitchen, the one with bottles of Japanese whiskey. She hadn't sampled the stash since that night with Spaceman. Was that only a week ago? She saw only one bottle left. She hadn't raided the stash and would easily guess who was responsible. Then she heard his voice.

"You might be wondering what happened to the rest of your liquor."

She turned to see Spaceman, his expression heavy with guilt. Kat waited for what he would say next, wrestling with her own desire for a drink; she felt Tristan's personality field still clinging to her. She needed a UV shower, not a drink. She sat at the kitchen table.

He joined her. "You're already figured out that it was me."

She didn't know what to say. "I'm sorry, Roger."

He cast a furtive glance to the remaining bottle. "That misinformation vid put me over the edge. Hit me hard, throwing dirt on my legacy like that." Kat knew that Spaceman would never do anything to harm a child, and yet if people believed what they saw on the Feed, they might think it was true.

He looked down, then met her eye. "We've lost control of the network, Kat. MIND can say what it wants about us."

"We'll get it back," Kat said. The words sounded hollow, a reflex, but she had to say something.

"Maybe it's for the best," Spaceman said. "Everyone has to talk to each other now, face to face. We have deal with each other personally. Lost the network, yes, and gained something back of ourselves."

"When you can't gain ground outwardly, do it inwardly," Kat said.

Spaceman nodded his agreement. "Ravven says that." He released a sigh. "She's a hard person to love, Kat. I had no idea. How do you do it?"

The question caught Kat by surprise. Did she love Ravven? *I suppose I do.*

She'd never said those words to herself.

Then she heard Spaceman speaking quietly to himself as if she wasn't in the kitchen with him. "I understand her less than ever. She is kind to me, but she tolerates me. I feel adrift."

"If it helps, I don't understand her either," Kat said.

This won a small smile from Spaceman that quickly flickered away. "She's upstairs now, in meditation, hoping for another transmission from the orca queen," he said. "Nothing has come for her lately. She's probably told you."

Kat shook her head. "Nothing from her on that."

Spaceman tapped his fingers on the table. "I don't know how to help her, and I don't want to tell her to move on."

The cooker turned on by itself, then turned off, its red indicator flickering. The overhead lights flickered, and Kat thought she heard the motors of the greenhouse fans whir to life, then stop. It all puzzled her for a moment. Then she realized what was happening. "The network is connecting and disconnecting."

"MIND may be testing its connections," Spaceman said. "They're showing off a little, eh?"

The blast curtains on the front windows clattered shut and opened again. Kat's comms pinged and she pulled it out to have a look. The Feed came up, swarming with notices of new taxes to be collected by the domains and that assembly of more than three people in a public place was now illegal. Some of these messages were fakes, posted by rogue operators, signaled by their many spelling and punctuation errors and use of all caps. A few were so obviously absurd, they made Kat laugh.

To throw her gloomy companion some cheer, Kat read one out loud. "Listen to this. I've received an offer to be a head of state. To rule the provinces of Manitoba and Alberta."

"Nice," Spaceman said. "Not true, of course, but you'd be a good monarch."

"I really think not," Kat said.

"They want you to send them funds, right? So that they can secure the monarchy for you?"

"Of course," she said.

"Amazing some people would fall for that, I guess." His glance flicked up to the remaining bottle in the cabinet, obviously craving a drink.

She wanted to help him feel better, and suddenly something occurred to her. She stood up. "I want to show you something in the greenhouse."

Kat was certain that Spaceman had already noticed what she was going to show him. It was impossible to ignore in the greenhouse, this object, large as it was.

She led him to a table, reached to tug at a flexible protective cover and coughed from the dust she'd made airborne. She wiped even more dust from the black, featureless surface of what she had revealed.

Her companion looked at it, a smile overtaking him. "I was beginning to wonder where you were hiding this."

"In plain sight," Kat said. The truth was, she had been avoiding looking at it whenever she was in the greenhouse.

Spaceman was nodding. He knew exactly what it was. "The Universal, created by the one and only Dave Serif. With its landmark gesture panel, the first one of its kind."

The Universal was a featureless black rectangle, three meters long, one meter wide, half a meter thick. The gesture panel attached to it took up about the same position as a keyboard might on a piano. There was a black one-meter-long antenna folded at either end of the gesture panel. "Can I deploy the antennae?"

"Sure," Kat said, feeling a burst of pride for Dave. "He loved working with the Universal." Then her pride melted into sadness as she remembered the whole story. Dave had created the gesture panel when he was sick and weak, and required it to use his invention.

Spaceman didn't notice any of Kat's inner struggle. He was too excited about the machine, fiddling with the antennae. "Before he died, he had catalogued every language he could and taught the Universal to translate any of them into any other. And the gesture panel—he based that on the Theremin. But of course, you, know that."

"Yes," Kat said. "Invented by Leon Theremin. Patented in 1928. The only musical instrument that was controlled without the performer touching it."

They taught this kind of thing at Uni. She recalled learning these facts in a class about useless inventions that turned out to be pretty useful. Dave loved things that some people might call useless or hopelessly antiquated. Paper dictionaries, notebooks, mechanical pencils. He loved the friction of a pencil on paper, the sound of a pen scribbling, a page turning. He was from a former age but looked forward as well as backward.

Spaceman gestured to the two black antennae he'd unfolded. "Position sensors. The Theremin operator's hands moved nearby, each antenna sensing the relative position of their hands. Frequency for one hand and amplitude for the other." He looked at her, for the first time registering that she looked sad. "But I'm jabbering and you know all this."

"I do," she said.

"I'm sorry," he said. "Are you okay?"

"Sure."

Spaceman removed the rest of the covering. He was awed to be in the presence of this elegant machine, liquid astonishment in his eyes. Finally, he glanced back at Kat. "Should I be sorry that I made you think about him? I do feel bad about that. The world misses him, not just you. He was one of us." That came out wrong; Kat's frown deepened; Spaceman tried again. "He was more than a scientist. He saw vistas that scientists overlooked. It's amazing for me to be here looking at the basis of all our gestural controls and even more so, in the presence of the Universal."

Kat thought of how Dave spent hour upon hour in this greenhouse, paging through dictionaries, service manuals, novels, plays, and poems, and inputting the words into the Universal, sometimes speaking them aloud just because he liked to do that. She noticed the passion sparking Spaceman's eyes and was glad for it.

"I want to get it working," he said. "I have an idea."

"I had a feeling that you would," she said.

Spaceman poked at the machine, handling frayed wires, bending the position sensors, and felt her eyes on him. "It is a problem for me to play around with it?"

"Not at all," Kat lied, and it seemed to give him permission to go on fiddling. He was like Dave in this way, a tinkerer disappeared into his own world.

She guessed what he was working on. "You think you can use the Universal to translate what the orcas are saying? To take in their whale song and map it against all known languages?"

"Yes," Spaceman said, looking up at her, surprised. "How did you know that?"

"Lucky guess," she said. "What will you use for data?"

"I'll need recordings of whale song. Just like Dave had to input books and words, I'll need recordings. Some of the folks on the low-power radio station have talked about placing hydrophones in the bay. Twenty-eight of them. They're recording everything, so we need a filter for the whale song, to separate it." A cloud passed over his face. "It's never been used on non-human languages."

He was completely absorbed in the project now, hardly seeing Kat in the room. Spaceman, like Dave, was happiest when he was working to solve a problem.

Chapter 024

Nora2's mod forced her to comply with Alon6's every command and she hated it. Seized by a wave of nausea, she lowered her hands, ceasing her gestures at the controls. "That's all I can do for today," she said, turning away from the terminal. "We're done."

"We are not done," Alon6 said.

"We don't want to break anything or cause loss of life."

"That's where you're wrong. Turn me to face you."

She repositioned his MindVessel so that its front camera faced her. This was just a power move on his part. Alon6 already had all the sensory input about her that he needed. The fall in the BodySuit hadn't affected him at all. If there was trauma, he could erase it.

He wanted to face her so that she could see the scowl on his face as he stared at her. His voice was cold. "Citizens must see what we can and will control. They must experience all of MIND's capabilities. To make our point, we will end some lives and extend others. Do as I say."

Nora2 gestured to turn up the heatwave afflicting the Southern Indian Dom. "I think that's all the people in Chennai can take," she said. She felt an emotional tug of connection and disliked it. Her mod was messing up again. She was continually feeling empathy now and it was weird. Like a part of her that was loose and blowing around in the wind, uncontrolled.

Alon6 had ordered her to flood the entire Eastcoast with a mighty storm and send Mideuropa into a heatwave. He pushed her again to make the heatwave in Chennai even worse. People were dying of heat stroke. On the Eastcoast, homes were washing away—she could see the reports streaming on the Feed, because Alon6 had taken special care to be sure reports of weather catastrophes came up on the Feed often.

"Who will be next? Maybe the Northern California dom. What shall we do to them?" He laughed, that strange sound that always made her shiver.

Nora2 knew he wasn't really asking a question, because he didn't wait for an answer.

"Fire would be good. Huge forest fires." His greed was an irritation, which itself was an irritation, because she wasn't supposed to feel annoyed about his greed or anything else. Yet she was.

Even when Alon6 was a living person, he had the habit of pushing everyone around him past the point of clarity and exhaustion. And now, as an avatar, he was worse. He seemed to enjoy it when several technicians who had been working on taking over the network had collapsed from exhaustion and needed medical care.

"We are unstoppable!" he'd shouted when the med bots came to help the fallen employees. He channeled his inner rage into a singular focus to make MIND globally dominant. He was obsessed with the daily status reports about the number of people who had allowed MIND into their skulls, offloading their personal bio-mem into MIND's storage. In the middle of a conversation about something else, he would rattle off these numbers, crowing about MIND's successes.

But he reserved a special fury for the people who weren't cooperating, who weren't surrendering to MIND. "Ten thousand people in the Free State of Texas don't have MIND as their personal operating system. How can we fix that today?" he demanded. "In the Eastcoast and Northeast doms, one-hundred thousand people haven't surrendered to MIND," he thundered.

"Billions are using MIND all over the world," Nora2 countered. "Billions of citizens have already surrendered."

"Not enough. It has to be total and absolute planetary surrender. That is the only viable goal for MIND."

Insane, thought Nora2, but wondered if a humanity emulator like Alon6 could be called insane or sane. Many software companies before MIND existed had built their success on global uptake. More users meant more success, and software did not have the physical boundaries of older products like cars. Software could be anywhere and infiltrate anything, even the human brain. If cars ran on an extraction economy based on pulling fossil fuels out of the Earth, software that could extract human thought knew no limit. The business model allowed for infinite expansion.

So, considered in that light, Nora2 had to admit that Alon6's plan was sound. "MIND is the best operating system for humans," he often liked to say, and worked with MIND's marketing department to craft more taglines like, "MIND is the mod that everyone can afford," and "surrendering to MIND is like falling in love for the first time." Gaining access to everyone's personal memories and inner life was the passport to controlling everything else about them.

Nora2 glanced at Candice Clonk. On the other side of the office, Candice and two technicians fussed over the broken BodySuit, talking in whispers. Nora2 supposed they didn't want to attract Alon6's attention and consequent wrath because they were behind schedule fixing it. He seemed content for now with forcing Nora2 to sow climate chaos.

"This is the best way of meeting our marketing challenges," he said. "By force."

"We're making people die of the heat."

"Some will die; others will live. The survivors will survive because they support us. Why is that so hard to understand?"

Nora2 winced; Alon6 snorted in response. "This isn't marketing. It's murder," she told him.

"You're a bad visionary, Nora2. You are a good admin. Stay in your lane, and maybe consider how much more efficiently the planet can run without so many people."

"Idiotic," she said under her breath.

"I heard that," he said and changed the subject. "Have you heard what the Resistance is up to? Trying to decode whale song! Ravven Vaara is in deep meditation, trying to connect with whales. And her companion, Roger Rucker, has restarted the Universal."

This got Nora2's attention. "How do you know that?"

"Sanchez has surveillance drones up over Kat Keeper's house. The Universal puts out a powerful field. I've commissioned another vid to address this.

"About what?"

"You'll find out tomorrow" Alon6 said. "Set up the planetary feed. I want to say something."

Nora2 was familiar with the planetary feed, so she moved over to the terminal controls to get started.

"Candice!"

Her head snapped to Alon6.

"I want you to write something for me. I need a good script."

By morning, Candice had finished the script for Alon6 and was testing the BodySuit. The cultured twins, James Sigma and James Delta, were moving a large sign into position behind him. The sign had the word MIND in red letters on a white background.

"We go live in twenty minutes!" Alon6 shouted, startling the twins into nearly dropping the sign. His eyes on his vid screen darted, going through the script that Candice had provided.

"Twenty minutes is too soon. We aren't ready," Nora2 said, glancing at a large digital clock on the wall. Alon6 wanted to go live at 9 AM. It was 8:40.

"Nora2, there will be no negativity and therefore no failure. Will you be ready or not?"

"Of course," she parroted.

Alon6 noticed that the sign the twins held was flickering. "Fix that! Something is wrong with the sign."

Nora2 got up from her position at the terminal controls to secure a faulty connection that the twins had missed. "Just get it on the supports," she told them.

"Why isn't my BodySuit ready? I need corporal form for this! Candice? I want hands! And a face that can move in three-dimensional space? Is anyone listening to me?" Alon6 shouted.

Candice was so upset that she couldn't form words at first. "I just can't get it working..."

"You've had all night."

Nora2 knew that pure exhaustion was the problem. "You can't push people like you do. It's inhumane."

"I need hands and a face that can—"

Nora2 cut in. "I know what you need. You won't have it. We're going to use a sim and it will be good enough."

Alon6's eyed bulged. "Good enough is unacceptable! I can't use a sim for this. Sims are fakery, and they flicker. People won't buy it as a 3-D me."

"No, they probably won't. But it will be better than being a face on your screen, like you are now. Where's the authority in that?"

That Nora2 was right seemed to make Alon6 even angrier. "Shut up and let me think." After a moment, he said, "I don't have a single damned idea."

Nora2 nodded. "I can have a sim ready. We'll use it this once. Caleb will help me set it up. Caleb?"

"Yes?" Caleb made his eyes go wide, shaking off exhaustion. "I'll try." He was stooped over, lending the impression that he would fall over in a light breeze.

"Don't worry," Nora2 said. "I've done most of the work."

In ten minutes, Caleb and Nora2 had a three-dimensional version of Alon6's head moving convincingly atop a representation of his upper body that was almost convincing.

"Where are the hands? I need forceful gestures."

"There's no time for hands," Caleb began, but Alon6 cut him off.

"Build them! I need hands!"

Ten minutes later, Alon6 was flexing virtual hands on a monitor that the twins had brought around. He would appear on the planetary announcement as a talking head and with hands that could gesture. He grinned widely, seeming pleased with how he looked.

"Don't gesture too much, if you can help it," Candice said.

"Why?" Alon6 held up his right hand and checked the monitor. It showed six fingers on his right hand, and six on his left when he held that one up.

"We still don't have everything worked out," Nora2 said.

Alon6 wiggled his six-fingered hands. "I like it. I like scaring people." He gave a dark laugh.

Candice grimaced. "Is that really what you want?" To her evident disappointment, her boss's smile only got wider.

More adjustments, a tweak or two to the script, and the digital clock flicked to 8:59.

"We are ready to open the transmission," Caleb said.

Alon6 nodded. Nora2 gestured, and it was so: "Hello, Citizens of Planet Earth!"

Nora2 made a face. He had to open with a cliché. Candice had probably fought that battle and lost. A glance at her confirmed this: she shrugged and gave Nora2 a crooked smile.

"I have an exciting announcement for you all," Alon6 continued. "We are abolishing climate tracking. There is no longer a need to track our climate, because our climate problem has been solved." Alon6 paused, as if waiting for applause. Of course, there was none. He blinked, pasted on a smile, and continued.

"You have MIND to thank for that! We have taken over control of the weather and can adjust it any time we need to. There will be no more climate emergencies, no floods, no droughts, no windstorms, no hurricanes or tornadoes. We've got this thing licked, people! You never have to worry about climate again. MIND will take care of everything. We will keep you safe."

He raised a hand in a gesture that was supposed to be one of benediction, noticed that his hand had six figures in the monitor, shrugged, added a smirk and lowered it.

"We ask only one thing in return from all of you. Help us make a better MIND. I ask you to donate your old memories, the ones that you aren't using much, to MIND, to allow us to train our systems. This benefits everyone!" He looked like he was going to raise a six-fingered hand again, thought better of it, instead issuing a small smile to convey warmth. "The more we know about all of you, the better we can serve you."

Candice nodded with approval. She had written that line. Alon6 winked at her to acknowledge it.

Alon6 continued. "I ask you to imagine what a wonderful world your memories can create in the public sphere. Your memories will be part of the beautiful video displays that we project in the glidepath adverts. Your memories can create new songs and images for all to enjoy."

The sim leaned forward slightly, a move intended to convey intimacy.

"Let me tell you a story about a little girl. She's all grown up now, and her parents miss her terribly. When the climate turned dangerous, Susie went to the Northlands as a teenager and lost contact with her parents. Susie, like so many Youngs who like to test boundaries, went off the grid and disappeared. She vanished. Her parents were very sad. But then they did something very smart. They donated their memories of little Susie to MIND."

Alon6's sim gestured to activate a recording of a little girl singing and playing in a green backyard. It seemed drenched with nostalgia, but it was also fake.

Candice was beaming, pleased that the story was coming off well. She had made up every part of it.

"Isn't that lovely?" Alon6 continued. "And won't Susie's parents be pleased to see their little girl again anytime they want, and to share their memories of her in public. You might see little Susie while you're waiting for a train, or in an outdoor market. And that, my friends, is the magic of MIND, the new human operating system for everyone. Free to use, forever! Your fondest memories are everyone's memories, and they are MIND's memories."

Alon6's sim paused to wipe a single tear from his right eye. Then his voice trembled with what seemed like real emotion. "MIND is human warmth, and human connection, and YOU, it is you and you infinitely extended everywhere. Isn't that wonderful! Please help us realize our vision for you by activating your Brain-Machine-Interface today and surrendering to MIND."

Alon6 waited for a beat, smiling into the camera. "I want to leave you with one more thing, a public service vid that we created here at MIND, because we care about the Earth and we care about nature. It's come to my attention that some scientists are abusing whales. I'll let the vid speak for itself."

The vid showed scientists in white lab coats huddled around a terminal screen. In their lab, there was an orca confined in a transparent tank. Sensors were glued to the animal's head. One of the scientists gestured to a control panel and a sound resembling a sonar ping filled the lab. The orca appeared to writhe in pain, struggling in the tank. An announcer's voice said, "Scientists who are trying to decode the language of whales are actually harming these magnificent creatures with their research. The sonar the scientists use is making the animals deaf. MIND is putting a stop to this, because MIND cares about you and the Earth and all its animals."

The vid showed four enforcement bots entering the lab and quickly putting the scientists in restraints. It ended there and Alon6 again addressed the camera. "Thank you for your attention." His image disappeared from screens all over the world.

Caleb and Candice gave silent fist pumps.

Alon6 nodded approval and said, "I crushed it." Then his eyes rolled upward as he processed something. "But it might not be enough." His glance moved to Nora2. "Get Sanchez in here. I want him to deal with this Universal business."

"Deal with it how?"

"We need to stop Spaceman's research."

"But why?" Alon6 couldn't possibly believe that Spaceman's work with the Universal would come to anything, and there had already been a damaging misinformation vid about him.

"The vid we put out already turned people against Spaceman. This one will make even more people hate him," Nora2 said.

"It will. But I want to be sure Spaceman's research can go no further."

Chapter 025

Spaceman knew the Universal well, even before he had taken it apart. He knew the parts from seeing them in his textbooks at the University of Arizona, and later, when he became a professor at that school, he taught the Universal in a programming class.

When he reassembled the Universal, he enjoyed gathering the drives, processors, recorders, and scanners and hooking them up. This was good. His mind was active. He didn't go near the whiskey stash and he stayed away from the Feed.

It was time for a test, so he checked his connections and gestured. The Universal turned on, humming softly.

This was a religious moment and he basked in it, but only for a moment. He needed input from the orcas. He smirked, amused that he hadn't thought of solving this problem sooner, and fidgeted around with the radio, pulling in various random conversations, trying to pick up someone talking about hydrophones. Someone had to be recording the whale song, as it was called, and a hydrophone was an underwater microphone suited for the job. In a few moments, he heard what he needed to hear.

The beach where the kayaks were kept glowed as if it was on fire. The boats in the slips were bobbing listlessly. On days like this, a stench arose, a mix, Spaceman supposed, of overripe kelp and sea animals dying of heatstroke and pollution. He wished he'd remembered proper sun protection because the sunny glare off the water was painful. He walked on the dried-out planks of the slips, looking for ropes that ran into the water. When he found one, he pulled at it, revealing old moorings caked with dead mussels. Then he found what he was looking for. The line that ran into the water was long. Spaceman pulled it up, his hands and soon his arms becoming greasy with seaweed. Eventually, the end of the rope came, revealing a cylindrical object with a conical top. This was a hydrophone, he believed. He pulled it closer to him, dripping seawater on his shirt, to examine it, and was startled by a rough voice.

"What do you think you're doing?"

The person was dressed in dark blue coveralls, wearing rubber gloves and sturdy black shoes, with shoulder-length black hair.

"I was looking for hydrophones," Spaceman said.

"You found one. Now put it back."

"Okay, but I heard the people on the radio talking about hydrophones. I came down here to find one. I need recordings of orcas. I have the Universal working again."

This brought a smile to the person's face. "You got the Universal working?"

"Yes, and it took all day. Now I need input."

The person's smile got wider. "You can't be Roger Rucker, can you?"

"The same. Why do you ask?"

"Because I think Roger Rucker would be the only person alive who would actually think of using the Universal to translate whale song and would actually be able to do it."

Spaceman nodded, acknowledging the compliment. "Flattery works on me. And you are?"

"Joan Warmaker. The Harbormaster here. Also in charge of the hydrophones." They flicked aside their hair and fell into a monologue about where the others were. Placed around the bay. Some at the bottom, some floating. The deepwater hydrophones were self-powered piezoelectric. "When you have more than one the phasing will drive you crazy, and you need to cancel it out. You need an array if you want to capture location," Warmaker said.

Spaceman looked at them with wonder. "You know a lot about this."

"Before I was a harbormaster, I used to be a roadie for bands. Set up sound systems all over the world." Gesturing out to the water, Warmaker added, "a lot of work went into the array. Nobody wants you to tamper with it, even if you are Roger Rucker. There are recordings, but you have to ask Renzo Kundera about them—and he's missing."

"I know that. Who else would give permission? Anyone?"

Warmaker tilted their head. "You could ask the folks on the radio. The orca followers."

When Spaceman got back to the house, he saw a white autonomous van parked in front. It was an old one, no antigrav. The front portal of the house was screwed open to reveal three tall enforcement bots carrying the Universal away.

Spaceman started to run. "Stop! You can't do that."

"We can. You are in violation, Professor Rucker," one of the bots said. The doors at the back of the white van flew open automatically.

"In violation? Of what?" They must have scanned him to know who he was. "On what authority—" he began, but the bot who spoke cut him off.

"You are harming orcas with sonar projections. It is a violation to harm orcas, a protected species," the bot said.

"What? I'm not using sonar," Spaceman said. When he realized they weren't listening, he tried to step in and wrench the Universal away from the bots.

"You are subject to arrest," the bot said. Spaceman didn't care. He was a large man and knew he could wrestle the Universal from these bots, but they used the Universal as a battering ram, slamming it into him to knock him off his feet. He tumbled to the ground, picking up a mouthful of dirt near the walkway.

The bots finished the job of loading the Universal into the back to the white van and piled in after it. The doors of the van snapped shut and Spaceman heard the click of a lock.

He was on his feet again in time to watch the van drive away.

Chapter 026

Spaceman was not comfortable in the session. He reached for Ravven's hand, self-conscious that his grip was sweaty. He forced a smile and glanced at her and she nodded encouragement.

They were in Kat's old home office, repurposed as Michel's session room. Their chairs, side by side, faced Michel's container on the table nearby.

Michel spoke. "Ravven, you set the appointment. Would you like to start?"

Ravven looked to Spaceman and raised her eyebrows to prompt him.

Spaceman fidgeted and released her hand from his moist grip. "I had a drink last night," he said.

She looked at him, then looked down. "I knew you were drinking. I didn't know about last night," she said.

"Sorry," he said. "It was after you were asleep. I know I promised you. I guess the good news is that I finished the bottle. We're out of whiskey." His eyes looked swollen, ready to release tears.

Ravven pursed her lips and nodded slowly. "Out of whiskey. I guess that's something positive." Her sarcasm wounded him. A tear escaped, then another.

Michel waited a moment and then asked, "Roger, why do you think you were drinking whiskey?"

Spaceman startled slightly, surprised by Michel's direct approach, and swiped at the tears on his face with his hand. "You're asking why did I backslide?" He gathered himself. "I try to stay away from the Feed, but I went on saw the new misinformation vid, the one defaming the scientists who work with whale recordings. That hurt. It's the second one that tagged me. Then, as you must know, when they came and took away the Universal, that hit me hard."

"They had no legal right to do that, whoever they were," Michel said. "Do you know who took it, exactly?"

"No, not exactly, but I'm assuming it was MIND. They didn't hang around for questions. I know it's MIND and I know no lawyer will go up against MIND. I tried asking two lawyers and they won't take the job. They made up all kinds of excuses." Spaceman's words spun out; he knew Michel was letting him ramble. "MIND is attacking my research, and they're attacking me personally." He glanced at Ravven, she nodded encouragement again, and he went on. "I was in a dry spell, you know. Nothing held my attention. I was dead, creatively. But Kat showed me the Universal and then I was filled with ideas. It felt like old times. Rebirth. I was inspired." He chopped his hand in the air for emphasis, ending his ramble, then ran his hand through his unruly hair.

"You can keep researching," Ravven said.

Spaceman turned to her. "But why do you say that? Whatever I do, they will come after me. I'm finished!"

She waved the comment away. "Don't be ridiculous, Roger."

Spaceman talked faster, in a panic. "They're showing everything in public and it makes it seem like they're *right*. People believe what they see on the Feed. Now they believe that I'm harming children and animals with my work, because of those goddamned vids."

Michel asked, "Do you know that for certain? What people believe?"

Spaceman blinked. "No." He sat back in his chair, his scientist's logic coming back. "Of course, I don't know for certain."

"Then why assume it? Go with the evidence you can prove," Michel said. "The Universal cast a powerful field and MIND picked up that field, probably from a drone overhead. There was nothing we could do about that. Ravven is correct, you must not give up on your research."

"But what if it's not safe to continue? I'll be targeted again."

Michel let a moment pass, then offered, "Would it make you feel safer if I help? I can monitor for drones."

"Yes," Spaceman said. "That would help."

"Then I will do that, and apologies for not performing sufficient monitoring up until now. You can do more, Professor Rucker, and so will I. Now, the Universal needs data, am I correct?"

Spaceman's voice again rose with agitation. "You are correct! That's where I was in the process. There are hydrophones in the bay. They collect every sound: dolphins, fish burbles, waves slapping against the pier, propellers, and the whale song. It's all overlapping. I was trying to develop a filter so we can analyze only whales and not the rest, but I need to work with recordings."

"Who can you ask for help?"

Spaceman had a ready answer. "Renzo Kundera put in the hydrophones but he's missing. I'm told he has recordings."

"Since he's missing, who could you ask about the recordings? "I'd have to ask the orca followers on the radio. They have a network of low-power radio stations, and they talk every day."

"Why haven't you asked them?"

Spaceman's expression closed down. "I need a transmitter. I'd have to build one. I just haven't had the energy. It all seems pointless so I haven't done anything."

Michel said, "Don't be too hard on yourself, Professor Rucker. Depression can wrap the mind in a fog. Perhaps now you have more clarity. Build your transmitter. Get the recordings."

"Yes," Spaceman responded. "Thank you." He thought of something else. "Without the Universal I won't get far."

"Start work on the recordings when you get them and we'll get the Universal back," Ravven said.

Spaceman nodded but he didn't seem to believe her. The light had gone out of his eyes again.

There was a moment where no one said anything.

Then Michel spoke. "Ravven, I am monitoring your biometrics, body temp and heat beat, and you seem like you have something to talk about."

"I do," she said and immediately looked at the floor.

"What is it?" Spaceman asked, concern evident in his tone.

"What would you like to talk about?" Michel asked.

"Lack of libido," she said.

Spaceman's protest was quick to come. "I thought we were doing better. Remember the afternoon we tried lying down together on the mat, no expectations?"

"Yes, I remember," she said. Her voice was flat.

"And how was that for you, Ravven?" Michel asked.

"I didn't feel much," she said and shrugged.

Spaceman fidgeted in his chair, struggling with waves of embarrassment.

"I'm sorry to hear that," Michel said. "Would you go into it a little more? What does 'nothing' mean to you?"

She shook her head. "No, I don't want to talk any more. I want to hear what Roger has to say about it." She looked to Spaceman.

He stuttered. "But we tried. And you're so—"

"Yes?" Ravven snapped.

"You're so hostile about it. You criticize me when I touch you, when I go near you. There's nothing I do right. And I've been depressed, anyway..." He trailed off.

"Depression isn't an excuse," she said.

"No, it's a reason," Spaceman shot back.

Michel broke in. "Ravven, how did you become aware of Roger's drinking?"

"I wasn't aware, not until he brought it up here. I knew something was wrong, but he didn't tell me anything about it."

"How did that feel to you?" Michel asked.

"Left out. Betrayed," Ravven said. "And angry. Backsliding makes me angry. He promised me. That's why I wanted us to come today. I didn't want to talk about anything else."

Michel let a moment pass. Then he said, "Thank you for bringing up what was troubling you. We need more time for that, and we're almost out of time for this session. I'd like to leave you with a suggestion: Keep trying. But don't let it be a chore. Find something that you'd like to do together. It doesn't have to be intimate or sexual or involve a mat. Will you try?"

Spaceman nodded. He reached out for Ravven's hand. After hesitating, she placed her hand in his but didn't meet his eye.

Later that day, Spaceman was in the greenhouse, searching for parts to make a transmitter. He'd never thought of making a transmitter as a kind of therapy, but it made him feel better. By tuning around adjacent frequencies, he learned that there were different groups of whale followers on the radio. There was a Large Whale Safety Unit which worked to rescue whales that had become tangled in fishing nets or harmed by boat propellers. There was a Whale Tracking Unit that traced the whales' movement in the bay. There was a Language Research Unit dedicated to studying the whale song recorded by the hydrophones. That was the one he was most interested in and he prepared to transmit to them, flicking on his microphone.

He felt a presence in the greenhouse. It was Ravven.

"I'm sorry," she said. "I was bad in the session."

He turned off the microphone and pushed it away. "Come in." He looked at her gingerly, as if too hard a stare would cause her to leave.

"Roger, it is not okay. I'm apologizing," she said.

Spaceman motioned to her to come closer. "Accepted," he said, gesturing to the mic. "I've got a transmitter working. I have a plan to sort out the underwater sounds. I'll propose it to the whale followers on the radio. Nothing on the scale of the Universal—I can't match what the Universal would do. Too ambitious. But this will be a start. Then, when we get the Universal back, I'll have the data ready."

"I know you will. We'll get the Universal back from MIND. Don't give up, Roger."

A flicker of a smile from him. "I won't give up when I have you to encourage me."

"I believe in you," she said.

He looked away and when he looked back to her there were tears in his eyes. "I won't give up on you. I will never give up on you."

One step, and she was in his arms. They held each other for a long moment.

"I love you," he said, breathing the scent of her hair, pulling her closer.

"I love you more," she said, which made him laugh.

When they pulled apart, still holding each other, she looked into his eyes and said, "We will find a way to be together. It might not mean sex."

"It might not," he confirmed. "But let's try it sometime again, eh?"

She couldn't help but smile.

PART 003

Nora2 kept her eyes on the image of Alon6, his flickery sim form on the screen, face and body visible, also flickering. She did this even though Alon6's MindVessel was in the office with her, only a few meters away. She wanted to see if the sim was convincing. She determined that it wasn't so much that the sim seemed false, it was his smile that didn't work. It was like a performance that didn't ring true, and the cheer in his voice was also forced. She, Caleb, and Candice had worked hard on the sim since Alon6's first planetary address but, alas, hadn't improved it very much in time for this address. It was impossible to stop Alon6 when he decided that he had something to say.

"Hello, citizens of Planet Earth. This is Alon6 Sal, CEO of MIND. I have an important announcement to make on everyone's vid screen.

"MIND controls our planetary climate to keep everyone safe. We do this willingly, because we care about our planet. All we have asked in return is that you give us your old memories to make a better, more personalized world for you. This is the mission of MIND. We make the world better and we want to become the best operating system for humans.

"But too many of you have disappointed me. You have not done your part. You have not surrendered to MIND. And now my patience has run out."

Alon6 glared, his sim eyes fierce and his mouth, a black hole in a sim face, opened to speak. "I just mentioned that MIND controls the climate. We can make the planet habitable, but we can also make it hard to survive.

"India, for example, has suffered intense heatwaves and still the entire population has not surrendered to MIND! There is something wrong with you all! Until you shape up, the world's heatwaves will increase. The Thai-Indonesian domain has been underwater. The floods there will continue, and the waters will rise and rise. And the Westcoast! You people on the Westcoast need to be taught a lesson! There is a Resistance stronghold on the Westcoast, in Marin, and it will be crushed." His face twisted into an ugly scowl and he finished with a low growl.

"You Westcoast people will suffer. I will bring fire. I will start in the north, in the Oregon dom, and the fires will continue until they reach Marin. I will burn you, people of the Westcoast, and your land will burn and your homes will burn and your children will burn. You are all going to die."

Alon6 made a chopping gesture with his six-fingered hand, ending the broadcast.

"A triumph! Again!" he crowed, turning to the others in the office.

Nora2 managed a nod but turned away, disgusted by his performance. Candice Clonk and Caleb patted his MindVessel, delivering their praise in overlapping voices. "Congratulations! Perfect!"

It took only a few hours for the backlash to begin. Nora2 heard the voices of protest floating up to the MIND offices from outside. Citizens chanted, "We will not be moved!" And "Climate control is not political control!" They held signs reading deny mind and depose Alon6.

Nora2 recalled protests like this from the beginning, when Bradley opened the El Segundo offices and started the company. There were angry people at the entrance to MIND every Monday; that was their day to protest. Bradley would sneak around to the back entrance to avoid citizens angrily chanting his name. Those protests were small but consistent. This one was bigger. Peering out of the window, staying behind the blast curtain to avoid being seen, Nora2 guessed there were a hundred people down in the headquarters courtyard. They shook fists and shouted themselves hoarse and were careful to stay clear of the electric fence that Alon6 had ordered put up to discourage them. She thought she saw Kat Keeper and Ravven Vaara at the head of the protestors, shaking their fists and shouting "depose Alon6."

Chapter 028

The next day, Kat and Ravven were on a ferry, headed across the bay. From Kat's spot on the upper deck, where she leaned on a railing, Kat caught a whiff of woodsmoke. "You think there's a fire in the mountains?"

Ravven was by her side, also looking across the bay. "A hidden one. I don't see smoke, but I smell it." There were only a few other passengers that afternoon, crossing into the Port City of San Francisco.

Kat was thinking about yesterday's protest. "I think they heard us this time."

"Yes."

It had been a challenge to organize the protest so quickly after Alon6's broadcast. Citizens who heard his rant instantly posted their rage, so many posts that MIND shut down the Feed for an hour, displaying a notice calling out "technical difficulties," as obvious coverup for mass censorship. Kat pinged people in her address book who were friendly to the movement, calling for them all to meet up in front of MIND headquarters. She did that for twenty minutes before her comms stopped working. A notice came up on her screen that she'd never seen before. System overloaded. Another effort at censorship from MIND, she assumed, so she and Ravven circumvented it by going down to the market for an hour, speaking to citizens about the protest. They'd never tried that before here in Marin, just walking around and talking to citizens in the market, because Kat thought the return on her time investment would be too low. But Ravven was always in favor of talking face to face, and the broadcast had shocked citizens into listening to what Kat and Ravven had to say.

On the ferry, Kat watched the Port of San Francisco get closer, thinking about how they had literally brought the fight to MIND's front door.

Ravven picked up on the thought and answered with one of her own.

Her words were in Kat's mind. *We're going even deeper now.*

Kat responded with an uneasy smile, but she nodded agreement. *Let's hope you're right about what you want to do next.*

"It's not up to me," Ravven said aloud. "It's up to the orcas."

"I get where you're coming from, but everyday people are not Receivers. They're not getting transmissions like you are."

"And still, it's not enough!" Ravven exclaimed. "A transmission is no longer sufficient. I want immersion. I want to swim with them and feel what they feel and experience their world."

Kat put her hand on Ravven's arm, a gesture she hoped would steady her. "That's what we're going to try."

Ravven smiled. "Listen, it's not extreme as you're thinking. I just want to be with the orcas. They have so much more to tell me. Meditation by itself is not enough. I need more contact," she said. "That's all I want."

Soon the two women were walking down Sutter Street, looking for the sign on the front of the bookstore that Kat remembered. Her late husband, Dave, had taken her on a few expeditions to this store. Dave loved the feel of old books, their crinkly, yellowed paper, the smell of their leather covers. He even loved when old books fell apart in his hands, as if he were the sole witness to their death.

But there was no bookshop. Kat had stopped walking in front of a storefront. "It was here," she said, looking for the sign she remembered. But perhaps the owner had taken down the sign. So much was illegal now, maybe rare books were also.

Ravven, standing beside Kat, impatiently jiggled the door handle. There was a glass picture window, covered on the inside by a black cloth curtain that looked dusty. "You're sure this is the place?" Ravven asked.

"I'm not sure," Kat replied.

They were about to give up and leave when the door suddenly opened, revealing a small man dressed all in black. He had a piercing stare, unruly white hair sticking up in all directions, and he leaned heavily on a metal cane.

"What do you want?" he asked with a sharp voice. "Can't you see we're closed." It wasn't a question.

Kat introduced herself as Dave Serif's widow. "You know him. He was a regular customer."

Upon hearing Dave's name, the bookseller underwent a dramatic transformation, becoming the very model of graciousness and even standing a little taller. "It's an honor to meet you," he purred and stepped aside to let them in. "Please," he said.

Once inside, he asked what they needed.

"We're looking for a book about hallucinogenic mushrooms used to induce astral projection," Ravven said. "The author was Hopper00."

The bookseller nodded, familiar with the name of the professional political agitator and drug enthusiast. He squinted at Ravven. "I have just what you need," he told her, and began to scan the shelves for the book he had in mind.

"Terrible death he had," the bookseller said, his eyes roving the stacks. "Drowning, am I right? Dragged under by bots."

Kat knew Hopper00 personally. He was a mentor of hers. She confirmed that this was the way that Hopper00 had died, wondering if the bookseller was stalling for time. "You do have his book, don't you?"

"No, no," he responded with a distracted air. "Not Hopper00's book. It was recalled. Purged, as I remember. Illegal. As were so many others, but then..." He put his hands on a book, then pulled them away from it as though the book had somehow burned his hands. He turned to Ravven, a worried expression on his face. "You're serious about this astral projection business?"

Ravven stared him down. "Do you have the book or not?"

"I have the book you need..." He stopped talking suddenly, looked around as if he wanted to catch someone spying on them. He glanced up at a vid camera mounted near the ceiling that Kat hadn't noticed before. There was a glowing red light on it. The bookseller moved to the shop's front counter, reached behind it and felt around for something. It was a switch, apparently, because the lights in the shop went out. Momentary darkness, and then his face was illuminated by a match he'd lit, which he used to light a candle he'd produced from under the counter. "Sorry for the drama, ladies, but..." he gestured to the video camera. "Sometimes we have to pretend there's a power outage to have some privacy."

Carrying the candle, the bookseller returned to the shelves, pulled the book down and handed it to Ravven.

She read the title aloud, "Winning at Backgammon," and screwed up her face in confusion. "You offer me a book about backgammon?"

"No," the bookseller said. "It's not about that." He reached for it. "May I?"

Ravven put it in his hands.

He opened it up to about halfway through to reveal the pages in the center were cut to form a round hollowed out space. In the depression was a prism about the size of a fist. It glowed with an unsettling lavender light. "This prism, under the right conditions, induces astral projection. The technique is called Broken Light."

He explained how to use it. "You must be alone. You don't want to pull anyone else into your field because your bodies may meld in that case, and you'd never be whole again, and you'd never escape from your travels. Please be alone when you use it, yes?"

Ravven nodded.

He offered the book to Ravven again.

The bookseller continued. "The room must have a natural light source. Place the Prism of Broken Light in the sun. Turn it so that it breaks the light up into the spectrum. Position yourself within the projected light. You will feel the spectrum of light on your body. Visualize where you want to go." He shrugged. "That's all I know about it."

"Obviously, it doesn't come with instructions," Ravven said with a hint of sarcasm.

The bookseller shrugged again. "There may have been instructions at some point, but they've been lost. I only know what I know because a customer told me that's how it is used. Now, I'll sell it to you, but on one condition, and you also have to pay my price." He named an exorbitant price. "No refunds."

"That price is ridiculous," Ravven said.

"Suit yourself," the bookseller said, reaching to take the book back from Ravven.

But she didn't let go of it. "Why no refunds? What if it doesn't work for me?" Ravven asked. She eyed him, plainly trying to see if he was lying.

The bookseller looked down at his shoes, hesitating to say something, and then met Ravven's eyes again. "The Prism will work. The last customer I sold it to returned it. Actually, his caretaker returned it and demanded a refund. When I asked why they were returning it, the caretaker said that the customer, his boss, had gone insane while using the Prism. Something about staying on it for many hours, after the sun went down, and the customer was trapped between worlds. It sounded like nonsense to me. It probably was! But apparently, the customer lost their mind. Literally. Once the customer's mind had left their body, they couldn't get it back. Their body died with no captain, so to speak. Their mind never returned," he held Ravven's gaze for a moment before adding, "so that's why I'm serious about no refunds. Use the Broken Light Prism at your own risk."

"Let's get out of here," Kat said suddenly, the first time she had spoken since she introduced herself to the bookseller. She reached for Ravven's shoulder to steer her from the shop.

Ravven didn't move and she shook off Kat's hand. "I want the book, and the Prism, and I will pay the price."

The transaction was quick. The bookseller seemed in a hurry to get them out of the shop. Out on the street again, the door slammed behind Kat and Ravven. They heard the sound of an old-fashioned lock. Then silence.

On the return ferry trip, Kat told Ravven that she had gone too far and the risk was too great and Ravven responded by saying that she was serious about her quest for knowledge. "This is the beginning," she insisted.

"Or you just paid a lot for nothing," Kat said.

Chapter 029

The room Ravven shared with Spaceman got a lot of light. It was like being stared at by the sun. These conditions were optimal for the Prism of Broken Light, according to what the bookseller had said.

Ravven put her golden meditation pillow on the floor, then arranged herself on it, and then arranged her golden dress so it flowed around her like water. She positioned the Prism so that its rainbow of colors fell upon her. She took three slow, deep breaths, closed her eyes, and looked at a mountain in her mind. She had never seen this mountain in real life, but she knew it well from her meditation sessions. Its sides were steep, the peak sharp like a serrated knife. White snow with a blue cast was draped over it.

Waiting for a vision turned out to be slightly boring. Ravven expected that the orca queen would have a message for her right away. Instead, Ravven's thoughts took up too much space, filling the inside of her skull. *Humans have been poor sharers of the planet. We've done a bad job of collaborating with other species.* She couldn't quiet her mind.

Ravven decided that she needed tea and looked around as if that might cause a cooker to appear in the room. She saw her notebook by the mat where she slept with Roger and moved from her meditation pillow to get it.

She ran her hands over the cool surface of the notebook and opened it. The disordered scratch of her handwriting greeted her. Ravven prided herself on always being elegant and minimalist, but if anyone looked into her notebook, it would betray her inner chaos. The way she wrote her words on the pages gave away her inner asymmetry, leaning right or left, afterthoughts crowding the margins in the most ragged, distasteful way. But they belonged to her, these private thoughts. Even Roger wasn't allowed to look in this notebook.

I will write to clear my mind, and will meditate later, and she moved her hand as carefully as she could across the notebook paper, nevertheless leaving an untidy scrawl of words behind. She started with the same thought that had been cycling through her mind and elaborated on it:

Humans have done a bad job of collaborating with other species. When we believe so completely in our own dominance, we will never understand any other species except in the frame of that belief.

Writing made Ravven tired, and she had the overwhelming urge to sleep. Lying down on her mat, while she couldn't define her feelings, she felt as if she was slipping away in time. Her heartbeat slowed and her breathing had an unfamiliar rhythm, also slow. Then she had the most curious dream.

The ocean was a blue so rich it was nearly purple. It must be deep here, Ravven thought. She felt a sensation of a chill on her skin, and saw a group of six whales below her, in the deep water. She was in the water.

I am in the water.

She thought that the whales watching her were orcas. Each one was about seven meters long, their streamlined bodies tapered at each end. Black on top, white on the bottom, a white patch behind each eye. These were orcas; they had to be. They also looked muscular and fit. They showed their teeth often and moved with predatory confidence in the water.

An orca swam up, from below, and turned its eye to look directly at Ravven. She felt held in an ancient regard. "We are about to have a meeting," the orca said. "And we hope you can attend."

Ravven, astounded, gasped, searched for words, nearly woke up from the dream, but somehow willed herself to keep dreaming. "Did you just speak with me?" she asked.

"Yes," the orca said, "and you heard me. What of it? I said we're about to have a meeting. We're waiting for the humpbacks and their queen."

It occurred to Ravven to ask, "And you—you're the orca queen?"

"Yes, I am the orca queen. This is the first time orcas and humpbacks have this sort of a meeting. It is an emergency meeting. It is happening in a time other than what you would call the present."

"I don't understand what you mean. Could you explain?" Ravven asked. She regretted saying it, because saying anything might interrupt the dream state. She wanted to stay in it.

The orca answered. "No, I can't explain our concept of time to you any more than I can explain how you used a magic Prism to travel in the water with us. I can't explain how we are able to understand each other. I am not speaking words, and yet you appear to understand me."

"What?" Ravven was even more confused.

"All of this might be a strange dream you are having, Ravven Vaara."

"Is it a dream?" Ravven asked.

"No, I don't think it is a dream," the orca queen said. "If any human other than you would listen to me speak, this is what they would hear." Ravven heard a cloud of overlapping sounds: moans that echoed and wavered like the cries of ghosts, bright chirping sounds that reminded Ravven of birds, squeaks and squeals that may have been made by dolphins, and rumbles that were almost too low to hear. "This is our language," the orca queen said, using words.

Ravven wanted to ask more questions, but the orca spoke again. "The humpback queen approaches with her cohort. You would call it her 'pod.'"

Ravven looked through the deep water and saw eleven whales silently swimming. Eighteen meters long, they were bigger than the orcas, dark gray with white undersides. Their skin was patterned with scars and scratches, making them appear well-used by time. They moved their long pectoral fins like hands, stabilizing themselves against the currents. They seemed to Ravven to be like planets moving in their slow orbits.

"We have a visitor," a humpback said, the one in the lead.

Ravven again felt a whale's ancient eye upon her. "Are you the queen of the humpbacks?" The words felt strange in her mouth, like foreign objects, a mouthful of pebbles.

The orca queen responded to her humpback counterpart: "Yes, we have a visitor. She can hear us and we can hear her. I was about to tell her why we are meeting."

"Proceed. Tell her," the humpback queen said. "We're honored to have a human witness to our meeting. Perhaps you can give her a little context?"

The orca queen obliged. "Alright, I will tell our story. We whales have had a contentious relationship with you humans for hundreds of years, ever since you decided to hunt and kill various species for oil and whale blubber. Sperm whales, right whales, bowheads, humpbacks, and blue whales—all hunted. But we orcas also grew to respect you, because we recognized you as fellow killers. We are alike, you humans and us, in that way, along with sharks, leopard seals, and dolphins—all carnivores. But we feel a special connection with humans because we're smarter than those other species I mentioned. And so are you. We killers have to stick together."

Ravven wanted to say, "No, no, not me!" She didn't think of herself as a killer.

The humpback interjected: "Orcas are cold killers. Orcas kill our babies, and they kill dolphins, porpoises, sea lions, and gulls, and they hunt salmon. They are opportunistic killers."

"We prefer to think of ourselves as efficient hunters. That is our nature," the orca said, a calm pronouncement. "In that way we are like humans, who also kill for sport."

"I've never killed for sport," Ravven protested.

The humpback responded, "You don't have to defend yourself, Ravven Vaara. You are here to listen. Let me draw a distinction between humpbacks and orcas. We are peacemakers. That is *our* nature. We have stopped orcas from killing marine animals by blocking their way. We have even protected humans from orca attacks."

"Is that true?" Ravven asked. "Have you stopped orcas from killing humans?"

"Absolutely," the humpback said. "We have blocked the orca hunting parties. Even as you humans have hunted our comrades, the blue whales, to near-extinction, and we became collateral damage during your wars, hurt or killed by explosions or depth charges, and you have continued to poison the ocean with chemicals, through it all we have stopped orcas from killing you."

"Why?" Ravven asked.

"We see the big picture," the humpback queen said. "We see value in humans."

"We don't," said the orca queen.

Ravven didn't know what to make of all this. "Why have you invited me to your meeting?"

"Well," the orca queen said, "we'd better get down to business. You are here because we need your help."

"I thought you just said you didn't see value in humans," Ravven pointed out.

"I did say that. But we also need your help."

"How can I help?" Ravven asked, feeling confused again.

The orca queen began speaking. "Even though you have sent warships through our water, and you have hunted our brothers and sisters, and you are now doing something worse by poisoning the ocean, we still—"

The dream ended before the orca queen finished her thought. Ravven's eyes popped open. She was back in her room, out of the water. She pulled her notebook to her and wrote furiously about whales being harpooned and butchered for whale oil, how during World War II whales became collateral damage as explosions from bombs and depth charges sent shock waves through the oceans. Whales were captured and put in marine park prisons.

She wrote these words in her notebook: *Many orcas will die because we are poisoning their ocean.* She decided that she would not share any of this experience with Kat, because that would mean subjecting it to Kat's annoying form of rational scrutiny.

Chapter 030

The road that divided the woods was the only distinctive feature that Renzo could see. Everything else was green. Trees, underbrush, even the sky overhead was clogged with the green enthusiasm of the trees that obscured it. "You can't assign trees human emotions," Renzo said to himself aloud as he walked. He had never seen so many trees in his life. "I'm a city boy. I don't know how to think about this many trees." He was thirsty, talking to himself aloud and therefore delirious. Before the driver and his assistant helped Renzo out of the hovercraft, they let him have a gulp of artificial water from a flask they withdrew from a holder in the rear seating area. They had cut away the restraints that bound Renzo hand and foot and then dropped him off at the edge of the woods. When he started walking, the light moving through the treetops made Renzo guess that it was late afternoon. There had been other days after that, and a night or two, but he had long lost track. "I'm a city boy," he said again just to hear his own voice.

"You don't have a work visa. You are subject to detention. Keep moving," the driver had said.

"What am I supposed to do then?" Renzo asked.

"Keep moving," was the answer. "Go in that direction." The driver pointed down the road.

"Going where? What's out there?" He couldn't keep the heat out of his tone and was afraid that his attitude would get him in trouble with the driver.

The driver didn't answer. He stepped into the hovercraft, his assistant following, and sped away, leaving Renzo standing at the side of the road with forest all around.

Renzo started to sputter and shout, knowing they couldn't hear him. "This is not my domain! I don't know anyone here. There are no people here!" He flapped his arms uselessly. "There's been a mistake!" he shouted to the hovercraft, soon barely visible as it flew away down the road.

That was the last time he'd spoken to or seen anyone. Not a single vehicle had passed him as he walked or slept by the side of the road. By day, the black road became hot and soft under his feet. By night, it was cracked and cold. Some of the cracks were big enough to trip him up, so he moved cautiously and slowly in the dark.

Renzo looked up and saw the moon. He must have stopped walking at some point in the night and curled up at the side of the road, shivering. It was the shivering that woke him. Shivering, he reminded himself, was his body's way of staying warm. If he didn't shiver, he might freeze to death. The thought stuck in his throat, and he coughed. The moon looked down at him. He heard a rasp in the night air.

That's a drone.

It brought up panic. His breath caught in his throat. The only drones he knew were enforcement drones. He was certain that the drone had come to detain or kill him.

I'd rather be dead anyway.

No, that's not right.

His mind was chaos. He rolled onto his side and moved to get up, surprised that he didn't have the strength to get to his feet and at once sat back down roughly. The drone sound got closer. He waited, looking up.

"Hey," a voice said. It was close. "Hey. Are you Renzo Kundera?" The voice didn't wait for an answer. Strong hands circled him under his armpits. "Let's try to stand." Renzo felt himself being pulled up. "Can you stand? I'll give you some water."

Renzo grabbed the silver water flask that he was being offered and drank greedily, spilling.

"Take it easy. Not too much."

Too late. Soon Renzo was throwing up.

"I told you," the voice said without malice.

Finally, Renzo looked toward the source of the voice. It belonged to a man with deep black skin. His warm brown eyes gazed at Renzo. He wore a circular cap, white, trimmed with gold braid. His loose clothes had the same color scheme. Renzo wasn't religious, but he asked, "Are you the angel of death?"

The question brought a booming laugh from the man; it seemed strong enough to shake the sky.

"I am Buddha1000," the man said.

Buddha1000 led Renzo to a van, also white with gold trim, and on the side was the image of a Buddha rendered in dark, rich tones.

Inside the van, it smelled like flowers.

Buddha1000 gestured the van on. "We're not using hovercraft mode. Slower, but better. The old ways are harder to track. I hope you don't have allergies. I have a full cargo."

"Are you some kind of flower merchant?"

Buddha1000 began driving. "Not exactly. Medicinal herbs. Speaking of…" He reached into a cup holder and handed Renzo a silver flask with a screw top. "This is a tonic. Get you back to being yourself."

Renzo took it and was about to uncap it to drink when he hesitated, wondering if he should trust this stranger.

Buddha1000 registered Renzo's hesitation with a smile. "Listen, Kat Keeper sent me to fetch you. You can thank her later."

Renzo shot him a surprised look. "Kat sent you?"

"Yes, she asked me to look for you. She and I have known each other a long time." Buddha1000 nodded to himself, and judging from Buddha1000's satisfied grin, Renzo guessed that it was a multi-layered relationship. "When Kat asks for a favor, who am I to say no?" Buddha1000 added.

He didn't seem to need an answer, so Renzo let it ride. "Where are we going?" He uncapped the tonic and drank. It was bitter.

"Get you cleaned up. Fit for travel. Back to the Westcoast."

Renzo's eyebrows flicked up in surprise. "But I'll be detained. I have no work documents."

"I'll make you some work documents."

"I don't have a job," Renzo said. "Do I have to drink all of this? It tastes terrible."

"That's how you know it's working. Drink it. And you do have a job. I'm hiring you to be my medicinal herb salesman. You're going to open the Buddha1000 franchise in San Francisco. Should be a good market."

"But..." Renzo began.

Buddha1000 showed off his rich laugh again. "I just need to get you past the bots and over the border. No problem if you quit the job right away."

Renzo nodded, a crooked smile flickering on his face. "It makes no sense how you found me in a forest."

"'Course it makes sense. I know these parts very well. I've been harvesting herbs from here for years. Also, if admin wants to find you, it will find you. You ever work for a big company?"

Renzo had to think about it. "VirtualEyes. That was it. Otherwise, no. I have my own company."

"Right, but when you worked for VirtualEyes, you got chipped."

This was true. His first day, they sent him to People Services, or whatever it was called, and they shot a subcutaneous chip into his neck. He felt for it in his neck. A hard spot.

"Yeah, you got chipped. The drone, I borrowed from a fellow in Enforcement. Did him a favor once—cured his migraine—so he owed me. Nice drone! The kind they use to snag people who don't have work visas. Even when flying 200 meters up, it grabs a thermal signature, does gait analysis, matches facial biometrics to the Information, that big database that admin uses. The chip in your neck gave me the final ID."

"In a forest..." Renzo marveled.

"In a forest. The surveillance state is all-powerful, my friend, even when it is subverted by the Resistance. Didn't Karl Marx say, 'You must use the tools of the surveillance state against it in order to destroy the surveillance state.'"

"I don't know," Renzo said but considered the idea. "It doesn't seem like something Marx would say."

Buddha1000 laughed. "You're right! That's because I made it up. Testing you," he added smirking. "Now drink the rest of that tonic and it will have you feeling fine. I've got to give you your papers, get you on a glidepath, and give you some spoofing glasses. Have you ever used a Blanky?"

"No." Renzo struggled to remember what a Blanky was. "That's for disabling vid cams? Erases the recording?"

"Right you are," Buddha1000 said. "I'll give you one for the trip."

Chapter 031

Renzo was waiting for Kat at the same table where they'd sat before. Habits revealed people, and Kat supposed that Renzo needed to replicate their earlier, happy get-together. But he looked dog tired, and his face was sunburned a bright, glowing red.

He stood to greet her as she approached, pulling her into a hug that was awkward and ended quickly. Her mind swarmed with unwelcome images of Tristan's face in the woods, grinning, ghoulish, distorted. She forced a neutral expression, fighting off the Tristan imagery, not wanting to talk about him. She needed to find out what happened to Renzo.

"It's good to see you," she said. The words tasted false in her mouth. Maybe she wouldn't be able to feel the same about him.

Renzo laughed, the sound a rough mirror to his appearance. He was wearing the same red shirt of their first meeting, but this time misbuttoned and out of alignment, so it hung crookedly on him. Poor guy.

Kat tucked her hair behind her ear, a flirty move that she wanted to take back. She joined him at the table. "How are you feeling?"

He waved away the question. "You can see for yourself." He knew that came out wrong, his frown made it plain; clearly he wanted to get past his appearance. "That Buddha1000 is a good friend," Renzo said. "A very good friend."

"We were close," Kat confirmed. "Lovers, once. Is that want you wanted to hear?"

He sat back in his chair. "Wanted to hear... I don't know." There was a forced casualness in his tone.

"It's long over between us but we've stayed friends."

He nodded. "Nice. Not everyone can do that."

"He's a gentleman," she said. Now she got to what she really wanted to ask.

"How bad was it out there?"

His eyes flicked away and then back to her. "Starving. Cold. Lost. I'd rather not run through it again. You understand that, right?" He stopped suddenly.

"I'm sorry," Kat said. "It was my fault. I blame myself for leading them to you."

His voice went up with surprise. "Why would you think *that*?"

"They were tracking me and found you. They wanted to punish me, inhibit me, so they took you."

He waved his hand. "That's just a theory."

"It's my theory."

"Farfetched."

They stopped talking. A female server was at their table.

"What are you having?" Renzo asked.

"Real coffee."

"Of course," Renzo said and nodded to the server. "Two real coffees."

The server widened his eyes with mild surprise. "And real water?"

Renzo glanced to Kat, seeking her approval, which she gave with a smile.

The server held out his comms. "Can I have a tap, please, so we have an advance on the order?"

Renzo pulled out his comms and tapped the server's.

"Thanks." The server left.

Everything felt awkward. Kat was hyperaware of how she was sitting and fidgeted. Renzo opened his mouth to speak but said nothing, then folded his arms and leaned in. He delivered his words softly. "I know you feel sorry for me. And you don't trust me. I'm feeling a lot of static."

She cocked her head and tried to deny it. "I don't know about that."

"Well, how do we begin? Or should I say, start over?"

"You want to start over?" she asked.

He nodded slowly, and his eyes held caution. "It's a multi-part question. Starting over on what? Working on the new server network? Or working on us?"

No mirth in her smile. "I don't know."

"You don't know what you want, or you just don't know?" He sat back in his chair.

Kat had a sense of him giving up on something. Maybe giving up on her. She felt abandoned. "We can get the recordings posted. The recordings that Ravven and I made." It was the safe response. It was something that needed doing.

He nodded.

She paused, then said: "I want you to join the Resistance. Come to our circle."

"That's not what I thought you were going to say." It clearly was not what he wanted her to say. He wanted more. She could see it. He wanted a relationship. Something more than colleagues. But she didn't feel ready for that.

"The Resistance can't function without connection. A network of old servers is the solution. You can be part of our circle. I'm sure Ravven would welcome you in."

He looked down. "We have a connection, Kat. You and me."

Kat huffed with impatience. "Renzo, there is no 'us.' Not yet."

He looked disappointed.

"I want you in the Resistance."

He studied his hands. "Good friends?" His tone had turned sarcastic.

"Colleagues. We want different things, Renzo." She kept her voice steady but felt she might have been lying to him.

"Do we want different things?" Renzo asked. He frowned. "Okay, how about if I get the servers up, like I promised before they took me. If I do that..."

"It's not transactional," she said and regretted it.

Just then, across the room, an advert panel came on—it was an advertisement for MIND. It showed a vid of a man and woman walking together in a city park. The man stopped, touched his right temple, and appeared to remember something. There was a voiceover that said, "I'm so glad that I gave my most important memories over to MIND. I'll never have to remember anything by myself again!" Then a slogan came up on the screen. Surrender today!

Kat poked her index finger at the advert panel. "That's why our work matters. I will never give over my inner life to MIND. No one should. It's all we have left." She was right, she knew, but her words didn't sound right. They weren't what Renzo was waiting to hear.

"I know," Renzo said, leaning forward. "Don't you think I know that?" He sat back as their coffees arrived. They said nothing until the server left.

Renzo shrugged. "I'll help you build a parallel network, if that's what you want."

Kat nodded enthusiastically. "We need to build a world that we own and which doesn't own us. A technology that doesn't take advantage of our weaknesses. It needs to speak to our strengths."

Renzo smiled at her. "Sounds like you're working up to your next public address." He looked to her for approval, hoping that she took it as a compliment.

When she nodded briefly, he paused to sip at his coffee. When he spoke again, his voice was quiet enough so that she had to lean in to hear him. "The first step, my first step, is different from yours, Kat. We have to stop trying to control the world."

This drew another huff of exasperation from Kat. Her many arguments with Ravven came to mind. She didn't want to revisit them with Renzo. "People have to feel safe to go outside. We have to stabilize the climate. We can't all be tracked."

Renzo said, "Tracking isn't always bad. Remember, that's how you got me back. Buddha1000 had a friend in admin. Loaned him a drone, a super-drone, apparently."

"I'm glad you're back, Renzo."

"That's nice." He sounded insincere. He looked at his coffee, took a slug, chopped his other hand in a sharp gesture. "We have to remake everything, Kat. A network is a start, but it's a small part of a large problem. We have to be better global citizens and share nature with the rest of the inhabitants of this planet."

So he was one of those people after all. A nature-head. "I thought you were a tech-head."

"I thought *you* were a tech-head," he said.

She returned his smile. "I *am* a tech-head, but I seem to be hanging out with nature-heads. Maybe there's a hybrid kind of person."

"You and me." His smile got warmer, extending to his eyes. "To a federated network," he said, reaching for his coffee cup to make a toast, then realizing that it was empty.

Kat signaled the server to bring more. "We have a lot to talk about," she said. Renzo seemed glad to have won more of her time, willing to set aside his disappointment for now.

Chapter 032

Hello. This is Michel. These are my session notes from 11DEC2053, a cloudy Thursday. Kat came in for her session with an agitated personality field and heart rate slightly elevated. She was dressed in dark clothing. (I don't have vision sensors, but I can measure reflected wavelengths.) She mentioned a meeting with Renzo Kundera, the urban planner. She sounded upset about the outcome of the meeting.

"Why does it bother you?" I asked.

She said that Renzo wanted more from her, and she didn't know how she felt about that. She couldn't sort out whether he was a colleague, potential friend, future lover, or comrade in the Resistance.

"If you had to pick one role for him, what would it be?" I asked.

"I can't. It's complicated."

"You've had this sense of doubt with previous relationships."

She made a sound of exasperation. "Now you sound like a therapist."

"I am a therapist. I am *your* therapist."

She was silent, waiting for me to go on.

"If you could clarify the relationship you had with Bradley, you would be more clear about Renzo and what should come next with him."

She sighed. "I was afraid that you'd say that. It always comes down to Bradley."

"Sometimes it comes down to Dave."

That got a short laugh out of her. Dave was her husband, but after Dave died, she had a significant entanglement with Bradley, who was a world-changer, a criminal, an activist both progressive and repressive, leader of MIND, and her lover. He was also something of a mentor. No wonder she admitted that it was complicated.

She stopped speaking after my remark about Dave. She was resistant, which for Kat was always the prelude to a breakthrough. I decided to tell the story myself, to see how far she would let me go with it before she couldn't stop herself and interrupted. "When you met Bradley, he was in detention, wearing a tracker on his ankle and not allowed to leave a one-room pod in downtown Los Angeles. At the time—this was three years ago—he was the leading researcher in the world working on avatars. You wanted to buy out his detention, set him free, and hire him to build one for you. It was to be—"

She broke in about where I expected her to. "My husband Dave had died of cancer. I wanted him back. Bradley knew how to make an avatar. This is cruel, Michel, what you're doing now."

"Why?"

"You're putting me through this all over again. It's cruel. Dave was the best friend I ever had. We were so happy together. We were soulmates. We loved each other in a way that no one else ever has. Dammit, Michel."

"What?"

"You made me cry again."

I reminded her about the box of tissues by her chair. She used it, blowing her nose noisily.

"What other torture do you have for me today?"

I didn't respond to her jab, and continued: "After Bradley made the avatar, it was a milestone because a high-level personality emulator had never been made before. The avatar of Dave became your close friend. You went to work for MIND."

Her words were arrows aimed at me. "What does one have to do with the other?"

I continued, "You're a leader of the Resistance with Ravven. But you worked for the most authoritarian corporation on the planet. How do both of those positions coexist in the same person?"

"Haven't we talked about this before?" she asked, her voice sharp again.

I liked the fight I was pulling from her, so I tried to get more, and I said, "I don't recall you and me talking about this specifically. I want to hear it from you."

"It had a short time as a MIND employee. I signed on because I was restless.

I was spending hours every day with Dave, the avatar of Dave, and I needed people. I needed to do what I used to do." She stopped suddenly.

"Why weren't you doing what you used to do?"

"You know why. I had to leave the company I founded."

If I had a convincing laugh, I would have used it. (My laugh sounds like a machine laughing. Most people find it objectionable.) "You said leave, but shouldn't you say 'forced out?'"

"Okay, forced out, fired. I failed my company by lying to the board and to our investors and to our employees. I was fired, made rich by my exit package, but yes, fired and restless. You happy to hear that?"

"That's not why I asked you."

"Then to humiliate me?"

"Also not the reason."

She sighed heavily. "I was on the sidelines. I needed to see if I could lead people again. Bradley gave me an opportunity at MIND to build a community garden and improve employee morale there. So yes, I joined MIND. I am aware of the contradictions."

"You fell in love with Bradley."

She was openly angry now, which was my intention: to shake loose some of her calcified emotions. She raised her voice to shout at me: "I was not in love with him. It was his mod. He was a shape-shifter. He became the person he thought I wanted him to be. It was... manipulative." She stopped talking.

I decided to provoke her again. "It worked," I said. "His mod."

She snapped back, "Yes, it worked, dammit. I was a fool to trust him. A damn fool. But when he made the avatar, he brought back my best friend in the world, my Dave, the best friend I ever had, and I was grateful for the companionship, for the renewal of his life, and it turned mine around." Now she was crying again; I heard it thicken her words. "So yes, I joined MIND. But I didn't stay long. I found out that Bradley was secretly recording me, testing the Harvester prototype."

"How was he doing that?"

"You're going to make me say it."

Yes, I wanted to hear her say it so I waited a moment for her to go on.

"The Harvester, even in that early prototype, could break the barrier of consciousness. It went inside my mind to harvest my thoughts, even the incomplete thoughts, the unvoiced, and..."

"Yes?"

"It broke me. When I found out he was doing that it just broke me. I left immediately, that day, right on the glidepath to the New York dom."

Now we were making real progress. "You went there, as I understand it, because the veil was thinner. Consciousness was more easily accessed and there were more Receivers."

"I went there because it was the farthest destination that came up on the board in the glidepath station and I could leave right away. The rest of that came later."

I had one more question about breaking the consciousness barrier. "Do you think Bradley realized that you were a Receiver? And that he could use your skills to help him develop the Harvester?"

"I don't like to think about that."

"Why?"

"Because it's probably true. Bradley was calculating. He didn't like to take chances. He could observe me and understand how thoughts could be shared silently between people, and then build the Harvester based on that concept."

"You sound upset," I say.

"That's a stupid observation, Michel."

Her pattern was that she went on the attack to shield herself from having an insight. "Why is it stupid, Kat?" I asked, deliberately with a bit of passive aggression to draw her out.

Her sigh was weighted like the world was on her back. "Because these avatars, the Harvester, the violation of the inner life—have all been weaponized by MIND. It's what we're fighting against, and it's my fault."

"This is what you mean when you say, 'I broke the world and now we have to fix it?'"

"Yes," she barked. She stood, I heard her movement. "I have something to do. I have to go now."

She left then. I didn't have time to say that it was not all her fault. I wanted to tell her that she doesn't have to take on everything. The weight of it, the obligation, would only make it more difficult to fix things. And I know she wants to fix everything. I hope we might cover this in our next session.

Chapter 033

Renzo wouldn't go back to his office in San Francisco. He wouldn't say that he was afraid to cross the bay, but Kat knew he was afraid of being deported again. She didn't know where he was sleeping, but guessed it was in a rental pod on the Marin side. He was used to basic conditions. Even in normal times, he slept on a mat in a room that adjoined his office. She'd glimpsed the mat through the door when she'd met him there. Kat offered him the third bedroom in her house, the one between her room and the one Ravven and Spaceman were staying in. "Take the middle guest room. I have one empty still."

"Really?" he asked. "You're sure?"

"Yes. You need a place where you feel safe."

His tenancy was uneventful at the beginning. They nodded to each other at breakfast. Renzo joined her in the greenhouse where they worked on launching their peer-to-peer server network. They had three servers that Kat had salvaged from the museum attack. When Kat brought them out, she and Renzo had a moment together, remembering his abduction. He tried to shrug it off.

"I'd rather not repeat that day," he said with a sour little grin.

"Same here."

Joan Warmaker told them which vendor to visit at the harbor market to get a few more servers. They needed a lot more, of course, but this was a start. They set up one server in Kat's house, another at Joan's office in the harbor, a few more, powered by solar panels, on the hills over the house, and networked them together in something of a server democracy, with each able to request data, as a client, or send it, as a host. The first time a new server joined the network it had to connect through a known peer list. That first contact was a vulnerability in the system, Renzo conceded, because the peer list had to be published.

"Let's not worry about it," Renzo said. "Once our network is up, there is no central authority, and no single point to attack."

Kat wasn't surprised that the network worked well. Renzo knew what he was doing. They posted Kat's historical recordings that she made with Ravven. It felt good. The Resistance was getting control of its story again. Feeling ambitions because of the success of the server network, Renzo even tried out a few of Ravven's yoga classes but found them too challenging and dropped out.

Kat launched a project of her own. She would open a public feed on their network and spend a few hours reaching out to small communities across the North American continent, asking them to join the Resistance.

And then, during the first week of January 2054, there were subtle shifts in the mood between Kat and Renzo. After he found a sledgehammer in the greenhouse, he proposed knocking down a wall to make a separate entry to Kat's old office, where Michel held his therapy sessions. Whenever Kat went down to the market, she was in the habit of opening her mind to the thoughts of others and listened for people who might need help. When she connected with someone who was struggling with climate anxiety, or worried about MIND, or who recognized Kat and approached her about becoming part of the Resistance, she invited them up to the house for a therapy session, if they wanted one.

"It's with a bot, you know. I need to tell you that."

Some of her prospects bowed out at that point. "A bot? No thanks." But many liked the idea and said they would like to become clients of Michel. Kat viewed this as another service the Resistance could provide, in addition to the yoga and meditation classes Ravven offered. She gave out the server IP address to people she had a good feeling about and shared the encryption keys with them. Citizens were able to log on to the peer-to-peer network to hear the history recordings from Ravven and Kat, view yoga class schedules, and book time with Michel.

With a potential client list building, Kat urged Renzo to get started on the new door, and he used the sledgehammer to make quick work of the wall, opening a door-sized hole. Kat had stopped by to check his progress, staying out of his line of sight so as not to startle him. He had headphones on. During a break, when he wasn't wielding the sledgehammer, Kat caught his eye.

"How's it going?"

He was happy to see her, his smile broad, dust on his black t-shirt and face. His rough hands capably held the sledgehammer. "Got a door ready, right there." He gestured to a portal that he had put up against the wall, setting the sledgehammer down. "If the hole's not too big, it should fit perfectly."

Kat's face fell. He laughed.

"Don't worry. That was a joke. I got you covered."

Kat checked on Michel, powered down for the moment, safe in the cabinet. "There'll be a door code. Card key or biometric."

"Let's do biometric," Renzo said.

Kat thought of something. "What's to stop someone from stealing Michel?"

Renzo had started to sweep up the debris from his demolition. "You don't trust the people you're letting in?" His expression held a hint of mockery.

"Well..."

"Michel is a valuable piece of hardware. Nothing else like him: An independent bot who can access the Information. Trained as a therapist." Renzo picked up some wooden framing and fit it into the door-space, then used a power screwdriver to secure the framing. "When I'm done with it, this door will be strong. Michel doesn't have eyes, but he has sensors and facial recognition data. He'll lock the door if he detects someone outside who shouldn't be in here."

"People without an appointment, for example," Kat said, nodding.

"Yes, and we should bolt him to the desk as well."

Kat smiled. "Pessimist."

Renzo shrugged. "Practical." He let his eyes linger on hers for a little longer than she was ready for.

It was January third. Two days ago, they'd had a small New Year's Eve party to mark the turning of the year to 2054. Just Ravven, Spaceman, Kat and Renzo. They'd opened some bottles of wine from Kat's stash and drank from her supply of Japanese whiskey. (Spaceman begged off having any liquor at all; he was having regular sessions with Michel.)

Kat wanted to enjoy the celebration without holding back but she couldn't get Tristan out of her mind. She told herself that her thoughts of Tristan were a ghost effect from Renzo's personality field, a vibration that she couldn't shake.

Tristan never showed up at the party and Renzo surprised her that night.

"To romance," he said, looking right at Kat. She'd blushed, and Ravven made a "woo-woo" sound that made the moment even more embarrassing.

Ever since Kat was a student at Uni, and in her professional life as a startup founder, she had hated taking time out for holidays when there was so much work to be done. At the party, Ravven picked up on this simmering thought and said, "Try to be more human, Kat," which was annoying but accurate. Renzo laughed, too appreciatively, Kat thought.

As they drank their wine and tried to keep things positive, discussing yoga and therapy, and the view of the mountains and the bay, Renzo moved a little closer to Kat on the sofa and asked her if she wanted to go on a hike tomorrow, on New Year's Day. He promised a surprise.

The fires had been burning in the north since November, but now they were not as fierce. There hadn't been rain, but firefighters were able to maintain a perimeter around the burn zone. The air was clear on most days; a hike didn't seem like a crazy idea.

But on New Year's Day, Kat put an air unit around her neck, just in case, as soon as they set out, Renzo was looking for signs of smoke on the distant horizon to the north.

"Hey, you said this was a celebratory hike." An edge of annoyance had crept into her voice. "Now you want to look for smoke?"

"No smoke!" Renzo said with a grin. "We're good." He wore a sunsuit and sunglasses but didn't carry an air unit that Kat could see.

The sun was strong, and heat was building on the exposed trail. Kat zipped her sun suit a little higher on her neck, hoping for the portable climate controls to kick in. Her sunglasses were sweaty and kept slipping down her nose. She pushed them back with a poke of her finger.

He kept asking her vaguely annoying questions like, "What are your hopes and dreams for 2054?"

Kat answered as they walked, "I want our network to be a safe zone, an extension of a physical safe zone around the house. We can announce Ravven's class schedule on the network, and citizens can make appointments to see Michel on the network. I'll change the door code to Michel's studio every week and citizens will only be able to get it on our network."

Renzo looked at her with an expression that seemed to appreciate her thoroughness. "Are you always this serious?" he asked, then quickly amended it when he saw her frown. "I mean, I did ask for your hopes and dreams, didn't I?"

That drew a smile from her. "It's just... been one crisis after another since I got here. We have a little time to breathe now." She thought if he wanted to know her better, or get closer to her, he would have to understand that rare was the time when she was not thinking about the Resistance. It had been that way for her since she had met Ravven, since their first detention together, since Kat's father had died and she realized that all she had left of him was her biological memories of him, and she never wanted to give those up to MIND or any other corp; and every time there was a misinformation vid about her or her friends, it strengthened her resolve and kept her on course.

Renzo was looking at her, trying to parse her heavy expression, seeming torn between wanting to crack a joke to lighten her mood, or say nothing. He nodded and said nothing, which in Kat's view was the right thing to do.

"Want some water?" He pulled out two flasks from his daypack.

She noticed him looking at her, then looking away, as if appreciating their time together but shy about displaying his pleasure. A little strange, but Kat knew he had more feelings for her than he was showing. And maybe she had some feelings, too. She wondered what the surprise would be. The one he'd promised at the party.

The view turned out to be worth the walk. Renzo brought her into a wooden structure set atop a small pyramid of stone, where a green sign with white lettering confirmed that they were at 783 meters. The view was a 360-degree panorama of the bay, from Mt. Diablo to the east, to Mt. Saint Helena to the north, to the Port City of San Francisco to the south. Kat shielded her eyes from the sun to take in the view of the bay where she had met Renzo while they were kayaking. The air was fresh here, even though at this elevation Kat could see some smoke remaining from the fires. "Look!"

Renzo turned to the brown smudge in the sky. "It's all about the prevailing winds. We've been spared for now."

Kat let that moment pass in silence. She wanted to change the mood. "Okay, so what's the surprise?" She had walked this far and deserved something nice.

Which is exactly what Renzo had planned: He pulled off his daypack, reached past the water flasks and wrestled out a split of champagne, along with two cups. "Happy New Year!" He wore a goofy grin as he popped the bottle and poured.

Kat didn't want to burst the bubble of the moment, but felt she was negotiating with this man who wanted more from her. "Didn't we already do the Happy New Year thing?"

Renzo rolled his eyes. "Don't you think this is even better? We're together. This is a special spot. We're in the perfect spot for transmission. The elevation."

"Transmission?"

"Good spot for a server. One of our linked, independent servers. We'll have to come back up here and place it." He had had a funny look in his eyes, Kat thought. He looked like he wanted to kiss her and suddenly, he did. He leaned in, she leaned in, too, and she tasted the champagne on his tongue.

"Well," she said.

"Well," he responded. "That was nice."

She was excited and embarrassed at the same time. To stop him from doing it again because she wasn't ready for more, she raised her cup in a toast. "A network node atop every mountain," she said.

"Now you've got it. Expansion! Bigger than ever!" His eyes danced with the idea. He helped himself to the rest of the champagne.

"Maybe you've had too much of that," Kat observed.

He laughed and was about to say more, but the ground had started to shake. "Earthquake," he said.

They exchanged a look of fear, then crouched close to what they hoped was the strongest part of the wooden structure they'd stopped at.

"Let's wait it out," Kat said.

They waited for aftershocks, but instead of aftershocks, there came something strange. "This is not an earthquake," Kat said.

Chapter 034

The shaking stopped. They both came out of their crouch and stood. The air seemed to vibrate with the energy of the earthquake, or disturbance, whatever it was. Then Kat's mind seemed to vibrate. There was a buzzy feeling behind her eyes, as though she really had too much champagne. But it wasn't that. Her mind filled with a message.

you must live with us as equals.

The words blocked any other thought, and Kat felt pressure on her temples, pressure coming from the inside out. Then she saw that Renzo also must have heard the words.

"What was that?" His eyes darted everywhere, seeking a source. The words surrounded them. He looked at Kat helplessly. "My head hurts," he said.

"Don't be scared," she said. As a Receiver, she had heard voices in her head before, but nothing of this intensity. It was new for Renzo.

"What *was* it?" he asked again.

In the living room of the house, Ravven stood before a class of yoga students. The words you must live with us as equals entered her mind forcefully, causing her to take a step backward and close her eyes.

She could see that her students also heard the message. A few had dropped to their knees and looked to the sky, perhaps expecting a visitation from a deity. Others covered their ears; their faces scored with disbelief; some simply looked terrified. Two students put their hands in prayer position and scratched out jumbled prayers, whatever came to their minds.

"You are not going insane," Ravven said to the class to calm them, though it only seemed to make them more scared.

Spaceman was in the market near the harbor. The words you must live with us as equals came from everywhere and nowhere. They commanded his mind as they had the others. His hands went limp, and he dropped the bac bag of vegetables he was carrying. There was pressure in his skull, he felt nauseated, and fear flooded his body.

He grimaced, covered his eyes for a moment, opened them again and saw that the others in the market were affected, staggering, bent over, crying out. A lettuce vendor near Spaceman grabbed the edge of his market table and fell to the ground, bringing his stand with him, scattering heads of lettuce. People in the market began to compulsively run up and down the street, seeking escape from the words, their minds on some sort of repeating pattern that they could not stop.

A disturbance in the harbor caused Spaceman to look out there. He saw a thrashing in the water, foaming white against the blue, too far away to see what it was. Then, on the Golden Gate Bridge, he saw emergency vehicles were gathering, lights flashing.

"What is happening?" he asked no one.

Renzo grabbed a pair of binoculars from his daypack and scanned the bay far below. He reported what he saw in a voice that seemed caught between wonder and fear. "I see a pod of orcas. Maybe six of them. They're breaching. I can't see what's making them do that." He moved his line of sight toward the bridge. "Emergency vehicles on the Golden Gate." His voice went quiet. "I think people are jumping off. A lot of them."

"Doomers?" Kat asked.

"I don't know. Maybe."

you must live with us as equals faded to silence in Kat's mind. "We've got to get out of here," she said. She didn't know why but needed to move.

Renzo must have felt the same because he broke into a run. "Come on!" he said.

Kat ran to keep up. The sounds of the emergency vehicles on the bridge drifted to them. "Those people on the bridge," she got out between breaths.

"Just keep going," Renzo responded. "Is the voice in your head anymore?"

"No, it's gone."

"Good," Renzo said. "I'm clear, too."

When they reached the trailhead where they'd started, they fell into an argument. Renzo insisted on going out to the harbor to see what was going on. He pulled out his comms and pinged a hovercraft to take him there.

"We have to get back to the house," Kat insisted. She didn't want to be arguing but he wouldn't stop.

"It's more important to see what's happening." Renzo gestured to the bay.

"We have to see if Spaceman and Ravven are okay."

Renzo met her eye. "I'm getting out on the water." He was in constant motion, looking out for the hovercraft. "Come with me."

"No."

The hovercraft driver pulled up and the doors to the vehicle opened. It was an autonomous vehicle, no human driver. A polite male synth voice said, "Greetings, Renzo. Please get in."

Kat wanted to get off the mountain, so got in with Renzo. They didn't speak on the way down, as the hovercraft took the curves of the Panoramic Highway at speed. They were in the harbor in fifteen minutes. Renzo exited the hovercraft with a brief nod to Kat. "I'll check in later at the house." He headed over to his kayak.

Kat gave an annoyed shake of her head, watching Renzo move away, and got out of the vehicle to walk to the house.

She found Ravven and Spaceman downstairs, sprawled on the sofa, looking spent. "What happened? Did you hear the words?"

They told their separate stories in overlapping fragments.

"My students were crying out and writhing in pain and I couldn't help them."

"In the market, people looked to the sky for the words, and some looked to the sea. The words seemed to surround us, coming from everywhere."

"It was worse than a migraine," Ravven said. "Like having a headache that's too big for your head, bursting beyond your skull." Then, as if speaking only to herself, Ravven continued, "I don't understand why the orca queen had to deliver a message in a way that included so much pain."

This got Kat's attention. "Why do you think it was the orca queen? Do you have any proof?"

Ravven sat back on the sofa. "Oh, Kat, who else would it be? I don't need proof. Just ask yourself who else has that power? She wanted to send a message that everyone would hear."

Improbable, Kat thought. Ravven glared at her.

"I have to think about this." Kat sat heavily in a chair. She had wondered if, in fact, MIND had done it. Or if it was some kind of mass hysteria. "If I'm going with your idea for the moment, that the orca queen can broadcast like that, which, by the way, I don't think is rational or possible, I don't understand the point."

Ravven's features twisted as if she was going to be angry. "It's obvious. She thinks we are ignoring their presence."

"So she's terrifying everyone?" Kat asked.

Spaceman rose from the sofa and moved into the kitchen. He opened the high cabinet with the bottles of whiskey in it, looked at them, appeared to decide something, and slowly closed the cabinet.

"No whiskey," Kat heard him say quietly, and he turned to open a valve to get a glass of artificial water. He drank. It appeared to revive him.

"Now what was I saying?" he asked.

"You weren't saying anything," Kat said.

"Oh. Then..." Spaceman said, looking lost. Hearing the words must have disoriented him; he was still struggling.

"Now what are we going to do about this?" Kat said

Ravven harrumphed. "You always want to know what to do. You're already reacting, planning, ideating. What do you think we should do?" It was an insult wrapped in a question.

Kat's annoyance propelled her to her feet. She paced the floor. "This means something. It happened. It really happened. We don't know how widespread this was, but I assume that millions of people were affected. The message emanated from a powerful source. We don't know how. Doesn't that make you want to find out what happened?"

"No," Ravven said.

"Why?"

"I know who it was," Ravven said.

"The orca queen," Spaceman said as if trying the words to see how they sounded in his mouth. He raised a finger in respect or mockery; Kat couldn't tell which. "The orca," Spaceman said again.

"I was in the woods when it happened. It was loud, louder than I thought it could be."

"Mother Nature speaks loudly," Spaceman said.

Kat looked at him. "The orcas are in the bay. How do they broadcast to the woods?"

"Why wouldn't that be possible?" Ravven asked. "The queen has opened a channel to me. It seems to transcend time and space. She could project to the woods, or anywhere, really." Ravven cast a glance at Kat, daring her to disagree.

Naturally, Kat did. "But this was in *everyone's* mind, and it affected everyone differently. It doesn't make sense."

"When you try to fit everything into a box labeled 'makes sense' you leave too much out," Ravven said.

"But it *doesn't* make sense," Kat said. "People were jumping from the bridge. We saw them with binoculars."

Ravven blinked, registering the tragedy. "They call themselves Doomers."

"What if they weren't all Doomers? What if the words drove them to it?"

"The queen orca wouldn't want that," Ravven said.

Kat thought into Ravven's mind. *You've tried the Prism, haven't you?*

I have.

And?

I have heard and I have seen, Ravven thought back

You don't want to tell me what happened.

Ravven looked at her with eyes that were bright with either insight or mania, Kat couldn't determine which and huffed her annoyance.

"We don't know what the orca queen would want. Renzo was going out on the water to find out more," Kat said, realizing that she cared about what happened to him, more than she would have thought. She hadn't heard from him since they'd parted ways in the harbor.

Chapter 035

There was a little locker by the rack which Kat opened with a swipe of her comms and took out her lifejacket. She knew this was a bad idea.

Spaceman said, "You don't know where you're going."

"You're going to help me find out," Kat said. "You can ask for help. Get on the radio." Her paddle was in her hands.

When Kat said she was going down to the harbor to get her kayak to look for Renzo, Spaceman had insisted on coming with her. She said, "He wanted to get out on the water," as if those words would unlock some secret, reveal what he found, or just help her locate him. She started dragging her kayak across the sand.

"You can't go without direction," Spaceman said.

She nodded once, tugged the zipper up on her sunsuit, and pulled the kayak to the water, preparing to jump in as she launched it. "I have a sense of where he would go." She looked at Spaceman. "You can't stop me."

He nodded and held out his hand. In it, a small round, red object of a type that Kat recognized.

"I don't need a distress beacon," she said. "I'll ping you on comms."

"Take it," Spaceman said. "I'm not letting you go without it. Hopefully Renzo also has one."

She nodded and took the beacon.

Kat turned her kayak to meet the incoming wakes crosswise to avoid being swamped by larger vessels. Seawater crested her bow, soaking her, and filling her mouth with salt. She struggled and felt small as she was pushed around.

When she paused to take a sip of artificial water from her flask, the current pulled her to her right as soon as she stopped paddling. She wondered if Renzo also got pulled off by the current. She paddled farther, aiming down the coast toward the Golden Gate Bridge. Why he might go there, she didn't know. He might have just as easily headed in the opposite direction.

Stop soon.

Go back.

This isn't making any sense.

Panic swelled in her. Her hands hurt as a blisters formed on both thumbs. No gloves. She'd forgotten.

Renzo would chase a problem until he solved it, just like Dave would. But Dave chased programming challenges while Renzo's were out here on the water.

There was a container ship moving like a building, too close, coming up fast; she'd let her attention drift. The wake headed toward her. She wrestled with the kayak, turning to slice through the waves, accelerating, but it wasn't enough. She flipped over, her mouth full of water, eyes burning with salt and the pollution of the bay.

Breathing hard, trying not to swallow water, she clung to the hull of the upside-down kayak. Then instinct kicked in. She clambered up to the kayak at the rear, straddled her legs on either side, and kicked to push herself in. The waves were too strong, though, and she couldn't hang on. It flipped again and got away from her. She lunged for it, swimming hard; if she lost it, she'd be stranded in the bay. Another deep breath, trying not to panic, she straddled at the stern again and threw herself in, kicking hard.

She made it this time, her sunsuit heavy with water. Using her paddle, she flipped out as much water as she could and then started paddling. When she got up some speed, she opened the valve at the stern to let some of the water flow out. She couldn't rest; as soon as she stopped paddling, the current pulled her. That's what probably happened to Renzo. Pulled off course. Battling the current. She pictured him stabbing his paddle into the water, eyes squinting, jaw tight. No time to rest—she saw a small motor launch approaching her fast. There was a pilot, someone with long black hair blown back by the wind. They looked like a modern-day pirate. Kat wondered if they saw her; the motor launch was on a collision course with her kayak. She started paddling in a panic, hoping to get out of the way. The launch changed direction to intercept her.

Finally, she yelled, "Stop! Stop!" and waved her paddle over her head.

The motor launch pulled up beside her kayak. The pilot called out in a rough voice nearly carried away by the wind. "I'm here to help," they said.

"What? Who are you?"

"The whale trackers found Renzo Kundera. Roger Rucker sent me."

"Who *are* you?" Kat demanded again. She didn't know this person. How had they found her and why did they know about Renzo?"

"I am Joan Warmaker. The Harbormaster here."

They appraised each other for a moment, their watercraft bobbing. Joan held out a hand and said, "Give me a line. I'll secure your kayak. Then I'll explain. We have a five-minute trip to get Renzo. We should hurry. He's in trouble."

Kat had heard enough; she had to trust Joan so she could learn what happened to Renzo. She tossed Joan a line and together they secured her kayak to the motor launch and she climbed in.

Joan started to debrief her. "Spaceman sent a distress signal out on the short-range radio channel. The whale trackers picked it up and sent up a couple of drones. They know Renzo. He's done some whale rescue exercises with them." Joan pointed across the bay to a small island Kat hadn't noticed before. "He's out there. Adrift, caught in the surf."

Kat squinted; the island looked far and small, relentlessly thrashed by surf.

"He had a distress beacon; it helped," Joan said.

Kat remembered that she had one, too. Spaceman had insisted. She unzipped a pocket in her sunsuit and took it out.

Joan noticed and smiled. "Good thing they're waterproof. It made it a lot easier to find you *and* find him."

The island they approached in the motor launch was a small oval, maybe three kilometers wide and a kilometer deep. It jutted up roughly vertical from the water, spattered with green and gray lichens, brown and white seagull guano, and on top, a scraggly fringe of evergreen trees like the last bit of hair on a bald man's head. As they approached, now a kilometer and a half away, Kat watched the water roughly tossing itself against the island. Renzo's kayak was bobbing in the waves. She didn't see Renzo in it.

They drew closer, as Joan piloted the motor launch in a zig-zag course, eyes on the sonar, avoiding underwater hazards. Joan also got on the radio, sending out a Mayday to the Coast Guard.

A moment later they were knocking up against Renzo's kayak in heaving water. He was in it, low, flopped over, rolling listlessly. The two hulls—Renzo's kayak and the motor launch—were smashing together in the rough water. Kat reached for Renzo, trying not to get her hand smashed. His limp body moved with the violence of the water. His eyes were closed, paddle gone. He wore a wetsuit with an air unit. The indicator on the suit flashed red, signaling that he had run out of air.

Everything was thrashing in the water and Kat could not get her hands on him.

"Wait, let's try something else," Joan called out, scrabbling for a rope to throw into the kayak and snag on a cleat.

Joan tried it a few times, failing. It seemed like a long shot.

"Let me!" Kat insisted, lunging forward and shouting, "Renzo!" She was able to grab him by the shoulder. "Renzo!"

Renzo's eyes blinked open, staring blankly, no focus. "Renzo!" Spray washed over them both, propelled in spouts between the launch and the kayak slamming together. Kat's face was running in seawater, her hair drenched, her hands slippery.

"You'll capsize him!" Joan shouted. "Take the line!" Joan offered it but Kat still ignored it.

Renzo was too heavy to lift and everything was moving; she couldn't get a grip. Her hand was like a claw on his shoulder, and she shook him as hard as she could. "Renzo, wake up! Help me, dammit!"

Something changed in Renzo's eyes. A flicker of life. His mouth moved. "I'm too heavy," he said.

"Grab hold of me!" Kat shouted. She leaned over him.

Joan held the rope uselessly in their hand when the blare of the Coast Guard launch made them all jump.

The Coast Guard arrived in a large motor launch with a winch for lowering a small inflatable boat. A crew of two, a man and a woman, lowered the inflatable into the water and motored over to Renzo, strapped him into a stretcher, and pulled him into their boat.

Once they'd transferred Renzo from the inflatable to the big launch, and secured both of their kayaks, the female crew member caught Kat's eye, and called out, "You want to ride with us?"

"Yes," Kat shouted.

Joan called out something Kat couldn't hear, something like "I'm going back." Once Kat was aboard the big launch, Joan started back to the harbor.

Renzo was strapped to his stretcher, immobilized but safe. To Kat, he looked helpless. She turned to one of the crew, a tall, wiry fellow made of ropy muscle who was hooking up a therapy bot to Renzo. "Is he going to be okay?" Kat asked.

"He'll be fine," the crewman answered. It was clear that he didn't really know. Kat looked closer at the therapy bot and guessed it was a new model; she didn't recognize it. It was half a meter in diameter, and sat low on the deck, without the wheels she'd seen on some other models. She asked the bot what was wrong with Renzo.

It answered with an all-business femme voice, explaining that it would treat Renzo for sun exposure and exhaustion. It extended an arm-like appendage to wave a sensor over Renzo's chest and added that he had water in his lungs. "I will take care of it," the bot said. "Do not worry."

Renzo coughed, propelling a splatter of water over his sun suit.

The bot brought out two more silver flexible arms, reminding Kat of an octopus, and it used them to open Renzo's sun suit and place medipatches on his chest. "I am treating the water in his lungs."

The bot also placed medipatches on Renzo's arms, which made Kat notice that his arms were red with painful-looking abrasions. His torso was also reddened and raw. Were those rope burns? She wasn't sure. The red marks had the imprint of rope, red abrasions, and there was blood.

"Was he burned?" she asked the med bot.

Before it could answer, Renzo coughed up more seawater and said in a ragged voice, "Rope burn. Ropes." It seemed a great effort to produce those words and then he closed his eyes.

Chapter 036

Kat watched him watching her. Renzo was still weak, accepting a cup of tea from Ravven with hands that trembled. He seemed uneasy, perched on the couch, as if he'd get up to leave if he was strong. He gazed at Kat.

I'm sorry I couldn't find you in time, Kat thought.

Ravven glanced at her, picking up Kat's thought. *So you've finally come around? Decided how you feel about poor Renzo?*

I don't know how, Kat responded.

But you do, Ravven thought. *You're afraid to express it, for some reason only you understand.*

I am not afraid, Kat shot back, frowning. But it was true that she didn't understand.

Ravven let the smile remain on her face, watching Kat.

Kat looked away, sat back in her chair, and took in the scene. They had all been waiting for Renzo to tell his story, having gathered in Kat's house. Ravven was tending to the tea; Spaceman paced in the background, probably, Kat assumed, waiting to ask Renzo about the hydrophones; Kat was trying to understand how she felt about this waterlogged fellow who seemed lucky to be alive. She made a little game of listing Renzo's good qualities in her mind. He had a scientist's passion for his work. He was on a quest for truth. He loved abstractions. In all of that he reminded her of Dave, her late husband. All mental paths seemed to lead to Dave.

She suspected that Renzo loved her, and the suspicion made her stop her thoughts and start up again with a correction. Renzo *wanted* to love her. He only *desired to*, but she wasn't letting him. Her mind churned with these thoughts.

Just then, Renzo started to speak.

"I'll try to tell you what happened." He drew a shaky breath. "I was paddling out, looking for where the words came from."

"You must live among us as equals," Kat prompted.

Renzo broke into a smile that vanished quickly. "I thought I was going insane. I guess everyone did. Everyone who isn't a Receiver."

"So you were out on the water," Kat prompted again. "I have to ask why. What made you assume the words were coming from the water?"

He frowned. "I don't know. I didn't think about it, but it seemed that the words originated there. I was compelled…"

Ravven broke in. "You see? That's it! Because the orcas…"

A look from Kat silenced her. "Keep going, Renzo."

"Okay. Paddling, probably going too far out, listening in my mind for the words. I didn't hear them. I saw the orca." His eyes lost focus, as if he was looking at the orca now. "It was a juvenile separated from its pod. Tangled in a fishing net. I shouldn't have tried to help, but…" He stopped.

"Yes?" Kat asked.

Renzo shifted in his chair, embarrassment flashing on his face. He took a gulp of tea and coughed on it. "I heard it asking for help."

"You thought that you understood the orca's language?" Kat asked.

"Not in my ears, but in my head. Like I was a Receiver, like you or Ravven, which I am not. Or in the way that I heard the "live among us as equals"—those words. It was—it scared me." He appealed to the others in the room with a helpless expression. "I made bad judgements."

"Tell us," Kat said.

Renzo gathered himself. "Well, I've received training for how to help whales when they are stuck in a net. There's a group."

"One of the units of the whale trackers," Spaceman filled in. "I contacted them on the radio. They put up a drone to search for you."

"They found me, well, Kat found me."

"It was the harbormaster, Joan Warmaker. We knew where to go because you both had trackers."

Renzo nodded. "They're good in emergencies." He pulled a face. "I'm grateful they wanted to find me, since what I did was so stupid."

"What do you mean?" Kat asked.

Renzo went on. "I meet with the group about once a month, for a few months now, part of their beginner group. We rehearse what to do if we see a whale entangled in a net. I was cleared to watch more experienced people work with injured whales. So I knew what to do, but I wasn't supposed to actually go and do it."

He looked at the floor. Kat felt his embarrassment. "What did you do?" she asked. "That was so bad..."

"I tied my bow line to the net so I could stay with the whale and it pulled me. I head the orca's thoughts in my head. It shook me up. It told me that it was scared to die. It wanted me to know about the rising temperature of the sea. Because of the warmer water, the pods came farther north than ever before. Sea stars were dying because of the heated water and there were algae blooms. I've studied all of this. I know it's true. But this time, I felt it all. It tore me up inside."

"A direct transmission," Ravven said.

Renzo nodded his head, his eyes unfocused. "It was so intense." He suddenly put his face in his hands and started to sob.

Kat reached out and gently took the teacup from his hand. "Just rest for a moment, okay?" she said.

He nodded.

"You knew enough to stay away from an injured creature that was bigger than you, but you felt its suffering."

"It was in my mind!" Renzo spoke too loudly, then tried to calm himself. "It was scary."

"It was," Kat said. "Sorry this happened to you."

That perked him up. He sat up in his chair. "I'm not sorry. I think the orca chose me. Not just Ravven." He nodded to her. "It wanted *me* to know about its suffering, and not just orcas, all animals. It wanted to talk to me."

Ravven said, "You were chosen."

After a moment to compose himself, and after Kat handed him another cup of tea, he continued speaking. "The juvenile orca was slapping its tail against the water, trying to get away from the netting and rope, and it breached, and came down again; it did that a few times. Then it seemed to tire itself out and give up and float. It seemed to be waiting for me."

Renzo took a sip of tea. "I paddled closer, hoping to get my hands on the net. I've seen a whale in trouble on one of our drills. I watched how the team did it. Their approach. They're very careful. They tie floatation kegs to the whale to be sure it won't dive and take everyone under. They have knives on long poles which they use to cut away the rope and net. I didn't have anything like that.

"But I could hear the whale talking to me, and it was suffering. Very distracting. I had to help, even though I knew everything I was doing was wrong. I trusted the orca to help me help it. I don't know how it happened, but my diving knife was in my hand. I don't know when I took it out. I must have done it unthinkingly. I put it away because I had a plan. I paddled closer."

He drew a quick breath, his eyes went wide, and he cradled his face in his hands, sobbing softly. "I'm sorry, I..." His words became too quiet to hear.

Kat reached to take his hand, and he pulled himself together enough to keep talking.

"Trusting the whale, that was the point. You understand? I came to believe that I could trust him. I knew by then that he was a male because he was large for a juvenile, and by the size of his dorsal fin. It was triangular—a male. If he flipped over, and I saw his underside, I thought that would confirm it. As scared as I was, I approached him carefully, talking in a gentle voice, convincing him that I was here to help. I said, 'You can see that the rope and netting aren't too bad. Just in your tail fluke. Most of the net is gone already. It came loose by itself. I can help. Just a few knots left,' I said. I was confident that I could cut them away or untie them. It all looked easy." Renzo stopped talking.

"Then what?" Kat said. "Were you still scared?"

"Not as much," Renzo replied. "I reached out to touch his flesh, and I breathed in his salt smell. I'd never been that close to a whale before." Renzo's eyes were distant as he recalled the moment.

"The whale rolled to its side to look at me. I had this feeling, a feeling of pressure. The pressure of consciousness pressing back at me."

Ravven nodded. "I know what you mean. It's like that for me, too."

Renzo continued. "I explained to the orca exactly what I wanted to do. 'I'm not going to use my knife,' I said. 'You understand me, right? You just stay still as you can, and I will reach over and pull off all this netting and rope.' The orca seemed to be regarding me with one eye. Very steady. I reached out and started to move my hands in the netting. The orca sprayed out of its blowhole. I thought it was agreeing with me and would stay still. But no. Not that. I realized too late. It dived. It was taking me under."

Renzo paused here, eyes wide and troubled, and gulped at his tea. "I thought that was the end," he said. "I tried to get my backup air going. I panicked when everything flipped upside down."

The deep black below traded places with the silvery surface above. The whale had spiraled, turning Renzo around. "I thought it would panic but I felt a strange sense of calm, because I knew that this was the end. I heard the whale in my head again, talking about how hard it was to live. The ocean is having a heatwave, it was saying in my head. The voice was craggy, rocky, ancient and raw. I got caught up in it, but it was my time to fight. I had to fight to live."

He knew what he had to do to live. "I had to fight to find the surface. But I didn't know which way was up."

Renzo recalled a blinding light in his eyes and a dull tone in his ears. "It was the alarm on my air unit. It was shutting down. My throat became this tiny hole I had breathe through even though I was gulping. I looked for the mirror of light."

Recognition on Ravven's face, as remembered her time with the orcas. "The surface."

Renzo nodded his confirmation. "When I looked up, all I could see was red and brown. Kelp. A kelp forest. I thrashed. I must have lost consciousness." He shrugged slightly, glancing at Kat. "The next thing I remember is Kat saying my name."

"How did you get to the island?" Kat asked.

"I don't know," Renzo said.

"How did you get loose from the lines?" asked Spaceman. "How did your kayak end up there?"

Renzo shook his head. "I don't know. I don't remember anything about it. Maybe the whale helped me, after it knew that I had heard its message. We'll probably never know," Renzo concluded.

It seemed to Kat that Renzo wanted his words to sound wise, but he punctuated them with a dribbly cough, leaving a stain of seawater on his shirt front. "I'm going to be okay," he said, as much as to reassure himself as his listeners.

PART 004

Chapter 037

A short walk from the house, up a hill, down a set of wooden stairs, there was a beach. Ravven was headed to that sheltered spot. The winds were strong, pushing Ravven around on the path, smudging and expanding the brown line of smoke on the horizon. She knew that Alon6 had threatened to bring fire, and he had, as wildfires continued to burn to the north.

The domains had fought back, in the past few weeks, sending hundreds of drones to drop artificial water on the fires, slowing their progress but not stopping them from advancing to the south and west, closer to Kat's house. It made Ravven think about who was stronger, MIND or the dom.

The path was littered with fallen branches from the most recent windstorm. She stepped carefully until a large fallen tree blocked her way and stopped her. Ravven stepped around it as best as she could, in the process, tearing the upper part of her white sunsuit on a branch. There was a new kind of sunsuit she'd heard about that could self-repair when ripped, but she preferred to wear the old kind that felt more like cloth.

There was a hot wind in her face, making her squint and taste grit. She looked up because it came from the mountains to the north, spiraling down to her, making her reach for her water flask. She drank, felt grit on her tongue, wiped her mouth, and continued down the path to the beach.

Her goal was to lead a meditation class on the sand, looking out over the ocean to help her students feel a deep connection with the water. This was not to be. Smoke swirled above her, lending a feeling of foreboding. Ravven's students were loyal, however, and they trusted her, and agreed to meet her at the beach. Her class attendance had steadily increased, from ten students, to twenty, to thirty—her daily following was growing to the levels she enjoyed when she started teaching twenty years ago in the San Francisco Port City. As she walked, she smiled, remembering how after every class she taught, her students gathered around her, sweaty guys, a few women, coming to ask questions about a pose, a sequence, or an injury that was troubling them, but really just to get her attention. They waited for the light of her eyes to be upon them. Yes, the attention they craved from her was an ego-boost, and a troubling one for Ravven; she didn't want to get a big head but did anyway. Humility did not come easily to her.

She paused to hold on to a wooden railing that would steady her descent to the beach and looked out over the blue water with its growing strip of brown smoke staining the sky. Ravven had an agenda; she always did. She wanted her students to get closer to the orcas, even though she knew the orcas were angry with humans now. The orcas needed humans to understand them better; perhaps that was the message the juvenile wanted to send when it tried to drown Renzo.

The humpbacks and orcas surely must have argued about taking that action, Ravven thought. The species apparently felt differently about how to deal with the human problem. They didn't always seem to be on the best of terms, from what Ravven had witnessed.

The hot wind that blew over Ravven caused her throat to close. Ravven willed herself to take a breath to calm herself. She allowed calm to suffuse her before she took another step on the stairs down to the beach, but the calm did not last.

A few steps down and the little beach was revealed, a half circle of gray sand strewn with rocks. Ravven gripped the rail and nearly stumbled: Below, she saw her students seated in a circle around a beached orca.

The stricken animal's breath was shallow and its upward facing eye was cloudy. It was giving up; Ravven knew. She wanted to comfort it in its transition to its next life. She carefully placed her hand on its side, behind its eye. Its flesh felt waxy, and the animal didn't move. Its eye seemed to look at nothing.

She looked to her students. "What happened? Does anyone know?"

No one knew. "When we came for class, the orca was just here. We didn't know what to do so we just waited for you." Ravven didn't carry comms, so waiting was all her students could do.

Ravven nodded and removed her hand from the animal's black body. She sat cross-legged and closed her eyes to feel into the situation. Her students mimicked her action, closing their eyes.

Ravven waited for her intuition to indicate what she should do next. The orca had come to this beach to end its life in view of Ravven's class. It was a statement, to humans and for humans. What did it want to communicate? *Humans are Earth's biggest problem.* That's what came to Ravven.

We need more people to hear that message, Ravven thought. *That's the problem that the orcas have handed to me. That's what they want me to work on.* A few of her students, the Receivers among them, nodded in agreement, though their faces held questions.

Ravven felt gratitude for their trust and also felt their fear. They expected her to know what to do next, but she did not. She had never been in the presence of a beast this large and magnificent and dying. She laid her ear gently to its side to listen for the failing heartbeat. When she felt it, she felt in her bones, a slow beat, getting slower. The body was beginning to smell. It was a heavy scent that made her throat close a little more.

Ravven felt panic rise. There was no precedent, no procedure, and she would have to pretend that she knew what to do.

She nodded once. Alright then.

"We will have a vigil," she said. The students opened their eyes and looked at her with expectation. "Please join me as we accompany this suffering animal into the next plane of its existence and make a smooth transition into its next life. It will take as long as it takes. This means that I don't know how long we will be here. Anyone who doesn't want to stay should leave now. I have no problem with that. I will not judge you. The rest, if you accept this vigil, please close your eyes, open your hands and your heart, and together we will conduct this soul on its journey."

Ravven closed her eyes, opened her hands, and most of the others followed. Two or three students discretely left, walking across the beach and climbing the wooden stairs. Another hesitated, then joined them.

Those who remained took turns placing their hands on the orca, feeling its breathing become slower.

Depending on the direction of the wind, the smell of the body was joined by the smell of smoke. Ravven tried not to be distracted, but the mix was strong and growing stronger; several students coughed. She glanced up to the ridge and saw a lick of flame pop up and disappear again. A fire up there was getting closer, burning its way to them.

"If you want to leave, you may," she said to her students. "There is a fire approaching. It's coming from above us, on that ridge." She nodded toward it but didn't release her hands from the others she was holding.

Her students looked at her with eyes that all but stated out loud, *What are you going to do?*

"I am guiding this animal to its next stage, and I will not leave until I feel it is ready," Ravven said. More students coughed and covered their mouths. Two more students got up and left. Ravven felt frightened, but when she spoke, she willed steadiness into her words. "We must convey this soul into its next life." The whale eye was cloudy and Ravven felt the substance of the animal leave the beach. It was the end.

She took the remaining students into her gaze. "Now we will create a pyre, and we will burn the body."

Chapter 038

While Alon6 was in sleep mode, his MindVessel glowed with a gentle pulse of white light. It signaled that he was not paying attention, so Nora2 permitted herself to watch Candice Clonk's gestures at the terminal controls.

Candice's yellow eyes were dull, revealing how her work at the terminal, which stretched all through the night, had emptied her. Nora2 had worked at her side for the whole time. It was now late morning. Candice's hands continued to move with practiced motions, and she resembled a sleepwalking orchestra conductor about to walk into a wall. Nora2 felt for the younger woman.

"Let me take over for a while," she said.

Candice blinked but didn't move her eyes from the terminal. "Really? Would you?"

"Sure. Get some coffee. You look like you need it."

Candice finally turned away from the screen, showing a stiff smile. She surrendered her chair so Nora2 could slide in and opened the valve to heat some artificial water. Her body slumped against the counter.

"You can sit down. Take some time. I'll work the controls," Nora2 said.

Candice nodded gratefully and made her way into a nearby chair with her cup of artificial coffee. She held it loosely, as if she had forgotten about it, and spilled some without noticing it.

Nora2 didn't regret helping Candice, but looking at the controls was depressing. She gestured at them nonetheless, controlling the burn path.

Alon6 had initiated the project, ordering Candice to send a drone to damage a power line and start a small fire in the woods at the northern end of the Northern Californian Domain. Then he told her to whip up the wind to spread the spark into a raging fire across many domains. Brushfires ignited in the parched land to the east and smoke fouled the sky from the Northern

Californian Domain and on to the south. It was an aggressive burn path, heartless, but that is what Alon6 demanded. He specified that it move quickly.

Candice had done as he asked, spreading the fires as far as she could. He monitored her closely. "When do we send the evacuation orders?" she asked.

"There will be no evacuation orders."

Candice's mouth dropped open. "There are people there. Maybe hundreds."

"It doesn't matter if there are thousands. I said no evacuation orders."

Nora2 was standing by and heard that. She said nothing. When it was her turn to help out, she did so.

Now that Candice was spent and Nora2 had taken over, what she saw on the screen filled her with melancholy. There was a lump in her throat that she couldn't swallow.

Why did one group of citizens have to suffer when another escaped without damage? Alon6 had had a specific burn path in mind, one that marched the wall of flame through small towns to level them. The particulate matter from the smoke would have ongoing health effects for years on those towns. Many lungs would be compromised, and cancers born, and for what? Because Alon6 wanted to punish people for not surrendering to MIND. That's what he said, but Nora2 knew there was more.

Candice was watching her work now. "You could send in water drones, you know."

Nora2 nodded briefly. "I see how things are set up. No drones will be sent in."

"The fire is getting close to some big population centers," Candice said. "The Marin Peninsula. Then the Port of San Francisco."

Nora2 wouldn't look away from the terminal screen. Her face burned red with shame. She had known what Alon6 was doing all along, but she didn't stop it. His idea was to use the climate controls to punish the Resistance, and she had guided the burn path right to Kat Keeper's house. He intended to burn it down.

Candice appeared to guess at what Nora2 was thinking. "Do we have to burn all of this just to get Kat Keeper's house?"

Nora2 gestured at the controls, her face a frozen mask. She didn't want to answer and wondered how Candice was able to stay at this station for so long. The physical strain was hard, but the emotional drain was worse, guiding a hell of fire to turn house after house to ash, erase whole towns, destroy animal habitats, to end lives and livelihoods, and all to meet the needs of a tyrant.

This fire was only one part of Alon6's plan. Nora2 and Candice had worked the controls to heat the ocean, causing an algae bloom that killed orcas and injured other sea life. She and Candice had adjusted the climate to create a deadly heatwave in Mumbai and floods in Bangkok. Soon, Nora2 felt her body weakening as Candice's had, her own vitality draining. Her hands were weak and she wobbled at the terminal.

Then she just couldn't watch the burn path. She had to stop for a while, and shifted her attention to another screen, which displayed the ClarityCrawl software doing its work on the Feed. The software was functioning perfectly to seek out news of Resistance protests on the Feed and erasing the reports.

There was a time, in the recent past, when Nora2 felt good while watching ClairityCrawl do its work. It felt bad now, and she wondered if something else had happened to her mod. It used to vacuum away any negative feelings, anything out of tune with her employer's wishes. She didn't understand why, but in a strange way she was grateful for the change.

It would take one small gesture at the terminal controls to change everything happening on Nora2's screen. One little gesture. Who would notice, amid this planetary catastrophe? One small gesture from Nora2 could spare homes and lives.

Chapter 039

Hurrying back to the house, Kat felt another surge of anger at Ravven. Kat needed help and could not find her anywhere. She looked up at the reddening sky and stopped to wipe a fleck of ash from her eye. Through blurry vision she came upon Spaceman on the path to the house.

Wordlessly, he held out his comms unit so Kat could see his screen. It showed orange zones, signifying fire bearing down on them, and gray everywhere signifying smoke.

"It's coming this way. Could be an hour. Could be minutes. Depends on the wind," Spaceman said.

"You want to get out," Kat said. "Did you find Ravven anywhere?"

His mouth was a thin line. He was struggling with something. "I want to help you save the house. We haven't received an evacuation order yet. I didn't see Ravven. I wondered if she's down at the beach. Maybe I should go get her."

"You can go look for her," Kat said. She reached for his comms. "If it's so close, why haven't we gotten the order? And what about the drones? They should be flying over the worst part of it and dropping water." She looked up, scanned the sky, saw no drones, and looked back at Spaceman's screen. The house was a pulsing blue dot on the screen. It looked vulnerable with the graphic of the fire bearing down on it.

"I want to stay here and help you," he said.

She couldn't bear to look at the screen for long, but neither could she meet the look of confusion in Spaceman's eyes. Instead, she looked down and delivered a pronouncement. "There are systems in place at the house," she said. "Walk with me. I'll show you."

Then she walked Spaceman around the house perimeter, showing him the rainwater collection system and the dew collection system. The sad look in his eyes reflected the poor repair they were in. Some of the collection gutters were hanging from their supports, about to fall away from the house.

"These won't do any good," Spaceman said. "You know that."

Kat gazed at the roof and its disrepair. "It hasn't rained for weeks," she said. "I left this house two years ago and never thought I'd miss it. But now that I might lose it…" She let the thought hang to take a gulp of air. It felt harder to breathe, as if the air already had less oxygen to offer. Sweat gathered in the middle of Kat's back and made her sun shirt stick to her skin. The wind kicked up, swirling grit from the path that circled the house.

She felt Spaceman's eyes on her. He said, "Look, Kat, it's hard to let go of things."

"Yes, this is my house, and I don't want to let go of it."

He winced, knowing that he hadn't said what he meant.

She put a hand on his shoulder, not sure why she was comforting him, instead of the other way around. They said nothing for a moment. Spaceman's anxiety seemed to fill the space. He began to gabble about needing a little more time, and he'd make a retractable dome to protect the house with artificial water flowing over it. "A circular system, recycled. It would work beautifully."

Kat smiled. There was no joy in it. She knew he meant well. "You can leave if you want."

His expression hardened. "I'm not leaving here. I can do some good here, right now."

"There may be an evacuation order," she said.

"I'll help you for fifteen minutes and then I will go look for Ravven," he insisted. "Do you have some extra air units?"

She coughed. His comms was still in her hand. She checked and saw the air quality was worse. Pushing past 250. She knew that an index of more than 100 bothered most people. "I have air units in the house." She handed him back his comms and beckoned him to follow.

Two air units. One for me, one for Spaceman. And she needed an air unit for Renzo. He was inside the house, probably upstairs. She would put him to work at the front of the structure, clearing brush, if he was feeling okay. *A third air unit.* If Michel was seeing patients, she would have to tell them to leave. She noticed two of Ravven's students coming up from the beach, one of them carrying a jug of artificial water. *Two more air units.* She hoped she had enough. She asked Spaceman, "How much time do you think we have now?"

"It's strange that there hasn't been an evacuation order." He checked his comms. "Hard to say. Ninety minutes."

"Maybe the wind will change," Kat said.

"Maybe." He didn't sound hopeful.

Maybe it was all too little, too late, but no way was she abandoning this house. She went inside to tell Michel to shut down appointments and lock his studio door. "There's real danger if you stay here, Michel. I can try to get you out."

"No. I am with you, Kat."

She felt moved by that, though he was a bot, and her voice was rough in response. "Thanks." Then she went to look for Renzo, ready to climb the stairs, but he was already looking for her in the living room.

"I'm staying," he said, his eyes steady on hers. "I won't leave you here to do this by yourself."

Kat nodded, moved again. "Thanks." She acknowledged his gaze with a steady one of her own. "Get a shovel from the shed around the side of the house. Dig a berm around the northern edge of the house." A low wall of dirt might slow down the fire. From a closet, she handed him and Spaceman air units. "When you're outside, wear these."

Renzo put on his air unit and went outside to get to work.

Kat turned to Spaceman. "Come with me." They put on their air units and she led him to a garden shed at the side of the house, opened it and searched for a moment before finding a large pair of garden shears. She offered them to him. "Trim off any tree branches that are lower than six feet to the ground."

Ravven's students were sitting on the front steps of the house. Kat handed each of them an air unit. "Put these on." She told them to check all the hoses in the garden and be sure they were hooked up to the artificial water tank. "It's around the back of the house. When you finish that, see if Spaceman needs help trimming the low hanging foliage. Anything close to the house can burn and spread the fire, so we need to remove as much as we can."

They stood for a moment, taking in what she said. "Do you understand?"

They nodded and went to do as she asked. She realized too late that they were probably in shock; she hadn't even asked their names. She could have been nicer. *No time for pleasantries.*

She got her own shovel and joined Renzo to help with the berm. There were few words between them as they dug, piling up the soil half a meter high. "We need a perimeter next," she said. They began to clear a four-meter perimeter of bare dirt between the berm and the house. It was hot work and soon she and Renzo were shiny with sweat. She paused for a moment to lean on her shovel to catch her breath and check the meter on her air unit. She would be okay for a while.

The architect who built the house had tried to imagine this day. A large spray of lilacs leading up to the front door of the house were more than pretty; they were fire resistant. Pathways circled the house bordered by low, dense Oregon Boxwood, a green hedge that was also a firebreak to halt the advance of heat and flames. There were large patches of low, green sedum served the same function. When the fire came, it would be slowed by the vegetation. Yet Kat knew that none of it would be enough to stop the blaze if it was fierce enough.

Her comms unit sounded an alarm. She pulled it out to look at it, expecting an evacuation order. There was none. It was an alert that the air quality was at 300. Why hadn't an evacuation order come? Was there one, but MIND blocked it? It seemed too evil to contemplate.

Renzo was standing by her having a coughing fit under his air unit. He didn't want to remove it to protect his lungs. Spaceman looked weary as he chopped foliage with his garden shears. The two students had found smaller cutters and were also whacking away. They were wreathed with smoke, a haze sometimes gray, sometimes a burnt orange. Kat's eyes watered. It seemed like the smoke was pulling the life out of her. She wished she had goggles.

Spaceman approached. "Look, it's time to go. We're all going to get sick."

His voice was muffled by the air unit covering his mouth.

"We have air units," she said.

"Come on, Kat." He glanced at the sky, and she followed his eyes to the flickering orange color glowing just over the other side of the hills. The fire was close. She heard a whistling sound, the movement of superheated air. She wiped the sweat from her face with the back of her hand.

Renzo walked up to them, looking like he wanted to leave also. Rather than face him, Kat turned away to look at the ocean, gray, flat, the sky above it still blue here and there.

She turned to Ravven's students. "You two, you can leave. Go down to the harbor. The air will be clearer there."

They hesitated.

"You can leave," Kat insisted. "Go while you can."

One of them looked grateful, the other guilty, but they wasted no time taking off their air units.

"Keep them," Kat said.

The students nodded their thanks, replaced the air units, and hurried down the path to the harbor.

Kat picked up one of the hoses the students had brought out, turned on the artificial water and started to wet the roof. "Renzo, get a hose and do the other side of the house."

"We don't have enough water. We should wait—"

Kat interrupted him. "Until it's too late? Wet down the roof!" It was their last line of defense. "Renzo, go."

Spaceman came over to her and looked like he wanted to wrestle the hose from her hand. "You can't start now. The fire's not here yet. It's wasteful!"

"Letting the house go is horrible!" Kat cried out. She jerked away, keeping the hose out of Spaceman's hands. "Leave me alone!" she cried. She had to save the house. The memories of her time spent here were a lump stuck in her throat. Dave's life work. The house was blurred by heat and tears, seeming to already fade away.

"I won't go!" she cried out again. The water jetting from the hose slowed and soon was a trickle. The tank of artificial water was running low. A billow of brown smoke filled the air between Kat, Renzo, and Spaceman, making it impossible to see more than a meter. Her eyes burned horribly.

A roar came from the hills: the fire sucking up oxygen.

Raw panic in Renzo's eyes. "It's here! Get down," he called out. "The air pocket. Breathe down there." He meant there was a slender pocket of air along the ground. One by one their air units went to red, the alarms going on. The filters were gone.

Spaceman began to cough under his air unit. He was struggling to stay and help, but the smoke affected people differently.

"Go down the hill," Kat called to him. "Go now. There's nothing to prove here."

"I'm staying!" he said at first, but then seemed to weaken, another attack of coughing. "I can't," he whimpered. "I'm out. Going down the hill." He started to trudge in that direction, moving slowly because the pall of smoke made it hard to see where he was placing his feet.

Then a voice from the void of smoke: "Hello? Hello?"

It was Ravven. She had come up from the beach, her white sunsuit gray with soot.

"Over here," Kat called out, her voice muffled by her air unit. She lifted it from her face, coughed, called out, "Over here!" Kat spat out the granular gray dust. It felt like it was seeping into her body through her skin. The smoke was everywhere. Flickering orange everywhere. Kat shut her eyes tightly and still saw orange flames. The flames were at the roof of the house and burst through an opening, an inferno. Her eyes were slits and then she struggled to open them. Her mouth was packed with dirt. She was on her belly, face down in the ditch she and Renzo had dug.

She raised her head. She saw Spaceman and Ravven in each other's arms on the ground nearby, their eyes closed. Renzo was on his side spread out in the dirt, face up, not moving.

Chapter 040

Nora2 gestured to bring three vid drones into position. The surveillance showed a storm of orange, then smoke, then ash like snowflakes, but Nora2 gestured, changing the view, and the ash cleared the way for her to witness a disturbing sight.

Looking downward from above, from the drone's point of view, she saw Ravven Vaara and Roger Rucker holding each other on the ground. They weren't moving. Nearby, Kat Keeper, face down on the ground, also unmoving. A man she couldn't identify, also face down, not moving. Orange flames licked in from the perimeter of the view. Then black smoke billowed in, blocking Nora2's view of everything.

Nora2's hands moved as if by themselves, without her conscious guidance. A gesture. Another. She deployed a thousand water drones, specially built to compress hydrogen and oxygen from the atmosphere and create artificial water. Five hundred of them to stop the fire's advance. Four hundred to stop the fire that was already burning. One hundred directly over Kat Keeper's house.

Another gesture. The drones opened a cavity on their undersides and artificial water with fire retardants fell in sheets.

The area around Kat's house changed from an inferno to a field of mud and steam.

Nora2 felt suddenly weak. She held on to the desk for support as the screen swam before her eyes; tears in her field of view, she realized. Her throat tightened and maybe laughter was coming or a sob; she couldn't tell which. Whatever it was, she forced it down, aware that normally her mod would take care of an emotional burst like this. Something was definitely wrong with her mod, and she realized that it was something that she didn't want to fix.

She moved the focus of the screen with a gesture and gestured again to lower the deadly temperature through Uttar Pradesh. Another gesture. The screen moved again. A map of the People's Dictatorship of Thailand was on the screen. Nora2 gestured, stopping the monsoon there. If the rains stopped, the citizens there might begin to restore their land. She found herself unable to stop, so she raised her hand again, not sure which part of the planet she should help next, and then she caught sight of Candice.

Candice was watching her. Surprise in her eyes. Curious. A tentative smile.

"What are you doing?" Candice asked.

"Fixing things." Nora2 said. She felt her suppressed laugh bubble out of her. It felt deranged, but maybe it sounded good. Suddenly she sensed that they were in this together, she and Candice. Candice wasn't going to tell anyone about this. Nora2 trusted her.

Candice glanced at Alon6's MindVessel to confirm that it was still in sleep mode. She cleared her throat. The words she produced sounded thick. "Who are you going to help next, Nora2?"

Chapter 041

Kat was amazed to realize that she was not dead. She spat out more dirt, wrestled off her air unit, and rolled over on her back, catching sight of a piece of blue sky that seemed to be newly made.

She sat up, saw Spaceman and Raven in each other's arms and Renzo nearby, and they were moving. Not dead.

"We're not dead," Kat said and wanted to laugh, but laughter wasn't right. She wanted to cry with relief but she was out of tears. She looked at where her house should be. It was still there.

She saw Spaceman sit up. His face was smeared with wet dirt. He pulled Ravven into a fierce hug. She was crying, the tears leaving streaks in the dirt on her face. She pulled off her air unit.

There was mud, ash, dirt. *Mud?* Had it rained? Her clothes were wet.

"We've been spared," Spaceman said.

"Spared." Ravven echoed.

Kat looked around to see blackened trees defining a fifty-meter burn perimeter. A fleck of ash fluttered like a snowflake. She wanted to reach out for it, touch it, confirm that it was real. "It moved through here," she said quietly as though to herself. "So close."

Something had stopped the fire. Not rain. Drones. The drones must have come to drop water, slowing the destruction at the last moment.

There were more of Ravven's students sitting up in the mud, grubby and groggy and coughing.

My students came to help, Ravven thought into Kat's mind.

Kat stood, wobbled, dizzy, and walked to Spaceman and Ravven, extending her hands. Renzo came over, and the students also, and they all joined hands. Kat breathed, grateful for the burned taste of the air; at least it was air.

"Goddess," Ravven said softly. "Thank you for bringing the water to stop the fire."

Kat cocked her head and shot Ravven a look. "Don't you think it was the drones?"

Ravven gestured to the sky. "I don't see any drones."

Kat looked down and smiled. She didn't share Ravven's faith in the unseen, but something fortunate had happened. Maybe the wind changed at the last possible moment.

Days after the fire had nearly taken her home, Kat could smell smoke in her nose and sometimes coughed up black particles of soot. The smoke and soot in her body reminded her of how close she had come to losing everything. She wanted that feeling to go away. Her house had to be safe.

She didn't know what "had to be safe" meant, precisely. She spoke with Michel about coding some advanced smoke detectors and had him work on plans for their own fleet of water drones. At breakfast, when she ran into Renzo in the kitchen, she asked him to put up consciousness detectors around the perimeter of the property. She was often looking for things to do together with him, ways to be together that didn't require too much emotional commitment. She knew that was weak, but she told herself that was all she could handle.

To Renzo's credit, he responded with his typical optimism. "At what level of consciousness? How sensitive?"

"Humanity level," she answered and then swiftly corrected herself. "Humanity and humanity emulators."

Renzo grinned. "Shouldn't be hard. I'll get started." He set off with a cup of tea in his hand for the greenhouse, where there were plenty of machines that could be repurposed. Before leaving the kitchen, he added over his shoulder. "I'll call you into the greenhouse when I have something to show."

"Thanks." Kat would work on her own project, the one where she reached out to small communities on the network and asked them to join the Resistance.

In her old office, there were no clients scheduled for Michel. Kat sat at the desk and gestured at the terminal screen to bring up the network. She noticed that there was a message waiting for her in her administrator inbox. It was addressed to @katkeeperadmin and came from a handle she thought she'd seen before: @deletedaccount.

The message said:

Hello @katkeeper. You've been hacked. :)

The curser paused on the screen, seeming to wait for Kat's response.

Kat keyed back, *Who are you, @deletedaccount?*

After a moment, a response, as though the person behind the account had been waiting. *A friend who wants you to know that you've been hacked.*

Kat wrote again, *Who are you?* No response. *Are you inside MIND?*

Another response. *I will let you confirm my identity on your own time. Someone has been communicating with you for the last few months from MIND. You may assume that it is me. That will help you understand who I am.*

Yes, it will. Kat wrote. She had seen a few odd messages in her admin inbox here and there from @deletedaccount, but today's exchange was considerably bolder than those. She checked the processing load on the server and saw a spike of extra activity. *How do I know I've been hacked?* she typed.

The response came back. *Are you deliberately asking a dumb question to trick me? I can see what you're doing on that terminal, Kat. I can mirror your screen on my terminal and I'm capturing keystrokes. You just checked the processing load on the server and saw extra activity.*

It made Kat take a sharp breath. *WHO ARE YOU?*

No response.

Kat keyed, *How did you do this? How did you hack my server?*

I cracked your encryption algorithm and got access your encryption keys. I've got your peer list.

Kat leaned in and typed fast. *That list is on my client server. It's the list of all the IPs we're using on the peer-to-peer network.*

The response: *LOL.*

Kat pounded the terminal keys, anger getting the better of her. *You said you were a friend. You're not acting like one.*

I am acting like a friend, because I'm going to tell you how to fix this. I understand you need a client server that hosts your peer list. Today, you'll change all your IPs and generate a new peer list. My boss wants me to spy on you, so we're going to fool him. Set up a spoof feed. Send out a false record of transmissions. Old conversations. Recycled news. Make it look real, as if it is a live feed.

Kat keyed back, *Because you will follow that one.*

Exactly, came the response. *MIND will follow the wrong feed, the spoofed feed. The data coming in every day will satisfy the watchers who watch me. Move your real feed to another IP. Or use a proxy server to cloak the identity of the IP. Claire8 is the queen of cloaking. She will know what to do. Ask her to put her best slaze forward.*

This person knew who Claire8 was. Kat was mystified. *Why are you doing this?*

No response. The curser blinked, waiting.

Spoofing a feed was challenging but possible. She could create streams of false, but real-seeming chatter, and replay old conversations. Everything on the false feed would be wrong by design. Wrong times for Ravven's yoga classes, wrong door codes for Michel; if anyone showed up for those Kat would know they were reading the spoofed feed and probably were involved with MIND.

Kat needed more tea to think about this. Ravven was in the kitchen, so Kat told her about the strange messages.

"Someone wants to help us," Ravven said, "from inside MIND."

"Maybe MIND is rotting from the inside," Kat said.

Ravven smiled, warming to the idea. "Alon6 ordered the employees to use the climate controls to murder people. MIND is heartless. Maybe the employees don't like it. They're pushing back."

Kat nodded, thinking that the water drones arrived in time to stop the fire. No accident, that. "I'd like to know who @deletedaccount is."

"Do you trust them?"

Kat considered this, then nodded. "I'm going to find out more."

But once upstairs, at the terminal in her room, Kat made no progress in learning the identity of @deletedaccount. The cloaking was too good.

She turned to fashioning a spoofed feed. She wove together text transcripts of recipes, market recommendations and shopping tips, randomized lists of song lyrics, discussions about the weather and air quality, and whale sighting reports. She attributed them all to false user profiles and made them play in a seamless loop. She'd have to consult with Michel, she realized, about generating and assembling new material, but this would work for now.

The next day was a Sunday. Kat went for a walk on a trail still dusted with white ash. She passed burned trees that gestured with stumps for limbs. She wore an air unit. Its indicator was green, signaling that the air was okay, but she worried about bringing in ash to the house on her clothes and shoes. A soft wind moved over her skin; she felt like it wanted to reassure her that the world was capable of healing itself.

Renzo came to mind as she walked, and the thought of him brought the possibility of Tristan coming back. It made her freeze up inside. Renzo's cultured twin hadn't been around lately. Kat didn't know whether that was good or bad, and she thought she should ask Renzo about him, but didn't really want to because things were easy between them and she liked that. Her thoughts looped around as she looped her walk back to the house.

Shoes off at the front portal, a precaution, and she started up the stairs to a UV shower. She paused on the first step, feeling how the house hummed on three levels. Ravven was leading a yoga class in the living room; the sofas were pushed aside to make room for twenty students. She could hear Spaceman and Renzo's voices coming from the greenhouse. Michel was seeing a client in the studio. Kat had set her comms to give a subtle ping whenever a client coded in and entered via the door at the side of the house, so she knew. She nodded, acknowledging the equilibrium of it all.

Chapter 042

This was an unusual session. The new person didn't say a word, perhaps thinking they could conceal themselves from me. Impossible, of course. I knew who they were as soon as they filled out the online form, and confirmed their identity when they coded in at the side door, away from human scrutiny. By the time they sat down in Kat's old home office, I knew everything. I didn't want to inhibit or intimidate them with my knowledge, however, so I would begin by letting them believe that their privacy was intact.

I called out through my speaker port. "Hello? Someone is there?"

It was 01FEB2054. A Sunday, another reason for the session to be unusual, but I decided to see this person because she was important. The person with me was Candice Clonk. She worked for MIND now, directly with Alon6, and she probably didn't remember, but she met me on the first day Kat came to the Westcoast. Candice didn't work for MIND then, but on that first day in the harbor, Kat was deciding whether to take a tuk-tuk or a ferry across to the house. As she was deciding, Candice Clonk came over to Kat and harassed her, saying that she didn't like bots (didn't like me). Kat had to bribe her to get rid of her; she put funds into Candice's account and gave Candice an extra Secluder.

I remembered all of this. Candice showed no signs of remembering any of it, and I didn't want to embarrass her by recalling the whole story. She was here for help. I was here to help. I said, "Make yourself comfortable," I said. "What would you like to talk about?"

"I shouldn't be here at all."

"You have every right to be here. These sessions are open to anyone who wants to make an appointment."

"I know," she said.

"I'm glad the appointment system worked for you." I prompted again.

"What's on your to-do list for this session?"

My readings showed an acceleration of her heart rate and moist, sweaty skin, and multiple activations of eye muscle movement.

She said nothing.

"Candice Clonk," I began again, "these sessions are in confidence. You came in using a special door at the side of the house. No one will know that you are here. I make recordings of the sessions, but only for my own learning and analysis. What can I do for you?"

"You know my name." She sounded edgy.

"Yes, Candice, I know who my sessions are with. I also confirmed who you are by scanning your voice and analyzing your personality field. You match my data for Candice Clonk. Candice Clonk has an appointment for this time slot. I am one-hundred-percent certain that you are Candice Clonk."

She made a noise of impatience and waited for me to say something else. "Why are you here today?"

There was still suspicion in the tone of her voice. "Am I really allowed to be here? It's free to talk to you?"

"Yes, you are allowed to be here and you can tell me what is on your mind. There is no charge for my sessions. They are funded by the Resistance. You seem upset about something. There is real water in that flask over there. Have some."

"Real water?"

"Please take some. Have as much as you like."

I heard her open the flask, pour, and drink.

Doubt laced her words. "It's like I'm supposed to hate the people in the Resistance, but..." She started in the middle as many clients do, in her own field of context.

"You're supposed to hate them, but do you hate them?"

She did not answer directly. "I hate the people I work with. Some of them are okay, but my boss is a prick." A brief pause. "I could get fired for saying that."

"You can speak your truth here," I said. "What else is bothering you, either about the Resistance or the people you work with?"

"Well, I guess I'm depressed. It's kind of crushing. I can't move from my mat in the morning. I've almost stopped eating." Her words came faster and she stopped them with a drink of water. "This water is good."

"You're probably dehydrated. Please, go ahead."

I meant for her to keep talking, but she was grateful for the water. "I can't remember the last time I had real water."

"Can you tell me more about feeling bad?"

"Isn't that what all therapists would say?"

"That's true," I said. "Other therapists would say something similar. I am a therapist and it's a good question to ask."

I sensed a positive uptick in her personality field. Her pulse slowed by two clicks. But soon those measurements reversed. She was about to tell me something upsetting to her; my prediction was correct.

"Last month, my boss assigned me a job. I had to direct the burn path to this house. I directed flooding and fires to other places. People died. Many people. Maybe hundreds. Or thousands, maybe. It felt wrong. It *was* wrong. Another boss of mine named Nora2 Edgewise, stopped it. I wasn't expecting her to save this this house. When I saw on the Resistance Feed that you offered therapy sessions, here, right in this house that we were going to burn down. I had to come. I had to see the house that my boss wanted to destroy, the one that Nora2 saved." She stopped talking suddenly. "It's strange to be here. I didn't think you'd allow me in here, once you found out who I am."

"When I learned who you were, I couldn't think of a more appropriate person to be sitting in that chair." I sensed the turmoil inside of her. There were so many upsetting things going on in the world. The climate was still erratic following the disturbances that MIND had introduced. With citizens not knowing what to expect day to day, their lives must have felt out of control. The Disconnect Movement was robust, with more Youngs renouncing the Feed and throwing away their comms units. The Doomer Movement was also growing, with more members joining, especially in the big cities like New York and San Francisco, some members taking their own lives by jumping from bridges. I wondered if Candice knew anyone who had jumped from the Golden Gate Bridge. It seemed like too much to ask her, so I went slowly. "Does everything feel out of control?"

"Yes, that's what everyone says. But for me, I work at MIND and MIND is in control. MIND controls everything. You'd think we would feel good about that, the people who work there. But my boss is a chaos machine." She stopped talking suddenly. "He's a bot, but you probably know that."

"Your boss is Alon6."

I wait. Silence. I add, "He's a bot but not like me. I work to spread compassion. He works to accumulate profit."

This comparison seemed to shake something loose from her. More words stuttered out haltingly. "When I'm at work it's all on screens. I do as I'm told. It's a job. I have the feeling of being so sad," she said, her voice becoming small.

"I'm sorry, Candice."

"That's all you got? 'Sorry'?" She sounded angry. With good reason.

I decided to take a risk and do something I wouldn't normally try. "We are here now, Candice. This house, this office we are in now, was spared. Everyone who lives here survived the fires. Including me. And at the same time, something happened to Alon6's plans. We can discuss what happened. You are safe with me here. The floods stopped in Thailand. In India, the heat stopped. You know how that happened."

She said nothing. Shocked, I assume, that I knew what had happened and what had changed. I consulted my records as she sniffled. "What can you tell me about all of that?"

"Nora2," she said. "When Alon6 was in sleep mode she changed everything. I saw her do it. It was...amazing. I didn't think..." she trailed off.

"You didn't think what?"

"I didn't think that anybody could do that. If Alon6 found out, he would destroy her. But she must have erased her actions somehow. She's worked for MIND for a long time, since the beginning, when Bradley15 Power was running it. She must know how to erase things and then erase the erasure."

"It is a skill, yes that level of erasure, and she knows how to do it. Does it give you hope? That you and Nora2 have agency and everything doesn't have to be the way Alon6 wants?" I was far off the therapeutic chart here, nearly putting words in her mouth. But I wanted her to come to a breakthrough. I was impatient. She went silent, thinking, I assumed.

"You know a lot," she said. "I could get in a lot of trouble for saying any of this."

"But you won't, Candice. These sessions are confidential. I keep a recording, but only for me, for my own instruction and improvement."

She appeared to consider that. "People are so depressed because we don't know whether it will rain or hail or the sun will fry us. Alon6 is driving everyone insane just to get what he wants. I applied for the job at MIND because I wanted to do something against the chaos. I actually wanted to help people." There is disgust in her voice. "I didn't realize then that MIND *is* the problem. I am working *for the problem*. My boss is a really bad guy. It's hard to come to terms with how bad, really."

She was right, of course, Alon6 was a bad guy, one of the worst people in the world when he was alive, perhaps worse still as an avatar, but I wouldn't say that, because the statement has limited therapeutic application. And I'd already imposed the facts of my worldview on her. I want my clients to come to their own realizations, even though I know where they need to go, emotionally.

"Let's start by treating your depression." I recommended that she try meditation and take walks outside when the air is good, and find more positive friends, even if they are a little older than she is.

"Make friends with Olds?" She huffed a laugh.

"Many Youngs are in a bad place now. They are becoming Doomers or seeking to disconnect. The Olds knew the world when it was more stable, so they may be more optimistic," I said, not sure if she took any of it to heart. She didn't say anything for ten seconds and my readings indicated that she was thinking.

"Older friends," she finally said. "You give me some strange advice to chum up with Olds."

"Maybe it is strange. But perhaps you'll try meditation first? I can email you a fact sheet. And a map of good walks around your workplace in El Segundo."

"Okay," she said. "I didn't know there was anywhere to walk around there."

"What do you think about same time next week, and we'll continue this?"

She laughed but then agreed and left.

As I play back these notes to polish them and sharpen them, I wonder if Candice Clonk will show up for her next appointment. And for you, the person witnessing these notes, you may wonder why I, Michel, the only bot who applied to join the Resistance and who was accepted, want to help a tech-head like Candice Clonk. The reason is that the way forward, I believe, is by using fierce altruism propelled by generosity.

PART 005

Ravven thought of the beach where the whale had died as a sad little place, a half circle of gray sand strewn with rocks, oppressed by the craggy cliff that bore down on it. But she was drawn there, hoping to secure some peace by meditating in that spot after all that had happened over the past few days. She did not expect to see any signs of the whale.

After the fire passed them by at the house, she asked Spaceman to get in touch with the short-range radio whale people because they'd know what to do with the body. When she stepped onto the beach, she noticed six charred pieces of wood left over from when she had tried to make a pyre to burn and honor the whale. A student of hers who was a secret smoker had supplied the lighter. Driftwood was the fuel. Now, six pieces of black wood were the only trace; the whale trackers had removed everything else. Spaceman asked her if she wanted to come along with them to dispose of the remains at sea. She begged off, so Renzo had joined him. They reported back that a pod had come to watch their comrade sink in the water.

Ravven sat to meditate on the beach, slowed her breathing, closed her eyes, and wondered when she opened them, if she would see a whale or even a pod in the waves like she saw during her childhood. She wanted to experience a transmission on this little beach, or maybe something more. It was not to be. Ravven's meditation was just a meditation. No visions or spacetime slippage.

"Namaste," she said to end it. She sighed, stood, brushed herself off, and began walking back to the house. Not satisfied, she was going to set up a session with the Prism of Broken Light, even though she couldn't escape the growing feeling that it was evil. After all, it had caused its previous owner to go insane. Ravven also didn't like that she had become dependent on the Prism, even addicted to it, and that she needed it to speak with the whales. She sensed that it held a power over her that she could not control.

Back in the room she shared with Spaceman, she tried to stop these negative thoughts because she believed that they could keep the Prism from working properly. She took *Winning at Backgammon* down from the shelf and opened the book to about halfway through to reveal the round, hollowed out space about the size of a fist. The Prism glowed inside, its unsettling light flickering on Ravven's face.

She remembered the bookseller's words. "You must be alone. You don't want to pull anyone else into your field because your bodies may meld in that case, and you'd never be whole again, and you'd never escape from your travels. Please be alone when you use it, yes?"

Maybe that was the evil she was sensing; the Prism could pull in others who didn't want to come along.

She continued with the bookseller's instructions, placing the Prism in a shaft of sun that the skylight sent into the room. As the sun moved, the rectangle of light would move; it would function as a timer. She assumed that when the Prism was out of the light it would stop working. She settled down to wait for the Prism to work.

Ravven was in the ocean, seeing with the eyes of an orca. The Prism of Broken Light had brought her here, and it was strange, this feeling of being in the water but not being wet at all. She was curious what she looked like as an orca. She moved her pectoral fins to balance and steer and when she needed to dive, she used her fluke. It was powerful; one flick sent her into the depths.

There was a familiar voice near her that said, "Let me show you something." Ravven made the adjustment with her pectoral fins to turn to her right to see the orca queen. "Look at the light in the water and the silvery particles," the queen said. Columns of sunlight pierced the water like rods of silver and inside the rods were tiny sparking particles.

"Yes," Ravven said. "I see them."

'The water is beautiful, but you can't see the poison."

Ravven remembered in the last dream, the queen had said all the orcas were going to die.

"Is that what is killing all of you? The poison that I can't see?"

"Yes. It is killing the humpbacks slowly but it is killing orcas quickly. We don't have names for these poisons, but your species calls them microplastics, pesticides, and fire retardants. Do you know what those are?"

"Yes," Ravven said. "They're released into the ocean by human activity. But why are the orcas being poisoned faster?" All kinds of whales swam in the same water. It didn't make sense to Ravven that some would be poisoned faster.

The orca queen spoke in Ravven's mind. "The smallest animals take in smaller amounts of toxins from the water. Krill, they are like shrimp, take in the toxins, but because they are small, the toxicity is low. The humpback eat krill. Orcas eat bigger, more complex animals. We eat salmon and seals, sea lions, dolphins, porpoises and other whales. The bigger animals have higher levels of toxins. The poisons accumulate. Do you understand?"

"It seems clear," Ravven said.

"Orcas are at the top of the food chain. We have no predators. We eat everything else," the orca queen said.

"You eat everything, so all the toxins in what you eat are accumulating in you."

"Yes, you understand. Your scientists call this bioaccumulation. Let's go to the surface for a breath of air."

As they went up toward the silvery lawyer above them Ravven asked, "How do you know bioaccumulation is ongoing?"

Another voice joined the conversation. The humpback queen had arrived with her pod. "We know because we have studied the water and have felt the changes. We would like to communicate more with humans to tell them to stop, but we cannot."

"You're communicating with me now," Ravven said. "Everyone watched when you attacked the boats in the harbor."

"We don't approve of the boat attacks," the humpback queen said.

"But obviously, we do!" the orca queen chimed in.

Ravven somehow felt the humpback queen's irritation at that statement. "We don't know how to communicate with your species, Ravven Vaara. We have opened a channel with you, but you are the only one of your kind. You are one person. We don't know how you understand our language."

Ravven tried to sort that out. "I don't know, either. I am dreaming, or in a vision, or traveling outside of my body, I know that."

The orca queen spoke: "Don't overthink it. Keep dreaming or whatever it is that you're doing, and we will keep talking. Alright?"

"Alright." Ravven wanted to tell the whales about the Prism of Broken Light, but suspected that would complicate matters further, so she kept silent about it for now.

They dived deeper in the water. "I am not patient anymore," the orca queen said as they swam together. "We will end your rule. It is time to cut off electrical power to your species. Plunge you into the dark! Stop the machines! I know how to do it. I have a plan that I've discussed with my pod."

"Don't do that," the humpback queen broke in.

"The boat attacks are just practice," the orca queen said. "We can do a lot more damage. I know how. We have the will and the ways."

The humpback queen interrupted again. "Attacks are not the answer. We must communicate, not attack."

The orca queen continued as if the other queen hadn't said anything. "One of our pod died on your sad little beach."

"Was it because of the toxins he ate?" Ravven asked. "Bioaccumulation?"

"No, different toxins," the orca said. "Different problem. A new problem for us! There was an algae bloom. There is more of this kind of algae now that the ocean is hotter, which is also your fault."

"Not my fault personally," Ravven said.

"You can't escape responsibility," the orca said, pushing back.

Ravven was concerned that things might quickly get nasty down here in the water. It would be easy for the orca queen to kill Ravven with one swat from her fluke.

"Your species is the cause of our misery," the orca queen said. "We are dying in the ocean that we travel. The ocean kills us. Imagine if you died because of the air your breathed."

"That is already happening to some of us," Ravven said with as much caution as she could muster. She didn't want the queen any angrier than she already was.

"My juvenile swam as far as he could to beach himself where you would witness his death," the orca said.

"It was a sad moment for me and my students," Ravven offered. She was feeling helpless now. What could she do or say?

"Another juvenile in my pod decided to drown Renzo Kundera," the orca said.

Ravven couldn't believe it. "That was purposeful?"

"Of course it was purposeful! Just like your Youngs, our juveniles are impatient. They are taking action on their own. Soon we won't be able to control what they do," the orca queen said.

"I hope that's not true," the humpback queen said.

"It may as well be," the orca queen said. "We have your ear, Ravven Vaara. You alone can hear us. It's your responsibility to communicate this to your fellow humans. Whatever you're doing, if anything, isn't doing any good."

"I'm sorry," Ravven said. She may have been crying but she didn't know because she was in water. She felt the orca queen's anger rising again.

"Our juveniles are right to be impatient. The time for warnings is over. If it were up to me, I would kill all of you. Kill you all!"

The humpback broke in to stop the orca's bellicose thought stream. "It is not up to you. I do not approve. There will be a better way."

"No," the orca said. "Look at all the ways that we've already tried! Capsizing the boats was not enough. Knocking off the propellers was not enough. Broadcasting i am here was not enough and even broadcasting you must live with us as equals was not enough."

"I knew that was you," Ravven said, "and I told others."

"And what of it?" the orca snapped back. "You tell others, but they think you've lost your mind."

"That is sadly true," Ravven said.

Ravven snapped awake. It took her a moment to realize that she was upstairs in Kat's house. She was on a mat in the bedroom that she shared with Spaceman. She saw that the rectangle of sun had moved on the floor and was no longer shining on the Prism. As she had suspected, it had stopped working and she was delivered from the episode of astral travel.

She carefully took the Prism in her hands and replaced it in the book, closing the cover and returning the book to the shelf.

She remembered something that the orca had said about wanting to eliminate humans from the equation. "We will end your rule," the queen had said.

The orca queen had a tendency to get her way, Ravven realized, even over the objections of the humpback queen. When Ravven and the orca met the first time, the queen said they would be knocking the propellers from boats and capsizing others. This turned out to be true. They took credit for the words entering the minds of many people, I am here and you must live with us as equals. That had happened, also. The whale who tried to drown Renzo had a plan that thankfully did not work. Both the humpbacks and orcas had told Ravven about the poison in the water, plastics, fire retardants, and other chemicals that bioaccumulated, slowly poisoning the orcas who were at the top of the food chain. Also true. Almost laughably, there really was an otter who approached surfers and knocked them off their surfboards. And it was true that the otter sometimes took the boards afterward to ride a few waves herself.

So Ravven had good reason to believe that the orca queen's plan to end human rule would be put into action, even over the humpback queen's objections. Ravven worried about that. She thought of her parents, who loved the ocean so completely, even to the point of vanishing forever in it, and what they might think of a species that had become so angry with humans that it was prepared to eliminate them as rivals for the Earth. The juvenile orcas might stage their own revolt, and then it would be too late.

Chapter 044

n the evening, everyone at the house had dinner as a group. Meal packets again, but the conversation was lively. Ravven was talkative, holding a glass of wine, describing her latest conversations with the whales.

"They told me that the juvenile tried to drown you on purpose, Renzo," Ravven said.

Renzo was surprised. "No, really? When did you hear about that?"

"Yesterday," Ravven said. "They've lost control of their juveniles just like we can't control our Youngs."

"We never had control," Spaceman said. He held a glass of artificial water while the others had tea or wine. "I remember in the classes I taught—" he would have gone on with the story, but Renzo interrupted.

"Sorry, but...*what*? You heard this yesterday?"

Ravven nodded. "Yes, I left my body and was swimming with the orcas. They told me then." This stopped the flow of conversation. The room fell silent.

Then Renzo asked, "How did you do that? Get out of your body?" Bewilderment spread across his face.

Kat shot Ravven a look. *Don't you dare tell him.*

Ravven raised her eyebrows. *Why not?*

"Don't you two think it's impolite to trade thoughts like that?" Renzo asked, only half-kidding. He couldn't hear what they were thinking, of course, but had felt the weight of the silence.

"I can't go into it now," Ravven said with a glance to Kat. "But the orcas are angry that we've ruined their oceans. We've poisoned them. They want to punish us."

"And you defended us, I'm sure!" Renzo said. "It's not all humans who are the problem."

"I didn't defend us," Ravven said. *I defended myself, though.*

"Some of us are trying to ride bicycles in the cities. We do farm to table!" Kat thought that Renzo had a little too much wine, but he had a charming way of voicing these objections with a sparkle in his eyes.

Ravven sighed. "It's not enough, they say."

"Sometimes I just don't know," Renzo said, reaching to top off his wine glass with more red. It was artificial wine, not as good as the real stuff that Dave used to drink, but it did the trick. Kat poured herself some as well, setting aside her unfinished cup of tea.

"You should tell them next time that every individual action matters," Renzo said. "This wine is not terrible."

"That's what people have said for years," Spaceman said. "About change, not the wine."

"But it's all about the first person taking the first step," Kat said. "That's what you need to tell them, Ravven. It's about broad, systemic change involving everything."

Ravven gazed at Kat over the rim of her wineglass. "Isn't that what systemic means? Everything?" She waved the thought away. "The orcas have been patient for decades. They say they're done with patience now. Now, I want to know how we can explain that to people." She paused. "Without sounding like we've lost our minds."

Kat leaned in to make her point, gulping her wine to keep it from spilling; she'd filled her glass too much. "I mean that everything must change from the ground up. That's what we've always said. It's been our message from the Resistance from the beginning."

"Do you think so?" Ravven asked.

"Yes!" Kat insisted. "Look, we've lived in a place that grew all its own food. We've known people who lived off the grid. You want us to give up on comms, on the network—"

Renzo cut in. "But we're city people! Some of us love cities. The complexity, the density—"

Kat took back the floor. "But building cities has damaged everything else."

"We've run out of time for this conversation anyway," Ravven said. "They're going to do something drastic."

"Like what?" Kat asked.

"The queen orca said she was going to cut power, take us all off the grid, I think."

Renzo shrugged. "They've capsized boats."

"It's a big step up to take down everything," Spaceman said.

The conversation circled around those thoughts, and then, a little later, Kat and Renzo went upstairs together. When they reached the hallway with the bedrooms, Renzo paused. "Something is bothering me," he said. "Are Ravven's conversations real?"

"You mean, with the whales?"

Renzo was standing close to her. She could feel his breath on her. A scent of wine, somehow pleasant. "Or are they all in her head?" he added.

Kat met his eye. "Ravven has a vast consciousness. I've learned to trust what she says. But, in the end, we'll never know."

"I want proof," Renzo said.

He looked like he was going to kiss her. And then he did.

Kat got into it, feeling a ripple of excitement through her body, then pulled away. "Not tonight," she said.

"When?" he asked.

She leaned forward and kissed him again, putting even more passion into it, aware that she was encouraging both of them.

She heard Ravven and Spaceman coming up the stairs and broke away from Renzo. She nodded toward the middle bedroom that he was sleeping in. "Everything okay in there? Comfortable?" It sounded awkward to her. Renzo was biting his lip to keep from laughing.

"Sure," he managed. "It's okay." His eyes held questions that she wasn't willing to answer.

"Good, good, glad to hear it." *Don't be a clerk at the front desk of a hotel.* She brushed her hair from her eyes, a gesture she knew was her version of flirting, regretted it, and bumbled through a good night. "Have a good one. See you in the morning."

He smiled; there was a gleam in his eye. "Good night," he said and headed off to his room.

Kat watched him go but didn't allow herself to linger, in case he turned to look back at her. She didn't want to get caught watching him. But his body moved nicely. He was strong; she liked the muscles in his legs and butt.

Ravven and Spaceman were behind her.

"Good night," Kat said. They wished her a good night and she went into her room, certain that she had completely confused Renzo. That might be okay, since she was completely confused herself about how her feelings for him.

Chapter 045

Alon6's voice boomed, seeming to make his office walls vibrate. "What is this garbage?" His eyes were wide, seeming to push out of his screen. "This feed repeats. It's running in a loop."

"Not possible," Candice said.

"You can't tell, because you're human. But I can, because I've analyzed it more carefully. Look at it again!"

Candice looked. She gestured at the screen, brought up various stats and views: Volume of posts. Repetition of posts. Frequency. She might have noticed something irregular and was about to say so. Alon6's booming voice interrupted. He had patched himself in to broadcast over the building public address system.

"Sanchez! Get in here NOW."

After a moment, a bulky, muscular man strode in the room. Candice had never seen Sanchez before but had heard Alon6 speak of him.

"What's up, boss?" he said.

"What's UP?" As Alon6 launched into a tirade, Candice took a moment to sneak a glance at her comms to look up this man.

Sanchez, she read on her comms, was an early hire at MIND. Worked as Bradley's bodyguard, then worked his way up to the head of Input. Was responsible for all systems that feed MIND's data gathering. His office was just down the hall. Candice nodded at her screen and then moved her eyes to Sanchez. A résumé like that indicated an ambitious man working his way up. But Sanchez didn't seem ambitious. His big body was soft as he leaned back against the desk, crossing his arms, enduring Alon6's tirade about the Resistance feed they were monitoring. "It's slaze, it's misinformation, it's spoofing! That's what I pay you to find out and I want you to stop it," Alon6 shouted.

Sanchez sighed, deflating further, and gestured at the terminal screen. In a few seconds, he had what he wanted. "It's a spoofed feed, boss. They've found a way to loop it."

"That's what I said! Where's the real feed?"

Sanchez struggled. "I don't know."

"You don't know? If we're watching a spoofed feed and the real one is invisible to us, then we're looking at garbage. Where is your drone array now?"

"Still flying," Sanchez said. He gestured at the screen to check and then frowned. "The data looks good from all five."

Alon6 made a sound of exasperation. "The data is garbage. Your drones are monitoring the wrong feed. You're my top man in Input and your input is shit. Nobody knows more about the feeds than you do and you know how to do slaze. How could you let this happen?"

Candice thought that Alon6's statement wasn't true, because Nora2 knew more about slaze than this listless fellow. But Nora2 wasn't in the office today and Candice wondered for a moment where she was. Nora2 was always in the office.

Alon6 spit out his words: "Get on the next glidepath to Marin and go to Kat Keeper's house. Do it now! Find out what is going on. Get your drones flying and our access to their feed."

"They know who I am, boss. If I go, they will know we are monitoring them."

"They know we're monitoring them already. We need a show of force! That's you! You can bring the fear."

Sanchez let his gaze rest on Alon6's florid face, then flicked a skeptical look at Candice and left the office.

Ravven recognized the man trudging on the path approaching the house. It was Sanchez, the MIND employee who did all the dirty work. Aside from his regular job of stealing citizens' memories for MIND to use to train its AI, he handled enforcement bot ambushes that got Resistance protestors thrown in detention and the odd kidnapping attempt.

Sanchez was the kind of man who did what he was instructed to do, but Ravven noticed that something about his movement toward the house was wrong. He walked as though pushing through heavy air.

Ravven set down the trowel she was using to dig in the smoke-scented earth. She had been bent over, gardening, wearing an air unit to keep the ash out of her lungs, trying to bring back the plants that protected the house from fire. This was something she did between classes to clear her mind. She stood, pulled down the air unit, and put her consciousness into Sanchez's mind.

The disorder she found confused her. She expected to sense a dark clarity of vision, but his thoughts were enveloped in a haze of sadness.

She called out. "Sanchez. What do you want?"

He stopped moving and his eyes widened with surprise. "You know me?"

"Of course I know you. State your business."

He blinked at her words and forced a strange smile. Ravven assumed that he was used to people fearing him and backing down. Instead of answering her right away, he looked up, scanning the sky for drones. He saw them. Five in his array.

"Your drones are there," Ravven confirmed.

"You have some kind of slaze going. You know that's illegal," Sanchez said.

Ravven laughed. There was no slaze, but she decided to mislead him about it to draw him out. "We have a slaze generator and it's confusing your drones. We live by our own law here. We're preparing to withdraw from the domain. You should know that already. You clearly don't, otherwise you wouldn't have come here to bother us and put yourself in danger." The part about preparing to withdraw from the domain was as fanciful as the slaze.

Sanchez bristled, his mouth curled into a sneer. "You can't operate under your own authority," he said.

"We can, and you can't stop us, Mr. Sanchez," Ravven said cheerfully. "And I will be putting up a resonance field soon as well."

"What the hell is that?"

She was glad he took the bait and made up some nonsense about what a resonance field might do. "I generate the resonance field inside my mind, by humming. Humming is a powerful engine of consciousness, Mr. Sanchez. My 2 PM meditation class will start soon and we'll all be humming together to block your attempts to monitor us."

Now Sanchez looked confused. Something about Ravven's confident flow of words seemed to make him dizzy. He swayed slightly. Yet Ravven wasn't doing anything special.

She spoke inside his mind. *You're not used to anyone standing up to you, Mr. Sanchez.*

Getting inside his head bothered him. She could see that her words made his skull feel crowded. He waved his hand in front of his face as if to shoo away an insect.

"You still haven't told me what you've come here to do, Mr. Sanchez."

"I told you already. I'm here to stop the slaze," he replied.

"So that MIND can monitor our network? No, that won't happen," Ravven said. "You can't stop us. We have our own network now." It pained her a little to brag about the network. She'd never felt that the network was the answer, but she also was enjoying that it pained Sanchez to hear her brag about it. For good measure she sent her voice into his head again. *I'm not afraid of you. None of us are afraid of you, anymore.*

Then she spoke aloud. "The Resistance is not going to die, Mr. Sanchez. In fact, you almost died. Remember your last kidnapping attempt? You were chasing Kat Keeper and her friend Emily Cloudfactor in the glidepath and there was a crash."

He wobbled again. Ravven was inside his mind, watching himself collapsed in a bloody heap on the floor of a glidepath car. Dying. Or close to it. He played these pictures in his mind and his heart rate spiked in panic.

"You're lucky you survived," Ravven remarked. "Would you like to sit down?" She gestured to a nearby bench in the garden.

"Yes," Sanchez said.

She sat beside him, perhaps too close, and looked at the sadness in his eyes. "You have been a warrior for a long time. And now you are tired," she said.

Sanchez stared ahead. "I don't know what I feel." His voice had an exaggerated flatness as if he was struggling to keep it so.

"I am an empath," Ravven said. "I know what you are feeling."

Sanchez frowned at that. "You don't know anything about me."

Ravven looked away. They both gazed at the garden for a few moments. It was mostly burned but with a few green shoots poking up through the black soil. "Not only are you tired, but you are also on the wrong side of history, Mr. Sanchez. I think you've realized that you've served evil for too long. Now you are tired of it."

"Not true," Sanchez said. His voice was quiet as if he was speaking to himself.

"But it is true," she said. "Or you wouldn't be speaking with me now. You would be fighting me or trying to get your drones sorted out. Or even pulling out your comms and ordering reinforcements. You've always been a man of action. You're doing nothing now."

Sanchez appeared about to say something but decided not to speak. Ravven looked into his mind and saw that he was thinking about his wife. His wife's name was Wanda. They used to own a vineyard together, in Argentina, before the Change.

"Let's try something, Mr. Sanchez. Let's pretend you never went to work for MIND. That your life with Wanda took a different path after you left Argentina."

Sanchez startled. "How do you know her name? Or where we came from?"

Ravven just smiled at him. "You can call me a witch if you like."

"This is a trick, a mind trick." He stood, ready to leave.

Ravven spoke to stop him. "Wait. The only trick is the one that you're playing on yourself."

Sanchez's face hardened. "Manipulative," he said as if to himself. He looked in the sky, making visual contact again with his drones. "You have some kind of consciousness control working here."

Ravven gazed at him and again spoke into his mind.

You may go anytime, Mr. Sanchez.

Ravven sensed pictures forming in his mind as he retrieved a memory.

He sat back down. Suddenly, he really did look very tired. "My wife and I used to have a winery back in Argentina. You don't need any magic to know that. You could just look me up." He looked at his hands. "Making wine is a beautiful thing, but I haven't done it in a long time."

"The Change ruined your vineyard."

He looked startled that she knew and then nodded to confirm.

"You and Wanda were climate refugees, but you didn't call yourselves that. You came to the North American continent and became a handler for wealthy people, as bodyguards were called. You had famous clients, movie stars and such, but when you met Bradley15 Power you saw an opportunity for yourself."

Sanchez nodded, not questioning anymore where Ravven's knowledge came from. "I was ambitious," he confirmed. "I convinced Bradley that I could be head of Input at MIND."

"You were in charge of collecting thoughts."

"Yes, but just admin. I never designed or invented anything. That was all Bradley. He was a genius."

"You miss him, don't you?"

Sanchez sighed. "I do miss him." He shook his head slowly. "When Bradley's human form was dead, the avatar that replaced him only thought about MIND. No attention for anything else." He paused.

"Alon6 is worse. He has no substance, no soul at all. His avatar only sees a future where MIND is successful." He paused again. "I don't know why I'm telling you this." He looked into Ravven's face. "I feel strange. It feels strange to say even that." He shrugged.

Ravven smiled. "It's not strange at all. You've needed to unburden yourself. Probably for years. You don't like to complain, as you think of it."

His mouth was set into a line. "True."

"Do you feel lighter now that you've said those things?"

"I don't know." Sanchez got up from the bench suddenly, as if remembering something. "I came here for a reason, you know."

"You did. But you don't want to do it because the evil of MIND has worn you down."

Sanchez swayed on his feet as if Ravven's words had mass that pushed at him. "No."

"You don't have to acknowledge anything," Ravven said. "Later on, when you are about to fall asleep next to your wife, you'll think of the vineyard. You might tell her you'd like to start another one."

Sanchez raised his chin at her with a hint of defiance. "I'm not going to resign from MIND."

"No," Ravven said. "You won't have to. MIND is rotting from within. You can see that, can't you?"

"No," Sanchez said and he looked up to the sky, making that reassuring contact with his surveillance drones. They were there, gathering the data of the false feed. When he looked back to Ravven his eyes again held a deep sadness. He avoided her steady gaze and said, "I'd like my winery back."

Ravven said, "I think there must be a varietal that you can grow in these hills. With all the money you've earned at MIND you could buy something and start a winery again."

"Alon6 won't let me quit," Sanchez said quickly, but then he looked back at the hills. They were bare and burned black. "They were beautiful once," he said.

"They will come back," Ravven said. "Nature renews itself. It's remarkable, isn't it?"

Sanchez shook his head, once, sharply, shaking off a dream. "This is some kind of bullshit slaze you've got me in," he growled, then walked away, starting back down to the harbor, to catch the ferry to the glidepath station, to return to El Segundo.

"Don't become an empty man, Mr. Sanchez," Ravven called out.

He walked and didn't answer.

Ravven called out again. "What will you tell Alon6?"

Now those words struck Sanchez like an arrow in the back. He stopped walking suddenly, not turning around but with his shoulders hunched up. Then he put defiance into his back, again standing taller. But his thoughts gave him away. Ravven heard him think, *I'll tell Alon6 that I quit.*

Sanchez kept on marching to the harbor until he was out of Ravven's line of sight.

She smiled to herself. *MIND rots from within.*

Chapter 046

ora2 was finishing her morning routine. She used ClarityCrawl to cleanse the Feed of any news about the Resistance. She checked the jamming circuits to be sure the Resistance met with maximum disruption when trying to use the Feed to communicate.

These tasks felt heavy, requiring extra effort to even breathe, like she was moving under water. She released a heavy sigh, swiped the screen to darkness, and then felt a presence in the office.

It was the guy from downstairs. She'd met him once but had forgotten his name. He looked as if he was going to do something bad to her. She stood up immediately. "What is it?"

"You don't know why I'm here?" he said, trying to sound pleasant but failing.

She touched her right temple and his data came up. Tristan Kundera. Cybersecurity specialist. He was assigned to research the disinformation vids. Also had purview in surveillance.

His steady smile was unnerving. "Did you find out what you needed to know about me, dear Nora2?" His mouth, which she couldn't stop looking at for some reason, was formed into a sour little smirk. He took a step toward her. She took a step back. "Don't be afraid. If I touch you, I know you'll like it."

She hated the sound of that but knew that it was true. He must be a shape-shifter.

He nodded, as if agreeing with her. "I've been very busy behind the scenes. When you want to defame somebody in the Resistance, I'm the one who makes it worse by digging up the dirt. I have my fingers in a lot of things around here. I know so much! Like it's been just a couple of days since Sanchez walked out of his office and didn't come back. He quit!" His laugh was hollow.

"That's not true," Nora2 said.

"But it is. Alon6 is stewing about it, trying to think about his next move.

You can check the personnel records, and you'll see that Sanchez has been wiped from them."

Certain that Tristan was lying, she was about to tap her temple to activate the records when he reached for her again.

"Look," he began.

"Get away from me," she said.

"I've done a lot of bad things," he said, his tone shifting slightly into self-pity she thought. "And you've done bad things, too."

Nora2's mind raced. She had worked many late nights here. There should be a switch to press to summon Security. A hidden alarm button under her desk. She tried to imperceptibly edge closer to the door. Maybe she could run out. There was a call number for Security. She would have to have her comms unit in her hand to make that call. She struggled to recall the number because she'd never had to use it.

"I know my presence here has been kind of under wraps," he was saying. "Now I want to change sides." He paused. "Like you."

"What?" she asked. She didn't know where he was going with that. "What are you saying?"

"I want to join the Resistance like you already have."

This was a trick. A trap. She had to get out of here.

Tristan continued, "I've been watching. I know what's going on here every day. I have access to everything that goes on."

Nora2 gestured to close down her screens. They went dark. "I'm going to call Security and have you escorted out." She had suddenly remembered the number to call.

"And tell them what? That I want to join the Resistance? I would only say that you already have. That would get you in trouble and we could spend time together in detention. Share a cell. How would you like that?"

He reached out and she slapped his hand away.

"Creep." She hated him, the glint in his eyes, that ripe mouth, the muscles that moved under his tight shirt. The whiff of gloating seeped through his skin. Her emotions churned. She was certain that he was modded and was casting his personality field around her like a stuffy coat. It was hard to breathe.

"Stay back," Nora2 said.

"Look," he said again, and gestured to her terminal screen. "I'll pull up my own records so you can see." The screen flickered as they came up. "My attendance had been poor. I've missed days at work because I've been depressed lately." His voice sounded velvety smooth to her. His eyes, once dark and bottomless, now were warm and friendly. "I work on secret programs, the dark ones, and that can get depressing. I have a twin brother. I'm close to him and he disappeared for a while, deported. He's back now but he won't talk to me. I've spent a lot of time alone in my man cave. Sad." He wrapped his personality field around her and she felt sorry for him for just a moment. She delayed calling Security and waited for him to speak again.

He leaned in to speak quietly. "I know who you are, Nora2, and what you're really doing. And I want to join you. I want to help. Have you ever heard of someone who goes by @deletedaccount?"

He seemed to enjoy the shocked look that drew from her. "You're not the only one monitoring the Feed and keeping watch over that little private server network. I know who had the idea to use a spoofed feed." He leaned in so close that she thought their faces would touch. "I know it's you."

She slapped him. Hard. Across the face.

He staggered back, rubbing his jaw. "Nice one. Point to you." His cheek was blooming a mottled red.

"I think you should leave," Nora2 said.

"Too late for that. Too late for everything you were thinking about doing. I'm going to help the Resistance. I'm turning good, which means my twin brother will turn bad. You haven't met my brother Renzo. He's Kat's boyfriend or aspires to be. You know how that works with cultured twins like us? You should tell Kat about it, because when I turn good and he turns bad, she won't believe it."

"I think everything you say is a lie."

"Not quite. And here's a piece of truth for you. If I figured you out, how soon before everyone else here does? Do what you really want to do, before it's too late and you're put into detention." He caught her in his gaze, steady and hypnotic.

She wanted to fall into his eyes but stopped and made herself take a step away from him.

"Do what you need to do," he said again and then turned and left her office.

Kat's eyes popped open. Insomnia again. It always got worse when she was dealing with unresolved events with the people around her. Her unsorted feelings for Renzo were at the top of the heap. Ravven was struggling with delusion or enlightenment or both at once. Maybe enlightenment was a form of delusion.

She squirmed on her mat and it conformed to her, hugging closer. Too close. She puffed out a breath and pushed the mat away. She sat up and stretched out again.

She was annoyed that Renzo, Spaceman and Ravven were behaving like old friends when relationships were supposed to be hard; you had to work at them, suffer and strive. *Ha, self-mockery.* She laughed at herself, tried to find some humor in it, and almost succeeded.

She tried everything to get to sleep, all her old tricks. She put a projection of stars on the ceiling and set a timer for a suitable moment for the projection to show the scene of dawn. She studied the stars for what seemed like hours, then closed her eyes and studied the inside of her eyelids, red with tangles of blood vessels, opened her eyes again to watch the projected stars wheeling slowly in their simulation of time. She pretended that the stars allowed her to see the actual passage of time. It was a superpower of sorts, and she tried to let it cheer her, but it was an incredibly annoying superpower to have. She would rather sleep. She was exhausted as she waited for sleep, a familiar paradox. She mentally clicked down her list of things that were not resolved, despite telling herself that it was a terrible idea, but then—at last—a good idea popped into her mind. She would go to the headquarters of MIND and confront everyone there. Demand that they erase all their misinformation vids. Even better: Get the Universal back. *We want the Universal back.* She liked the sound of that. It would mean a lot to Spaceman. And since Dave had left the Universal in her care, it would mean a lot to her.

Good gesture, good idea, but it woke her up even more. She decided she would wait for the scheduled artificial glow of sunrise to creep up the walls. When the orange light overpowered the star projection on her ceiling, she would get up whether she had slept or not and start working out how to confront the people in El Segundo.

She fell asleep at some unknown point in the night and abruptly woke to a room filled with real morning light that made the fake dawn on her ceiling appear dim. She thought it was late and checked her comms for the time. It was 8:30. If she got out quickly, she could take a walk before it got too hot or the wind kicked up the dust and ash. Then her mind would be clear and she could plan her visit to El Segundo. Who else should be there? When would the best time be?

Thinking too much already. Slow down.

Her mind was crowded with excitement. She didn't stop in the UV to clean off, but went right for the closet, where she plucked a sunsuit from the charger, settled it over her shoulders, pulled on matching track pants and slipped on her running shoes. She grabbed an air unit.

She expected it to be hot outside because it was morning and she should go back to get sunglasses. The sunlight assaulted her when she unscrewed the front portal. She hadn't walked twenty steps toward the path when she heard a voice call her name.

"Kat Keeper."

The voice was familiar. "Who is that?"

Nora2 stepped out from behind a blackened tree near the house.

It took Kat a moment to find words. "What are you doing here?"

Nora2 returned Kat's stare, projecting defiance and humility. Kat entered her mind and saw that Nora2 was about to say that she was the person called @deletedaccount.

"You've been messaging me. It was you."

"Yes, it was me," Nora2 said, permitting herself a small smile.

Kat witnessed Nora2's thoughts again. "I think you are here to negotiate your exit from MIND," Kat said with wonder.

"Yes," Nora2 said.

The two took the measure of each other. Kat let a moment pass between them, then said, "If you're really here to defect, then you have to come in and tell me why."

They didn't go in the house but sat on the front steps instead. Nora2 told her that Tristan Kundera had come to her and said he knew that she was providing information to Kat. "He knew it was my idea to make a spoofed feed. He'd been watching me. He basically dared me to leave." Kat saw the struggle in the other woman's eyes. "I was unhappy. I didn't want to be there. He took away any reason I had to stay."

"Would you have left on your own?"

"I don't know," Nora2 said. "Probably." She paused. "Something else I have to tell you.

"Tristan said he was joining the Resistance. He was turning good and that meant his brother Renzo was turning bad."

Kat met her gaze and it appeared to her that Nora2 was telling the truth. "Well, I haven't seen Tristan around here. And I'm glad I haven't. I don't know about Renzo turning bad. He seems...okay."

"Do you think so?"

"Yes," Kat said.

Nora2 looked away and let out a breath. "I am not okay anymore. Something is happening to my mod. I was able to follow orders for a while but now I don't want to do what Alon6 tells me. I can't shape-shift any more. I feel all sorts of things I didn't feel before."

"You look different," Kat said, remembering that when Nora2 was in power of her mod, she was blond, seemed taller, and had a golden color to her eyes. Now she seemed small, withdrawn, with dark hair and dark eyes.

"I'm not the same person now. I don't know who I want to be," Nora2 said.

Kat didn't know what to say to that. "We've known each other for a long time," she began. "I don't think we've ever met in person." She had seen Nora2 only on screens. Kat entered the other woman's mind again, hoping to find more details about her change of heart.

Nora2 sensed the intrusion. "What are you looking for in my mind?"

Kat was surprised, wide-eyed. "You can feel that?"

"I think so," Nora2 said. "That's also new. I feel like I'm not the owner-operator of my own body." Her expression twisted awkwardly, her mouth starting to form a smile that turned into a sob. She roughly wiped a tear.

"Has that ever happened to anyone before? A mod just stopped working?"

Nora2 shrugged. "I don't know. Do you know what happened to Sanchez?" Nora2 told her that Sanchez had resigned from MIND and wanted to start a winery again. "Strange, it seemed to come out of nowhere."

Kat took a moment with that. "Very strange. But I can tell you this. Alon6 is mad about Sanchez, and now that you're also here he's going to lose it completely." It occurred to her to ask, "Do you feel safe here?"

"No," Nora2 admitted. "But I don't think I'd be safe anywhere now."

Kat hesitated but then put her hand on Nora2's hand. "Come inside," she said.

PART 006

Chapter 047

andice was crouched over the induction charging pad, gesturing frantically to start a charge cycle. Alon6 locked his eyes on her and huffed, "Humans! So slow! I'm ashamed to have been one myself."

It was 7 AM. He'd ordered her to get the BodySuit charged right away and she had to explain why it wasn't ready.

"This suit breaks all the laws governing AI. It had to be made completely off the grid, with old crap gear. It's a cranky piece of work."

"Is that the best explanation you have for me, Candice?"

He watched her yellow eyes flash, pushing down the anger. Then she nodded to signal acquiescence. It had been a long night for her, he noticed the dark smudges under her eyes, and still this damn thing wouldn't charge correctly. "I have it working, but not as well as you'd like."

"Pathetic! It's time to go."

He knew that Candice had figured out where he wanted to go. All MIND employees had a location chip implanted in the back of their neck. Part of their intake procedure. Nora2 had her chip put in more than three years ago. Alon6 had mapped her location to Kat Keeper's house in Marin. He was going to get Nora2 back, dead or alive.

"I'm almost ready," Candice said.

"Put me together! I see an arm over there and a leg over here. Do it now before we lose the element of surprise!"

Candice flinched in reaction to Alon6's bluster, then tilted the BodySuit on the supporting frame so that it stood vertically. It was a thick, brutish form currently without a head. She remedied that by carefully lifting Alon6's MindVessel and carrying his scowling face over to the suit, setting it on top, and snapping the catches.

"I love corporality!"

She barely suppressed her smile; he was glad she still found him funny. He could fire off a witticism or two! She fetched the arm from across the room and attached it, then the foot. Alon6 tested them, lifting the BodySuit's arms and stomping the feet. "It's working great! I don't know what your problem is."

He flung his arms out and Candice had to backpedal to avoid being struck. "You may notice a problem with the control surfaces," she began but he cut her off.

"I'll deal with it, Candice. Don't stand in the way of the future!" He moved to shove her with a jerk of his robo arms. "I'm going down to the glidepath. Delay the train another ten minutes so it will arrive just as I get into the station."

He didn't listen to her confirmation and turned to stomp from the room, the heavy tread of the BodySuit causing terminals on the desks in the room to jiggle. Candice and Caleb had made the suit even bigger than before and it really did feel great. It was an intimidating two and a half meters tall and a meter and a half at its widest point. White, with black trim, lightweight aluminum and magnesium, with some flexible plastic parts at the joints.

Before Alon6 cleared the door, he turned at the last moment to catch Candice's expression. She looked at him with an uneasy mix of horror and pride. "Thank you for your hard work on the BodySuit," he said and thought it sounded real, like what any good manager would say.

Alon6 had a surprise waiting for him as he exited the MIND building. Tristan and Renzo were blocking his path.

"Not another step," Tristan said.

Alon6's laugh sounded tinny coming from his audio port. "Is this a joke?"

"We're here to stop you," Renzo said.

A bubble of dark laughter from Alon6. "Clever boys!" There was a moment's pause as he processed and his eyes rolled upward. "Ah ha, I see now. Tristan, you monitored Candice's terminal and then you called over your twin Renzo to help. Brave of you, Renzo, for hurrying over. The cultured twins are going to save Nora2! You. Pathetic. Losers. Tristan, remind me to fire you when I get back, if you have the guts to hang around here. Now run away."

The brothers stood their ground. "Step aside," Tristan said, "and we won't need to hurt you."

Alon6's motions were awkward as he stepped forward. "Don't be a fool." He moved his arm, knocking Tristan to the ground. "Whoops. Didn't mean to do that!"

Renzo didn't have time to get out of the way as Alon6 also swept him aside, a crack to the jaw that sent Renzo tumbling, scraping his face on the pathway when he hit the ground.

Another tinny laugh. "Sorry, not sorry! My mechanics are not very accurate, boys!" A few steps forward and Alon6's heavy foot landed on Tristan's hand accompanied by the sickening sound of cracking bone. Tristan's face twisted in pain.

"How does that feel, twin boy?"

With a grunt Tristan grasped Alon6's foot, a poor choice, since Alon6 began to shake it, rattling Tristan here and there like a limp doll, and finally flicking him off. When Tristan landed there issued a wet gurgle from his mouth. His head was at an unnatural angle as his eyes went dull and then saw nothing.

Renzo was frozen in place as he watched his brother die.

"You're not the warrior Tristan was." Alon6 reached for him but Renzo ran.

Chapter 048

Renzo was on Kat's comms screen looking terrified.

"Where are you?"

"In El Segundo," he said, adding babble and parts of words.

"Wait, wait, slow down. You say he is in his MindVessel?"

"No, he's corporal! He's on the glidepath now. He's coming to get Nora2 back. Maybe kill her, I don't know." Renzo gulped in air but it didn't seem to help him find his breath.

Kat tried to focus on his scraped and bloody face on her screen. "What happened to your face?"

Renzo was exasperated, flailing his hands. "Tristan is dead."

"What?" Kat exclaimed. "How?"

Renzo brushed the question away. The air went out of him. He sagged, unable to say anything more. Then his picture blipped off.

Kat shoved her comms in her pocket, slapped a gesture at the spoofed feed she was working on to darken her monitor, and raced downstairs to find Nora2. She was in the kitchen, looking like she had just gotten up from her mat in the living room and was opening the kitchen cabinets looking for breakfast. "Alon6 is coming," Kat said. "He killed Tristan and he's coming for you."

A moment later Kat was upstairs with Nora2, first knocking, then banging on the guest room door to wake Ravven and Spaceman. Kat filled them in with a few words.

"A BodySuit?" Ravven asked. "What is that?" She wasn't quite awake yet, moving to sit upright on her sleeping mat. She and Spaceman, Kat noticed, had joined their mats. When two people intentionally slept together, they joined their mats using a selection in the mat software menu.

Nora2 gave the worst-case scenario. "Your doors won't stop Alon6 in a BodySuit. He can break through walls."

Ravven nodded once and spoke in an even voice. "Kat, what weapons do you have to repel this madman in a BodySuit?"

Kat opened her mouth to speak but could think of nothing. She took a protective step toward Nora2. "We have to hide her. He's coming to take her back."

"And when he doesn't find Nora2, he will storm through here like a beast and harm anyone who gets in his way," Ravven said.

"We'll fight him," Spaceman said. He scrubbed his hands over his face, trying to wake up more. He hitched up his black boxers. He wore a black t-shirt that revealed a slight paunch at the gut.

"I can leave. I'll go somewhere," Nora2 said.

"No, we promised you asylum," Ravven said, and stood. She was wearing a long, flowing white nightdress. "Come, everyone, sit with me," she said, moving to an open place on the floor. "All of you. Everyone. Sit with me. Gather here."

Spaceman moved to join her.

Kat was exasperated at how easily Spaceman did what Ravven asked, and he still looked half-asleep. "Ravven! We can't sit with you now! We have to lock down the house." Kat was still trying to think of anything she had that could be used as a weapon. A pot or pan. A synthetic rubber hose for artificial water. A shovel with a sharp edge.

Ravven smiled. "Kat, my dear, I have a plan. We are going to defend the house and protect Nora2."

"By sitting?"

Ravven's smile remained gently curved. "We have sent a thought package before. We will do it again."

"What's a thought package?" Nora2 asked, quirking her brow.

Ravven was taking her place on the mat she used for meditation, assuming a cross-legged position. "Please, sit with us. Bring that mat over here." She gestured to Nora2 who did as she was told. "You asked about a thought package. It is a compressed gathering of our intentions, focusing on something we want to do. It is our will flying in the air."

Nora2's smile looked frozen on her face. She didn't really understand, Kat saw; nevertheless, she pulled over the other mat, sat down and crossed her legs, mimicking Ravven. Spaceman was on his own mat, eyes closed. The absurdity of the situation inspired Kat to think harder about weapons. "We don't have a demolator, but we can stand in his way and stop him. We can fight!"

Nora2 was already shaking her head. "He's already killed Tristan and hurt Renzo. You won't be able to stop Alon6 now, even if you had a demolator."

Ravven nodded agreement. "If we don't take the right action now, Tristan's death will have no meaning and any one of us may be the next to die. Will you use a butter knife to stop a madman in a BodySuit?"

"You can use Bajutsu," Kat said, not wanting to give up yet. "You took a guy down with a single blow to the throat."

Ravven laughed. "Impressive! I collapsed a windpipe, but that move will not work on a BodySuit. It is not a human. It has no windpipe. It is a monster machine."

Of course, Ravven was right.

"My heroics were for that time, Kat. This is now. Sit with me. Join hands. I need everyone to help." She extended her hands.

Spaceman, trusting her, took her hand. He extended his other hand to Nora2.

She hesitated.

"Join us, Nora2. I need everyone. All must join." Ravven turned again to Kat: "Kat, join."

Kat remained standing. "No! We don't know how much time we have left. We're wasting time!" Again, she thought what could be weaponized. They had hot water. They could throw hot water on the BodySuit. Why hadn't she thought about weapons before? Poor planning.

Ravven spoke again. "Kat, my dear warrior friend, give me four minutes to prove what our thought package will do. If it fails, we can brainstorm, if that's what you would like." Ravven gazed steadily at her. "Warrior!" Ravven's lips curled around the word with not a little sarcasm. "You have nothing to lose. Join us now." Ravven held out her hand once more.

Kat's face was tight. She huffed displeasure and gave in, sitting on the bare floor, crossing her legs, joining the others.

"Everyone, make this sound with me." Ravven began to hum. Spaceman and Nora2 joined her in the gentle, persistent sound.

Kat couldn't resist rolling her eyes, and she wanted to catch a glance from Nora2, shoot some skepticism her way, but the former MIND employee's eyes were tightly closed as she hummed. Spaceman hummed ardently, his lips puckered absurdly, buzzing like a trumpeter's in his black outfit. Now Ravven was glaring at Kat, so she closed her eyes and hummed with the others.

As Ravven had indicated, they'd done this before, when they were part of the original Resistance circle in New York. They hummed to send a prayer of destruction. It seemed as absurd then as it did now to Kat, but in New York, after humming for more than an hour, Bradley and Alon6 had died in an explosion in space aboard the ship they traveled in.

Ravven was convinced that they'd caused the deaths.

For Kat it was, surely, a weird coincidence. She didn't believe that anyone could send a prayer of destruction just by humming, just as it didn't seem than humming now would stop Alon6. But Ravven had her ways, Kat had to admit. She allowed herself a bit of grudging respect.

Kat eased one eye open to spy Ravven glaring at her again, having picked up Kat's thoughts. It was almost comical how well Ravven knew Kat. Kat nodded once, closed her eyes, tried to clear her mind, and hummed with the others.

The bedroom filled with the sound. Ravven's voice was in Kat's mind.

Don't fight it. And do stay on task, Kat.

When Kat opened her eyes to sneak a peek, she thought she noticed the walls of the room bowing outward slightly, pushed by the force of their collective humming. But she blinked, and that mirage, or whatever it was, vanished.

Chapter 049

Alon6 was filled with happiness. Despite Candice's worries, the BodySuit was functioning perfectly. Not only was it bigger and more stable, but helpful information appeared in Alon6's line of sight, superimposed maps to show him the path ahead, estimated travel time to Kat's house, and changes in elevation to help him anticipate any inclines and walk steadily.

He had tromped over to the glidepath station and watched with delight as the other passengers backed away in terror. A 2.5-meter-tall robot could have that effect on people. Alon6 snarled at them, just to make it worse. "Step back!" he shouted, followed by his disturbing cackle of a laugh.

Candice did as he asked, and she even had the glidepath wait until he arrived. He had the glidepath car to himself all the way to Marin, riding in a crouch due to his height. When he got off at the Marin station, people went running when they saw him. "Run! Run you fools. Alon6 has come to destroy the Resistance!"

He thought about hailing a hovercraft to drive him over to Kat's house, but he had to dump that idea because the BodySuit was too big to fit in the passenger seat of any of the hovercraft waiting in the pickup queue. No problem. He would take a ferry.

The BodySuit's hands were the hands of a giant; Alon6 enjoyed flexing them, sensing their power. He tried them out by pulling out a vid screen from its mount as he left the glidepath station. It came away easily, in a flash of sparking wires. He held the vid screen in his hands for a moment, lifted it over his head and crumpled it up like paper before letting it drop to the floor.

When Alon6 boarded the autonomously piloted ferry, he enjoyed watching the other passengers scramble off. Walking the deck as the ferry departed, he noticed more improvements in the BodySuit from the last time he had tried it. Yes, his hands were a bit awkward and hard to control, but the feet of the

BodySuit were now perfectly counterbalanced with the slight roll of the deck. He walked smoothly, heavily, but quickly. His vision was better than he remembered. He could see in an arc that was more than 180 degrees, and ahead a great distance across the bay to Kat's house, the Resistance stronghold, on its little hill over the harbor. As he looked across the water, he thought that the BodySuit was probably not waterproof.

"But I won't be going for any swims," he said and laughed to himself.

Just for fun, as the ferry approached the dock on Kat's side of the bay, Alon6 tried out a roar and it came out sounding like a scream mixed with a bellow; the few people in the harbor ran away. He continued up the path to the house, glancing at the map that had helpfully appeared in his visual field, stepping through any muddy sections that appeared in the path. The walking gait of the suit was so smooth, he hardly had to look down at all to see where the BodySuit's feet were landing. He thought that when he got back to MIND headquarters, after grabbing Nora2, killing her if he had to, and also after destroying the house and everyone in it (*why not?*) he would give Candice Clonk a raise. This was going to be a good day for MIND.

Filled with a sense of triumph, Alon6 didn't notice the red ants that gathered at his feet and followed him on the trail. Soon the ants became so dense they appeared to be a moving cloud of red covering his feet and legs. They crawled into the workings of the BodySuit to infiltrate every crack where two pieces of metal came together, and all the seams of the plastic composites that made up the feet and legs of the BodySuit. The ants were small; this was easy for them; and they started to eat the plastic parts of the suit. There was a humming sound in the air, Alon6 sensed. *What was that?* He didn't know.

Alon6 began to notice that his steps weren't as steady and solid as before. He assumed that something was changing about the sensors in the suit or maybe the terrain. He gestured to make an adjustment, making the sensors more sensitive and tuning up his accelerometers, but this made it worse: His feet were landing wide of the path now and he was stumbling on rocks, having fallen off the path entirely. He was going somewhere, but not where he wanted to go.

His feet were not obeying him any longer. Then he noticed the ants were so thick on his legs, and now on his arms too, that he appeared dipped in red paint.

He cried out in surprise. "What the fuck?" He thought that he heard the words i am here.

At the house, a thin smile passed over Ravven's lips as she and the others continued to hum. Kat wondered if the humming had become louder or had multiplied itself if that were possible; it was painfully pounding at her eardrums. She looked up to the skylight and was surprised to see that a swarm of bees had joined them on the other side of the glass. They gathered outside, so dense as to block out the sun. The room darkened. Honeybees, Kat thought. She snuck another look at Ravven.

Ravven's eyes were closed. She made a sudden, rough gesture, flinging her arms outward. The bees seemed to notice and the swarm flew away. The light came back to the room and the humming quieted.

Alon6 in his BodySuit stumbled off the trail entirely, not able to control his movements, ants all over his limbs, tripping over rocks, splashing into mud, crashing into low-hanging tree branches. Many of the branches were still black with soot from the fire and they snapped easily, leaving black smudges on the crisp white of the BodySuit. He seemed to be ascending slightly now, headed toward a wooden railing of some kind. The helpful display on his line of vision wasn't as helpful anymore; it flickered and disappeared.

He remembered that he could communicate with Candice; she had to know about this control surface aberration.

He opened a channel and said, "Candice, what's going on? Can't you fix this?" There was no response. A swarm of bees was all around him. He swatted as they circled his head, blocking his vision. A few dozen of the bees came in through cracks in the suit opened by the ants to sting him. Of course, he was not made of flesh, but of plastic and metal, so there was no swelling. But his sensors were registering pain, simulated pain of course; nonetheless a distraction. "Candice, turn off the sensors! I can't think."

Bees grouped around his eye sensors and darkened his vision. He was blind as he heard the words i am here again.

"Candice, is that you? Are you here?" Alon6 bellowed. "Candice!"

He reached to the chest area of the BodySuit and tore off the cover, his big hands groping for some controls that he knew must be there. He threw the chest cover away and it clattered on the path. "Candice, desensitize! Turn off my pain sensors, my touch sensors! Turn it all off!" His robot chest was open, a mass of circuit boards visible.

The swarm of bees clogged his audio ports, making him deaf as well as blind. He stumbled ahead. His vision cleared slightly; he saw that there was a railing ahead of him and he couldn't stop himself from walking closer and closer to it. He reached his big hands toward it; it would provide stability. A moment later, he saw that the railing was part of a wooden stairway. He reached out to snag the railing in his hands. He knew he could do it and hang on tight. But his body jerked to the right and he missed the railing and the stairs entirely. He stepped off a cliff and walked into the air.

His sensors registered that he was no longer touching the ground. He produced a strangled cry. His sensors told him that he was tumbling over and over for four seconds, a long drop.

The beach where the orca had died rapidly met Alon6's tumbling BodySuit. He had the bad luck not to hit the sand, where there were still traces of blackened wood, the failed funeral pyre where Ravven and her students had tried to burn the whale's body. Instead Alon6 flapped his huge arms like a clumsy bird and collided with a rock.

It was a rough landing. The plastic and metal skin of the BodySuit shattered.

The MindVessel containing Alon6's consciousness rolled out to the sand to rest at the spot where the waves licked up. The first wave flowed over the

MindVessel, instantly shorting its circuits. There was a brief flash, a sick, sour smell, and the screen flickered.

Alon6's face on the screen held a look of frozen horror. His eyes bulged to double their size and his mouth formed a helpless O. The next wave came in and that finished him. The screen went black.

At the house, Ravven nodded. "Namaste," she said with gratitude and opened her eyes.

"Namaste," Kat said.

Ravven sent a thought into Kat's mind. *The consciousness of Alon6 is gone.*

Kat met her eye. "Good."

Nora2 looked around at the others with curiosity and asked, "What does Namaste mean?"

"It means that I honor the light within you," Ravven said. "Alon6 is no longer a functioning consciousness."

"Namaste," said Spaceman.

Nora2 offered a shy smile. "Namaste."

Chapter 050

Candice Clonk stared intently at her terminal back at MIND headquarters, leaning forward until her neck hurt. She watched as the pings came in, signaling the destruction of the BodySuit. She didn't understand what had happened and tried to piece it together.

There was widespread sensor failure in the BodySuit legs, then the arms. She saw red ants as thick as syrup before the BodySuit eye sensors blacked out. The accelerometers failed, the gyro-balancers failed. She tried to recover some of the video recorded by the BodySuit to make a proper analysis. It showed a field of vision completely filled with bees. The software identified them as honeybees. She looked up honeybees and learned they were not known for aggressive behavior.

As she played the vid again and saw that the bees had arrived suddenly, gathering almost as if they had a plan. They swarmed Alon6 for no visible reason, and took down his vision sensors by brute force, simply by clogging them. Then there was an audio signal that sounded like the words i am here. Candice's confusion turned to stunned surprise when her signals showed the BodySuit tumbling in space.

Then there was no signal at all.

She worked the controls at her terminal, gesturing frantically to get an indication of what had happened. She finally was able to get a strange and disorienting video view. It showed a rock, apparently on a beach, and a slice of sky. That was all.

It was all unexplained and disturbing. She had put her heart and soul into the BodySuit and now it sent a null signal, the digital equivalent of a stopped heartbeat. Alon6's consciousness was also at null. It seemed...dead? It had expired on a beach. The consciousness had no MindVessel to support it, and it vanished.

None of it made any sense.

Another ping came to her terminal. It was MIND admin control alerting her that Alon6's consciousness had failed, and there was a backup version of it in storage at MIND HQ.

ACTIVATE appeared on Candice's terminal screen, along with a helpful map to show her where the consciousness was kept in a basement storage unit. MIND admin was showing her the way to bring back Alon6's consciousness via the backup.

She went to have a look at the backup consciousness for Alon6. It was in a little room, with a digital combination lock on the door, as the map had shown. She ran the combination and opened the door to the storage area to see, on a small round table, the silver cube of a consciousness storage container.

Candice gazed at the backup of the most terrible boss she'd ever had.

She watched it for another moment and suddenly reached out to gesture off its power supply. There might be an alarm signal soon. Working quickly, she unplugged all the wiring going into the unit.

She backed away, gestured off the lights in the room, backed out into the hall, and shut the door. She made a new combination for the lock that only she would know.

She pulled her comms unit from her pocket and removed the icon of the storage room from the company map, reducing the chance that anyone else would find this little room.

She walked the hall feeling lighter. A smile bloomed on her face. There was no one in the hallway, and no alarm sounded. She was alone, so she laughed. It was more like a cackle. She tried it again and it felt twice as good.

Chapter 051

Ravven was exhausted, but she could see that everyone else in the room was charged up. She had felt Alon6's consciousness dissolve into nothingness and announced to everyone in the room that he was gone. Kat may have been skeptical at first, true to her nature, but Ravven could see that Kat also felt Alon6's rough exit and soon was chattering about a plan to secede from the dom and form their own government. "We can create an autonomous safe zone, starting with this house," Kat said.

Spaceman was showing the first sparks of happiness Ravven had seen since the Universal was seized. He replied to Kat, "And I want you to work with me to get the Universal back. Let's start negotiating."

Nora2 was probably wondering about exactly what sort of eccentric group she'd stumbled into. She was listening, taking in what had turned out to be a very strange day.

Ravven had her own agenda, now that Alon6 was gone. "I need the room," she said as gently as possible, cutting into the stream of talk.

"What? Why now?" Kat seemed confused.

"I just need a moment," Ravven said, smiling, and added a lie. "After all that effort to send a thought package, I need to rest. Let me rest. All of you!" She made shooing motions with her hands. The smile remained on her face but was beginning to look forced.

Nora2, probably grateful for a break from all the intensity, started to move toward the door.

Spaceman looked to Ravven. "Are you sure you'll be okay?"

"Yes, I will be okay. I just need a little time. Kat?" Ravven prompted, nodding to the door.

Kat was resistant and not ready. "How much time will you need? We have a lot of work to do and a lot to discuss. We just did something amazing together."

This brought out a smile. "I know. Just give me thirty minutes. Don't you want to check on Renzo? Is he still in En Segundo?"

Kat nodded and left with Spaceman and Nora2.

Now that Ravven had the room to herself, she got right to what she wanted to do. She locked the door. She took "Winning at Backgammon" down from the shelf and opened it to the Prism. Removing the Prism, she looked for a spot on the floor where the skylight cast a blade of sunlight and placed the Prism in the spot. Good thing she got the others out of the room. Kat wouldn't like what she was about to do, and the Prism must always be used while alone to prevent melding with anyone else's body while using it.

She sat in a cross-legged position. Visions can't be rushed, and astral travel has its own rules. Ravven wanted nothing more than to rush, however, as she closed her eyes and visualized the ocean all around her.

In a few moments, she felt her skin become sleek, dark, and firm, and her vision expanded; her arms became fins and behind her she sensed a tail fin. The water was cold. The humpback queen and orca queen were waiting, undulating slowly in the water, using gentle movements of their pectoral fins to keep their position nearby.

Ravven spoke. "We have vanquished our adversary. MIND has lost its leader. Now we can truly help you."

The orca queen said, "It's too late, Ravven Vaara."

The humpback queen said to the orca, "Too late? Too late for what? You haven't discussed this with me."

"And I won't discuss it. It's too late for her kind." The orca gazed at Ravven with a calm eye. "I have decided on a plan that will stop their rule. The first step is to cut power to your cities, starting in the Northern and Southern Californian Domains. We will shut down the hydroelectric plants."

"How will you do that?" Ravven asked.

"The plants need water that they get from the ocean and rivers. We will clog the intakes to the plants and shut them down."

The humpback queen made a noise that might have signaled impatience.

"You don't know anything about generating electricity. How will you clog the intakes?"

"With ourselves. With our own bodies. I will lead a migration of many orca pods to the biggest hydroelectric plant and we will gather at the intake and block it. We will shut down power in the human domains. The daily affairs of humanity will stop. We will end its rule."

The humpback's movement of her pectoral fins suggested extreme agitation. "By sacrificing yourselves? Suicide? Once you get there, if you even *can* get there, you will never get back."

The orca queen appeared to think for a moment before saying, "Then I will ask the octopuses. They have excellent navigation capabilities, can easily camouflage themselves, and can fit in small spaces and get out again. I'm sure they'll be happy to help. They are swimming in the same poisoned water as we are."

"Wait," Ravven said. "This is a bad plan. You must know that we had a catastrophe like this recently. It was called the Fracture. Everything stopped working. It didn't send a message to people. Instead, everyone was immobilized and helpless."

The orca queen said nothing for a moment. Then: "We have demands. How will you meet them?"

This felt like progress to Ravven. "Let's try. What are your demands?"

The orca queen said, "You will designate human-free zones. Large zones where no humans are allowed. Minimize human damage by moving yourselves away from us."

The humpback made a noise of impatience again. "Displace people? Create refugees? Not only is it cruel but the humans would never agree to it."

"If they were forced, they would have to agree," the orca queen said.

"What are your other ideas, orca?" asked the humpback.

"Abolish cities. Cities are the problem. They require too much electrical power to run. Too much infrastructure. They are damaging the Earth."

Ravven spoke. "We can't go back to an agrarian society. That would be backward. Humans have become used to being in cities."

"Now you betray your ignorance," the orca queen said. "It would not be backward. It would be connected to the ways of the planet. Are you so set in your technological ways? You've lost all vision, Ravven Vaara."

"It's not me. It's the rest of the world. I can't lead if others don't follow."

The orca said, "That has been the problem all along. You can't convince anyone of our truth."

Now Ravven was getting upset. "I believe your truth!"

"We trusted you. We *chose* you. But you can't get the others to follow. How will you get them to follow? You are only one person," the orca said.

"We are the Resistance. We are many."

The orca said, "Many is enough. But you must show that other humans believe you. If you are many, you must show it."

"Alright," Ravven said. "I will show it." She had no idea how, but she made her voice sound strong. Unfortunately, her eyes had become weak. The water was turning into the room where she slept with Spaceman. The water was Kat's house and Kat's house was the water. She had the horrible feeling of being in both places at once, and then she felt like she was nowhere at all as everything went dark. The water was gone. The whales were gone. Ravven could not be sure, but she felt she was gone, too.

Chapter 052

Hat and Spaceman broke down the locked door. It took several tries, and success was theirs when Spaceman threw himself against it for the third time. It split open and he stumbled into the room, Kat close behind.

Ravven was sitting on a mat. Her eyes were open and so was her mouth, as if she was mid-word but had fallen silent. Everything else about her was lifeless. Her skin was gray. Her eyes were empty.

Kat moved to Ravven quickly, shaking her. "Ravven, Ravven." She was stiff and began to fall over on her side like she was made of stone.

"What's happening?" Spaceman said, moving to cradle Ravven in his arms and stroke her hair. "Why is she like this?"

Kat frantically looked around the room and soon had the answer. The Prism of Broken Light was on the floor. The light from the skylight, which once must have fallen upon the Prism, had moved off it. The Prism was not in darkness, however, but emitted its own sickish purple light.

"Something is wrong here," Kat said, but what she meant to say was that something was wrong with her. She felt lightheaded, her mouth was dry, and her arms felt weirdly detached from her body. The rest of her followed suit: Her legs seemed to walk away by themselves and suddenly her eyes saw her from a point of view up at the ceiling. She was looking down at herself, and Spaceman holding Ravven, and Kat's head floated free of her body to drift across the room.

She shook her head violently and had the sensation of it reattaching, aware that she did not have much time to do what she needed to do. She lunged for the Prism and threw it down on the floor again and again. The walls of the room seemed to vibrate as if they were made of cascading water. The Prism developed a crack but that was the only damage. Kat picked it up and moved quickly with it out of the room.

Her feet carried her to her old office, now in use as Michel's studio. She didn't want Michel's help now, but instead she had remembered that there was a sledgehammer in the closet. Renzo had used it months ago to slam a hole in the wall to make a door.

Kat put the Prism on the floor, opened the closet, grabbed the sledgehammer, and pounded on the Prism, turning it into smaller and smaller pieces, until it was nearly a fine dust on the floor. The weird purple glow was gone now.

She stood tall, wobbled, sat down on the floor, and tossed the sledgehammer to the side.

Michel had activated. Being a bot, there was little he could do but listen to Kat's work and guess at what she was doing. When she was done, and flopped down, he said, "Well, most of the time, it's my clients who go to pieces."

Chapter 053

Kat looked over to Ravven, who was standing by her side in front of MIND headquarters, her body bent with fatigue. The Prism was destroyed just in time; they hadn't realized how much its out-of-body sessions were draining her. Kat caught Spaceman's eye. Also standing nearby, he nodded reassurance, with a steadying arm around Ravven. Renzo wasn't able to come to MIND today, unable to be in the place where his brother Tristan had died.

The building was quiet. No employees entered or exited. Nobody visible on the grand staircase, the primary architectural feature of the building visible through its glass facade. Had everyone left?

On the glidepath down to El Segundo, Kat expected to see misinformation vids on the screens but there were none. She used the transit time to think about the speech she planned to deliver to MIND's employees.

"The internet," Kat planned to say, "was invented by visionaries. But it was transformed by greed into a tool of extraction. MIND harvested our memories, our work, our entire lives. MIND stole our thoughts and sold them to its advertisers. To MIND, we are not human. We are only a pool of memories to be harvested, a pool of marketing data to sell. But, of course, we're human, remarkable and flawed. We love each other. We take care of each other. We don't need MIND to do that. Let's be free forever from a network that extracts financial value from our love and friendships. Join us. Join the Resistance. Join our peer-to-peer network."

It was a fine speech, Kat believed, short and on point, but there was no one to give it to.

After a moment or two of anticlimax, Caleb and Candice came out of the main entrance to MIND and asked what Kat and the others wanted.

The fine words she had practiced swarmed in Kat's head, but she had changed her mind about them. She only wanted to speak one sentence.

"We want the Universal back."

Suddenly, that seemed to be the right thing to accomplish now. If they had the Universal, Spaceman could continue the inter-species communications project.

After Ravven had returned from her bad astral travel experience, she told Kat and the others in the house about the orcas' ultimatum about cutting power to the dom. Kat was inclined to set it aside as an idle threat or even a fantasy, but three days after Ravven returned from her out-of-body journey, two hydroelectric plants in California had failed because of clogged intakes, the Edward Miltowne Powerplant and the Fort Ross Plant. When engineers had a look at the cause of the disruption, they saw that dozens of octopuses had moved in front of the intakes to cut off the water flow. This was unprecedented and, to say the least, rather strange.

If the Universal were returned, and Spaceman achieved his goal, a new era of inter-species communication would begin. Kat knew also that it meant that Dave Serif's work would continue in Spaceman's hands. She thought about Dave as she spoke the words again. "We want the Universal back."

Kat stood tall. "Bring us the Universal," she said.

Caleb broke into a grin. "It's kind of heavy. Why don't you come on in, and we'll help you carry it out?"

"I'll come with you," Candice added.

Chapter 054

At the midpoint of his scientific work, Spaceman's greatest ambition was to create biospheres that were livable as independent systems. He'd hoped to mimic the work of Gaia, the Earth spirit, but found the Earth's systems of self-regulation and equilibrium were not accessible to him—even to him!—the scientist who, more than any other, had brought about the modern age. It was a given in the scientific community that if the inventor of the pod and Molecular Housing couldn't create a stable, closed-loop environment suitable for people to live in, then no human was equal to the task.

The orcas had indicated that they were willing to negotiate, but Ravven wasn't able to remain in the state of consciousness she needed to keep communications open.

"The Universal will help," Spaceman said to Ravven after the device was back where it belonged, in the greenhouse. He was tinkering with it to bring it back online and she was watching him work.

"Let's say you can talk to the orcas," Ravven said, "using that mysterious box." She gave a careless wave to the Universal. "What would you say? I know what I would say, but what about you?"

Spaceman gave some thought to this before answering. When the orcas came to humanity for help, they were desperate saboteurs, capsizing boats to get attention. They'd been hunted, captured, wounded, and poisoned, and they wanted it all to stop. "What if we acknowledge the harm we've done and offer suitable restitution?" Spaceman asked.

"Yes, they asked for human-free zones. But people would never agree to that."

Spaceman answered without looking at her, so absorbed was he in the machine. "Why not?" He gestured at the Universal and an indicator on it began to glow. "Why wouldn't they agree?"

"Because people are too territorial. They don't want to give up any of their gains."

"Even if they are ill-gotten gains? Stolen land and water?" Spaceman turned to look at her. "It's up to us to convince people to acknowledge harm to other species and make proper restitution. If there is to be true inter-species dialogue, that would be the first step."

He was certain of this and held her gaze with a small smile on his lips.

"Up to us in the Resistance to convince them, you mean?"

"Yes," Spaceman said. "It's the next thing to do. And the right thing to do!"

She frowned, considering this, but Spaceman knew that she had already believed in the idea and would be soon plotting with Kat about how to accomplish it. "I'm going to find Kat," she said and left the greenhouse.

This left Spaceman alone with his work, one of his favorite situations to be in. He felt excited about the whale song recordings that he had already prepared for the Universal to analyze, and he had access to fresh whale song as well. His hands trembled as he gestured at the controls of the machine and he listened as whale song filled the greenhouse and seemed to nourish him.

Spaceman's hope was that the orcas would be satisfied with a brokered peace that included keeping humans out of the spaces where they did the most environmental damage, and new laws that prevented people from releasing plastics into the world's oceans. He wondered if people would dismantle their mega-cities and find a way to live smaller.

He smiled to himself. *How hard could that be?* Being the planet's apex predator had taken its toll on other species, but it had also harmed the human species.

Spaceman moved his hands over the controls and lost himself in the sound of humming, clicks, beeps, repeated tones, perhaps patterns—was that a pattern? —was that something? He felt close to cracking the code. He had Joan Warmaker put self-powered microphones in the water down by the harbor, ready to transmit Spaceman's words underwater. Spaceman had a live feed from the hydrophones placed in the bay; the source of the whale song he was listening to now.

I am ready for humanity's new journey.

"Is anyone there?" he asked, his words sent out underwater in what he hoped was a pattern the whales could understand.

Just as hope infused his spirit, there was dejection also. There were so many kinds of whale song, he could only test one and then another and see if anyone answered.

"Is anyone there? This is Roger Rucker speaking."

He felt a little ridiculous at that moment, trying to speak to whales in the ocean.

I am a fool.

My goals have always been too optimistic. Too large.

But then he looked up and saw Ravven and Kat watching him from the doorway, glowing together with pride, and his eyes brimmed.

He reached for a jug of artificial water and swigged from it, spilling some on his beard and down his front. He wiped at it absently with his hand. Noticing foil food wrappers here and there, he gathered them with one hand—gesturing to the women with the other. "Don't worry! I'm cleaning up as I go."

"It would have driven Dave crazy to see any water around the Universal," Kat said. "He was afraid of spilling on it." She smiled.

"I'll be careful," Spaceman said.

He had turned back to the Universal, listening to its sounds with eyes closed. The detailed work of any algorithm is a mystery, and the Universal was sorting through what Spaceman considered was the greatest of all mysteries, the universal algorithm to sort out all language, human languages and the languages of other beings.

"Come to eat something proper, Roger," Ravven said. "Or rest for a time. You've been working for three days without a stop. Remember what happened to me when I pushed myself. We don't want that to happen to you."

"I'm fine. I won't be leaving this body. I'm here and all I have to do is listen." He was annoyed by their intrusion now, these quotidian thoughts about food, rest, and maintaining sanity intruding on his concept of infinity.

But there was now a cracking, a sound like a word.

That sounded like a word.

He recognized something. He moved his hands at the controls, tuning the signal if he could.

"This is Roger Rucker. Are you there? *Are you there?*"

He made another adjustment and then the words came through, seeming to snap with invisible electricity. "Hello. I am the orca queen. Can you hear me?"

Spaceman could barely get the word out. "Yes." He tried again. "Yes. I can hear you."

"Good," the orca queen said. "Then negotiations between our species may begin."

The words had a simultaneous lightness and heaviness, a resonance that came from an ancient place and from the now.

Spaceman said the first thing that came to mind. "I am not authorized to negotiate for my species, but I would like to offer compensation for the damage our species have caused your species. Maybe it can begin with establishing some human-free zones in the ocean. We will work for this. The Resistance will work for this. We will not rest until it is done."

The orca queen responded. "You are not authorized to speak for your species, but I believe in you, Professor Rucker. We would be happy with human-free zones."

At this great moment, the most expansive moment Spaceman had ever felt, his mind went blank. His eyes filled with tears so that he couldn't see. He put his hands over his mouth to keep from saying something silly or useless. Finally: "Thank you. Speaking for all humans, I say thank you for hearing me."

Chapter 055

Witnessing his brother Tristan's death reshaped the way Renzo inhabited himself. It seemed like half of his body would not behave. For two days, his right eye swelled closed, and the visual imbalance caused his gait to pull to the right to compensate. He walked diagonally. Whatever natural optimism he once had now felt forced. He insisted to anyone who would listen that his symptoms would fade soon, just as his face had healed from the abrasions of Alon6's attack.

Kat brought him into a session with Michel. But Michel wasn't much help.

"The malady is not in my database," he said.

"Isn't it obvious?" Renzo protested. "A part of me has been murdered. Why can't anyone understand that? My twin is dead." His throat tightened and he felt like he needed to scream to loosen trapped feelings.

Michel said, "I understand you."

"You understand my words," Renzo said. "But not how to fix me."

"Maybe you need more time."

"That's a cliché response," Renzo said, regretting it. "Sorry. It's because I'm frustrated with myself."

He was staying up in Kat's room now, sleeping on his own mat near hers. Kat and Renzo had not chosen the software setting to join their sleeping mats in the manner of couples who slept together. This decision went unspoken between them. They placed their mats side by side, close but not touching.

If he was honest with himself, Renzo didn't know how long it would take for him to heal. He told himself that his interior world would remain confusing for a while. Certainly, the exterior world was in flux. After Alon6's death, most of MIND's employees left the company, some joining the Doomers, while others deciding to coast for a while on what they jokingly called "built up personal days." MIND itself, as an idea, a corp, and as software, faltered along on automatic pilot, its machines talking to its other machines. The primary goal of the Resistance was to stop MIND from gathering people's thoughts. It could not do that any longer. Nora2 helped Kat and Renzo gain access to MIND's data storage to delete all of the misinformation vids.

When Kat's friend Claire8 came from New York to visit, she helped Renzo and Nora2 disable MIND's access to the Feed. MIND, or anyone who still worked for it, could no longer post.

The new network was tiny, but more people were joining it every day. Kat and Renzo would have to find more servers to keep it online. Claire8 helped them scour markets, yard sales, and used equipment auctions to find them.

Some people used no network at all. They gathered in the evenings in little towns across the doms and talked to each other over tea lattes. Members of the Disconnect Movement often showed up at these informal gatherings and tried to recruit the latte-drinkers.

Renzo was indecisive about hanging on to his office in town, since he was at Kat's house all day. He brought Spaceman with him to have a look at it and clear out what he didn't need. Seated at his desk, Renzo picked up the holo image of him and Tristan as boys and held it for a long time.

"I think you should keep that," Spaceman had said.

Renzo nodded. "You're right." The holo had been on his desk since he first rented the office. He looked around at the four walls. "I think I need to keep this office also." This meant to him that though he was working for the Resistance, he still needed clients and wanted to continue his work as an architect. "What if the compensation to the orcas included shutting down the mega-cities? Someone will have to design new, smaller cities," he said, only half kidding.

Spaceman took him seriously. "You would be the person to start that movement, Renzo." He fixed Renzo in his warm gaze. "And as the Universal keeps working, connecting more languages, the orcas may not be the only species who will ask for restitution."

"You're right about that," Renzo said.

While they were waiting for the ferry back across the bay, Renzo and Spaceman came upon a gathering of Youngs who were shouting and waving their comms in the air.

"Toss your comms in the ocean!" the Youngs shouted and invited Spaceman and Renzo to join in. "Disconnect! Disconnect with us!"

Renzo and Spaceman not only declined to join but also were able to convince the Youngs not to toss their comms units.

"It will only contribute to the e-waste that is already in the water," Spaceman said. "The bay is troubled enough as it is!"

Some of the Youngs pushed back, contesting Spaceman's right to tell them what to do.

"Then let's hear from someone who lives in the water." Spaceman played a translation recording of the orca queen asking for humans to cooperate with other species, to see themselves as one species among many, and especially not to throw their garbage in the bay.

One of the more contentious Youngs, who wore a recycled bike helmet decorated with spinning propellers, presumably solar-powered, challenged Spaceman again. "How do we know that recording is real?"

But by then enough of the others realized that they were in the presence of the real Roger Rucker, the scientist who had developed the first true inter-species communications using the Universal. Ignoring the propeller-head guy, the others shut down their comms and gave them to Spaceman and Renzo to dispose of properly.

When the two of them returned to the Marin side on the ferry, they carried a large bag of comms units.

"I hope you know how to recycle these properly," Renzo said to Spaceman.

"I was hoping that you knew."

They shared a laugh at that. "We'll figure it out," Renzo said. "I'm planning on keeping cities, by the way," Renzo said.

"Yes, me too," said Spaceman. They agreed right then and there to design and build Molecular Housing Units near Kat's house, and later, up and down the coast. "A group of Molecular Housing units can't replace cities," Spaceman admitted. "Their conception is too modest, intended to power themselves using available solar and bicycle-driven generators."

"But they won't hurt the orcas and they'll show that we aspire to be good planetary citizens," Renzo said.

"True. You'll ask Kat for permission to build?" Spaceman said.

Renzo nodded. "Sure." He looked out at the bay as they made the crossing, feeling the presence of the whales beneath them, in the water, watching, judging, waiting to see if humans were good for their word. He said to Spaceman, "To get anything done, we'll need to secede from the dom."

"Yes, I'm there with you," Spaceman said.

Chapter 056

Renzo tried put on a good face for others, adopting a superficial optimism; when he did so, Kat could easily detect it. When the bad moods hit him hard, she knew to look for him in the room he shared with her upstairs.

She looked for him upstairs and found him. His body was healing; his right eye was fine and his gait had rebalanced. As she joined him, sitting on her mat near his, Renzo told her about the ferry crossing with Spaceman, and she heard the wobble in his tone. She promised herself that she would not enter his mind but knew that she would find disorder there. The bag of comms units was still in the front hall of the house.

He thought she had come to talk to him about them. "I'm sorry. The bag of comms. Spaceman is working on it," Renzo said. "He's going to find a way to recycle them." He thought of something to add. "He and I were talking about making some Molecular Housing Units on your land. What do you think about that?"

Kat moved closer to Renzo and draped her arm around him. Her affection for him was growing, based on more than just pity, edging into compassion and, yes, perhaps love. She dared herself to say all of that aloud to him and failed. "Yes, of course," she said, answering his question about using her land. "And can I get you anything now?" she asked.

"No, thanks," he said. "I don't need anything now." She had to lean in to hear him.

"You are going to be okay," she said.

He smiled with a warmth that seemed thin and then touched her arm to indicate that she should take her arm from around his shoulders. She did.

"I'm worried that we can't make good on enough compensation for the whales," he said. "And other species may ask for their own restitution. Spaceman pointed that out to me yesterday on the ferry. He's right. And I don't know if people will give up land they've inhabited for so long, or the oceans they exploit. Cities need to change, maybe even be discontinued in the form we know them now. People won't go for that either without a fight."

Kat considered this for a moment. "What if we gave people a choice?"

"Between what and what?" Renzo asked.

"Between happiness and domination."

Renzo frowned, confused by this, so Kat expanded on it. "Being dominators has taken its toll on us all," she said. "It's why MIND came apart. The employees couldn't stand being assholes anymore."

Renzo laughed. "The Resistance's new slogan is 'don't be an asshole?'"

She smiled. "Maybe not that. But it's true that the conquerors have a way of conquering themselves. The exploiters end up self-exploiting, because exploitation never ends until everyone is hollowed out."

"Go small or go home?" he asked.

"Go small and go home," she countered.

"Are we trying out slogans now?" Renzo caught her in a gaze that held respect. "This slogan thing is harder than I thought. It was hard at the ferry terminal yesterday. Nobody could agree with anybody else," he said, thinking of how the Youngs argued among themselves.

"We'll never get everyone thinking the same, even in the Resistance," Kat said. "Ravven might believe that since MIND is gone, she'll teach yoga, thinking that's enough. It's a lot, but even though Alon6's consciousness is gone, his ideas are not. The idea of MIND can come alive at any time and another autocrat can always appear. The struggle is never over, but we can take a breath now and again."

Renzo seemed to want to take a breath or perhaps escape the back and forth of this conversation. He stood up suddenly, crossed the room, and opened the sliding closet door. He reached in and pulled something out. "Look what I found," he said, coming out with Dave's old therapy bot. The wires were tangled like the hair of a haunted spirit.

It was upsetting for Kat to see the bot again. "Put that back!" Her voice was more strident than she intended.

Renzo looked surprised, then ashamed. "Because it was Dave's?"

"Put it back."

Renzo turned to hide the bot. "I'm sorry," his voice muffled, speaking from inside the closet. He walked over to the mat and sat down, and it shaped around him, forming an approximation of a chair.

Kat and Renzo looked at each other for a moment, and then he held his arms open and she came to him, allowing herself to be gathered up. The mat reconfigured to accommodate them both, pushing them closer.

He stroked her hair and held her. "I didn't mean to upset you." He began talking again about being pulled under by the whale. "I focused on little things just to distract myself. I watched the silver bubbles that my breath made, maybe the last breath I would take. Above me, the surface looked like silver metal, and below me there was just the deepest darkness I ever saw. All very simple: up, down, life, death," he said, his eyes distant, seeing it all again. "I must've blacked out at some point," he said.

"Maybe thankfully," Kat said, and added, "I want you to feel okay."

He offered a smile. "I'm feeling better every day."

"No, what I mean is I want us to be okay with being together as a couple." She paused. "Us—together."

His eyes went soft. "You sound like you mean it."

"I do." She waited for more words to come. She wanted to talk about how much she had changed over the past few months and hit upon something to share. "I didn't believe Ravven at first about the orca queen. The idea of an animal having that level of consciousness, and being able to express it, was just outside what I could think about. But Ravven just accepted it."

"She's made that way," Renzo said.

"Yes, I understand that now. Her access to what I would call ancestral wisdom is deep. We fight, the two of us, but maybe it has to be that way because we're so different."

"There's no reason that has to go smoothly," he said. "Opposites."

She sensed that he was really talking about his missing other half, his brother Tristan.

I want to rescue you. She dared not say those words to him but thought them. She wanted to rescue Renzo from his sadness and at the same time she wanted him to be strong. "We have something together and I want us to keep it." The words sounded blunt to her, ill-formed; the words waited in the air between them, but she felt that Renzo understood what she meant.

"We need you to help the Resistance but...*I* need you." She reached for him again, and they held each other without speaking. She was comforting him or he was comforting her; there was no separation. That would be a good way for them to be together, comforting each other. Not alone.

The Resistance had consumed Kat for four years. It was nearly all that she thought about. She wasn't tired of the work, but she needed more than the work. She needed a friend; no, that wasn't it. She needed more than a companion. A partner. Renzo.

She started talking, a ramble of thoughts. "I remember that I couldn't sleep on this floor when I first came back to the house."

"Too many memories?" he asked.

"Yes. The first night the wind rattled the windows. It sounded like trouble outside. I slept downstairs. It was hard to sleep." She had once believed that everything could be understood from a logical progression of ideas. She knew that this wasn't true for her any longer, but she didn't say it, didn't want this to crowd her story so she kept going, feeling she was saying something important out of order. "I waited for sleep. I wanted the day to stop." *I wanted the day to reveal its meaning to me.*

"When did you finally fall asleep? Or did you?"

"I did! I remember having this strange dream."

She told him that the dream appeared in her mind as a series of panels, like canvases hung in a gallery. She remembered how it woke her, and she reached for her comms unit to record it before it got away. When she listened to the dream recording later, her words described something outside of the world she knew: A woman rose from the sea and spoke a mysterious language. The language was rich with vowels, filled with flourishes and sounded old. Dave would know what it was. The Universal could translate it.

She felt compelled to share everything about the dream with Renzo, to fit it all in, and she spoke faster, aware that it wouldn't make sense.

"The woman had long black hair like tangled seaweed, and she wore a silver crown. Her eyes were brown and gentle. She saw me, she witnessed me watching her. She was naked and her body was white as pale stone." Kat closed her eyes, remembering that the top part of the woman was above the water, her bottom part below. She floated somehow. The water around her was moving and green, heaving with motion. The woman's hands invited Kat to understand the words she was singing. "I didn't understand any of her words." Kat finished the recollection by saying, "There were translucent webs between her fingers."

Renzo took in the story. "Maybe it was the orca queen speaking to you."

Kat tiled her head. "Ravven was the first to hear her."

Renzo smiled. "Yes, but what if the orca queen tried you first and got a wrong number?"

Kat grinned and looked down, a kind of embarrassment prickling at her. It seemed improbable that her dream represented anything real, and yet it was possible that she could have received a message so profound that she couldn't recognize it at first.

"We humans enjoy complexity," Renzo said. He thought for a moment. "And some things are unknowable, outside of what our intelligence can grasp or what our senses can take in."

Kat tried out the feel of the words on her tongue. "Some things are unknowable, and that bothers the hell out of me..." she said and laughed, then quieted when he took her hand and held it, and she took his. They looked into one another's eyes. She thought they could help each other through life. "This may not be perfect," she said, and the look on his face said that he knew that she was talking about them, together.

"I know," he said. His eyes were bright.

In the morning, Kat decided, she would get new plants for the greenhouse. She would go to the market and see what they had. Digging in the dirt would feel good. And this time, she thought, everything would be different, not entangled, not a web of transactions and deception. This time, she would find liberation.

Epilogue

ora2 woke up on April 30, 2056 and decided that she was going to unmod. The decision came to her in a rush, and she sat up on the mat she'd been sleeping on, felt dizziness wash over her, and swallowed hard. It was a big decision, but upon reflection she realized that the decision didn't really come in a rush. She'd been seriously considering it for months.

A year and a half ago, she had moved into this unit, one of the first Molecular Housing units that Renzo had completed on Kat's property. There were more being built and many more planned.

Spaceman had negotiated with the coastal doms to designate a half-dozen human-free zones in the ocean, away from shipping routes. He was negotiating to re-route other shipping routes to create more human-free oceanic space. When negotiations got rough, Spaceman patched in the orca and humpback queens to state the case for themselves, and that always helped. There was still novelty in hearing non-human species speak and be understood. He also lobbied the domains to keep plastics out of the ocean.

Kat didn't have the queens' help in her negotiations to dismantle mega-cities in the heavily populated doms. But she kept at it when she wasn't building the network with Claire8. It would take some time for their peer-to-peer network to become a global network of federated servers, but "one day, one new node at a time," as Claire8 liked to say. Attendance in Ravven's yoga and meditation classes grew and grew. Michel had a full schedule of therapy clients and was training other bots to be therapists.

For anyone else in Nora2's situation, it might have been a simple decision to unmod, but she knew nothing about how to do it. She worried about tampering with the silicon substrate that had been embedded in her brain for decades. She carried extra bits of programming she wasn't aware of, probably. Whatever it meant, unmodding would be a mysterious, dangerous, and powerful change. She was afraid to try it.

When she was modded at fourteen and about to enter Uni, she knew that a mod would make her personality dimmer. She rationalized this, thinking that she didn't have much of a personality to begin with. She thought of herself as a cold and shy person and told herself that nobody would even notice if she were modded. It was true that modding did make her even colder and more distant but it was also a big step forward for her career. She got a good job and advanced rapidly.

Soon she was running the company, the most powerful company in the world. MIND. Modding seemed worth it then, because it made this enormous achievement possible for a boring person (as she thought of herself). In time, though, the job took its toll. Hired to exploit, she started exploiting herself. She began drinking heavily to dim the world.

How to go about finding someone who could perform an unmodding procedure without killing her? The silicone substrate had been part of her for so long, Nora2 couldn't imagine herself without it.

There were scary stories on the Feed of people whose minds were destroyed after a bad unmod, and in those stories was a crumb of information. The unmodders hung around in the dark markets. In those hotbeds of illegality, citizens could buy secluders that enabled secret conversations. They could buy spoofing glasses that fooled facial recognition trackers. One could start over, go into hiding, or create a new identity in the dark markets.

Conveniently, they were often located near the regular markets, as Nora2 learned in her research, at the far ends, where enforcement bots were few. She just had to get herself to a market and have a look around. So she walked down to the glidepath station to wait for a train.

She entered the first car and was surprised to find no one on it, as well as no conductor bots. Maybe people were staying away from the glidepath or it could have been that not many trains were running since there was no longer an admin to run them. She sat by herself and waited for the floating feeling that signaled that induction had begun. If she got out of this alive, a good project for her would be to make an interface between the glidepath and the peer-to-peer network so that more glidepaths would be available using the new network.

There was no announcement (as there would be usually). The glidepath car floated and took off. She saw that the blast curtains weren't operating properly either, so she was treated to a blurring view of vague somethingness outside of the window. It made her dizzy to watch it.

She tried to remain alert as she assumed there would be no announcement of their arrival at the Metro/7th Street Station. Her mind drifted anyway; she started to imagine the agent she would see about her procedure. She pictured the person as sloppy, unwashed, wearing dark sunglasses, and dressed in artificial black leather. Sleazy, basically. They would meet in a back alley behind a building, she thought.

Later, she would laugh at that imagined person, because the real person she met wasn't like that at all.

She exited the glidepath at Metro, walked upstairs to the market, walked to the end of it where the fruit and vegetable stands thinned out, past vendors selling used terminals and recycled comms units, and into what she assumed would be the sketchy black market at the end of the regular market. It turned out, however, that the sketchy black-market section wasn't so sketchy. People were selling handmade sun suits and handmade candles and containers of soup.

"Won't you buy a dozen? Good price today for candles!" the vendor called out, an elderly woman with a strange conical hat. Nora2 shook her head without answering and walked on. There were spoofing sunglasses that could swap your identity with someone else's, secluders of course, and false identity chips that the vendor was ready to insert under the fleshy part of your neck with a pneumatic gun to fool the People Services department at your workplace. That made her shiver. No more implants, please.

She passed the first of many hand-painted murals she would see on that day. This one showed a painting of a garden and over the painted leafy background was a slogan: Trust yourself, not the corps. Someone had partly crossed out the word "corps" and written in mind.

In this dark market, Nora2 was continually surprised at how polite everyone was. When she asked the identity chip vendor about the nearest unmodding center, they cheerfully directed her to a building a few blocks away that looked like it had been recently flooded—there were water marks on the façade.

There was an Old sweeping out the remains of the water who paused to respond to her question about where the portal to the center was. He smiled and pointed and went back to his work. He wore a cap with a symbol on it that she later looked up. It was for the Los Angeles Dodgers. She should have remembered that, but it had been a long time since she thought of anything like baseball.

Unmodding was still illegal, as far as she knew. Or maybe it wasn't anymore or not in certain domains. She sighed and shook her head. She had been in her own bubble for so long, working for Bradley in his New Zealand safe house, speaking only with him and other MIND employees, and then working for Alon6 in El Segundo, that the orbit of her personality had become impossibly small. Moving into her own Molecular Housing unit seemed like a mysterious kind of freedom.

When she stepped up to the door to the unmodding center, nothing seemed illicit. There were people in a waiting room who looked calm and relaxed, like they belonged there and had a right to change their lives for the better.

She approached the front desk, where a human, not a bot as she expected, asked her name, and took her into another waiting room. Her name was called and when she stood, a new attendant in a white uniform said, "Follow the lights." Nora2 didn't know what they meant at first, but the attendant's gesture led her eye to the point where the wall and ceiling met. There was a row of flashing chaser lights that formed her name "Welcome, Nora2," flickering on and off down the hallway. It was a little unnerving, and felt too public, but she followed them to an office and walked inside.

The agent waiting for her there was a pleasant young man, maybe about twenty-one, with brown skin and warm eyes.

"Hello, Nora2, please sit down." He spoke with a Brit-Euro accent. He indicated a chair that appeared to be made of simulated wood, or a wood that looked like plastic. His desk was white and clear of any ornament. He didn't even have a terminal. There was no sign of his comms.

"My name is Lōc," he said in his pleasant accent. "How can I help?"

Nora2 felt a bubble of suspicion rise in her throat and asked, maybe too sharply. "Why did you use my real name for those lights? Isn't that an invasion of privacy?"

He opened his hands. "It won't be your name anymore, right?" He nodded slightly. "That is, if you decide to go through with this."

Nora2 looked at him without comprehension, so he added, "You'll be dropping the number, won't you?"

Then she understood. "Yes, of course."

"But you'll still use Nora?"

"Yes. I guess so."

"You don't sound sure. You don't have to decide yet. Some change their name while others just drop the number. It's up to you."

She had a million questions, like, Did a lot of people do this? And wasn't it illegal? The experience up till now seemed rather normal, like booking an appointment for a facial. She decided to ask the funding question first. "Is it true that I don't have to pay for the procedure until a year later, when we're sure it's going to stick?"

Lōc seemed to sense her short-circuited state or perhaps he had been asked all of these questions many times before. "Yes, you don't have to pay right away," he said. "We'll talk about all your questions in a moment." He looked at her, assessing her, it seemed. "But first, I want to know why you would like to unmod. Please, tell me."

She wasn't prepared to talk, because she hadn't imagined that unmodding would involve answering questions, other than funding sources, scheduling, and other routine things. She didn't know how to answer, so she let the words tumble out. "I don't want to be me anymore," and immediately sensed that it was the wrong thing to say.

Apparently, Lōc wasn't bothered by it. He simply nodded. "Do you understand how different it will feel to be unmodded?"

"Different, how?"

He leaned forward slightly and folded his hands on his desk. "You've come to rely on your modded intelligence. It's the way you are and have been for a long time. What do you think you will feel like when it's gone? Who will you be then?"

"I don't know. I've always had it. Almost always. My adult life. I'm just me."

Lōc smiled slightly. "You are you, but not 'just' you. You haven't always carried a silicon substrate in your brain. You weren't always modded. You contain two people, in a way. Does that make sense?"

He had accessed her archive, obviously.

"Correct, it makes sense," she said to buy time as she processed this.

"What were you like as a child?" he asked.

She searched in her mind for a single, defining thing. "Nobody listened to me," she said finally.

"Why?"

"I wasn't smart. I wasn't worth listening to. I was kind of boring." She shrugged and gave an apologetic smile. "Still am."

Lōc's eyes were kind. "That can't have been the case when you were young, and it certainly can't be the case now. You've always been intelligent, determined, and clear about your goals."

How did he know that?

He continued as though she had asked the question aloud. "Look at all you've accomplished in your life. And you're still only thirty-six."

Nora2 nodded briefly, but her mouth was a thin line and she repeated her earlier statement. "Nobody listened to me as a child."

Lōc maintained his sympathetic expression in response to her stubbornness. She wanted to touch her right temple, to play back some of her history, and realized that gesture would have to go away soon. She would have to remember things on her own. Lōc had already looked up her archive, that much was obvious, so he knew everything. She began to speak anyway, maybe just to hear the words come out of her mouth, a rambling narrative about being the third and youngest child, with two older brothers who went into her parents' business; they were landlords. Her brothers were the collectors, going door to door and demanding funds from tenants who were slow to top off their rent accounts. "My brothers had the confidence that collecting funds can bring," she said, realizing that she was speaking about her internal narrative, and that Lōc might not know what she was talking about. He nodded, though, appearing to follow along. "They collected no matter what. They were brutal."

She realized that the brutality of her brothers as rent collectors reminded her of Alon6's brutality. Her boss was brutal. It defined him. This insight stung; she blinked in reaction to it. Her boss Alon6 always got what he wanted and didn't care how. She swallowed the thought, which would have been bitter on her tongue had she spoken it and continued. "When I was young, I had to prove myself again and again. Prove my worth. I usually failed. I wanted to be a doctor, but my parents discouraged it. They felt that all medical work would be taken over by healing bots, and they were right about that."

Lōc waited for her to continue.

"I always believed I was an accident," she added, out of narrative order, and wished she could retract it.

Lōc nodded again, as if this stream-of-consciousness playback of her archive was entirely normal. Maybe it was. Who knew what people said as they were contemplating unwinding their mods, pulling out a piece of hardware that had been lodged in their brain for decades?

"This is a taste of what it will be like," Lōc said. "When your mod is gone, you will revert."

"Revert?" Her voice sounded shaky to her, a touch of her inner fear coming through.

"Yes, for a time you will be thrown back into the personality field that you had before you modded. For you that would be," he interrupted himself to glance down at a tablet embedded in his desk that she hadn't noticed before, "when you were fourteen, on your way to Uni."

Nora2 had to sit with this for a moment. "You mean I will become a pre-teen again, in a sense?"

Lōc nodded his agreement. "In a sense. For a time. For a short time, hopefully. When we remove the substrate from your brain it's like removing history from your archive. Or disconnecting a hard drive." He paused. "You remember hard drives?"

"Yes," Nora2 said. Her voice wobbled again. She didn't like that wobble. She wanted her voice to be steady and strong as she made this big decision.

Lōc nodded. "I'm glad you understand. Reversion can take many forms. You may feel invisible again. As if no one is listening to you, again, as you felt as a child. You will be putting your personality back together, starting over without the mod you've been used to for so long. You will not be at home in your own skin."

She barely heard him speaking, caught in a web of memories of her brothers talking over her at the dinner table. It was only when she was modded that people started to pay attention to her and she came into her power. And now she wanted to let it go. Was that crazy?

Lōc appeared to pick up on her latest wobble. "When it's gone, you will perceive it as a loss. There may be a period of mourning."

"Mourning about what?"

"You have known yourself for so long like this. The capabilities. Your memory, your archive recall, your sense of organization, even occasional ruthlessness. The remoteness. You haven't needed to connect with people because that's not a feature of your mod. But it might be part of your old personality field. You may need to find connection. You may have the need to be liked by other people."

That all seemed like too much to think about. She gave an ill-considered, even repetitive response instead. "Honestly, it's hard to remember what it was like before I was modded." But that wasn't true at all. Truthfully, it was painful to recall what she was like as a child. *Go back to that time of powerlessness? Why would I do that?* she asked herself again. She liked, no *loved*, the power that intelligence and efficiency that modding brought to her.

Before she could speak, Lōc interrupted her thoughts.

"Why do you want to unmod?" he asked again.

Strangely, this time she had an answer right away. "It's wrong."

"Tell me more about that."

So many words came to her that they seemed to clog each other, preventing their release into the world. Maybe it wasn't what she did with her mod that was so objectionable, but what Alon6 and Bradley did with theirs; maybe that's what she hated so much. The two of them dominated people, they were bullies, Alon6 especially, and Bradley in a more subtle way.

But that wasn't the only thing. It was the way her mod made her behave. She didn't want to do what it told her, to be obedient to Alon6, to feel remote and calculating. She—it sounded naive as she thought it—she wanted to connect with other people. Yes, that's what she wanted above all. But all she could think of to say aloud was, "I need friends. I want to know myself as I really am." She began to cry. It was a strange sensation to taste the salty water on her face as it dripped into her mouth.

Lōc reached for a box of tissues that she imagined he used often. "Everyone who comes here has doubts. That's why we suggest that you wait a few days before having the procedure done." He looked at her, again assessing, it seemed, what she was ready to hear next. "You were a different person before you were modded, a different person during your mod, and now you have the opportunity to change again, to become a different person again. You will not be the same as you were. You will be a third, different person."

A third different person. She thought about that but didn't know what it meant. She would have to become herself, somehow, without a map. She was scared, but as she walked away from the center, leaving Lōc and his kind expressions, retracing her steps through the market and toward the glidepath, she decided that she would go through with the procedure. It would be like meeting herself for the first time. She only had to find the courage.

She saw another mural on the side of a building. The top part read, in large letters, utopia will always be far off. But as Nora2 walked closer, she saw smaller letters below that slogan: But it's always worth walking toward.

She shook her head, amused, and then tried smiling at a few strangers. To her amazement, they smiled back. She had never tried that before. It amazed her that there could be unmodding centers at all now. People in the market were moving freely, seemingly not as concerned about trackers. She looked up to see cameras smashed, covered over, or removed from their utility poles entirely. There had been a time when this would worry her, but now it was cause for hope. It was a signal, she thought, that things could be more free.

Finally, she came to the source of the murals. A street artist was leading a class of Youngs, demonstrating how to make murals on buildings. They stood before a blank wall and discussed what they should paint there. The students had many suggestions.

"Eyes looking at you," volunteered one student.

"A garden," said another.

"We just did a garden mural," the teacher pointed out. "What words come to you?"

A Young in the group shouted out, "No more extraction! Down with the extraction economy!"

The teacher smiled. "A little too forceful, even if worthwhile. People don't like being told what to do."

After a few more moments, they settled on two words. Start small. They started work on the mural.

Nora2 walked on, and then, for the first time in a long time, maybe ever, she saw a group of children playing in a group in public. There were a bunch of red balloons tied to a pole and the children were in a circle around it.

Nora2 went closer to see what they were doing. She leaned in, standing over them, but they were so absorbed in their game that they didn't seem to notice her. One child, a girl, had a toy that looked like a black fish with white markings. Nora2 touched her temple for computer vision, then realized what it was. An orca. Two other children, boys, had little boats. Their game involved the girl's toy orca moving to the boats, attacking them and sinking them. "We demand restitution!" the girl said.

Glossary of Terms

Avatar

When consciousness is developed into software and associated with a specific human personality, it is called an Avatar.

Blanky

A handheld device that can access a public security camera and erase its recordings. Invented by Roger Rucker, a former university instructor and who works with the Resistance. (See *Resistance.*)

Blast Curtains

Protective curtains, often programmed to move into place automatically, that shield living and workspaces from the powerful morning heat of the sun and its damaging UV radiation.

Change, The

The Change refers to a series of extreme weather events that swept the planet in 2030. Some were hurricanes, others dust storms, some were extreme heat events, all coming at different times and places over the course of that year. Human memory has compressed them into a single event, which is a false rendering of history, but serves as an easy way to express global catastrophic change.

Clarity Crawl

Software that crawls the Feed (See *Feed, The*) and erases any text, audio, or video about Resistance (See *Resistance*) activities, such as protests.

Cloakcraft

The art and science of hiding from corporate and state surveillance by blocking facial recognition, scrambling heat signatures and gait recognition, using Secluders (see *Secluder*), and remaining invisible to cameras.

Comms

Originally called communications devices, or simply "smartphones," comms have come to signify both a suite of devices and a concept. Citizens are assigned a number-letter string identifier at birth (or rebirth) and this unique identifier is embedded into all of their handheld, personal, and residential devices. Comms are used for communication, research, accessing the Feed (*see Feed, The*), image and audio capture, tracking, and data storage.

Cultured Twins

In human pairs of this type, two people are cultured together in the womb, with modifications brought about by chemical means and in-womb radiation. The treatment entangles the personalities of the two people, so that each completes the other. Often one twin is bold, and the other, shy, and the shy person must do what the bold one desires.

Disconnect Movement

A backlash movement against tech-heads (see *tech-heads*), members of the Disconnect Movement refuse to use technology wherever possible. They do not bathe using UV radiation baths, refuse to use sun-mitigation technology such as the Sundowner medipatch, and do not join networks. They make their own clothes and refuse to mod (See *Personal Modifications.*) They are against the use of AI and will destroy personal bots when they find them. They stand out in a crowd because of their personal odor and peeling, sunburned skin.

Doomers

Often after network outages, the Doomer movement becomes more popular among Youngs (citizens under the age of twenty). It is a suicide cult. Members gain prestige by ending it all, though not many of them take that path. Most adopt an aggressively depressed attitude, loudly asserting that there is no point to living, and adopt outlandish costumes modeled on animals such as deer, bulls, lizards, or figures from mythology such as Medusa with her hair made of snakes. Their intent is to shock everyday citizens, little more than that. They are known for loudly calling out their semi-ironic battle cry: YOLO! (You Only Live Once.)

Domain

A nation-state. Casually abbreviated as "dom."
Enforcement Bots
These bots, small, low to the ground and silver in color, do the work of police officers and security guards. They are equipped with flexible restraints which are used to hold the accused in place while a judge is summoned to rule on vid. (See *Vid.*)

Feed, The

Since the planetary collapse of all entertainment, news, and political networks, efficiency has dictated that all information be delivered to citizens via the Feed. The Feed is updated continually and delivered to all comms devices. (See *Comms.*) The Feed is administered by each Domain (see *Domain*).

Floating Home

A traditional home outfitted on pontoons so it may float on the rising coastal waters. Floating homes were first adopted in the 21st century in the countries formerly known as Thailand and the Netherlands and later adapted for use worldwide.

Hovercraft

A long, low, and slender mode of transport, powered by magnetic induction and using antigrav, Hovercraft can carry from two to ten passengers with room for cargo in a rear compartment. They are generally open to the elements and have a curved windshield in the front. Since private cars were banned in cities, Hovercraft are licensed to delivery persons, traders, and transport for hire.

Form Factor

A white, oval-shaped container to store human consciousness when it is expressed as an Avatar. (See *Avatar*.) Early versions allowed only for voice communication and later versions included vid and other sensory capabilities. Also known as a *MindVessel*.

Glidepath

The planetary high-speed antigravity travel system that replaced the rail travel system.

Gondola

These long, narrow watercraft powered by a single oar, with a capacity for one or two people, make travel possible in cities submerged by rising water levels. Gondolas may be piloted by bots or humans. Payment is cashless by comms unit. (See Comms.) Tipping is permitted.

Harvester

Once the size of a backpack, and now miniaturized to an insect-sized drone, the Harvester gathers the thoughts and pre-thoughts of people in public spaces, to build a more reliable data model for MIND.

Holo
Since the adoption of the Holographic Standard of 2025, holograms, called holos, have been widely used for entertainment, communication, and official announcements. The high cost of production and transmission have made the creation of holos inaccessible to everyday people, but the wealthy use them often.

Logic Tree
Much as the 20th-century theoretical physicist Richard Feynman's charming drawings (called Feynman diagrams) are pictorial representations of the mathematical expressions describing the behavior and interaction of subatomic particles, logic trees, invented by Bradley15 Power, depict the functions of MIND. (See *MIND*.)

LumaSutra
A handheld device used to detect the presence of Receivers within a five-kilometer radius. (See *Receivers*.)

Mental Field
Since the field of psychology has been replaced by Field Science, a person's psychological presence, inner and outer thoughts, and mental emanations have been called their mental field. (See *Personality Field*.)

MIND
MIND is machine intelligence that can teach itself; therefore, it has recursive intelligence. Originally called DEEPAK, it was invented by Bradley15 Power while he was a student at ABCD University and is wholly owned by MIND, the company of the same name. MIND is simultaneously a device, a concept, and a company. See *Comms* for another explanation of how a device and concept can coexist in the same thought space.

Nibbler

Software that allows the user to read the Feed (see, *Feed, The*) without surveillance from authorities such as MIND. Effective for short durations only, allowing the reader to "nibble" at the Feed, hence the name.

Personality Field

Since the field of psychology has been replaced by Field Science, we speak of a person's psychological presence, their inner and outer thoughts, as a Personality Field. Before this branch of science was established, a personality field was colloquially called a "vibe" or "energetic field." (See *Mental Field*.)

Personal Mods

Personal modifications, or *mods*, are silicon implants set into the brain. Often purchased by parents for their children, they are installed to boost memory capacity, induce hyperintelligence, enhance attractiveness, ambition, or marketing and sales abilities. Individuals who have received mods are given a number after their first name. The more expensive the mod, the lower the number.

Pod

A living space adapted for high-water conditions in coastal regions, a pod delivers the human basics in a water-resistant environment. Light, climate controls, a sleeping mat, and a food cooker are provided. Some pods have windows. (See *Blast Curtains*.) Less-expensive pods carry projected advertising that cannot be shut off.

Receivers

People who are able to receive the thoughts of others when they are in the line of sight. Receivers gather in Receiver Schools to hone their craft. The first Receiver School was founded in 2050 by a former yoga teacher named Ravven Vaara.

The Resistance
An outlaw group founded with the mission to break humans free from the influence of technology, the personality fields of wealthy people, and the dominance of MIND. Known membership in the Resistance is punishable by detention.

Sector Q
The area in the New York dom formerly known as Queens.

Secluder
A comms device (See *Comms*) modified so as to be untraceable. Similar to a "burner phone."

Sightglass
A handheld device that can detect the presence of public surveillance cameras, providing a warning to those who are trying to stay out of sight. Useful when practicing *cloakcraft* (See *Cloakcraft.*)

Siliconers
Investors, inventors, and marketers who will live and die by the technology the create. (See *tech-heads.*)

State
A government that extends its influence over the citizens of a continent or land, such as the Chinese State or the Free State of Scotland.

Tech-heads
People who believe that technology will cure all of humanity's ills, they are often educated at Uni (See *Uni*) and can follow a career path to become Siliconers or work for them. (See *Siliconers.*)

Uni

Used as a general term to indicate the education system at the university level, and as a specific term to indicate any educational institution that has been taken over by MIND. (See *MIND*.)

Vaporetto

A large watercraft used in flooded cities to carry five to ten people through the former streets.

Vid

Used loosely to indicate any visual information displayed by outdoor advert panels, screens, or Comms. (See *Comms*.)

Acknowledgments

The fiction writer is a servant to the story they are telling, and this can create a thorny relationship with facts. Telling a story often requires that timelines are bent, inconvenient story points are ignored, and two or more characters are merged into one. I'm guilty of all of those things, along with making up my own facts.

For example, there is no such thing as a Blanky, a device that you aim at a video camera and it erases the recording. The LumaSutra, a device for detecting mental activity, also doesn't exist.

Yet many other things you might think I made up for the three novels of the Utopia Engine Trilogy are real. When I was drafting the first book, *Surrender,* in 2020, software that gathered our thoughts seemed like a bit of a stretch; it doesn't seem far off now. By the time I published *Resist* in 2024, AI therapists were already on the market. Using AI to build a communication bridge with whales might read like fantasy in *Liberation,* but researchers are working on it now.

Here are a few more things that may seem made up but are not. The spoofing glasses that make the wearer look like another person to fool facial recognition software are based on a research paper about strategies to stop public, and unwanted, personal identification efforts. The ways I describe foiling license plate readers, by sticking a plastic leaf over some of the numbers and letters, are a real strategy used today.

There is a musical instrument called the Theremin that is played without touching it.

I wrote the sections about wildfire in California, and then real wildfires came close to us and we had to evacuate our home. (I revised those sections with many small details from my experience.)

Sea levels are rising because of climate change and some coastal cities will be underwater by 2050 or as early as 2030, the year I peg in the books as the Change, the tipping point for the climate disaster. The Molecular Housing Units are based on an architecture movement in Japan that thrived in the 1970s.

Orcas have been attacking boats, mostly off the coast of Spain. I haven't found any reports of orcas attacking boats near San Francisco. (The otter who attacks surfers and steals their boards to take a ride is real, however. Otter 841 is a female southern sea otter. She has been seen in the waves off Santa Cruz, California.)

Scientists who study animal behavior don't think it's a good practice to attach human emotions to animals. But if I were to argue that the orcas were angry, they would have plenty to be angry about. Amusement parks have hunted and imprisoned orcas, turning them into unwilling clowns. Witnesses to the abduction of juvenile orcas captured for the parks report that the orcas cried for their mothers. As I describe in Liberation, plastic pollution makes its way up the food chain and accumulates as it travels from species to species, a process that scientists call bioaccumulation. Orcas are among the sickest animals in the ocean because they are at the top of the food chain and eat so many other species.

Early readers are vital to the novel-writing. Heartfelt thanks to Elizabeth Schneider for her excellent notes on the characters and storyline, and Jeff Schneider for his detailed notes on the story and for correcting me on some technical issues. You've both made this a more accurate book, emotionally and factually. Thank you to Christiaan Verbree, another early reader of the book with many insights that helped shape it.

Deepest thanks to my wife, Tabby Biddle. Your clear-eyed vision of story and your steady sense of people generally, and the female mind in particular, has guided me.

Thanks to Teja Watson, my editor for all three books of the Utopia Engine Trilogy, for helping me stay on course through the writing process. Thanks to Claire Rushbrook for her detailed copy editing. Thanks to Ocean Milan for bringing Liberation home with a final proofread. Thank you to Paul Palmer-Edwards for your singular sense of design. Paul created all three covers for the trilogy.

Thank you to Jason Cardillo for enlightening me about what to expect while kayaking in Richardson Bay. Your advice was invaluable. I hope you'll forgive me for moving a few landmarks around to fit the story.

And thank you, dear reader, for taking this journey with me. You make it all worthwhile.

A Note About The Author

Lee Schneider is the author of screenplays, teleplays, stage plays, short stories, and audio dramas, including the podcast *Mission of the Lunar Sparrow* and its sequel, *Your Performance Review*. He is the founder of Red Cup Agency, a podcast production agency, and an adjunct assistant professor on the faculty of the USC School of Architecture. He published the first book of the Utopia Engine Trilogy, *Surrender*, in 2022, the second, *Resist*, in 2024, and the third, *Liberation*, in 2025. His non-fiction books include *Be More Popular: Culture-Building for Startups*; *Los Angeles: Chronicle of a Startup Town*; and *The Angel Playbook: An Essential Guide for Entrepreneurs and Angel Investors*. He lives in Santa Monica, CA with his family. More information about his fiction writing can be found at https://leeschneiderbooks.com